Charles Dickens

To be Read at Dusk, and Other Stories, Sketches and Essays

Charles Dickens

To be Read at Dusk, and Other Stories, Sketches and Essays

ISBN/EAN: 9783337097226

Printed in Europe, USA, Canada, Australia, Japan

Cover: Foto ©Andreas Hilbeck / pixelio.de

More available books at **www.hansebooks.com**

TO BE READ AT DUSK

AND OTHER

STORIES, SKETCHES AND ESSAYS

BY

CHARLES DICKENS

NOW FIRST COLLECTED

LONDON

GEORGE REDWAY

1898

CONTENTS

PUBLISHER'S NOTE

On the publication of a collection of occasional pieces from the work contributed by a great author to contemporary ephemera, some critics are too apt to damn it with faint praise, as a mere gathering of that author's immature essays.

Such criticism would not in any sense be applicable to the present volume, the contents of which were produced during a period of years when Charles Dickens was at the very height of his powers;—they range, indeed, from 1837 (the year of "Pickwick") to 1869, the year before the great novelist's death. Many are of peculiar interest as exhibiting the great writer of fiction as a serious man dealing directly with social and other·problems. Herein will be found the personal expression of Dickens's views on Capital Punishment, on Popular Education, on Copyright and other literary matters, as well as his verdict on some of his distinguished friends and contemporaries.

The insight and humour, the generous indignation at wrong-doing, and fervent appreciation of its reverse— in a word, the intense humanity of the man, Charles

Dickens, is perhaps the dominant note throughout this miscellany.

If, again, the captious critic should think that because Dickens himself did not re-publish these papers, therefore they are not worthy of preservation in book form, it should also be remembered that they were written while he was engaged upon his long series of famous novels, and were probably scarcely thought of again. How often is it thus with Genius, which scatters its riches with a lavish hand, conscious of the power to go on producing more! In many cases, indeed, the pieces in this volume may be looked upon as "sketches" and "studies"—essays towards the finished pictures which we know so well.

It is nearly thirty years since Death sealed the fount from which sprang so much of human wit and wisdom. All that Charles Dickens gathered up during his lifetime is now known to us by heart, and we assume that the discovery of even a few fresh pages cannot fail to prove an important event to a multitude of his admirers. The *trouvailles* which Mr. Kitton's life-long research here presents to us will, it is believed, be cordially welcomed not only by the "collector" and student, but by the general reader to whom the varied pieces were originally addressed.

INTRODUCTION

PERHAPS the most remarkable fact in connection with the Reviews, Sketches, and other papers here collected is, that they are now reprinted for the first time. It is true that a small number of them have recently seen the light in America, but for English readers the entire contents of the present volume will possess the charm of novelty, for here Charles Dickens is somewhat unexpectedly revealed to them in the rôle of essayist, critic, and politician. The majority of these fugitive pieces were actually produced at a period subsequent to the time when the name of the author of "Pickwick" became a household word, and are therefore essentially characteristic of his well-known literary style. Of the forty-six items of which this collection consists, no fewer than twenty-four have never been included in any Dickens Bibliography, the discovery and identification of these being the result of much investigation and research on my part among the archives at South Kensington Museum and elsewhere. The following notes concerning the more important of such occasional contributions to journalistic literature will not, I venture to hope, prove to be devoid of interest even to those who claim familiarity with the writings of the great novelist.

Mention must first be made of the short story entitled

"To be Read at Dusk", whence the leading title of this volume is derived. It was written in 1852 for "The Keepsake", in compliance with an earnest request from Miss Power, who succeeded the Countess of Blessington as editor of the then fashionable annual. During the same year this effective little story appeared in pamphlet form, and so scarce has it become that a copy (believed to be unique) was recently priced at twenty-five guineas!

When the "Sketches by Boz" were delighting innumerable readers, and the immortal "Pickwick" was in course of publication, that well-known publisher, Richard Bentley, conceived the notion of launching a monthly magazine bearing his name. He was quick to recognize that in the youthful "Boz", who had so suddenly taken the world by storm, a real literary genius had arisen and had "come to stay". Negotiations were immediately opened by the astute publisher, with the result that Charles Dickens was appointed editor of *Bentley's Miscellany* at a salary of twenty pounds a month, the agreement also stipulating that the future novelist should immediately furnish its pages with a serial story; hence the publication therein, during 1837-38, of that dramatic romance, "Oliver Twist", enriched by means of George Cruikshank's powerful illustrations. Besides editing the magazine, and contributing thereto an account of the numerous adventures of the unfortunate Oliver, Dickens occasionally supplied brief papers in a more or less humorous vein, such as those now known as "The Mudfog Papers", and others of a more quaint character. For example, the third Part of the *Miscellany* contains a curious production from his pen, which was inserted among the advertisements as a leaflet. It is entitled "Extraordinary Gazette", being written in a style parodying a Royal speech, while at the head of this remarkable announcement (herein reprinted) appeared a humorous wood-engraving designed by Hablôt K. Browne ("Phiz"), so long associated with Dickens as the illustrator of his novels. Special reference should be made to this little drawing,* for here is seen the youthful editor himself, leading by the lappels of his vest a burly, perspiring porter, who bears on his head a monster package containing copies of the *Miscellany*. Charles Dickens, who occupied the editorial chair nearly two years, marked his retirement therefrom with a genial valedictory paper which he designated, "Familiar Epistle from a Parent to a Child Aged Two Years and Two Months", where, as the "old coachman", he introduces to the readers of the magazine his successor, William Harrison Ainsworth. So valuable was Dickens's influence even at this early date, and so popular had his writings become, that Mr. Bentley offered him an honorarium equal to twice the amount of his editorial stipend, merely for lending his name to the *Miscellany* for a period of two years—a proposal to which the novelist not unwillingly assented, for it must be remembered that, at the time referred to, his fame had not long been established, so that the success of his writings did not then yield those substantial pecuniary returns which his later works secured for him.

To that now-defunct journal, *The Examiner*, Dickens anonymously contributed several articles (chiefly critical) during the editorship of his friend John Forster. He also enjoyed poking a little fun at Sir Robert Peel and the Tory Party, giving vent to his feelings in humorous and satirical verses such as "The Quack Doctor's Proclamation" and "Subjects for Painters", which amusing squibs

* *Reproduced as a frontispiece to the present volume.*

have already been reprinted by the late Mr. Richard
Herne Shepherd in his "Plays and Poems of Charles
Dickens". Among the novelist's prose writings in *The
Examiner* there is one—namely, a notice of Thomas
Hood's "Up the Rhine"—to which Mr. Forster directs
particular attention, but which both the indefatigable Mr.
Shepherd and I have failed to discover. There are
many others, however, that have hitherto escaped notice,
and which are here reprinted; indeed, it will probably
occasion some surprise when it is realised how much
valuable time Dickens must have devoted, during the busiest
part of his life, to the reviewing of books and to the
preparation of theatrical and artistic criticisms. Doubtless
these extraneous labours were undertaken *con amore*, and
chiefly with the object of benefiting those in whose welfare
he took a lively interest; as, for example, his remarks
upon the acting of his friend Macready, and those
delightful essays upon the Art of George Cruikshank and
John Leech. It is only fair to mention that Mr. Forster,
in his Life of Dickens, has quoted the more salient
points of these essays, but I am privileged to print them
in their entirety for the first time. A similar observation
applies to the paper descriptive of "The Chinese Junk",
the strange and incongruous appearance of which, as she
lay anchored in a London dock, so much impressed
the novelist that he wrote an account of her in a letter to
Mr. Forster, who tells us that "he could not resist the
temptation of using some parts of it at the time,"—hence
the excerpts in *The Examiner*. Commenting upon the
vigorously-worded notice of Lockhart's pamphlet, "The
Ballantyne Humbug Handled", Mr. Forster incidentally
alludes to the novelist's "hearty sympathy with Lockhart's handling of some passages in his admirable 'Life

of Scott' that had drawn down upon him the wrath of
the Ballantynes." It is perhaps superfluous to explain
that the mysterious composition, purporting to be a
"Report of the Commissioners" (which also appeared in
The Examiner) is intended as a burlesque. It will be
seen that Dickens enjoys a good-humoured laugh at a
book, the author of which (Henry Colman) hails from
Boston, U.S.A. The novelist was particularly amused
by the writer's constant references to his wonderful [?]
experiences as a guest at English country mansions, and,
in a letter to Mr. Forster, Dickens thus parodied the
Bostonian's peculiar idiosyncrasy: "Rockingham Castle:
Friday, thirtieth of November, 1849. Picture to yourself,
my dear F., a large old castle, approached by an
ancient keep, portcullis, etc., etc., filled with company,
waited on by six-and-twenty servants; the slops (and
wine-glasses) continually being emptied; and my clothes
(with myself in them) always being carried off to all
sorts of places; and you will have a faint idea of the
mansion in which I am at present staying." Rockingham
Castle, by the way, is to some extent reproduced in
Chesney Wold, of "Bleak House"; it was the residence
of his friends the Watsons, to whom he dedicated the
most delightful of all his books, "David Copperfield".

On March 10th, 1844, Dickens wrote to his solicitor-
friend, Mr. Thomas Mitton: "I send you a paper with
my first article in it, the second leader. When you have
read it send it me back, as I have no other." As, in
the same letter, he intimated his intention of furnishing an
occasional leader to the *Morning Chronicle* (the paper in
which several of the "Boz" sketches originally appeared),
a clue is at once afforded to the particular article referred
to, which was published the day preceding the date of

his missive. There is no evidence, however, that his intention to contribute subsequent leaders was really carried into effect.

Perhaps the most generous act ever performed by one author in behalf of another (and we do not forget Johnson's services to Goldsmith) is recorded of Charles Dickens, and took the shape of the writing of a Preface to a work comprising the literary efforts of a poor carpenter named John Overs, who, during his leisure moments, and while suffering from a fatal disease, had composed several poems and verses, hoping by their publication to leave some small provision for his wife and children. In his introductory remarks Dickens has given us the details of this pathetic picture, together with the facts which led up to his promise to edit the collection of poems, and to provide (gratuitously) a Preface which, bearing his familiar signature, would obviously direct public attention to the little volume. "Evenings of a Working Man" was appropriately dedicated to Dr. Elliotson, who had so carefully tended the sick man, and it is gratifying to learn that the venture proved fairly successful, although there is an added touch of pathos in the fact that poor Overs succumbed to his terrible ailment before he had long enjoyed the fruit of his enterprise. It is evident that, even when at the point of death, the generous assistance of Dickens was uppermost in his thoughts, for he suddenly demanded writing materials, and made up a small parcel, which it was his last conscious act to direct, and which was found to contain a copy of his little book, with the name of Charles Dickens inscribed therein, and the words "with his devotion",—a simple and touching act of gratitude for the help given to a lowly fellow-labourer in the field of Literature.

A matter which Dickens took seriously to heart was the education of the children of the poor. He therefore eagerly welcomed and warmly approved of the establishment of Ragged Schools, the institution of which was begun in 1843 by a shoemaker of Southampton and a chimney-sweep of Windsor, and carried on by a peer of the realm. The Schools also found a warm advocate in Lady (then Miss) Burdett-Coutts, to whom the novelist wrote a "sledge-hammer" account of them, at the same time demonstrating that (having seen her ladyship's name for a large sum in the Clergy education subscription-list) "religious mysteries and difficult creeds wouldn't do for such pupils,"—a point that still continues to provoke considerable discussion among educationists. One of the last things Dickens did at the close of the year 1843, was to offer to describe the Ragged Schools for *The Edinburgh Review*. "I have told Napier," he wrote to Mr. Forster, "I will give a description of them in a paper on Education, if the *Review* is not afraid to take ground against the church catechism and other formularies and subtleties, in reference to the education of the young and ignorant. I fear it is extremely improbable it will consent to commit itself so far." That his anticipations were well founded is proved by the absence of the article from the pages of the *Review*; but we find at a subsequent date, when his interest in the subject was revived, a lengthy letter in *The Daily News* bearing the familiar signature, and headed "Crime and Education", evidently a much-condensed version of the article intended for *The Edinburgh Review*.

It is well known that Charles Dickens's views respecting Capital Punishment were of a very pronounced character. In July, 1845, he intimated to Mr. Macvey Napier that he thought he could write " a pretty good and a well-timed article on the 'Punishment of Death', and sympathy with great criminals, instancing the gross and depraved curiosity that exists in reference to them, by some of the outrageous things that were written, done, and said in recent cases." He then briefly placed his views before his correspondent—an exposition, in fact, of the inferences to which the whole philosophy of his proposed paper must tend—by which he endeavoured to prove that Capital Punishment, especially when carried out in the presence of a degraded mob, was likely to brutalise and harden the feelings of men rather than act as a deterrent against crimes of violence and murder. Owing, however, to a " maze of distractions " which then seriously interfered with his literary work, he found it impossible to write the paper in time for the particular number in which it should have appeared; consequently its publication in *The Edinburgh* was, for some reason, found impracticable. This subject, like that of " Crime and Education ", was afterwards dealt with by the novelist in the form of letters, also addressed to the Editors of *The Daily News* (and here preserved in a more permanent form) while, at a still later date, he forwarded similar correspondence (since reprinted) to *The Times.* The extreme penalty of the law is now carried out within the precincts of the gaol, and in the presence only of the officials,—a result possibly brought about, directly or indirectly, by the novelist's forcible indictment of public executions and the mischief wrought by them upon the masses.

Many of the essays in the present collection were written for Dickens's own journal, *Household Words.* In some instances the existence of the original manuscripts testify to the authorship of these anonymous papers, while in

others there is sufficient internal evidence to satisfy the
student of Dickens as to their source. It is no easy matter,
however, to decide whether certain articles in *Household
Words* and *All the Year Round*, which apparently bear the
unmistakable impress of his hand, were really written by
Charles Dickens himself, or whether they are the productions of particular members of his clever staff of contributors
who, consciously or unconsciously, imitated the style of the
" Master." In such cases a most careful examination
has been made, and those papers where the authorship is
conjectural are rigorously excluded from the present
volume, only those concerning which there can be no
element of doubt being here printed. An article entitled
" One Man in a Dockyard " affords an instance of Dickens's
occasional collaboration with other writers, and of this
only the portion for which the novelist was responsible
is reproduced. It will be observed that in quite a number
of these fugitive pieces Dickens gives free play to his
opinions respecting politics generally and the "misgovernment" of the Tory Party in particular; reading between the lines one readily detects in him the predominance
of that Radical spirit which is conspicuous in his works
of fiction. The question of Sunday observance, too, was
ever uppermost in his mind, from the time when, under
the *nom de guerre* of Timothy Sparks, he penned that
severe onslaught upon Sir Andrew Agnew's Bill for enforcing
among the working-classes a Puritanic regard of the
Sabbath,* until we find him, twenty years afterwards,
reiterating his convictions respecting this important subject
in those *Household Words* papers entitled " The Sunday
Screw " and " The Great Baby."

---

* "*Sunday Under Three Heads*", by *Timothy Sparks, 1836.*

A peculiar interest attaches at the present time to one of the earliest articles in *Household Words*, explaining the aims and intentions of "The Guild of Literature and Art,"—a scheme which was intended to benefit necessitous authors and artists. Mr. R. H. Horne (the author of "Orion," etc.) was responsible for its inception, and subsequently Charles Dickens and Lord Lytton were most enthusiastic in promoting the success of so deserving an object. In 1850, some private amateur theatrical performances took place at Knebworth (Lord Lytton's Hertfordshire mansion), and the names of Dickens, Mark Lemon, John Forster, Douglas Jerrold, John Leech, and others distinguished in Art and Literature, appeared in the "bills"; and it was during the course of these entertainments that the idea of the "Guild" received practical development. A fund for the purpose of founding this Society was raised principally by means of a series of similar dramatic entertainments given in London and the Provinces by the novelist and his literary and artistic coadjutors, Lord Lytton having specially written a play for the occasion, entitled "Not so Bad as We Seem, or, Many Sides to a Character." Mark Lemon also composed an afterpiece called "Mr. Nightingale's Dairy", to which Charles Dickens contributed a considerable amount of humorous dialogue, the joint authors impersonating the principal personages in the little farce. The "Guild" project, however, was not favourably received by the public, and unfortunately resulted in failure. There is now a private Bill before Parliament, the aim of which is to provide for the winding-up and dissolution of "The Guild of Literature and Art", and, the necessary assent of the surviving members of the "Guild" being first obtained, to bestow the available assets upon the Royal Literary Fund and the Artists' General

Benevolent Institution. The property of the "Guild" consists of about two thousand pounds invested in stock, a small balance at Coutts's Bank, and the four houses at Stevenage, near Knebworth, erected on the land given to the "Guild" by Lord Lytton.

In "Whole Hogs" we discover a determined protest against the extreme views held by advocates of Temperance and Vegetarianism, a denunciation which excited much indignation in certain quarters. Both article and writer were severely criticised in a pamphlet (published at Middlesboro'), entitled "Mr. Charles Dickens on the Temperance Reformation"; and among those whose susceptibilities were wounded by Dickens's trenchant remarks was George Cruikshank, who had then become prominent in the cause of Teetotalism. Mention of this distinguished artist recalls to mind an attack, half-playful and half-serious, made by the novelist, in a paper called "Frauds on the Fairies", upon Cruikshank's version of the Fairy Tales, which had just been re-written by him (observes Dickens) "according to Total Abstinence, Peace Society, and Bloomer principles, and expressly for their propagation." Naturally, such comments very much incensed the artist, who attempted to defend his action by means of a statement on the wrapper of one of the story-books comprised in his "Fairy Library", as well as in the magazine bearing his own cognomen, where he addressed Dickens as "Most honoured, well-beloved, and trusted Sir," and signed himself "Hop o' my Thumb." It is said that the well-merited rebuke seriously affected the sale of the Fairy Tales, these little books being now treasured chiefly on account of their illustrations—for they are charming specimens of an art with which the name and fame of George Cruikshank will be ever associated.

The brief paper headed "The Worthy Magistrate" is very much to the purpose, and brings to one's memory the portrait of another "worthy magistrate", Mr. Fang in "Oliver Twist", who was drawn from the life, the original of Mr. Fang being a Mr. Laing, the magistrate then presiding at the Clerkenwell police-court, whose excessive coarseness and brutality while on the bench became notorious. We are told that the novelist's exposure of such conduct, in the pages of "Oliver Twist", was instrumental in procuring Mr. Laing's dismissal from the position which he so unworthily occupied and so consistently disgraced.

In April, 1855, Dickens wrote to Mr. Forster: "I have rather a bright idea, I think, for *Household Words* this morning; a fine little bit of satire; an account of an Arabic MS. lately discovered, very like the 'Arabian Nights'—called the Thousand and One Humbugs—with new versions of the best known stories." Mr. Forster is caught tripping when he says that this idea was abandoned, for the "little bit of satire" was immediately written and inserted in *Household Words*, whence it is now reproduced. This quizzical sketch is an amusing "skit" upon the House of Commons ("Howsa Kummauns"), in which political phrases and the names of prominent politicians are ingeniously translated into pseudo-Arabic.

The paper "On Mr. Fechter's Acting" was specially prepared for publication in *The Atlantic Monthly*, with the main object of introducing the great tragedian to the American public. Transatlantic caricaturists seized that opportunity of having a slap at the author of "American Notes", and a New York comic journal issued a humorous cartoon depicting the novelist inflating, with a pair of bellows, an indiarubber effigy of colossal proportions, purporting to represent the subject of his eulogy in a tragic attitude upon a pedestal. Between Dickens and Fechter there existed a very warm attachment, and it was this distinguished actor who presented the novelist with the pretty Swiss châlet, to which a pathetic interest attaches, for here were penned the closing words of "The Mystery of Edwin Drood." The article in praise of Mr. Fechter was Dickens's last contribution to magazine literature.

The first of the two letters at the end of the present volume speaks for itself; the other was received by the committee of the Metropolitan Drapers' Association in answer to an application made to Charles Dickens to take part in the proceedings at a meeting of the Association, and to accept the office of a Vice-President. This interesting communication has apparently never seen the light since its publication in "The Student and Young Man's Advocate," where, in 1845, it originally appeared.

St. Albans, December, 1897.   F. G. KITTON.

TO BE READ AT DUSK.

ONE, two, three, four, five. There were five of them.

Five couriers, sitting on a bench outside the convent on the summit of the Great St. Bernard in Switzerland, looking at the remote heights, stained by the setting sun, as if a mighty quantity of red wine had been broached upon the mountain top, and had not yet had time to sink into the snow.

This is not my simile. It was made for the occasion by the stoutest courier, who was a German. None of the others took any more notice of it than they took of me, sitting on another bench on the other side of the convent door, smoking my cigar, like them, and—also like them—looking at the reddened snow, and at the lowly shed hard by, where the bodies of belated travellers, dug out of it, slowly wither away, knowing no corruption in that cold region.

The wine upon the mountain top soaked in as we looked; the mountain became white; the sky a very dark blue; the wind rose; and the air turned piercing cold. The five couriers buttoned their rough coats. There being no safer man to imitate in all such proceedings than a courier, I buttoned mine.

The mountain in the sunset had stopped the five couriers

in a conversation. It is a sublime sight, likely to stop conversation. The mountain being now out of the sunset, they resumed. Not that I had heard any part of their previous discourse; for, indeed, I had not broken away from the American gentleman, in the travellers' parlour of the convent, who, sitting with his face to the fire, had undertaken to realise to me the whole progress of events which had led to the accumulation by the Honourable Ananias Dodger of one of the largest acquisitions of dollars ever made in our country.

"My God!" said the Swiss courier, speaking in French, which I do not hold (as some authors appear to do) to be such an all-sufficient excuse for a naughty word, that I have only to write it in that language to make it innocent; "if you talk of ghosts——"

"But I *don't* talk of ghosts," said the German.

"Of what then?" asked the Swiss.

"If I knew of what then," said the German, "I should probably know a great deal more."

It was a good answer, I thought, and it made me curious. So, I moved my position to that corner of my bench which was nearest to them, and leaning my back against the convent-wall, heard perfectly without appearing to attend.

"Thunder and lightning!" said the German, warming, "when a certain man is coming to see you, unexpectedly; and, without his own knowledge, sends some invisible messenger, to put the idea of him in your head all day, what do you call that? When you walk along a crowded street at Frankfort, Milan, London, Paris—and think that a passing stranger is like your friend Heinrich, and so begin to have a strange foreknowledge that presently you'll meet your friend Heinrich—which you do, though you believed him at Trieste—what do you call *that?*"

"It's not uncommon either," murmured the Swiss and the other three.

"Uncommon!" said the German. "It's as common as cherries in the Black Forest. It's as common as macaroni at Naples. And Naples reminds me! When the old Marchesa Senzanima shrieks at a card party on the Chiaja—as I heard and saw her, for it happened in a Bavarian family of mine, and I was overlooking the service that evening—I say, when the old Marchesa starts up at the card-table, white through her rouge, and cries, 'My sister in Spain is dead! I felt her cold touch on my back!'—and when that sister *is* dead at the moment—what do you call that?"

"Or when the blood of San Gennaro liquefies at the request of the clergy—and all the world knows that it does regularly once a-year, in my native city," said the Neapolitan courier after a pause, with a comical look, "what do you call that?"

"*That!*" cried the German. "Well, I think I know a name for that."

"Miracle?" said the Neapolitan, with the same sly face.

The German merely smoked and laughed; and they all smoked and laughed.

"Bah!" said the German presently. "I speak of things that really do happen. When I want to see the conjurer, I pay to see a professed one, and have my money's worth. Very strange things do happen without ghosts. Ghosts! Giovanni Baptista, tell your story of the English bride. There's no ghost in that, but something full as strange. Will any man tell me what?"

As there was a silence among them, I glanced around. He whom I took to be Baptista was lighting a fresh cigar. He presently went on to speak. He was a Genoese, as I judged.

"The story of the English bride?" said he. "Basta! one ought not to call so slight a thing a story. Well, it's all one. But it's true. Observe me well, gentlemen, it's true. That which glitters is not always gold; but what I am going to tell, is true."

He repeated this more than once.

Ten years ago, I took my credentials to an English gentleman at Long's Hotel, in Bond Street, London, who was about to travel—it might be for one year, it might be for two. He approved of them; likewise of me. He was pleased to make inquiry. The testimony that he received was favourable. He engaged me by the six months, and my entertainment was generous.

He was young, handsome, very happy. He was enamoured of a fair young English lady, with a sufficient fortune, and they were going to be married. It was the wedding-trip, in short, that we were going to take. For three months' rest in the hot weather (it was early summer then) he had hired an old palace on the Riviera, at an easy distance from my city, Genoa, on the road to Nice. Did I know that palace? Yes; I told him I knew it well. It was an old palace, with great gardens. It was a little bare, and it was a little dark and gloomy, being close surrounded by trees; but it was spacious, ancient, grand, and on the sea shore. He said it had been so described to him exactly, and he was well pleased that I knew it. For its being a little bare of furniture, all such places were. For its being a little gloomy, he had hired it principally for the gardens, and he and my mistress would pass the summer in their shade.

"So all goes well, Baptista?" said he.

"Indubitably, signore; very well."

We had a travelling chariot for our journey, newly built for us, and in all respects complete. All we had was complete; we wanted for nothing. The marriage took place. They were happy. *I* was happy, seeing all so bright, being so well situated, going to my own city, teaching my language in the rumble to the maid, la bella Carolina, whose heart was gay with laughter; who was young and rosy.

The time flew. But I observed—listen to this, I pray! (and here the courier dropped his voice)—I observed my mistress sometimes brooding in a manner very strange; in a frightened manner; in an unhappy manner; with a cloudy, uncertain alarm upon her. I think that I began to notice this when I was walking up hills by the carriage side, and master had gone on in front. At any rate, I remember that it impressed itself upon my mind one evening in the South of France, when she called to me to call master back; and when he came back, and walked for a long way, talking encouragingly and affectionately to her, with his hand upon the open window, and hers in it. Now and then, he laughed in a merry way, as if he were bantering her out of something. By and by, she laughed, and then all went well again.

It was curious. I asked la bella Carolina, the pretty little one, Was mistress unwell?—No. Out of spirits?—No. Fearful of bad roads, or brigands?—No. And what made it more mysterious was, the pretty little one would not look at me in giving answer, but *would* look at the view.

But, one day she told me the secret.

"If you must know," said Caroline, "I find, from what I have overheard, that mistress is haunted."

"How haunted?"

"By a dream."

"What dream?"

"By a dream of a face. For three nights before her marriage, she saw a face in a dream—always the same face, and only One."

"A terrible face?"

"No, the face of a dark, remarkable-looking man, in black, with black hair and a grey moustache—a handsome man, except for a reserved and secret air. Not a face she ever saw, or at all like a face she ever saw. Doing nothing in the dream but looking at her fixedly, out of darkness."

"Does the dream come back?"

"Never. The recollection of it, is all her trouble."

"And why does it trouble her?"

Carolina shook her head.

"That's master's question," said la bella. "She don't know. She wonders why, herself. But I heard her tell him, only last night, that if she was to find a picture of that face in our Italian house (which she is afraid she will), she did not know how she could ever bear it."

Upon my word I was fearful after this (said the Genoese courier) of our coming to the old palazzo, lest some such ill-starred picture should happen to be there. I knew there were many there; and, as we got nearer and nearer to the place, I wished the whole gallery in the crater of Vesuvius. To mend the matter, it was a stormy dismal evening when we, at last, approached that part of the Riviera. It thundered; and the thunder of my city and its environs, rolling among the high hills, is very loud. The lizards ran in and out of the chinks in the broken stone wall of the garden, as if they were frightened; the frogs bubbled and croaked their loudest; the sea-wind moaned, and the wet trees dripped; and the lightning—body of San Lorenzo, how it lightened!

We all know what an old palazzo in or near Genoa is—how time and the sea air have blotted it—how the drapery painted on the outer walls has peeled off in great flakes of plaster—how the lower windows are darkened with rusty bars of iron—how the courtyard is overgrown with grass—how the outer buildings are dilapidated—how the whole pile seems devoted to ruin. Our palazzo was one of the true kind. It had been shut up close for months. Months?—Years! It had an earthy smell, like a tomb. The scent of the orange trees on the broad back terrace, and of the lemons ripening on the wall, and of some shrubs that grew around a broken fountain, had got into the house somehow, and had never been able to get out again. There it was, in every room, an aged smell, grown faint with confinement. It pined in all the cupboards and drawers. In the little rooms of communication between great rooms, it was stifling. If you turned a picture—to come back to the pictures—there it still was, clinging to the wall behind the frame, like a sort of bat.

The lattice-blinds were close shut, all over the house. There were two ugly grey old women in the house, to take care of it; one of them with a spindle, who stood winding and mumbling in the doorway, and who would as soon have let in the devil as the air. Master, mistress, la bella Carolina, and I, went all through the palazzo. I went first, though I have named myself last, opening the windows and the lattice-blinds, and shaking down on myself splashes of rain, and scraps of mortar, and now and then a dozing mosquito, or a monstrous, fat, blotchy, Genoese spider.

When I had let the evening light into a room, master,

mistress, and la bella Carolina, entered. Then, we looked
round at all the pictures, and I went forward again into
another room. Mistress secretly had great fear of meeting
with the likeness of that face—we all had; but there was
no such thing. The Madonna and Bambino, San Francisco,
San Sebastiano, Venus, Santa Caterina, Angels, Brigands,
Friars, Temples at Sunset, Battles, White Horses, Forests,
Apostles, Doges. All my old acquaintance many times
repeated?—Yes. Dark handsome man in black, reserved
and secret, with black hair and grey moustache, looking
fixedly at mistress out of darkness?—No.

At last we got through all the rooms and all the pictures, and came out into the gardens. They were pretty
well kept, being rented by a gardener, and were large
and shady. In one place, there was a rustic theatre, open
to the sky; the stage a green slope; the coulisses, three
entrances upon a side, sweet smelling leafy screens. Mistress moved her bright eyes, even there, as if she looked
to see the face come in upon the scene: but all
was well.

"Now, Clara," master said, in a low voice, "you see
that it is nothing? You are happy."

Mistress was much encouraged. She soon accustomed
herself to that grim palazzo, and would sing, and play
the harp, and copy the old pictures, and stroll with master
under the green trees and vines, all day. She was beautiful.
He was happy. He would laugh and say to me, mounting
his horse for his morning ride before the heat:

"All goes well, Baptista?"

"Yes, signore, thank God; very well!"

We kept no company. I took la bella to the Duomo and
Annunciata, to the Café, to the Opera, to the village Festa,
to the Public Garden, to the Day Theatre, to the Marionetti.

The pretty little one was charmed with all she saw. She learnt Italian—heavens! miraculously! Was mistress quite forgetful of that dream? I asked Carolina sometimes. Nearly, said la bella—almost. It was wearing out.

One day master received a letter, and called me.

" Baptista!"

"Signore."

" A gentleman who is presented to me will dine here to-day. He is called the Signor Dellombra. Let me dine like a prince."

It was an odd name. I did not know that name. But, there had been many noblemen and gentlemen pursued by Austria on political suspicions, lately, and some names had changed. Perhaps this was one. Altro! Dellombra was as good a name to me as another.

When the Signor Dellombra came to dinner (said the Genoese courier in the low voice, into which he had subsided once before), I showed him into the reception room, the great sala of the old palazzo. Master received him with cordiality, and presented him to mistress. As she rose, her face changed, she gave a cry, and fell upon the marble floor.

Then, I turned my head to the Signor Dellombra, and saw that he was dressed in black, and had a reserved and secret air, and was a dark remarkable-looking man, with black hair and a grey moustache.

Master raised mistress in his arms, and carried her to her own room, where I sent la bella Carolina straight. La bella told me afterwards that mistress was nearly terrified to death, and that she wandered in her mind about her dream all night.

Master was vexed and anxious – almost angry, and yet full of solicitude. The Signor Dellombra was a courtly gentleman, and spoke with great respect and sympathy of mistress's being so ill. The African wind had been blowing for some days (they had told him at his hôtel of the Maltese Cross), and he knew that it was often hurtful. He hoped the beautiful lady would recover soon. He begged permission to retire, and to renew his visit when he should have the happiness of hearing that she was better. Master would not allow of this, and they dined alone.

He withdrew early. Next day he called at the gate, on horseback, to inquire for mistress. He did so two or three times in that week.

What I observed myself, and what la bella Carolina told me, united to explain to me that master had now set his mind on curing mistress of her fanciful terror. He was all kindness, but he was sensible and firm. He reasoned with her that to encourage such fancies was to invite melancholy, if not madness. That it rested with herself to be herself. That if she once resisted her strange weakness, so successfully as to receive the Signor Dellombra as an English lady would receive any other guest, it was for ever conquered. To make an end, the Signor came again and mistress received him without marked distress (though with constraint and apprehension still), and the evening passed serenely. Master was so delighted with this change, and so anxious to confirm it, that the Signor Dellombra became a constant guest. He was accomplished in pictures, books and music; and his society, in any grim palazzo, would have been welcome.

I used to notice, many times, that mistress was not quite recovered. She would cast down her eyes and droop her head, before the Signor Dellombra, or would look at him with a terrified and fascinated glance, as if his presence had some evil influence or power upon her. Turning from her to him, I used to see him in the shaded gardens, or the large half-lighted sala looking as I might say, "fixedly upon her out of darkness." But, truly, I had not forgotten la bella Carolina's words describing the face in the dream.

After his second visit I heard master say:

"Now see, my dear Clara, it's over! Dellombra has come and gone, and your apprehension is broken like glass."

"Will he—will he ever come again?" asked mistress.

"Again? Why, surely, over and over again! Are you cold?" (She shivered).

"No, dear—but—he terrifies me; are you sure that he need come again?"

"The surer for the question, Clara!" replied master, cheerfully.

But he was very hopeful of her complete recovery now, and grew more and more so every day. She was beautiful. He was happy.

"All goes well, Baptista?" he would say to me again.

"Yes, signore, thank God; very well."

We were all (said the Genoese courier, constraining himself to speak a little louder), we were all at Rome for the carnival. I had been out, all day, with a Sicilian, a friend of mine and a courier, who was there with an English family. As I returned at night to our hôtel, I met the little Carolina, who never stirred from home alone, running distractedly along the Corso.

"Carolina! What's the matter?"

"O Baptista! Oh, for the Lord's sake! where is my mistress?"

"Mistress, Carolina?"

"Gone since morning—told me—when master went out on his day's journey, not to call her, for she was tired with not resting in the night (having been in pain), and would lie in bed until the evening; then get up refreshed. She is gone!—she is gone! Master has come back; broken down the door, and she is gone, my beautiful, my good, my innocent mistress!"

The pretty little one so cried, and raved, and tore herself, that I could not have held her, but for her swooning on my arm as if she had been shot. Master came up—in manner, face, or voice, no more the master that I knew, than I was he. He took me (I laid the little one upon her bed in the hôtel, and left her with the chamber-women), in a carriage, furiously through the darkness, across the desolate Campagna. When it was day, and we stopped at a miserable posthouse, all the horses had been hired twelve hours ago, and sent away in different directions. Mark me!—by the Signor Dellombra, who had passed there in a carriage, with a frightened English lady crouching in one corner.

I never heard (said the Genoese courier, drawing a long breath) that she was ever traced beyond that spot. All I know is, that she vanished into infamous oblivion, with the dreaded face beside her that she had seen in her dream.

"What do you call *that?*" said the German courier, triumphantly: "Ghosts! There are no ghosts *there!* What do you call this, that I am going to tell you? Ghosts! There are no ghosts *here!*"

I took an engagement once (pursued the German courier) with an English gentleman, elderly and a bachelor, to travel through my country, my Fatherland. He was a merchant who traded with my country and knew the language, but who had never been there since he was a boy—as I judge, some sixty years before.

His name was James, and he had a twin-brother John, also a bachelor. Between these brothers there was a great affection. They were in business together, at Goodman's Fields, but they did not live together. Mr. James dwelt in Poland Street, turning out of Oxford Street, London. Mr. John resided by Epping Forest.

Mr. James and I were to start for Germany in about a week. The exact day depended on business. Mr. John came to Poland Street (where I was staying in the house), to pass that week with Mr. James. But he said to his brother on the second day, " I don't feel very well, James. There's not much the matter with me; but I think I am a little gouty. I'll go home and put myself under the care of my old housekeeper, who understands my ways. If I get quite better, I'll come back and see you before you go. If I don't feel well enough to resume my visit where I leave it off, why *you* will come and see *me* before you go." Mr. James, of course, said he would, and they shook hands—both hands, as they always did—and Mr. John ordered out his old-fashioned chariot and rumbled home.

It was on the second night after that—that is to say, the fourth in the week—when I was awoke out of my sound sleep by Mr. James coming into my bedroom in his flannel-gown, with a lighted candle. He sat upon the side of my bed, and looking at me, said:

" Wilhelm, I have reason to think I have got some strange illness upon me."

I then perceived that there was a very unusual expression in his face.

" Wilhelm," said he, " I am not afraid or ashamed to tell you, what I might be afraid or ashamed to tell another man. You come from a sensible country, where mysterious things are inquired into, and are not settled to have been weighed and measured—or to have been unweighable and unmeasurable—or in either case to have been completely disposed of, for all time—ever so many years ago. I have just now seen the phantom of my brother."

I confess (said the German courier) that it gave me a little tingling of the blood to hear it.

"I have just now seen," Mr. James repeated, looking full at me, that I might see how collected he was, "the phantom of my brother John. I was sitting up in bed, unable to sleep, when it came into my room, in a white dress, and, regarding me earnestly, passed up to the end of the room, glanced at some papers on my writing-desk, turned, and, still looking earnestly at me as it passed the bed, went out at the door. Now, I am not in the least mad, and am not in the least disposed to invest that phantom with any external existence out of myself. I think it is a warning to me that I am ill; and I think I had better be bled."

I got out of bed directly (said the German courier) and began to get on my clothes, begging him not to be alarmed, and telling him that I would go myself to the doctor. I was just ready, when we heard a loud knocking and ringing at the street door. My room being an attic at the back, and Mr. James's being the second-floor room in the front, we went down to his room, and put up the window, to see what was the matter.

"Is that Mr. James?" said a man below, falling back to the opposite side of the way to look up.

"It is," said Mr. James, "and you are my brother's man, Robert."

"Yes, sir. I am sorry to say, sir, that Mr. John is ill. He is very bad, sir. It is even feared that he may be

lying at the point of death. He wants to see you, sir.
I have a chaise here. Pray come to him. Pray lose no
time."

Mr. James and I looked at one another. "Wilhelm,"
said he, "this is strange. I wish you to come with me!"
I helped him to dress, partly there and partly in the
chaise; and no grass grew under the horses' iron shoes
between Poland Street and the Forest.

Now, mind! (said the German courier) I went with
Mr. James into his brother's room, and I saw and heard
myself what follows.

His brother lay upon his bed, at the upper end of a
long bedchamber. His old housekeeper was there, and
others were there: I think three others were there, if
not four, and they had been with him since early
in the afternoon. He was in white—like the figure—
necessarily so, because he had his night-dress on. He
looked like the figure—necessarily so, because he looked
earnestly at his brother when he saw him come into the
room.

But, when his brother reached the bed-side, he slowly
raised himself in bed, and looking full upon him, said
these words:

"JAMES, YOU HAVE SEEN ME BEFORE, TO-NIGHT—AND
YOU KNOW IT!"

And so died.

I waited, when the German courier ceased, to hear
something said of this strange story. The silence was
unbroken. I looked round, and the five couriers were
gone: so noiselessly that the ghostly mountain night
have absorbed them into its eternal snows. By this
time, I was by no means in a mood to sit alone in
that awful scene, with the chill air coming solemnly upon

me—or, if I may tell the truth, to sit alone anywhere.
So I went back into the convent-parlour, and, finding
the American gentleman still disposed to relate the
biography of the Honourable Ananias Dodger, heard it
all out.   [1852]

EXTRAORDINARY GAZETTE.

SPEECH OF HIS MIGHTINESS ON OPENING THE SECOND NUMBER OF "BENTLEY'S MISCELLANY."
Edited by "Boz."

ON Wednesday, the first of February, "the House" (of Bentley) met for the despatch of business, in pursuance of the Proclamation inserted by authority in all the Morning, Evening, and Weekly Papers, appointing that day for the publication of the Second Number of the Miscellany, edited by "Boz".

His Mightness the Editor, in his progress to New Burlington Street, received with the utmost affability the numerous petitions of the crossing-sweepers; and was repeatedly and loudly hailed by the cabmen on the different stands in the line of road through which he passed. His Mightness appeared in the highest possible spirits; and immediately after his arrival at the House, delivered himself of the following most gracious speech:

"MY LORDS, LADIES, AND GENTLEMEN:

"In calling upon you to deliberate on the various important matters which I have now to submit to your consideration, I rely with entire confidence on that spirit of good-will and kindness of which I have more than once taken occasion to express my sense; and which I am but too happy to acknowledge again.

"It has been the constant aim of my policy to preserve peace in your minds, and promote merriment in your hearts;

to set before you, the scenes and characters of real life in all their endless diversity; occasionally (I hope) to instruct, always to amuse, and never to offend. I trust I may refer you to my Pickwickian measures, already taken and still in progress, in confirmation of this assurance.

"In further proof of my sincere anxiety for the amusement and lightheartedness of the community, let me direct your particular attention to the volume I now lay before you, which contains no fewer than twenty-one reports, of greater or less extent, from most eminent, active, and intelligent commissioners. I cannot but anticipate that when you shall have given an attentive perusal to this general report on Periodical Literature, you will be seized with an eager and becoming desire to possess yourselves of all the succeeding numbers,—a desire on which too much praise and encouragement can never be bestowed.

"Gentlemen of the Reviews:

"I have directed the earliest copies of every monthly number to be laid before you. They shall be framed with the strictest regard to the taste and wishes of the people; and I am confident that I may rely on your zealous and impartial coöperation in the public service.

"The accounts and estimates of the first number have been made out; and I am happy to inform you that the state of the revenue as compared with the expenditure (great as the latter has been, and must necessarily continue to be) is most satisfactory; in fact, that a surplus of considerable extent has been already realised. It affords me much pleasure to reflect that not the smallest difficulty will arise in the appropriation of it.

"My Lords, Ladies, and Gentlemen:

"I continue to receive from Foreign Powers, undeniable assurances of their disinterested regard and esteem. The

free and independent States of America have done me
the honour to reprint my Sketches, gratuitously; and to
circulate them throughout the Possessions of the British
Crown in India, without charging me anything at all. I
think I shall recognise Don Carlos if I ever meet him in
the street; and I am sure I shall at once know the King
of the French, for I have seen him before.

"I deeply lament the ferment and agitation of the public
mind in Ireland, which was occasioned by the inade-
quate supply of the first number of this Miscellany. I
deplore the outrages which were committed by an irritated
and disappointed populace on the shop of the agent;
and the violent threats which were directed against
him personally on his stating his inability to comply with
their exorbitant demands. I derive great satisfaction from
reflecting that the promptest and most vigorous measures
were instantaneously taken to repress the tumult. A large
detachment of Miscellanies was levied and shipped with
all possible despatch; and I have it in my power to state,
that, although the excitement has not yet wholly subsided,
it has been, by these means, materially allayed. I have
every reason to hope that the arrangements since made
with my agent in the Port of Dublin, render any recurrence
of the disturbances extremely improbable, and will effectually prevent their breaking out afresh.

"I view with heartfelt satisfaction, the loyal and peaceable demeanour of the people of Scotland; who, although
they experienced a similar provocation to outrage and
rebellion, were content to wait until fresh supplies could
be forwarded per mail and steam.

"I feel unfeigned pleasure in bearing similar testimony
to the forebearing disposition and patriotic feeling of the
hardy mountaineers in the Principality of Wales.

"I have concluded treaties on the most advantageous terms, not only with the powers whose names are already known to you, but with others, to whom it might prove disadvantageous to the public service to make any more direct reference at present. I have laboured, and shall continue to labour, most earnestly and zealously for your pleasure and enjoyment; and, surrounded as I am, by talent and ability, I look most confidently to your approval and support."   [1837]

ADDRESS ON THE COMPLETION OF THE FIRST
VOLUME OF "BENTLEY'S MISCELLANY."

"AT the end of a theatrical season it is customary for the manager to step forward, and, in as few words as may be, to say how very much obliged he feels for all past favours, and how very ready he is to incur fresh obligations.

"With a degree of candour which few managers would display, we cheerfully confess that we have been fairly inundated with *orders* during our six months' campaign; but so liberal are we, notwithstanding, that we place many of the very first authors of the day on our free list, and invite them to write for our establishment just as much paper as they think proper.

"We have produced a great variety of novelties, some of which we humbly hope may become stock pieces, and all of which we may venture to say have been most successful; and, although we are not subject to the control of a licenser, we have eschewed everything political, personal, or ill-natured, with perhaps as much care as we could possibly have shown, even had we been under the watchful eye of the Lord Chamberlain himself.

"We shall open our Second Volume, ladies and gentlemen, on the first day of July, One thousand eight hundred and thirty seven, when we shall have the pleasure of submitting a great variety of entirely new pieces for your judgment and approval. The company will be numerous, first rate, and complete. The scenery will continue to be supplied by the creative pencil of Mr. George Cruikshank; the whole of the extensive and beautiful machinery will be, as heretofore, under the immediate superintendence of Mr. Samuel Bentley, of Dorset Street, Fleet Street; and Mr. Richard Bentley, of New Burlington Street, has kindly consented to preside over the Treasury department, where he has already conducted himself with uncommon ability.

"The stage management will again be confided, ladies and gentlemen, to the humble individual with the short name, who has now the honour to address you, and who hopes, for very many years to come, to appear before you in the same capacity. Permit him to add in sober seriousness, that it has been the constant and unremitting endeavour of himself and the proprietor to render this undertaking worthy of your patronage. That they have not altogether failed in their attempt, its splendid success sufficiently demonstrates; that they have no intention of relaxing in their efforts, its future volumes, we trust, will abundantly testify.

"London, June, 1837.   "Boz."

SIR WALTER SCOTT AND HIS PUBLISHERS.

WHEN the *Refutation*, to which this pamphlet[1] is a reply, was put forth, we took occasion to examine into the nature of the charges of mis-statement and misrepresentation which were therein brought against Mr. Lockhart, to point out how very slight and unimportant they appeared to be, even upon the refuter's own showing, and to express our opinion that the refutation originated in the overweening vanity of the Ballantyne family, who, confounding their own importance with that of the great man who condescended (to his cost) to patronize them, sought to magnify and exalt themselves with a degree of presumption and conceit which leaves the fly on the wheel, the organ bellows blower, and the aspiring frog of the fable, all at an immeasurable distance behind.

Much as we may wonder, after an attentive perusal of the pamphlet before us, how the lad, James Ballantyne's son, can have been permitted by those who must have known from the commencement what facts were in reserve, to force on this exposure of the most culpable negligence and recklessness on the part of the men who have been paraded as the victims of erring and ambitious genius, it is impossible to regard the circumstance in any other

---

[1] The Ballantyne Humbug Handled; in a letter to Sir Adam Fergusson. By the Author of "Memoirs of the Life of Sir Walter Scott."

light than as a most fortunate and happy one for the memory of Sir Walter Scott. If ever engineer were "hoist with his own petard," if ever accusations recoiled upon the heads of those who made them, if ever the parties in the witness box and the dock changed places, it is in this case of the Ballantynes and Sir Walter Scott. And the proof, be it remembered, is to be found—not in the unsupported assertions of Mr. Lockhart or his ingenious reasoning from assumed facts, but in the letters, accounts, and statements of the Ballantynes themselves.

Premising that Mr. Lockhart, in glancing at the "unanswerable refutation" and "the overwhelming exposure" notices of the Ballantyne pamphlet in other journals, might fairly and justly have noticed this journal [1] as an exception (in whose columns more than one head of his reply was anticipated long ago), we will proceed to quote—first, Mr. Lockhart's statement of his reasons for introducing in the biography detailed descriptions of the habits and manners of the Ballantynes, which we take to have been the head and front of his offence; and secondly, such scraps of evidence bearing upon the allegation that the Ballantynes were ruined by the improvidence and lavish expenditure of Scott, as we can afford space for, in a very brief analysis of the whole.

With regard to the first point, Mr. Lockhart writes thus :—

"The most curious problem in the life of Scott could receive no fair attempt at solution, unless the inquirer were made acquainted, in as far as the biographer could make him so, with the nature, and habits, and manners of Scott's partners and agents. Had the reader been left to take his ideas of those men from the eloquence of epitaphs—

[1] *The Examiner.*

to conceive of them as having been capitalists instead of penniless adventurers—men regularly and fitly trained for the callings in which they were employed by Scott, in place of being the one and the other entirely unacquainted with the prime requisites for success in such callings—men exact and diligent in their proper business, careful and moderate in their personal expenditure, instead of the reverse; had such hallucinations been left undisturbed, where was the clue of extrication from the mysterious labyrinth of Sir Walter's fatal entanglements in commerce? It was necessary, in truth and justice, to show—not that he was without blame in the conduct of his pecuniary affairs—(I surely made no such ridiculous attempt)—but that he could not have been ruined by commerce, had his partners been good men of business. It was necessary to show that he was in the main the victim of his own blind over-confidence in the management of the two Ballantynes. In order to show how excessive was the kindness that prompted such over-confidence, it was necessary to bring out the follies and foibles, as well as the better qualities, of the men."

Does any reasonable and dispassionate man doubt this? Is there any man who does not know that the titles of a hundred biographies might be jotted down in half an hour, in each and every of which there shall be found a hundred personal sketches of a hundred men, a hundred times more important, clever, excellent, and worthy, than Mr. James Ballantyne, the Printer of Edinburgh, and whilom of Kelso, regarding which the world has never heard one syllable of remonstrance or complaint.

Of Mr. John Ballantyne, the less said the better. If he were an honest, upright honourable man, it is a comfort to know that there are plentiful store of such characters living at this moment in the rules of our Debtors' Prison,

and passing through the Insolvent Court by dozens every
day.   As an instance of Mr. Lockhart's easy mode of assertion, we were given to understand in the *Refutation* that
Mr. John Ballantyne had never been a banker's clerk.
Mr. Cadell and another gentleman bear testimony that he
used to *say* he had been (which seems by no means conclusive evidence that he ever was), and if he were, as
Mr. Lockhart tells us he has since learnt, a tailor, or
superintendent of the tailoring department of the father's
general shop at Kelso, a previously unintelligible fragment
in one of Scott's letters becomes susceptible of a very
startling and simple solution.   " If it takes nine tailors to
make a man, how many will it take to ruin one? "

The descendants of Mr. James Ballantyne charge Sir
Walter Scott with having ruined him by his profuse
expenditure, and the tremendous responsibilities which he
cast upon the printing concern.   Mr. Lockhart charges Mr.
James Ballantyne with having ruined the business by
his own negligence, extravagance, and inattention.   Let us
see which of these charges is the best supported by facts.

Scott entered into partnership with James Ballantyne
in May, 1805.   James Ballantyne's brother John (being
then the book-keeper) enters the amount of capital which
James had invested in the concern, at £3694 16s. 11d.;
but of these figures no less than £2090 represents " stock
in trade," which it appears from other statements that the
same John Ballantyne was in the habit of valuing at most
preposterous and exaggerated sums; and the balance of
£1604 16s. 11d. is represented by " book debts" to that
amount.   Scott came in as the monied partner—as the
man to prop up the concern; even then his patrimonial
fortune was £10,000 or £12,000; he possessed at the
time, independently of all literary exertions, an income of

£1000 per annum; he advanced for the business, £2008,
"including in the said advance the sum of £500 contained
in Mr. Ballantyne's promissory note, dated 1st February
last"—from which it would seem pretty clear that the affluent Mr. James Ballantyne ran rather short of money
about this time—and £40 more, also advanced to Mr.
Ballantyne previous to the execution of the deed. Scott,
in consideration of this payment, was to have one-third of
the business, and James Ballantyne two; his extra third
being specially in consideration of his undertaking those
duties of management, for the neglect and omission of
which, throughout the long correspondence of a long term
of years, we find him apologizing to Scott himself in every
variety of humble, maudlin, abject, and whining prostration.

The very first entry in the very first "State", or statement of the partnership accounts, is a payment on behalf
of James Ballantyne, for "an acceptance *at Kelso*,"—at
Kelso, observe, in his original obscurity and small way of
business—"£200." There are advances to his father to
the amount of £270 19s. 5d., there are his own drafts
during the first year of the partnership to the enormous
amount of £2378 4s. 9d., *his share of the profits being only*
£786 10s. 3d.; Scott's drafts for the same period being
£100 and *his* share £393 5s. 1d.! At the expiration of
five years and a half, the injured and oppressed Mr.
James Ballantyne had *overdrawn* his share of the profits
to the amount of £2027 2s. 5d., while Scott had *underdrawn*
his share by the sum of £577 2s. 8d. Now let any man
of common practical sense, from Mr. Rothschild's successor,
whoever he may be, down to the commonest light porter
and warehouseman who can read and write and cast
accounts, say, upon such a statement of figures as this,

who was the gainer by the partnership, who may be supposed to have had objects and designs of his own to serve
in forming it, and in what pecuniary situation Mr. James
Ballantyne—the needy and embarrassed printer of Kelso—
must have been placed, when Scott first shed upon him
the light of his countenance.

"Scott, in those days," says Mr. Lockhart, "had neither
bought land, now indulged in any private habits likely to
hamper his pecuniary condition. He had a handsome
income, nowise derived from commerce. He was already
a highly popular author, and had received from the booksellers copy-monies of then unprecedented magnitude.
With him the only speculation and the only source of
embarrassment was this printing concern; and how, had
the other partner conducted himself in reference to it as
Scott did, could it have been any source of embarrassment at all? He was, I cannot but think, imperfectly
acquainted with James Ballantyne's pecuniary means, as
well as with his habits and tastes, when the firm was set
up. He was deeply injured by his partner's want of skill
and care in the conduct of the concern, and not less so
by that partner's irreclaimable personal extravagance; and
he was systematically mystified by the States, etc., prepared
by Mr. John. In fact, every balance sheet that has been
preserved, or made accessible to me, seems to be fallacious.
They are not of the company's entire affairs, but of one
particular account in their books only—viz. the expenditure
on the printing work done, and the produce of that work.
This delusive system appears to have continued till the
end of 1823, after which date the books are not even
added or *written* up."

In 1809, the bookselling firm started, Scott having one
moiety for his share, and the two brothers the remaining

moiety for theirs. He put down £1000 for his share, and
LENT Mr. James Ballantyne £500 for his; (!) and by the
month of June 1810 he had embarked £9000 in the two
concerns. Mr. James Ballantyne, even now, had no capital;
he borrowed capital from Scott to form the bookselling
establishment; he rendered the system of accommodation
bills necessary by so egregiously overdrawing so small a
capital as they staited with; and not satisfied with this,
he grossly neglected and mismanaged the business (by his
own confession) during the whole time of its superintendence
being entrusted to him.

In 1815 (the year of Mr. James Ballantyne's marriage)
the bookselling business was abandoned; there were no
resources with which to meet its obligations but those of
the printing company, and Scott, in January, 1816, writes
thus to him—

"The burthen must be upon you and me—that is, on
the printing office. If you will agree to conduct this
business henceforth with steadiness and care, and to
content yourself with £400 a-year from it for your private
purposes, its profits will ultimately set us free. I agree
that we should grant mutual discharges as booksellers,
and consider the whole debt as attaching to you and me
as printers. I agree, farther, that the responsibility of
the whole debt should be assumed by myself alone for
the present—provided you, on your part, never interfere
with the printing profits, beyond your allowance, until
the debt has been obliterated, or put into such a train
of liquidation that you see your way clear, and voluntarily
reassume your station as my partner, instead of continuing
to be, as you now must consider yourself, merely my
steward, book-keeper, and manager in the Canongate."

Now, could the dullest and most addle-headed man

alive be brought to believe—is it in human nature, in common sense, or common reason—that if Mr. James Ballantyne had the smallest ground of just complaint against Scott at this time, he would have listened to such a proposition? But he *did* listen to it, and eagerly embraced it; and in the October of that very year this same Mr. James Ballantyne, whose besotted trustees have dragged the circumstance to light from the concealment in which Mr. Lockhart mercifully left it—this same Mr. James Ballantyne, the plundered and deluded victim of Scott, announces to him that, being pressed by a younger brother at Kelso for a personal debt—not a partnership liability— a personal debt of £500, he had paid away to him a bill of the company, and, but for this bill being dishonoured by an accidental circumstance, Scott would, in all human probability have never heard one word of the matter down to the day of his death.

Does Mr. James Ballantyne brazen this proceeding out, and retort upon Scott, "I have been your tool and instrument. But for you I should have been by this time a man in affluent circumstances, and well able to pay this money. You brought me to this pass by your misconduct; it was your bounden duty to extricate me, and I had a right to extricate myself by the use of your name for my own purposes, when you have so often used mine for yours"? Judge from the following extracts from his letters on the subject:—

"It is needless for me to dwell on my deep regret at the *disereditable incident* which has taken place. * * * *I was not aware of the terrible consequences arising from one acting partner's using the copartnery signature for his personal purposes. I assure you, Sir, I should very nearly as soon* FORGE *your own signature as use one which implicated your* *credit and property for what belonged to me personally.*"

And then he goes on in a tone of great humility, endeavouring to excuse himself thus:—

"I respectfully beg leave to call to your recollection a very long and not very pleasant correspondence two years ago, on the subject of the debts due to my brother Alexander, and I may now shortly re-state, that the money advanced by him went into the funds of the business, and at periods when it was imperiously wanted. No doubt it went in *in my name, to help up my share of stock equal to yours;* but I honestly confess to you, that this consideration never went into my calculation, and that when I agreed that the name of James B. and Co. should be given to the bills for that money, I had no other idea than that it was an *easy mode of procuring money*, at a very serious crisis, when money was greatly wanted; nor did I see that I should refuse it because the lender was my brother. His cash was as good as another's. *Personally*, I never received a sixpence of it."

Personally he never received a sixpence of it! Oh certainly not. That is to say, Mr. James Ballantyne paid the money to the partnership banking account towards his share of the joint capital, and immediately set about drawing private cheques as fast as he could draw for three times the sum.

In 1821 Mr. John Ballantyne died, and Mr. James Ballantyne, petitioning Scott that a termination might be put to his stewardship, and that he might be admitted to a new share in the business, he becomes, under a deed bearing date on the 1st. of April, 1822 (the missive letter, in Scott's handwriting, laying down the heads of which, is given by Mr. Lockhart at length) once more a partner in the business. The circumstances under which his steward-

ship had been undertaken,—and this request for a new
partnership was conceded by Scott,—are thus stated by
Mr. Lockhart; and the statement is, in every respect in
which we have been able to examine it, borne out by
facts:—

"For the preparation of the formal contract of 1822,
Sir Walter selected Mrs. James Ballantyne's brother. We
have seen that this Mr. George Hogarth, a man of business,
a writer to the Signet, a gentleman whose ability and
intelligence no one can dispute, was privy to all the transactions between Scott and James, whereupon the matri-
monial negotiation proceeded to its close;—and that Mr.
Hogarth approved of, and Mr. Ballantyne expressed deep
gratitude for, the arrangements then dictated by Sir Walter
Scott. Must not these Trustees themselves, when confronted
with the evidence now given, admit, that these arrangements
were most liberal and generous? Scott, 'the business being
in difficulties,' takes the whole of those difficulties upon
himself. He assumes, for a prospective series of five or six
years, the whole responsibility of its debts and its expenditure, including a liberal salary to James as manager.
In order to provide him with the means of paying a *personal* debt of £3000 due to himself—and wholly distinct
from copartnery debts—Scott agrees to secure for him a
certain part of the proceeds of every novel that shall be
written during the continuance of this arrangement. With
the publishing of these novels James was to have no
trouble—there was no risk about them—the gain on each
was clear and certain,—and of every sum thus produced
by the exertion of Scott's genius and industry, James
Ballantyne was to have a sixth, as a mere bonus to help
him in paying off his debt of £3000, upon which debt,
moreover, no interest was to be charged. In what respect

did this differ from drawing the pen, every five or six months, through a very considerable portion of the debt? Scott was undertaking neither more nor less than to take the money out of his own pocket, and pay it regularly into James's, who had no more risk or trouble in the publication of those immortal works than any printer in Westminster. The Pamphleteers must admit that James, pending this arrangement, was not the partner, but literally the paid servant of his benefactor, and that while 'the total responsibility of the debts and expenditure of the business' lay on Scott, Scott had the perfect right to make any use he pleased of its profits and credit. They must admit, that after the arrangement had continued for five years, James examined the state of the concern, and petitioned Scott to replace him as a partner; that so far from finding any reason to complain of what Scott had done with the business while it was solely his, without one word of complaint as to this large amount of floating bills so boldly averred in the Pamphlet to have been drawn for Scott's personal accommodation, James, in praying for readmission, acknowledged that down to the close of that period (June 1821) he had grossly neglected *the most important parts* of the business whereof he had had charge as Scott's stipendiary servant;—acknowledged, that notwithstanding his salary as manager of the printing-office, another salary of £200 a-year as editor of a newspaper, and the large sums he derived from novel-copyrights given to him *ex merâ gratiâ*,—he had so misconducted his own private affairs, that having begun his stewardship as debtor to Scott for £3000, he, when he wished the stewardship to terminate, owed Scott much more than £3000; but that, acknowledging all this, he made at the same time such solemn promises of amendment for the future, that Scott

consented to do as he prayed; only stipulating, that until
the whole affairs of the printing business should be reduced
to perfect order, *debts discharged*, its stock and disposable
funds increased, each partner should limit himself to drawing
£500 per annum for his personal use. They must admit
that James made all these acknowledgments and promises;
that Scott accepted them graciously; and that the moment
before the final copartnership was signed, James Ballantyne
was Sir Walter Scott's debtor, entirely at his mercy; that
down to that· moment, by James's own clear confession,
Scott, as connected with this printing establishment, had
been sinned against, not sinning.

"The contract prepared and written by Mr. Hogarth,
was signed on the 1st of April 1822. It bears express
reference to the 'missive letter dated the 15th and 22nd
of June last,' by which the parties had 'concluded an
agreement for the settlement of the accounts and transactions subsisting between them, and also for the terms
of the said new copartnery, and agreed to execute a
regular deed in implement of said agreement;' and 'therefore
and for the reasons more particularly specified in the
said missive letters, which are here specially referred to,
and held as repeated, they have agreed, and hereby agree
to the following articles.' Then follow the articles of
agreement, embodying the substance of the missive. Scott
is to draw the whole profits of the business prior to Whitsunday, 1822, in respect of the responsibility he had
undertaken. Ballantyne acknowledges a personal debt of
£1800 as at Whitsunday, 1821, which was to be paid
out of the funds specified in the missives, no interest
being due until after Whitsunday 1822. Sir Walter having
advanced £2575 for buildings in the Canongate, new
types, etc., James is to grant a bond for the half of that

sum. It further appears by the only cashbook exhibited to me, that James, notwithstanding his *frugal* mode of living, had quietly drawn £1629 more than his allowance between 1816 and 1822, but of *this*, as it is stated, as *a balance of cash*, due by James at Whitsunday, 1822, Scott could not have been aware when with his own hand he wrote the missive letter. Sir Walter, I have said, was to be liable for all the debts contracted between 1816 and 1822, but to have the exclusive right of property in all the current funds, to enable him to pay off these debts, and as the deed bears, 'to indemnify him for his advances on account of the copartnery'—*i.e.* from 1816 to 1822. Finally, JAMES BECOMES BOUND TO KEEP REGULAR AND DISTINCT BOOKS, WHICH ARE TO BE BALANCED ANNUALLY. Now, on looking at the import of this legal instrument, as well as the missive which it corroborated, and the prior communications between the parties, whom would an unbiassed reader suppose to have been the partner most benefited by this concern in time past,—whom to be the person most likely to have trespassed upon its credit, and embarrassed its resources?"

How did Mr. James Ballantyne perform his part of *this* contract? From January, 1822, to May, 1826, when the affairs were wound up, he was entitled to have drawn in all about £1750. He drew in all £7581 15s. 5d. Of whose money? Assuredly not his own.

For Mr. Lockhart's explanation of the *Vidimus*, and of the refuter's construction and distortion of certain important items which go a long way towards accounting for the great increase in the accommodation bills, and show how improperly, and with what an appearance of wilful error, certain receipts and charges have been fixed upon Scott, which might with as much justice have been fixed upon the Chancellor of the Exchequer, or the Bank of Scotland, we must refer our readers to the pamphlet itself, and merely state these general results : That, in 1823, the accommodations of James Ballantyne and Co. amounted to £36,000 ; that there is no shadow or scrap of evidence to show that any of these accommodation bills had been issued for Scott's private purposes ; that it is made a matter of charge in the *Refutation* pamphlet that in 1826 they had increased to £46,000 ; that we now find that of this additional £10,000 Mr. James Ballantyne himself pocketed (calculating interest) more than £8000, and that all the expenses of stamps and renewals have to be charged against the remaining £2000 ; finally, that Scott, who is asserted to have ruined these Ballantynes by his ambition to become a landed proprietor, invested in all, up to June, 1821, £29,083 in the purchase of land, having received since 1811 an official income of £1600 per annum, and gained, as an author, £80,000. Let any plain, unprejudiced man, who has learnt that two and two make four, and who has moved in the world in the ordinary pursuits of life, put these facts together, read this correspondence with acknowledgments of error and misconduct on the part of the Messrs. Ballantyne repeated from day to day and urged from year to year—let him examine these trans- actions, and find that in every one which is capable of explanation now the parties are in their graves, the extravagance, thoughtlessness, recklessness, and wrong have been upon the part of these pigmies, and the truest magnanimity and forbearance on the side of the giant who upheld them, and under the shadow of whose protec- tion they gradually came to lose sight of their own stature, and to imagine themselves as great as he—let any man divest himself of that lurking desire to carp and cavil over

the actions of men who have raised themselves high above
their fellows, which unhappily seems inherent in human
nature, and bring to this subject but the calmest and
most plodding consideration of facts and probabilities—
and say whether it is possible to arrive at any conclusion
but that the Messrs. Ballantyne and the Messrs. Ballantyne's descendants owe a deep and lasting debt of gratitude
to Sir Walter Scott as the originator of all the name,
fame, and fortune they may possess, or to which they can
ever aspire—and that this attempt to blacken the memory
of the dead benefactor of their house would be an act of
the basest and most despicable ingratitude, were it not
one of the most puling and drivelling folly.

That Mr. James Ballantyne did not know at what time
Abbotsford had ceased to stand "between him and ruin,"—
that he did not know, and well know, that Sir Walter Scott
had made the settlement of it which he did upon his son's
marriage, is next to impossible. All Edinburgh rung with
it for days; the topic was canvassed in every bookseller's
shop and discussed at every street corner; gossips carried
it from door to door; advocates discoursed upon it in
loquacious groups in the outer house; and the very boys
at the high school bandied it from mouth to mouth. To
Professor Wilson, Mr. Sheriff Cay, Mr. Peter Robertson,
all the known men and women of Edinburgh, and all the
unknown men and women also, it was notorious as the
existence of Arthur's Seat or Holyrood. Is it to be
believed that Mr. James Ballantyne alone, shut up in his
printing-office in solitary admiration of his old critiques on
Mrs. Siddons or his improvements in Scott's romances,
was in ignorance of the fact while its resounded through
the city from end to end, or that he could have remained
so for the space of nine long months? The insinuations

put forth by "the trustees and son of the late Mr. James
Ballantyne respecting his marriage, and his throwing his
wife's portion into the partnership fund at Scott's command, are no less monstrous. How stands this fact? Why,
that but for Scott's kindness and goodness he never could
have contracted it.—" I fear I am in debt for more than
all I possess—to a lenient creditor no doubt; but still the
debt exists."—" I am, *de jure et de facto*, wholly dependent
on you."—"All, and more than all, belonging ostensibly
to me, is, I presume, yours."—God be praised *that, after
all your cruel vexations, you know the extent of your loss.
It has been great, but few men have such resources.*" Such
are the terms in which Mr. James Ballantyne addresses his
"dear friend and benefactor" when, being deep in love
as well as in debt, he solicits that aid from his lenient
creditor, which, after all the cruel loss and vexation, the
latter did not withhold.

Ruin! ruin brought upon the Ballantynes by Scott—by
Scott, who aided and assisted them at every turn, from
the first hour when he found Mr. James Ballantyne, a
poor and struggling tradesman in a small Scotch town,
down to those later days when the same patronage and
notice enabled him to affect criticism and taste, Shakespeare and the Musical Glasses, and to get a good business
—which would have been a better one if he had minded
it—and to leave it to this very son, who is made to talk
about his father having cast his bread upon the waters,
and so forth, in a style not unworthy of Mr. James Ballantyne's own extravagant solemnity! Ruin! Where are
the signs and tokens of this ruin? Are they discernible
in the position of Mr. James Ballantyne at any one time
after he had fluttered, butterfly-like, into Edinburgh notoriety
through the influence of Scott, but for whom he would

have lived and died a grub at Kelso? Are they manifest in the present conditon of his son, who has acquired and inherited an honourable trade which he will do well to stick to, disregarding the promptings of weak and foolish friends? Good God! How much of the profits of the last edition of the Waverley Novels has gone to the schooling, apprenticing, boarding, lodging, washing, clothing, and feeding of this very young man, and in how different a manner would he have been schooled, apprenticed, boarded, lodged, washed, clothed, and fed, without them!

There is nothing in the whole of these transactions, which, to our mind, casts the smallest doubt or suspicion upon Sir Walter Scott, save in one single particular. His repeated forgiveness of his careless partners, and his constant and familiar association with persons so much beneath a man of his transcendent abilities and elevated station, lead us to fear that he turned a readier ear than became him to a little knot of toad-eaters and flatterers.

[1839]

Much Ado about Nothing and *Comus* were repeated on Tuesday to a crowded house. They were received with no less enthusiasm than on the night of Mr. Macready's benefit; and are announced for repetition twice a week.

We are desirous to say a few words of Mr. Macready's performance of *Benedick;* not because its striking merits require any commendation to those who witness it—as is sufficiently shown by its reception—but because justice is scarcely done to his impersonation of the character, as we think, by some of those who have reported upon it for the nobility and gentry (not quite so limited a one as could be desired, perhaps) who seldom enter a Theatre unless it be a foreign one; or, who, when they do repair to an English temple of the drama, would seem to be attracted thither solely by an amiable desire to purify, by their presence, a scene of vice and indecorum; and who select their place of entertainment accordingly.

There are many reasons why a tragic actor incurs considerable risk of failing to enlist the sympathies of his audience when he appears in comedy. In the first place, some people are rather disposed to take it ill that he should make them laugh who has so often made them cry. In the second he has not only to make the impression which he seeks to produce in that particular character, but has to render it, at once, so obvious and distinct, as to cast into oblivion for the time all the host of grave associations with which he is identified. Lastly, there is a very general feeling abroad in reference to all the arts, and every phase of public life, that the path which a man has trodden for many years—even though it should be the primrose path to the everlasting bonfire—must be of necessity his allotted one, and that it is, as a matter of course, the only one in which he is qualified to walk.

First impressions, too, even with persons of a cultivated understanding, have an immense effect in settling their notions of a character; and it is no heresy to say that many people unconsciously form their opinion of such a creation as *Benedick*, not so much from the exercise of their own judgment in reading the play, as from what they have seen bodily presented to them on the stage. Thus, when they call to mind that in such a place Mr. A. or Mr. B. used to stick his arms akimbo and shake his head knowingly; or that in such another place he gave the pit to understand, by certain confidential nods and winks, that in good time they should see what they should see; or in such another place, swaggered; or in such another place, with one hand clasping each of his sides, heaved his shoulders as with laughter; they recall his image, not as the Mr. A. or B. aforesaid, but as Shakspeare's *Benedick*—the real *Benedick* of the book, not the conventional *Benedick* of the boards—and missing any familiar action, miss, as it were, something of right belonging to the part.

Against all these difficulties, Mr. Macready has had to contend, as any such man must, in his performance of *Benedick*, and yet before his very first scene was over on

the first night of the revival, the whole house felt that
there was before them a presentment of the character so
fresh, distinct, vigorous, and enjoyable, as they could not
choose but relish, and go along with, delightedly, to the
fall of the curtain.

If it be beyond the province of what we call genteel
comedy—a term which Shakspeare would have had some
difficulty in understanding, perhaps—to make people laugh;
then, assuredly, Mr. Macready is far from being a genteely
comic *Benedick*. But as we find him—*Signior Benedick* of
Padua, that is, not the *Benedick* of this or that theatrical
company—the constant occasion of merriment among the
persons represented in *Much Ado about Nothing;* "all
mirth," as *Don Pedro* has it, from the crown of his
head to the sole of his foot;" and as we find him, in
particular, constantly moving to laughter both the *Prince*
and *Claudio*, who may be reasonably supposed to possess
their share of refined and courtier-like behaviour; we venture
to think that those who sit below the salt, or t'other side
the lamps, should laugh also. And that they did and
do, both loud and long, let the ringing walls of Drury
Lane bear witness.

Judging of it by analogy; by comparison with anything
we know in nature, literature, art; by any test we can
apply to it, from within us or without, we can imagine
no purer or higher piece of genuine comedy than Mr.
Macready's performance of the scene in the orchard after
emerging from the arbour. As he sat, uneasily cross-legged,
on the garden chair, with that face of grave bewilderment
and puzzled contemplation, we seemed to be looking on
a picture by Leslie. It was just such a figure as that
excellent artist, in his fine appreciation of the finest
humour, might have delighted to produce. Those who

consider it broad, or farcical, or overstrained, cannot surely have considered all the train and course of circumstances leading up to that place. If they take them into reasonable account, and try to imagine for a moment how any master of fiction would have described *Benedick's* behaviour at that crisis—supposing it had been impossible to contemplate the appearance of a living man in the part, and therefore necessary to describe it at all—can they arrive at any other conclusion than that such ideas as are here presented by Mr. Macready would have been written down. Refer to any passage in any play of Shakspeare's, where it has been necessary to describe, as occurring beyond the scene, the behaviour of a man in a situation of ludicrous perplexity; and by that standard alone (to say nothing of any mistaken notion of natural behaviour that may have suggested itself at any time to Goldsmith, Swift, Fielding, Smollett, Sterne, Scott, or other such unenlightened journeymen) criticise, if you please, this portion of Mr. Macready's admirable performance.

The nice distinction between such an aspect of the character as this, and the after love scenes with *Beatrice*, the challenging of *Claudio*, or the gay endurance and return of the *Prince's* jests at last, was such as none but a master could have expressed, though the veriest tyro in the house might feel its truth when presented to him. It occurred to us that Mr. Macready's avoidance of *Beatrice* in the second act was a little too earnest and real; but it is hard dealing to find so slight a blemish in such a finished and exquisite performance. For such, in calm reflection, and not in the excitement of having recently witnessed it, we unaffectedly and impartially believe it to be.

The other characters are, for the most part, exceedingly well played. *Claudio*, in the gay and gallant scenes, has

an efficient representative in Mr. Anderson; but his perfect
indifference to *Hero's* supposed death is an imputation on
his good sense, and a disagreeable circumstance in the
representation of the play, which we should be heartily
glad to see removed. Mr. Compton has glimpses of *Dog-
berry*, though iron was never harder than he. If he could
but derive a little oil from his contact with Keeley (whose
utter absorption in his learned neighbour is amazing), he
would become an infinitely better leader of the *Prince's*
Watch. Mrs. Nisbett is no less charming than at first, and
Miss Fortescue is more so, from having a greater share of
confidence in her bearing, and a somewhat smaller nosegay
in her breast. Both Mr. Phelps and Mr. W. Bennett deserve
especial notice, as acting at once with great spirit and
great discretion.

Let those who still cling to the opinion that the Senate
of ancient Rome represented by five-shillings' worth of
supernumerary assistance huddled together at a rickety
table, with togas above the cloth and corduroys below, is
more gratifying and instructive to behold than the living
Truth presented to them in *Coriolanus* during Mr. Macready's
management of Covent Garden,—let such admirers of the
theatre track the mazes of the wild wood in *Comus*, as it
is now produced; let them look upon the stage, what time

> He and his monstrous rout are heard to howl,
> Like stabbed wolves, or tigers at their prey,
> Doing abhorred rites to Hecate
> In their obscured haunts of inmost bowers,

—and reconcile their previous notions with any principle
of human reason, if they can.   [1843]

REPORT OF THE COMMISSIONERS APPOINTED TO INQUIRE INTO THE CONDITION OF THE PERSONS VARIOUSLY ENGAGED IN THE UNIVERSITY OF OXFORD.

IT can scarcely be necessary for us to remind our readers that a Commission under the Great Seal was appointed some months since, to inquire into the deplorable amount of ignorance and superstition alleged to prevail in the university of Oxford; concerning which, the representatives of that learned body in the Commons' House of Parliament, had then, and have since, at divers times, publicly volunteered the most alarming and astounding evidence. The Commission was addressed to those gentlemen who had investigated the moral condition of the Children and Young Persons employed in Mines and Manufactories; it being wisely considered that their opportunities of reporting on the darkness of Colleges as compared with Mines, and on the prejudicial atmosphere of Seats of Learning as compared with Seats of Labour, would be highly advantageous to the public interest, and might possibly open the public eyes.

The Commissioners have ever since been actively engaged in pursuing their inquiries into this subject, and deducing from the mass of evidence, such conclusions as appeared to them to be warranted by the facts. Their Report is now before us, and though it has not yet been presented to Parliament, we venture to give it entire.

The Commissioners find:

First, with regard to EMPLOYMENT—

That the intellectual works in the University of Oxford are, in all essential particulars, precisely what they were, when it was first established for the Manufacture of Clergymen. That they alone have stood still (or, in the very few instances in which they have moved at all, have moved backward), when all other works have advanced and improved. That the nature of the employment in which the young persons are engaged, is, by reason of its excessive dust and rust, extremely pernicious and destructive. That they all become shortsighted in a most remarkable degree; that, for the most part, they lose the use of their reason at a very early age, and are seldom known to recover it. That the most hopeless and painful extremes of deafness and blindness are frequent among them. That they are reduced to such a melancholy state of apathy and indifference as to be willing to sign anything, without asking what it is, or knowing what it means; which is a common custom with these unhappy persons, even to the extent of nine-and-thirty articles at once. That, from the monotonous nature of their employment, and the dull routine of their unvarying drudgery (which requires no exercise of original intellectual power, but is a mere parrot-like performance), they become painfully uniform in character and perception, and are reduced to one dead level (a very dead one, as your Commissioners believe) of mental imbecility. That cramps and paralysis of all the higher faculties of the brain, are the ordinary results of this system of labour. And your Commissioners can truly add, that they found nothing in the avocations of the miners of Scotland, the knife-grinders of Sheffield, or the workers in iron of Wolverhampton, one-half so prejudicial to the persons engaged therein, or one-half so injurious to society, as this fatal system of employment in the University of Oxford.

Secondly, with regard to the PREVAILING IGNORANCE—

That the condition of the University of Oxford, under this head, is of the most appalling kind; insomuch that your Commissioners are firmly of opinion that, taking all the attendant circumstances into consideration, the Young Persons employed in Mines and Manufactories are enlightened beings, radiant with intelligence, and overflowing with the best results of knowledge, when compared with the persons, young and old, employed in the Manufacture of Clergymen at Oxford. And your Commissioners have been led to this conclusion: not so much by the perusal of prize poems, and a due regard to the very small number of Young Persons accustomed to University Employment who distinguish themselves in after life, or become in any way healthy and wholesome; as by immediate reference to the evidence taken on the two Commissions, and an impartial consideration of the two classes of testimony, side by side.

That it is unquestionably true that a boy was examined under the Children's Employment Commission, at Brinsley, in Derbyshire, who had been three years at school, and could not spell "Church;" whereas there is no doubt that the persons employed in the University of Oxford can all spell Church with great readiness, and, indeed, very seldom spell anything else. But, on the other hand, it must not be forgotten that, in the minds of the persons employed in the University of Oxford, such comprehensive words as justice, mercy, charity, kindness, brotherly love, forbearance, gentleness, and Good Works, awaken no ideas whatever; while the evidence shows that the most preposterous notions are attached to the mere terms Priest and Faith.

One young person, employed in a Mine, had no other idea of a Supreme Being than "that he had heard him constantly damned at;" but use the verb to damn, in this horrible connection with the Fountain Head of Mercy, in the active sense, instead of in the passive one; and make the Deity the nominative case instead of the objective; and how many persons employed in the University of Oxford, have their whole faith in, and whole knowledge of, the Maker of the World, presented in a worse and far more impious sentence!

That the answers of persons employed in the said University, to questions put to them by the Sub-Commissioners in the progress of this inquiry, bespoke a moral degradation infinitely lower than any brought to light in Mines and Factories; as may be gathered from the following examples. A vast number of witnesses being interrogated as to what they understood by the words Religion and Salvation, answered Lighted Candles. Some said water; some, bread; others, little boys; others mixed the water, lighted candles, bread, and little boys all up together, and called the compound, Faith. Others again, being asked if they deemed it to be matter of great interest in Heaven, and of high moment in the vast scale of creation, whether a poor human priest should put on, at a certain time, a white robe or a black one; or should turn his face to the East or to the West; or should bend his knees of clay; or stand, or worm on end upon the earth; said, "Yes they did:" and being further questioned, whether a man could hold such mummeries in his contempt, and pass to everlasting rest, said boldly, "No." (*See Evidence of Pusey and others.*)

And one boy (quite an old boy, too, who might have known better) being interrogated in a public class, as to whether it was his opinion that a man who professed to go to church was of necessity a better man than one who went to chapel, also answered "Yes;" which your Commissioners submit, is an example of ignorance, besotted dulness, and obstinacy, wholly without precedent in the inquiry limited to Mines and Factories; and is such as the system of labour adopted in the University of Oxford, could alone produce (*See Evidence of Inglis.*) In the former Commission, one boy anticipated all examination by volunteering the remark, "that he warn't no judge of nuffin;" but the persons employed in the University of Oxford, almost to a man, concur in saying "that they ain't no judges of nuffin," (with the unimportant exception of other men's souls); and that, believing in the divine ordination of any minister to whom they may take a fancy, "they ain't answerable for nuffin to nobody;" which your Commissioners again submit, is an infinitely worse case, and is fraught with much greater mischief to the general welfare. (*See the Evidence in general*).

We humbly represent to your Majesty that the persons who give these answers, and hold these opinions, and are in this alarming state of ignorance and bigotry, have it in their power to do much more evil than the other ill-qualified teachers of Young Persons employed in Mines and Factories, inasmuch as those were voluntary instructors of youth, who can be removed at will, and as the public improvement demands, whereas these are the appointed Sunday teachers of the empire, forced by law upon your Majesty's subjects, and not removable for incompetence or misconduct otherwise than by certain overseers called Bishops, who are, in general, more incompetent and worse conducted than themselves. Wherefore, it is our loyal duty to recommend to your Majesty that the pecuniary, social

4

and political privileges, now arising from the degradation and debasement of the minds and morals of your Majesty's subjects, be no longer granted to these persons; or at least that if they continue to exercise an exclusive power of conferring Learned degrees and distinctions, the titles of the same be so changed and altered, that they may in some degree express the tenets in right of which they are bestowed. And this, we suggest to your Majesty, may be done without any great violation of the true Conservative principle: inasmuch as the initial letters of the present degrees (not by any means the least important parts of them) may still be retained as Bachelor of Absurdity, Master of Arrogance, Doctor of Church Lunacy, and the like.

All which we humbly certify to your Majesty.

THOMAS TOOKE (L. S.)
T. SOUTHWOOD SMITH (L. S.)
LEONARD HORNER (L. S.)
ROBT. J. SAUNDERS (L. S.)

Westminster, June 1, 1843.

THE NIGER EXPEDITION.

It might be laid down as a very good general rule of social and political guidance, that whatever Exeter Hall champions, is the thing by no means to be done. If it were harmless on a cursory view, if it even appeared to have some latent grain of common-sense at the bottom of it—which is a very rare ingredient in any of the varieties of gruel that are made thick and slab by the weird old women who go about, and exceedingly roundabout, on the Exeter Hall platform—such advocacy might be held to be a final and fatal objection to it, and to any project capable of origination in the wisdom or folly of man.

The African Expedition, of which these volumes[1] contain the melancholy history, is in no respect an exception to the rule. Exeter Hall was not in its behalf, and it failed. Exeter Hall was hottest on its weakest and most hopeless objects, and in those it failed (of course) most signally. Not, as Captain Allen justly claims for himself and his gallant comrades, not through any want of courage and self-devotion on the part of those to whom it was entrusted;

[1] "Narrative of the Expedition sent by Her Majesty's Government to the River Niger in 1841, under the command of Captain H. D. Trotter R.N". By Captain William Allen, R.N., Commander of H. M. S. Wilberforce, and T. R. H. Thomson, M.D., one of the medical officers of the Expedition. Published with the sanction of the Colonial Office and the Admiralty.

—the sufferings of all, the deaths of many, the dismal wear
and tear of stout frames and brave spirits, sadly attest the
fact;—but because, if the ends sought to be attained are
to be won, they must be won by other means than the
exposure of inestimable British lives to certain destruction
by an enemy against which no gallantry can contend, and
the enactment of a few broad farces for the entertainment
of a King Obi, King Boy, and other such potentates, whose
respect for the British force is, doubtless, likely to be very
much enhanced by their relishing experience of British
credulity in such representations, and our perfect impotency
in opposition to their climate, their falsehood, and deceit.

The main ends to be attained by the Expedition were
these: The abolition, in great part, of the Slave Trade,
by means of treaties with native chiefs, to whom were to
be explained the immense advantages of general unrestricted
commerce with Great Britain in lieu thereof; the substitution of free for Slave labour in the dominions of those
chiefs; the introduction into Africa of an improved system
of agricultural cultivation; the abolition of human sacrifices;
the diffusion among those Pagans of the true doctrines of
Christianity; and a few other trifling points, no less easy
of attainment. A glance at this short list, and a retro-
spective glance at the great number of generations during
which they have all been comfortably settled in our own
civilised land, never more to be the subjects of dispute,
will tend to materially remove any aspect of slight difficulty
they may present. To make the treaties, certain officers
of the Expedition were constituted her Majesty's Commissioners. To render them attractive to the native chiefs,
a store of presents was provided. And to enforce them,
" one or more small forts" were to be built, on land to
be bought for the purpose on the banks of the Niger;

which forts were, "to assist in the abolition of the Slave Trade, and further the innocent trade of her Majesty's subjects." The Niger was to be explored, the resources and productions of the country were to be inquired into and reported on, and various important and scientific observations, astronomical, geographical, and otherwise, were to be made; but these were by the way. A Model-Farm was to be established by an agricultual society at home; and besides allowing stowage-room on board the ships for its various stores, implements, etc., the Admiralty granted a free passage to Mr. Alfred Carr, a West Indian gentleman of colour, engaged as its superintendent. By all these means combined, as Dr. Lushington and Sir Thomas Fowell Buxton wrote to Lord John Russell, who was then Colonial Secretary, the people of Africa were "to be awakened to a proper sense of their own degradation."

On this awakening mission three vessels were appointed. They were flat-bottomed iron steam vessels, built for the purpose. The Albert and the Wilberforce, each 139 feet 4 inches in length, and 27 feet in breadth of beam, and drawing 6 feet water, were in all respects exactly alike. The Soudan, intended for detached service, was much smaller, and drew a foot and a-half less water. They were very ingeniously conceived, with certain rudder-tails and sliding keels for sea service; but they performed most unaccountable antics in bad weather, and had a perverse tendency to go to leeward, which nothing would conquer. Dr. Reid fitted them up with what 'My Lords' describe as an ingenious and costly ventilating apparatus, the preparation of which occasioned a loss of much valuable time, and the practical effect of which was to suffocate the crews. "That truly amiable Prince," the Prince Consort, came

on board at Woolwich, and gave a handsome gold chrono-
meter to each of the three captains. The African Civilisation Society came down with a thousand pounds. The
Church of England Missionary Society provided a missionary and a catechist. Exeter Hall, in a ferment, was for
ever blocking up the gangway. At last, on the 12th of
May, 1841, at half past six in the morning, the line of
battle ships anchored in Plymouth Sound gave three cheers
to the Expedition as it steamed away, unknowing, for
" the Gate of the Cemetery." Such was the sailors' name,
thereafter, for the entrance to the fatal river whither they
were bound.

At Sierra Leone, in the middle of June following, the
interpreters were taken on board, together with some
liberated Africans, their wives and children, who were
engaged there by Mr. Carr as labourers on the model
Farm. Also, a large gang of Krumen to assist in working
the vessels, and to save the white men as much as possible from exposure to the sun and heavy rains. Of these
negroes—a faithful, cheerful, active, affectionate race—a
very interesting account is given; which seems to render
it clear that they, under civilized direction, are the
only hopeful human agents to whom recourse can ultimately be had for aid in working out the slow and
gradual raising up of Africa. Those eminent Krumen,
Jack Flying Pan, King George, Prince Albert, Jack Sprat,
Bottle-of-Beer, Tom Tea Kettle, the Prince of Wales, the
Duke of York, and some four-score others, enrolled
themselves on the ships' books, here, under Jack
Andrews, their head man; and these being joined,
at Cape Palmas, by Jack Smoke, Captain Allen's faithful
servant and attendant in sickness in his former African
expedition, the complement was complete. Thence the

Expedition made for Cape Coast Castle, where much valuable assistance was derived from governor MacLean; and thence for the Nun branch of the Niger—the Gate of the Cemetery. [1]

After a fortnight's voyage up the river the Royal residence of King Obi was reached. A solemn conference with this sovereign was soon afterwards held on board the Albert. His Majesty was dressed in a sergeant-major's coat, given him by Lander, and a loose pair of scarlet trousers, presented to him on the same occasion, and a conical black velvet cap was stuck on his head in a

---

[1] Most English readers will be as unwilling as the manly writers of these volumes, to leave one spot at Cape Coast Castle, without a word of remembrance.

"In passing across the square within the walls, an object of deep interest presents itself in the little space containing all that was mortal of the late Mrs. McLean; the once well known, amiable, and accomplished L. E. L. A plain marble slab, bearing the following inscription, is placed over the spot:

Hic jacet sepultum,
Omne quod mortale fuit
LETITIÆ ELIZABETHÆ M^cLEAN,
Quam egregia ornatam indole, Musis
Unice amatam. Omniumque amores
Secum trahentem; in ipso etatis flore,
Mors immatura rapuit.
Die Octobris XV., MDCCCXXXVIII. Ætatis XXXVI.
Quod spectas viator marmor vanum
Heu doloris monumentum
Conjux mærens erexit.

"The beams of the setting sun throw a rich but subdued colouring over the place, and as we stood in sad reflection on the fate of the gifted poetess, some fine specimens of the *Hirundo Senegalensis*, or African swallow, fluttered gracefully about, as if to keep watch over a spot sacred indeed to the Muses; while the noise of the surf, breaking on the not distant shore, seemed to murmur a requiem over departed genius."

slanting manner. The following extracts describe the process of

TREATY-MAKING WITH OBI.

On being shown to the after-part of the quarter deck, where seats were provided for himself and the Commissioners, he sat down to collect his scattered ideas, which appeared to be somewhat bewildered; and after a few complimentary remarks from Captain Trotter and the other Commissioners, the conference was opened.

Captain Trotter, Senior Commissioner, explained to Obi Osaï, that her Majesty the Queen of Great Britain had sent him and the three other gentlemen composing the Commission, to endeavour to enter into treaties with African Chiefs for the abolition of the trade in human beings, which her Majesty and all the British nation held to be an injustice to their fellow-creatures, and repugnant to the laws of God; that the vessels which he saw were not trading ships, but belonging to our Queen, and were sent, at great expense, expressly to convey the Commissioners appointed by her Majesty, for the purpose of carrying out her benevolent intentions, for the benefit of Africa. Captain Trotter therefore requested the King to give a patient hearing to what the Commissioners had to say to him on the subject.

Obi expressed himself through his interpreter, or "mouth," much gratified at our visit; that he understood what was said, and would pay attention.

The Commissioners then explained that the principal object in inviting him to a conference was, to point out the injurious effects to himself and to his people of the practice of selling their slaves, thus depriving themselves of their services for ever, for a trifling sum; whereas, if these slaves were kept at home, and employed in the cultivation of the land, in collecting palm oil, or other productions of the country for commerce, they would prove a permanent source of revenue. Obi replied, that he was very willing to do away with the slave trade *if a better traffic could be substituted.*

COMMISSIONERS.—Does Obi sell slaves from his own dominions?

OBI.—No; they come from countries far away.

COMMISSIONERS.—Does Obi make war to procure slaves?

OBI.—When other chiefs quarrel with me and make war, I take all I can as slaves.

COMMISSIONERS.—What articles of trade are best suited to your people, or what would you like to be brought to your country?

OBI.—Cowries, cloth, muskets, powder, handkerchiefs, coral beads, hats—anything from the white man's country will please.

COMMISSIONERS.—You are the King of this country, as our Queen is the sovereign of Great Britain; but she does not wish to trade with you; she only desires that her subjects may trade fairly with yours. Would they buy salt?

OBI.—Yes.

COMMISSIONERS.—The Queen of England's subjects would be glad to trade for raw cotton, indigo, ivory, gums, camwood. Now have your people these things to offer in return for English trade goods?

OBI.—Yes.

COMMISSIONERS.—Englishmen will bring everything to trade but rum or spirits, which are injurious. If you induce your subjects to cultivate the ground, you will all become rich; but if you sell slaves, the land will not be cultivated, and you will become poorer by the traffic. If you do all these things which we advise you for your own benefit, our Queen will grant you, for your own profit and revenue, one out of every twenty articles sold by British subjects in the Abòh territory; so that the more you persuade your people to exchange native produce for British goods, the richer you will become. You will then have a regular profit, enforced by treaty, instead of trusting to a "dash" or present, which depends on the willingness of the traders.

OBI.—I will agree to discontinue the slave-trade, but I expect the English to bring goods for traffic.

COMMISSIONERS.—The Queen's subjects cannot come here to trade, unless they are certain of a proper supply of your produce.

OBI.—I have plenty of palm oil.

COMMISSIONERS.—Mr. Schön, missionary, will explain to you in the Ibu language what the Queen wishes, and if you do not understand, it shall be repeated.

Mr. Schön began to read the address drawn up for the purpose of showing the different tribes what the views of the Expedition were; but Obi soon appeared to be tired of a palaver which lasted so much longer than those to which he was accustomed. He manifested some impatience, and at last said:—"I have made you a promise to drop this slave trade, and do not wish to hear anything more about it."

COMMISSIONERS.—Our Queen will be much pleased if you do, and you will receive the presents which she sent for you. When people in the white man's country sign a treaty or agreement, they always abide by it. The Queen cannot come to speak to you, Obi Osaï, but she sends us to make the treaty for her.

OBI.—I can only engage my word for my own country.

COMMISSIONERS.—You cannot sell your slaves if you wish, for our Queen has many warships at the mouth of the river, and Spaniards are afraid to come and buy there.

OBI.—I understand.

He seemed to be highly amused on our describing the difficulties the slave-dealers have to encounter in the prosecution of the trade; and on one occasion, he laughed immoderately when told that our cruisers often captured slave-ships, with the cargo on board. We suspected, however, that much of his amusement arose from his knowing that slaves were shipped off at parts of the coast little thought of by us. The abundance of Brazilian rum in Abôh, showed that they often traded with nations who have avowedly no other object.

It is not difficult to imagine that Obi was 'highly amused' with the whole 'palaver', except when the recollection of its interposing between him and the presents made him restless. For nobody knew better than Obi what a joke it all was, as the result very plainly showed.

Some of the presents were now brought in, which Obi looked at with evident pleasure. His anxiety to examine them completed his inattention to the rest of the palaver.

COMMISSIONERS.—These are not all the presents that will be given to you. We wish to know if you are willing to stop boats carrying slaves through the waters of your dominions?

OBI.—Yes, very willing; except those I do not see.

COMMISSIONERS.—Also to prevent slaves being carried over your land?

OBI.—Certainly; but the English must furnish me and my people with arms, as my doing so will involve me in war with my neighbours.

Obi then retired for a short time to consult with his headmen.

COMMISSIONERS (on his return).—Have you power to make an agreement with the Commissioners in the name of all your subjects?

OBI.—I am the King. What I say is law. Are there two Kings in England? There is only one here.

COMMISSIONERS.—Understanding you have sovereign power, can you seize slaves on the river?

OBI.—Yes.

COMMISSIONERS.—You must set them free.

OBI.—Yes (*snapping his fingers several times.*)

COMMISSIONERS.—The boats must be destroyed.

OBI.—I will break the canoe, but kill no one.

COMMISSIONERS.—Suppose a man of war takes a canoe, and it is proved to be a slaver, the officer's word must be taken by the King. You, Obi, or some one for you, can be present to see justice done.

OBI.—I understand.

COMMISSIONERS.—Any new men coming henceforth to Abòh are not to be made slaves.

OBI.—Very good.

COMMISSIONERS.—If any King, or other person, sends down slaves, Obi must not buy them.

OBI.—I will not go to market to sell slaves.

COMMISSIONERS.—Any white men that are enslaved are to be made free.

The Commissioners here alluded to the case of the Landers; and asked Obi if he did not remember the circumstance of their being detained some time as slaves. Obi turning round to his sons and headmen, appealed to them, and then denied all knowledge of Lander's detention.

COMMISSIONERS.—British people who settle in Abòh must be treated as friends, in the same way as Obi's subjects would be if they were in England.

OBI.—What you say to me I will hold fast and perform.

COMMISSIONERS.—People may come here, and follow their own religion without annoyance? Our countrymen will be happy to teach our religion, without which blessing we should not be prosperous, as a nation as we now are.

OBI.—Yes, let them come; we shall be glad to hear them.

COMMISSIONERS.—British people may trade with your people; but whenever it may be in Abòh, one-twentieth part of the goods sold is to be given to the King. Are you pleased with this?

OBI.—Yes—"makka".—It is good (*snapping his fingers*).

COMMISSIONERS.—Is there any road from Abòh to Benln?

OBI.—Yes.

COMMISSIONERS.—They must all be open to the English.

OBI.—Yes.

COMMISSIONERS.—All the roads in England are open alike to all foreigners.

OBI.—In this way of trade I am agreeable.

COMMISSIONERS.—Will Obi let the English build, cultivate, buy and sell, without annoyance?

OBI.—Certainly.

COMMISSIONERS.—If your people do wrong to them, will you punish them?

OBI.—They shall be judged, and if guilty, punished.

COMMISSIONERS.—When the English do wrong, Obi must send word to an English officer, who will come and hold a palaver. You must not punish white people.

OBI.—I assent to this. (*He now became restless and impatient.*)

COMMISSIONERS.—If your people contract debts with the English they must be made to pay them.

OBI.—They shall be punished if they do not.

COMMISSIONERS.—The Queen may send an agent?

OBI.—If any Englishman comes to reside, I will show him the best place to build a house and render him every assistance.

. . . .

COMMISSIONERS.—Obi must also give every facility for forwarding letters, &c., down the river, so that the English officer who receives them may give a receipt, and also a reward for sending them.

OBI.—Very good (*snapping his fingers*).

·COMMISSIONERS.—Have you any opportunity of sending to Bonny?

OBI.—I have some misunderstanding with the people intermediate between Abòh and Bonny; but I can do it through the Brass people.

COMMISSIONERS.—Will you agree to supply men of war with firewood, provisions, etc., etc., at a fair and reasonable price?

OBI.—Yes, certainly.

The Commissioners requested Mr. Schön, the respected missionary, *to state to King Obi, in a concise manner, the difference between the Christian religion and heathenism*, together with some description of the settlement at Sierra Leone.

MR. SCHÖN.—There is but one God.

OBI.—*I always understood there were two.*[1]

Mr. Schön recapitulated the Decalogue and the leading truths of the Christian faith, and then asked Obi if this

---

[1] Some former traveller—Lander, perhaps—had possibly bewildered Obi with the Athanasian Creed.

was not a good religion, to which he replied, with a snap of his fingers, "yes, very good" (makka).

Obi concluded the conference by remarking very emphatically "that he wanted this palaver settled; that he was tired of so much talking and that he wished to go on shore." He finally said, with great impatience, "that this Slave Palaver was all over now, and he didn't wish to hear anything more of it."

The upshot of the Slave Palaver was, that Obi agreed to every article of the proposed treaty, and plighted his troth to it then and there amidst a prodigious beating of tom-toms, which lasted all night. Of course he broke the treaty on the first opportunity (being one of the falsest rascals in Africa), and went on slave-dealing vigorously. When the Expedition became helpless and disabled, newly captured slaves, chained down to the bottoms of canoes, were seen passing along the river in the heart of this same Obi's dominions.

The following is curious:

OBI ON CAPITAL PUNISHMENT.

28th. Agreeably to his promise, Obi Osaï went on board the Albert this morning, where he was received by Captain Trotter and the Commissioners, with whom he breakfasted. His dress was not so gay as on his visit of yesterday, being merely a cotton jacket and trousers, much in want of a laundress, a red cap on his head, and some strings of coral, and teeth of wild beasts, round his neck, wrists, and ankles. He entered frankly into the views previously explained to him, and assented unhesitatingly to all required from him. It was, however, necessary that the Treaty, which had been drawn upon the basis of the draft furnished by Lord John Russell with the addition of some articles relating especially to the free navigation of the river, should be again read and explained to Obi and his principal headmen, especially the heir presumptive, and the chief Ju-juman, much to their annoyance; and as all this occupied a long while, apparently to very little purpose, he completely turned against ourselves the charge we made against the black people—of not

knowing the value of time.   In agreeing to the additional article, binding
the Chief and his people to the discontinuance of the horrid custom of
sacrificing human beings, Obi very reasonably inquired what should be
done with those who might deserve death as punishment for the commission of great crimes.

Something very like this question of Obi's has been
asked, once or twice, by the very Government which sent
out these 'devil-ships', or steamers, to remodel his affairs
for him; and the point has not been settled yet.

Now let us review this Diplomacy for a moment. Obi,
though a savage in a sergeant-major's coat, may claim
with Master Slender, and perhaps with better reason, to
be not altogether an ass. Obi knows, to begin with, that
the English Government maintains a blockade, the object
of which is to prevent the exportation of slaves from his
native coasts, and which is inefficient and absurd. The
very mention of it sets him a laughing. Obi, sitting on
the quarter-deck of the Albert, looking slyly out from under
his savage forehead and his conical cap, sees before him
her Majesty's white Commissioners from the distant blockade-
country gravely propounding, at one sitting, a change in
the character of his people (formed, essentially, in the
inscrutable wisdom of God, by the soil they work on and
the air they breathe)—the substitution of a religion it is
utterly impossible he can appreciate or understand, be the
mutual interpretation never so exact and never so miraculously free from confusion, for that in which he has been
bred, and with which his priest and jugglers subdue his
subjects, the entire subversion of his whole barbarous system
of trade and revenue—and the uprooting, in a word, of
all his, and his nation's, preconceived ideas, methods, and
customs. In return for this, the white men are to trade
with him by means of ships that are to come there one

day or other; and are to quell infractions of the treaty by means of other white men, who are to learn how to draw the breath of life there, by some strong charm they certainly have not discovered yet. Can it be supposed that on this earth there lives a man who better knows than Obi, leering round upon the river's banks, the dull dead mangrove trees, the slimy and decaying earth, the rotting vegetation, that these are shadowy promises and shadowy threats, which he may give to the hot winds? In any breast in the white group about him, is there a dark presentiment of death (the pestilential air is heavier already with such whispers, to some noble hearts) half so certain as this savage's foreknowledge of the fate fast closing in? In the mind's eye of any officer or seaman looking on, is there a picture of the bones of white men bleaching in a pestilential land, and of the timbers of their poor, abandoned, pillaged ships, shewing, on the shore, like gigantic skeletons, half so vivid as Obi's? 'Too much palaver,' says Obi, with good reason. 'Give me the presents and let me go home, and beat my tom-toms all night long, for joy!'

Yet these were the means by which the African people were to be awakened to a proper sense of their own degradation. For the conclusion of such treaties with such powers, the useful lives of scholars, students, mariners, and officers—more precious than a wilderness of Africans—were thrown away!

There was another monarch at another place on the Niger, a certain Attàh of Iddàh, 'whose feet, enclosed in very large red leather boots, surrounded with little bells, dangled carelessly over the side of the throne,' who spoke through a State functionary, called the King's mouth, and who had this very orthodox notion of the Divine right:

'God made me after his image; I am all the same as God; and he appointed me a King.' With this good old sovereign a similar scene was enacted; and he, too, promised everything that was asked, and was particularly importunate to see the presents. He, also, was very much amused by the missionary's spectacles, it was supposed; and as royalty in these parts must not smile in public, the fan bearers found it necessary to hide his face very often. The Attàh dines alone—like the Pope—and is equally infallible. Some land for the Model Farm was purchased of him, and the settlement established. The reading of the deed was very patiently attended to, 'unless,' say the writers of these volumes, with the frankness which distinguishes them—'unless we mistook apathy for such a laudable bearing.'

So much is done towards the great awakening of the African people. By this time the Expedition has been in the river five weeks; fever has appeared on board of all the ships in the river; for the last three days especially, it has progressed with terrible rapidity. On board the Soudan only six persons can move about. On board the Albert the assistant surgeon lies at the point of death. On board the Wilberforce several are nearly at the same pass. Another day, and sixty, in all, are sick, and thirteen dead. 'Nothing but muttering delirium or suppressed groans are heard on every side on board the vessels.' Energy of character and strength of hope are lost, even among those not yet attacked. One officer, remarkable for fortitude and resignation, burst into tears on being addressed, and being asked the reason, replies that it is involuntary weakness produced by the climate; though it afterwards appears that, 'in addition to this cause, he has been disheartened, during a little repose snatched from his duties, by a feverish dream of home and family.' An anxious consultation is held. Captain Trotter decides to send the sick back, to the sea, in the Soudan, but Captain Allen knows the river will begin to fall straightway, and that the most unhealthy season will set in, and places his opinion on record that the ships had better all return, and make no further effort, at that time, to ascend the river.

DEPARTURE OF THE SICK.

The Soudan was accordingly got ready with the utmost possible despatch to receive her melancholy cargo, and Commander W. Allen was directed to send his sick on board. That officer, however, feeling perfectly convinced from his former experience of the river, that in a very short time H. M. S. Wilberforce would be reduced to the necessity of following the Soudan, requested permission to send such only of the sick as might desire to go; especially as he considered,—in which his surgeon, Dr. Pritchett, concurred—that the removal of the men in the state in which they were, would be attended with great risk. Only six expressed a wish to leave, the others, sixteen in number, preferred to remain by their ship. One man, on being asked whether he would like to go, said he thought we had got into a very bad place, and the sooner we were out of it the better, but he would stay by his ship.

In order to have as much air as possible for the sufferers, and to keep them from the other men, Commander W. Allen had a large screened berth fitted on the upper deck, in the middle of the vessel, well protected from the sun, and the dews at night, by thick awnings, from which was suspended a large punkah.

Sunday, 19th.—The Soudan came alongside the Wilberforce to receive our invalids, who took a melancholy farewell of their officers and messmates.

Prayers were read to the crews of both vessels. It was an affecting scene. The whole of one side of the little vessel was covered with invalids, and the cabins were full of officers; there was, indeed, no room for more.

The separation from so many of our companions under such circumstances could not be otherwise than painful to all;—the only cheering feature was in the hope that the attenuated beings who now departed would soon be within the influence of a more favourable climate, and that we might meet under happier auspices.

In a short time the steam was got up, and our little consort—watched by many commiserating eyes—rapidly glided out of view.

Only two or three days have elapsed since this change was effected, and now the Wilberforce has thirty-two men sick of the fever, leaving only thirteen, officers and seamen, capable of duty. She, too, returns to the sea, on Captain Allen's renewed protest and another council; and the Albert goes on up the melancholy river alone.

THE WILBERFORCE ON HER RETURN.

We proceeded through these narrow and winding reaches with feelings very different to those we experienced in ascending the river. Then the elasticity of health and hope gave to the scenery a colouring of exceeding loveliness. The very silence and solitude had a soothing influence which invited to meditation and pleasing anticipations for the future. Now it was the stillness of death,—broken only by the strokes and echoes of our paddle-wheels and the melancholy song of the leadsmen, which seemed the knell and dirge of our dying comrades. The palm trees, erst so graceful in their drooping leaves, were now gigantic hearse-like plumes.

So she drops down to Fernando Po, where the Soudan is lying, on whose small and crowded decks death has been, and is still, busy. Commanding officer, surgeons, seamen, engineers, marines, all sick, many dead. Captain Allen, with the sick on board the Wilberforce, sails for Ascension, as a last hope of restoring the sick; and the Soudan is sent back to assist the Albert. She meets her coming out of the Gate of the Cemetery; thus:

THE ALBERT ON HER RETURN.

It was a lovely morning, and the scenery about the river looked very beautiful, affording a sad contrast to the dingy and deserted look of the 'Albert'.

Many were of course the painful surmises as to the fate of those on board. On approaching, however, the melancholy truth was soon told. The fever had been doing its direst work; several were dead, many dying, and, of all the officers but two, Drs. McWilliam and Stanger, were able to move about. The former presented himself and waved his hand, and one emaciated figure was seen to be raised up for a second.

This was Captain Trotter, who in his anxiety to look at the 'Soudan' again, had been lifted out of his cot.

A spectacle more full of painful contemplation could scarcely have been witnessed. Slowly and portentously, like a plague-ship filled with its dead and dying, onwards she moved in charge of her generous pilot, Mr. Beecroft. Who would have thought that little more than two months previously she had entered that same river with an enterprising crew, full of life, and buoyant with bright hopes of accomplishing the objects on which all had so ardently entered?

The narrative of the Albert's solitary voyage, which occupied about a month, is given from the journal of Dr. McWilliam, and furnishes, to our thinking, one of the most remarkable instances of quiet courage and unflinching constancy of purpose that is to be found in any book of travel ever written. The sickness spreading, Captain Trotter falling very ill, officers, engineers, and men, lying alike disabled, and the Albert's head turned, in the necessity of despair, once more towards the sea, the two doctors on board, Dr. McWilliam and Dr. Stanger—names that should ever be memorable and honoured in the history of truly heroic enterprise—took upon themselves, in addition to the duty of attending the sick, the task of navigating the ship down the river. The former took charge of her, the latter worked the engines, and, both persevering by day and night—through all the horrors of such a voyage, with their friends raving and dying around them, and some, in the madness of the fever, leaping overboard—brought her in safety to the sea. We would fain hope this feat would live, in Dr. McWilliam's few, plain, and modest words; and, better yet, in the grateful remembrance handed down by the survivors of this fatal expedition; when the desperate and cruel of whole generations of the world shall have fallen into oblivion.

Calling at the Model Farm as they came down the

Niger, they found the superintendent, Mr. Carr, and the schoolmaster and gardener—both Europeans—lying prostrate with fever. These were taken on board the Albert and brought away for the restoration of their health; and the settlement—now mustering about forty natives, in addition to the people brought from Sierra Leone—was left in the charge of one Ralph Moore, an American negro emigrant.

The rest of the sad story. is soon told. The sea-breeze blew too late on many wasted forms, to shed its freshness on them for their restoration, and Death, Death, Death, was aboard the Albert day and night. Captain Trotter, as the only means of saving his life, was with difficulty prevailed on to return to England; and after a long delay at Ascension and in the Bay of Amboises (in the absence of instructions from the Colonial office), and when the Expedition, under Captain Allen, was on the eve of another hopeless attempt to ascend the Niger, it was ordered home. It being necessary to revisit the Model Farm, in obedience to orders, Lieutenant Webb, Captain Allen's first officer, immediately volunteered for that service; and with the requisite number of officers, and a black crew, took command of the Wilberforce, and once again went boldly up the fatal Niger. Disunion and dismay were rife at the Model Farm, on their arrival there; Mr. Carr, who had returned from Fernando Po when restored to health, had been murdered—by direction of 'King Boy,' it would appear, and not without strong suspicion of coöperation on the part of our friend Obi—and the settlement was abandoned. Obi (though he is somewhat unaccountably complimented by Dr. McWilliam) came out in his true colours on the Wilberforce's return, and, not being by any means awakened to a proper sense of his own degradation, appears to have evinced an amiable intention of destroying the crew and seizing the ship. Being baffled in this design, however, by the coolness and promptitude of Lieutenant Webb and his officers, the white men happily left him behind in his own country, where he is no doubt ready at this moment, if still alive, to enter into any treaty that may be proposed to him, with presents to follow; and to be highly amused again on the subject of the Slave trade, and to beat his tom-toms all night long for joy.

The fever, which wrought such terrible desolation in this and the preceding Expedition, becomes a subject of painful interest to the readers of these volumes. The length to which our notice has already extended, prevents our extracting, as we had purposed, the account of it which is given in the present narrative. Of the pre-disposing causes, little can be positively stated; for the most delicate chemical tests failed to detect, in the air or water, the presence of those deleterious gases which were very confidently supposed to exist in both. It is preceded either by a state of great prostration, or great excitement, and unnatural indifference; it developes itself on board ship about the fifteenth day after the ascent of the river is commenced; a close and sultry atmosphere without any breeze stirring, is the atmosphere most unfavourable to it; it appears to yield to calomel in the first instance, and strong doses of quinine afterwards, more than to any other remedies; and it is remarkable that in cases of 'total abstinence' patients, it seems from the first to be hopelessly and surely fatal.

The history of this Expedition is the history of the Past, in reference to the heated visions of philanthropists for the railroad Christianization of Africa and the abolition of the Slave Trade. May no popular cry, from Exeter Hall or elsewhere, ever make it, as to one single ship, the history of the Future! Such means are useless, futile, and we will venture to add—in despite of hats broad-brimmed or shovel-shaped, and coats of drab or black, with collars or without— wicked. No amount of philanthropy has a right to waste such valuable life as was squandered here, in the teeth of all experience and feasible pretence of hope. Between the civilized European and the barbarous African there is a great gulf set.

The air that brings life to the latter brings death to the former. In the mighty revolutions of the wheel of time, some change in this regard may come about; but in this age of the world, all the white armies and white missionaries of the world would fall, as withered reeds, before the rolling of one African river. To change the customs even of civilized and educated men, and impress them with new ideas, is—we have good need to know it—a most difficult and slow proceeding; but to do this by ignorant and savage races, is a work which, like the progressive changes of the globe itself, requires a stretch of years that dazzles in the looking at. It is not, we conceive, within the likely providence of God, that Christianity shall start to the banks of the Niger, until it shall have overflowed all intervening space. The stone that is dropped into the ocean of ignorance at Exeter Hall, must make its widening circles, one beyond another, until they reach the negro's country in their natural expansion. There is a broad, dark sea between the Strand in London, and the Niger, where those rings are not yet shining; and through all that space they must appear, before the last one breaks upon the shore of Africa. Gently and imperceptibly the widening circle of enlightenment must stretch and stretch, from man to man, from people on to people, until there is a girdle round the earth; but no convulsive effort, or far-off aim, can make the last great outer circle first, and then come home at leisure to trace out the inner one. Believe it, African Civilisation, Church of England Missionary, and all other Missionary Societies! The work at home must be completed thoroughly, or there is no hope abroad. To your tents, O Israel! but see they are your own tents! Set *them* in order; leave nothing to be done *there*; and outpost will convey your lesson on to outpost, until the naked armies of King Obi and King Boy are reached, and taught. Let a knowledge of the duty that man owes to man, and to his God, spread thus, by natural degrees and growth of example, to the outer shores of Africa, and it will float in safety up the rivers, never fear!

We will not do injustice to Captain Allen's scheme of future operations, by reproducing it, shorn of its fair proportions. As a most distinguished officer, and a highly accomplished gentleman, than whom there is no one living so well entitled to be heard on all that relates to Africa, it merits, and assuredly will receive, great attention. We are not, on the ground we have just now indicated, so sanguine as he; but there is sound wisdom in his idea of approaching the blackman through the blackman, and in his conviction that he can only be successfully approached by a studied reference to the current of his own opinions and customs instead of ours. So true is this, that it is doubtful whether any European save Bruce—who had a perfectly marvellous genius for accommodating himself, not only to the African character, but to every variety of character with which he came in contact—has ever truly won to himself a mingled sentiment of confidence, respect,

and fear in that country. So little has our Government
profited by his example, that one of the foremost objects
of this very Expedition is to repeat the self-same mistake
with which Clapperton so astonished the King Boy and
King Obi of his time, by running head foremost at the
abolition of the Slave Trade; which, of all possible objects,
is the most inconceivable, unpalatable, and astounding to
these barbarians!

Captain Allen need be under no apprehension that the
failure of the Expedition will involve his readers in any
confusion as to the sufferings and deserts of those who
sacrificed themselves to achieve its unattainable objects.
No generous mind can peruse this narrative without a glow
of admiration and sympathy for himself and all concerned.
The quiet spot by Lander's tomb, lying beyond the paths
of guava and the dark-leaved trees, where old companions
dear to his heart lie buried side by side beneath the sombre
and almost impenetrable brushwood, is not to be ungrate-
fully remembered, or lightly forgotten.   Though the African
is not yet awakened to a proper sense of his degradation,
the resting place of those brave men is sacred, and their
history a solemn truth.   [1848]

THE CHINESE JUNK.

The shortest road to the Celestial Empire is by the Blackwall railway. You may take a ticket, through and back, for a matter of eighteen pence. With every carriage that is cast off on the road—at Stepney, Limehouse, Poplar, West India docks—thousands of miles of space are cast off too, the flying dream of tiles and chimney pots, backs of squalid houses, frowzy pieces of waste ground, narrow courts and streets, swamps, ditches, masts of ships, gardens of dock weed, and unwholesome little bowers of scarlet beans, whirls away in half a score of minutes. Nothing is left but China.

How the flowery region ever got, in the form of the junk Keying, into the latitude and longitude where it is now to be found, is not the least part of the marvel. The crew of Chinamen aboard the Keying devoutly believed that their good ship would arrive quite safe, at the desired port, if they only tied red rags enough upon the mast, rudder, and cable. Perhaps they ran short of rag, through bad provision of stores; certain it is, that they had not enough on board to keep them from the bottom, and would most indubitably have gone there, but for such poor aid as could be rendered by the skill and coolness of a dozen English sailors, who brought this extraordinary craft in safety over the wide ocean.

If there be any one thing in the world that it is not all a like, that thing is a ship of any kind. So narrow, so long, so grotesque, so low in the middle, so high at each end (like a China pen tray), with no rigging, with nowhere to go to aloft, with mats for sails, great warped cigars for masts, gaudy dragons and sea monsters disporting themselves from stem to stern, and, on the stern, a gigantic cock of impossible aspect, defying the world (as well he may) to produce his equal—it would look more at home at the top of a public building, at the top of a mountain, in an avenue of trees, or down in a mine, than afloat on the water. Of all unlikely callings with which imagination could connect the Chinese lounging on the deck, the most unlikely and the last would be the mariner's craft. Imagine a ship's crew, without a profile among them, in gauze pinafores and plaited hair; wearing stiff clogs, a quarter of a foot thick in the sole; and lying at night in little scented boxes, like backgammon men or chess pieces, or mother of pearl counters!

The most perplexing considerations obtrude themselves on your mind when you go down in the cabin. As, what became of all those lanterns hanging to the roof, when the junk was out at sea? Whether they dangled there, banging and beating against each other, like so many jesters' baubles? Whether the idol, Chin Tee, of the eighteen arms, enshrined in a celestial Puppet Show, in the place of honour, ever tumbled out in heavy weather? Whether the incense and the joss-stick still burnt before her with a faint perfume and a little thread of smoke, while the mighty waves were roaring all around? Whether that preposterous umbrella in the corner was always spread, as being a convenient maritime instrument for walking about the decks with, in a storm? Whether all the cool and

shiny little chairs and tables were continually sliding about
and bruising each other, and if not, why not? Whether
anybody, on the voyage, ever read those two books printed
in characters like bird-cages and fly-traps? Whether the
Mandarin passenger, He Sing, who had never been ten
miles from home in his life before, lying sick on a bamboo
couch in a private China closet of his own (where he is
now perpetually writing autographs for inquisitive barbarians), ever began to doubt the potency of the goddess of
the sea, whose counterfeit presentment, like a flowery
monthly nurse, occupies the sailors' joss-house in the second
gallery? Whether it is possible that the said Mandarin,
or the artist of the ship, Sam Sing, Esquire, R.A., of
Canton, *can* ever go ashore without a walking staff of
cinnamon, agreeably to the usage of their likenesses in
British tea-shops? Above all, whether the hoarse old ocean
can ever have been seriously in earnest with this floating
toy shop, or merely played with it in lightness of spirit—
roughly, but meaning no harm—as the bull did, with the
china-shop, on St. Patrick's day in the morning?

'Here, at any rate, is the doctrine of finality beautifully
worked out, and shut up in a corner of a dock near the
Whitebait-house at Blackwall, for the edification of men.
Thousands of years have passed away, since the first
Chinese junk was constructed on this model; and the last
Chinese junk that was ever launched, was none the better
for that waste and desert of time. In all that interval,
through all the immense extent of the strange kingdom of
China—in the midst of its patient and ingenious, but never
advancing art, and its diligent agricultural cultivation—not
one new twist or curve has been given to a ball of ivory;
not one blade of experience has been grown.

The general eye has opened no wider, and seen no

farther, than the mimic eye upon this vessel's prow, by
means of which she is supposed to find her way; or
has been set in the flowery-head to as little purpose, for
thousands of years. Sir Robert Inglis, member for the
University of Oxford, ought to become Ty Kong or managing
man of the Keying, and nail the red rag of his party to
the mast for ever.

There is no doubt, it appears, that if any alteration
took place, in this junk, or any other, the Chinese form
of government would be destroyed. It has been clearly
ascertained by the wise men and law givers that to make
the cock upon the stern (the Grand Falcon of China) by
a feather's breadth a less startling phenomenon, or to
bring him within the remotest verge of ornithological
possibility, would be to endanger the noblest institutions
of the country. For it is a remarkable circumstance in
China (which is found to obtain nowhere else), that although
its institutions are the perfection of human wisdom, and
are the wonder and envy of the world by reason of their
stability, they are constantly imperilled in the last degree
by very slight occurrences. So, such wonderful contradic-
tions as the neatness of the Keying's cups and saucers,
and the ridiculous rudeness of her guns and rudder,
continue to exist. If any Chinese maritime generation
were the wiser for the wisdom of the generation gone
before, it is agreed upon by all the Ty Kongs in the navy
that the Chinese constitution would immediately go by
the board, and that the church of the Chinese Bonzes
would be effectually done for.

It is pleasant, coming out from behind the wooden
screen that encloses this interesting and remarkable sight
(which all who can, should see) to glance upon the mighty
signs of life, enterprise, and progress, that the great river

and its busy banks present. It is pleasant, coming back
from China by the Blackwall railway, to think that WE
trust no red rags in storms, and burn no joss-sticks before
idols; that WE never grope our way by the aid of conventional eyes which have no sight in them; and that,
in our civilisation, we sacrifice absurd forms to substantial
facts. The ignorant crew of the Keying refused to enter
on the ship's books, until "a considerable amount of
silvered paper, tin-foil, and joss-sticks" had been laid in,
by the owners, for the purposes of their worship; but
OUR seamen—far less our bishops, priests, and deacons—
never stand out upon points of silvered paper and tin-foil,
or the lighting up of joss-sticks upon altars! Christianity
is not Chin-Teeism; and therein all insignificant quarrels
as to means, are lost sight of in remembrance of the end.

There is matter for reflection aboard the Keying to last
the voyage home to England again.   [1848]

THE DRUNKARD'S CHILDREN.

A 'SEQUEL to the Bottle'[1] seems to us to demand a few words by way of gentle protest. Few men have a better right to erect themselves into teachers of the people than Mr. George Cruikshank. Few men have observed the people as he has done, or know them better; few are more earnestly and honestly disposed to teach them for their good; and there are very, very few artists, in England or abroad, who can approach him in his peculiar and remarkable power.

But this teaching, to last, must be fairly conducted. It must not be all on one side. When Mr. Cruikshank shows us, and shows us so forcibly and vigorously, that side of the medal on which the people in their crimes and faults are stamped, he is bound to help us to a glance at that other side on which the government that forms the people, with all *its* faults and vices, is no less plainly impressed. Drunkenness, as a national horror, is the effect of many causes. Foul smells, disgusting habitations, bad workshops and workshop customs, want of light, air, and water, the absence of all easy means of decency and health, are commonest among its common, every-day, physical causes.

[1] The Drunkard's Children. A Sequel to The Bottle. In eight Plates. By George Cruikshank.

78

The mental weariness and languor so induced, the want of wholesome relaxation, the craving for *some* stimulus and excitement, which is as much a part of such lives as the sun is; and, last and inclusive of all the rest, ignorance, and the need there is amongst the English people of reasonable, rational training, in lieu of mere parrot-education, or none at all; are its most obvious moral causes. It would be as sound philosophy to issue a series of plates under the title of The Physic Bottle, or the Saline Mixture, and, tracing the history of typhus fever by such means, to refer it all to the gin-shop, as it is to refer Drunkenness thither and to stop there. Drunkenness does not begin there. It has a teeming and reproachful history anterior to that stage; and at the remediable evil in that history, it is the duty of the moralist, if he strikes at all, to strike deep and spare not.

Hogarth avoided the Drunkard's Progress, we conceive, precisely because the causes of drunkenness among the poor were so numerous and widely spread, and lurked so sorrowfully deep and far down in all human misery, neglect, and despair, that even *his* pencil could not bring them fairly and justly into the light. That he was never contented with beginning at the effect, witness the Miser (his shoe new-soled with the binding of his Bible) dead before the Young Rake begins his career; the worldly father, listless daughter, impoverished nobleman, and crafty lawyer in the first plate of the 'Marriage à la Mode;' the detestable advances in the Stages of Cruelty; and the progress downward of Thomas Idle! That he did not spare that kind of drunkenness which was of more "respectable" engenderment, his midnight modern conversation, the election plates, and a crowd of stupid aldermen and other guzzlers, amply testify. But after one immortal journey

down Gin Lane, he turned away in grief and sorrow—
perhaps in hope of better things one day, from better laws,
and schools, and poor men's homes—and went back no
more. It is remarkable of that picture, that while it
exhibits drunkenness in its most appalling forms, it forces
on the attention of the spectator a most neglected, wretched neighbourhood (the same that is only just now cleared
away for the extension of Oxford Street), and an unwholesome, indecent, abject condition of life, worthy to be a
Frontispiece to the late Report of the Sanitary Commissioners, made nearly one hundred years afterwards. We
have always been inclined to think the purpose of this
piece not adequately stated, even by Charles Lamb. "The
very houses seem absolutely reeling," it is true; but they
quite as powerfully indicate some of the more prominent
causes of intoxication among the neglected orders of
society, as any of its effects. There is no evidence that
any of the actors in the dreary scene have ever been
much better off than we find them. The best are pawning
the commonest necessaries, and tools of their trades, and
the worst are homeless vagrants who give us no clue to
their having been otherwise in bygone days. All are
living and dying miserably. Nobody is interfering for
prevention or for cure in the generation going out before
us, or the generation coming in. The beadle (the only
sober man in the composition except the pawnbroker),
is mightily indifferent to the orphan-child crying beside its parent's coffin. The little charity-girls are not
so well taught or looked after, but that they can take to
dram-drinking already. The church is very prominent
and handsome, but coldly surveys these things, in progress
underneath the shadow of its tower (it was in the year
of grace eighteen hundred and forty eight that a Bishop

of London first came out respecting something wrong in poor men's social accommodations), and is passive in the picture. We take all this to have a meaning, and to the best of our knowledge it has not grown obsolete in a century.

Whereas, to all such considerations Mr. Cruikshank gives the go-by. The hero of the Bottle, and father of these children, lived in undoubted comfort and good esteem until he was some five-and-thirty years of age, when, happening, unluckily, to have a goose for dinner one day, in the bosom of his thriving family, he jocularly sent out for a bottle of gin, and persuaded his wife (until then a pattern of neatness and good housewifery) to take a little drop, after the stuffing, from which moment the family never left off drinking gin, and rushed downhill to destruction, very fast.

Entertaining the highest respect for Mr. Cruikshank's great genius, and no less respect for his motives in these publications, we deem it right on the appearance of a sequel to the Bottle, to protest against this. First because it is a compromising of a very serious and pressing truth; secondly, because it will, in time, defeat the end these pictures are designed to bring about. There is no class of society so certain to find out their weak place, as the class to which they are especially addressed. It is particularly within their knowledge and experience.

In the present series we trace the brother and sister whom we left in that terrible representation of the father's madness with which the first series closed, through the career of vice and crime then lowering before them. The gin-shop, beer-shop, and dancing-rooms receive them in turn. They are tried for a robbery. The boy is convicted, and sentenced to transportation; the girl acquitted.

6

He dies, prematurely, on board the hulks; and she, desolate and mad, flings herself from London Bridge into the night-darkened river.

The power of this closing scene is extraordinary. It haunts the remembrance, like an awful reality. It is full of passion and terror, and we question whether any other hand could so have rendered it. Nor, although far exceeding all that has gone before, as such a catastrophe should, is it without the strongest support all through the story. The death-bed scene on board the hulks—the convict who is composing the face—and the other who is drawing the screen round the bed's head—are master-pieces, worthy of the greatest painter. The reality of the place, and the fidelity with which every minute object illustrative of it is presented, are quite surprising. But the same feature is remarkable throughout. In the trial scene at the Old Bailey the eye may wander round the court, and observe everything that is a part of the place. The very light and atmosphere of the reality are reproduced with astonishing truth. So in the gin-shop and the beer-shop; no fragment of the fact is indicated and slurred over, but every shred of it is honestly made out. It is curious, in closing the book, to recall the number of faces we have seen that have as much individual character and identity in our remembrance as if we had been looking at so many living people of flesh and blood. The man behind the bar in the gin-shop, the barristers round the table in court, the convicts already mentioned, will be, like the figures in the pictures of which the Spanish Friar spoke to Wilkie, realities, when thousands of living shadows shall have passed away. May Mr. Cruikshank linger long behind to give us many more of such realities, and to do with simple means, such as are used here, what the whole paraphernalia and resources of Art could not effect, without a master hand!

The sequel to the Bottle is published at the same price as its predecessor. The eight large plates may be bought for a shilling!

[1848]

THE AMERICAN PANORAMA.

A VERY extraordinary exhibition is open at the Egyptian Hall, Piccadilly, under the title of "Banvard's Geographical Panorama of the Mississippi and Missouri Rivers." With one or two exceptions, its remarkable claims to public notice seem scarcely to have been recognised as they deserve. We recommend them to the consideration of all holiday-makers and sight-seers this Christmas.

It may be well to say what the panorama is *not*. It is not a refined work of art (nor does it claim to be, in Mr. Banvard's modest description); it is not remarkable for accuracy of drawing, or for brilliancy of colour, or for subtle effects of light and shade, or for any approach to any of the qualities of those delicate and beautiful pictures by Mr. Stanfield which used, once upon a time, to pass before our eyes in like manner. It is not very skilfully set off by the disposition of the artificial light; it is not assisted by anything but a piano-forte and a seraphine.

But it is a picture three miles long, which occupies two hours in its passage before the audience. It is a picture of one of the greatest streams in the known world, whose course it follows for upwards of three thousand miles. It is a picture irresistibly impressing the spectator with a conviction of its plain and simple truthfulness, even though that were not guaranteed by the best testimonials. It is an easy means of travelling, night and day, without any inconvenience from climate, steamboat company, or fatigue, from New Orleans to the Yellow Stone Bluffs (or from the Yellow Stone Bluffs to New Orleans, as the case may be) and seeing every town and settlement upon the river's banks, and all the strange wild ways of life that are afloat upon its waters. To see this painting is, in a word, to have a thorough understanding of what the great American river is—except, we believe, in the colour of its water—and to acquire a new power of testing the descriptive accuracy of its best describers.

These three miles af canvas have been painted by one man, and there he is, present, pointing out what he deems most worthy of notice. This is history. Poor, untaught, wholly unassisted, he conceives the idea—a truly American idea—of painting "the largest picture in the world." Some capital must be got for the materials, and the acquisition of that is his primary object. First, he starts "a floating diorama" on the Wabash river, which topples over when people come to see it, and keeps all the company at the pumps for dear life. This entertainment drawing more water than money, and being set upon, besides, by robbers armed with bowie knives and rifles, is abandoned. Then, he paints a panorama of Venice, and exhibits it in the West successfully, until it goes down in a steamer on the Western waters. Then, he sets up a museum at St. Louis, which fails. Then, he comes down to Cincinati, where he does no better. Then, without a farthing, he rows away on the Ohio in a small boat, and lives, like a wild man, upon nuts; until he sells a revolving pistol which cost him twelve dollars, for five and twenty. With the proceeds of this commercial trans-

action he buys a larger boat, lays in a little store of
calicoes and cottons, and rows away again among the
solitary settlers along-shore, bartering his goods for bee's
wax. Thus, in course of time, he earns enough to buy
a little skiff, and go to work upon the largest picture in
the world !

In his little skiff he travels thousands of miles, with no
companions but his pencil, rifle, and dog, making the
preparatory sketches for the largest picture in the world.
Those completed, he erects a temporary building at Louisville, Kentucky, in which to paint the largest picture in
the world. Without the least help, even in the grinding
of his colours, or the splitting of the wood for his machinery,
he falls to work, and keeps at work; maintaining himself
meanwhile, and buying more colours, wood, and canvas,
by doing odd jobs in the decorative way. At last he
finishes the largest picture in the world, and opens it for
exhibition on a stormy night, when not a single "human"
comes to see it. Not discouraged yet, he goes about
among the boatmen, who are well acquainted with the
river, and gives them free admissions to the largest picture
in the world. The boatmen come to see it, are astonished
at it, talk about it. "Our country" wakes up from a rather
sullen doze at Louisville, and comes to see it too. The
upshot is, that it succeeds; and here it is in London, with
its painter standing on a little platform by its side explaining it; and probably, by this time next year, it and
he may be in Timbuctoo.

Few can fail to have some interest in such an adventure
and in such an adventurer, and they will both repay it
amply. There is a mixture of shrewdness and simplicity
in the latter, which is very prepossessing; a modesty, and
honesty, and an odd original humour, in his manner of

telling what he has to tell, that give it a peculiar relish. The picture itself, as an indisputably true and faithful representation of a wonderful region—wood and water, river and prairie, lonely log hut and clustered city rising in the forest—is replete with interest throughout. Its incidental revelations of the different states of society, yet in transition, prevailing at different points of these three thousand miles—slaves and free republicans, French and Southerners; immigrants from abroad, and restless Yankees and Down-Easters ever steaming somewhere; alligators, store-boats, show-boats, theatre-boats, Indians, buffaloes, deserted tents of extinct tribes, and bodies of dead Braves, with their pale faces turned up to the night sky, lying still and solitary in the wilderness, nearer and nearer to which the outposts of civilisation are approaching with gigantic strides to tread their people down, and erase their very track from the earth's face—teem with suggestive matter. We are not disposed to think less kindly of a country when we see so much of it, although our sense of its immense responsibility may be increased.

It would be well to have a panorama, three miles long, of England. There might be places in it worth looking at, a little closer than we see them now; and worth the thinking of, a little more profoundly. It would be hopeful, too, to see some things in England, part and parcel of a *moving* panorama: and not of one that stood still, or had a disposition to go backward.

[1848]

THE POETRY OF SCIENCE.

Judging from certain indications scattered here and there in this book[1], we presume that its author would not consider himself complimented by the remark that we are perhaps indebted for the publication of such a work to the author of the *Vestiges of the Natural History of Creation*, who, by rendering the general subject popular, and awakening an interest and spirit of inquiry in many minds, where these had previously lain dormant, has created a reading public—not exclusively scientific or philosophical—to whom such offerings can be hopefully addressed. This, however, we believe to be the case; and in this, as we conceive, the writer of that remarkable and well-abused book has not rendered his least important service to his own time.

The design of Mr. Hunt's volume is striking and good. To show that the facts of science are at least as full of poetry, as the most poetical fancies ever founded on an imperfect observation and a distant suspicion of them (as, for example, among the ancient Greeks); to show that if the Dryades no longer haunt the woods, there is, in every forest, in every tree, in every leaf, and in every ring on every sturdy trunk, a beautiful and wonderful creation,

[1] The Poetry of Science, or Studies of the Physical Phenomena of Nature. By Robert Hunt.

always changing, always going on, always bearing testimony to the stupendous workings of Almighty Wisdom, and always leading the student's mind from wonder on to wonder, until he is wrapt and lost in the vast worlds of wonder by which he is surrounded from his cradle to his grave; it is a purpose worthy of the natural philosopher, and salutary to the spirit of the age. To show that Science, truly expounding nature, can, like nature herself, restore in some new form whatever she destroys; that, instead of binding us, as some would have it, in stern utilitarian chains, when she has freed us from a harmless superstition, she offers to our contemplation something better and more beautiful, something which, rightly considered, is more elevating to the soul, nobler and more stimulating to the soaring fancy; is a sound, wise, wholesome object. If more of the learned men who have written on these themes had had it in their minds, they would have done more good, and gathered upon their track many followers on whom its feeblest and most distant trace has only now begun to shine.

Science has gone down into the mines and coal-pits, and before the safety-lamp, the Gnomes and Genii of those dark regions have disappeared. But in their stead, the process by which metals are engendered in the course of ages; the growth of plants which, hundreds of fathoms underground, and in black darkness, have still a sense of the sun's presence in the sky, and derive some portion of the subtle essence of their life from his influence; the histories of mighty forests and great tracts of land carried down into the sea, by the same process which is active in the Mississippi and such great rivers at this hour; are made familiar to us. Sirens, mermaids, shining cities glittering at the bottom of the quiet seas, and in deep lakes,

exist no longer; but, in their place, Science, their de-
stroyer, shows us whole coasts of coral reef constructed by
the labours of minute creatures, points to our own chalk
cliffs and limestone rocks, as made of the dust of my-
riads of generations of infinitesimal beings that have passed
away; reduces the very element of water into its constituent
airs, and re-creates it at her pleasure. Caverns in rocks,
choked with rich treasures shut up from all but the enchanted hand, Science has blown to atoms, as she can
rend and rive the rocks themselves; but in those rocks
she has found, and read aloud, the great stone book which
is the history of the earth, even when darkness sat upon
the face of the deep. Along their craggy sides, she has
traced the footprints of birds and beasts, whose shapes
were never seen by man. From within them she has
brought the bones, and pieced together the skeletons, of
monsters that would have crushed the noted dragons of
the fables at a blow. The stars that stud the firmament
by night are watched no more from lonely towers by en-
thusiasts or impostors, believing, or feigning to believe,
those great worlds to be charged with the small destinies
of individual men down here; but two astronomers, far
apart, each looking from his solitary study up into the
sky, observe, in a known star, a trembling which forewarns
them of the coming of some unknown body through the
realms of space, whose attraction at a certain period of
its mighty journey causes that disturbance. In due time it
comes, and passes out of the disturbing path; the old star
shines at peace again; and the new one, evermore to be
associated with the honoured names of Le Verrier and
Adams, is called Neptune! The astrologer has faded out
of the castle turret-room (which overlooks a railroad now),
and forebodes no longer that because the light of yonder

planet is diminishing, my lord will shortly die: but the professor of an exact science has arisen in his stead, to *prove* that a ray of light must occupy a period of six years in travelling to the earth from the nearest of the fixed stars; and that if one of the remote fixed stars were "blotted out of heaven" to-day, several generations of the mortal inhabitants of this earth must perish out of time, before the fact of its obliteration could be known to man!

This ample compensation, in respect of poetry alone, that Science has given us in return for what she has taken away, it is the main object of Mr. Hunt's book to elucidate. The subject is very ably dealt with, and the object very well attained. We might object to an occasional discursiveness, and sometimes we could have desired to be addressed in a plainer form of words. Nor do we quite perceive the force of Mr. Hunt's objection (at p. 307) to certain geological speculations; which we must be permitted to believe many intelligent men to be capable of making, and reasonably sustaining, on a knowledge of certain geological facts; albeit they are neither practical chemists, nor paleontologists. But the book displays a fund of knowledge, and is the work of an eloquent and earnest man; and, as such, we are too content and happy to receive it, to enlarge on these points. We subjoin a few short extracts.

HOW WE "COME LIKE SHADOWS, SO DEPART."

A plant exposed to the action of natural or artificial decomposition passes into air, leaving but a few grains of solid matter behind it. An animal, in like manner, is gradually resolved into "thin air". Muscle, and blood, and bones having undergone the change are found to have escaped as gases, "leaving only a pinch of dust", which belongs to the more stable mineral world. Our dependency on the atmosphere is therefore evident. We derive our substance from it—we are, after death, resolved again, into it. We are really but fleeting shadows. Animal and vegetable forms are little more than consolidated masses of the atmosphere. The sublime creations of the most gifted bard cannot rival the beauty of this, the highest and the truest poetry of science. Man has divined such changes by the unaided powers of reason, arguing from the phenomena which science reveals in unceasing action around him. The Grecian sage's doubts of his own identity, was only an extension of a great truth beyond the limits of our reason. Romance and superstition resolve the spiritual man into a visible form of extreme ethereality in the spectral creations, "clothed in their own horror", by which their reigns have been perpetuated.

When Shakespear made his charming Ariel sing—

"Full fathom five thy father lies,
  Of his bones are coral made,
  Those are pearls that were his eyes,
  Nothing of him that doth fade,
  But doth suffer a sea-change,
  Into something rich and strange;"

he little thought how correctly he painted the chemical changes, by which decomposing animal matter is replaced by a siliceous or calcareous formation.

Why Mr. Hunt should be of opinion that Shakespeare "little thought" how wise he was, we do not altogether understand. Perhaps he founds the supposition on Shakespeare's not having been recognised as a practical chemist or paleontologist.

We conclude with the following passage, which seems to us strikingly suggestive of the shortness and hurry of our little life which is rounded with a sleep, and the calm majesty of Nature.

RELATIVE IMPORTANCE OF TIME TO MAN AND NATURE.

All things on the earth are the result of chemical combination. The operation by which the commingling of molecules and the interchange of atoms take place, we can imitate in our laboratories; but in nature they proceed by slow degrees, and, in general, in our hands they are distinguished by suddenness of action. In nature chemical power is distributed over a long period of time, and the process of change is scarcely to be observed. By arts we concentrate chemical force, and expend it in producing a change which occupies but a few hours at most.   [1848]

COURT CEREMONIES.

THE late Queen Dowager, whose death has given occasion for many public tributes to exalted worth, often formally and falsely rendered on similar occasions, and rarely, if ever, better deserved than on this, committed to writing eight years ago her wishes in reference to her funeral. This truly religious and most unaffected document has been published by her Majesty the Queen's directions. It is more honourable to the memory of the noble lady deceased than broadsides upon broadsides of fulsome panegyric, and is full of good example to all persons in this empire, but particularly, as we think, to the highest persons of all.

I die in all humility, knowing well that we are all alike before the throne of God, and I request, therefore, that my mortal remains be conveyed to the grave without any pomp or state. They are to be moved to St. George's Chapel, Windsor, where I request to have as private and quiet a funeral as possible.

I particularly desire not to be laid out in state, and the funeral to take place by daylght; no procession; the coffin to be carried by sailors to the chapel.

All those of my friends and relations, to a limited number, who wish to attend may do so. My nephew, Prince Edward of Saxe Weimar, Lords Howe and Denbigh, the Hon. William Ashley, Mr. Wood, Sir Andrew Barnard, and Sir D. Davies, with my dressers, and those of my Ladies who may wish to attend.

die in peace, and wish to be carried to the tomb in peace, and free from the vanities and the pomp of this world.

I request not to be dissected, nor embalmed; and desire to give as little trouble as possible.

November, 1841.   ADELAIDE R.

It may be questionable whether the "Ceremonial for the private interment of her late Most Excellent Majesty, Adelaide the Queen Dowager, in the Royal Chapel of St. George at Windsor," published at the same time as this affecting paper, be quite in unison with the feelings it expresses. Uneasy doubts obtrude themselves upon the mind whether "her late Majesty's state carriage drawn by six horses, in which will be the crown of her late Majesty, borne on a velvet cushion," would not have been more in keeping with the funeral requests of the late Mr. Ducrow. The programme setting forth in four lines,

THE CHIEF MOURNER,
the Duchess of Norfolk
(veiled)
Attended by a Lady,

is like a bad play-bill. The announcement how "the Archbishop having concluded the service, Garter will pronounce near the grave the style of Her late Majesty; after which the Lord Chamberlain and the Vice Chamberlain of Her late Majesty's household will break their staves of office, and, kneeling, deposit the same in the Royal Vault," is more like the announcement outside a booth at a fair, respecting what the elephant or the conjuror will do within, by-and-bye, than consists with the simple solemnity of that last Christian service which is entered upon with the words, "We brought nothing into this world, and it is certain we can carry nothing out. The

Lord gave, and the Lord hath taken away; blessed be the name of the Lord."

We would not be misunderstood on this point, and we wish distinctly to express our full belief that the funeral of the good Dowager Queen was conducted with a proper absence of conventional absurdity. We are persuaded that the highest personages in the country respected the last wishes so modestly expressed, and were earnest in impressing upon all concerned a desire for their exact fulfilment. It is not so much because of any inconsistencies on this particular occasion, as because the Lord Chamberlain's office is the last stronghold of an enormous amount of tomfoolery, which is infinitely better done upon the stage in *Tom Thumb*, which is cumbrous and burdensome to all outside the office itself, and which is negative for any good purpose and often positive for much harm, as making things ridiculous or repulsive which can only exist beneficially in the general love and respect, that we take this occasion of hoping that it is fast on the decline.

This is not the first occasion on which we have observed upon the preposterous constraints and forms that set a mark upon the English Court among the nations of Europe, and amaze European Sovereigns when they first become its guests. In times that are marked beyond all others by rapidity of change, and by the condensation of centuries into years in respect of great advances, it is in the nature of things that these constraints and forms should yearly, daily, hourly, become more preposterous. What was obsolete at first, is rendered in such circumstances, a thousand times more obsolete by every new stride that is made in the onward road. A Court that does not keep pace with a People will look smaller, through the tube which Mr. Stephenson is throwing across the Menai Straits, than it looked before.

It is typical of the English Court that its state dresses, though greatly in advance of its ceremonies, are always behind the time. We would bring it up to the time, that it may have the greater share in, and the stronger hold upon, the affections of the time. The spectacle of a Court going down to Windsor by the Great Western Railway, to do, from morning to-night, what is five hundred years out of date; or sending such messages to Garter by electric telegraph, as Garter might have received in the lists, in the days of King Richard the First, is not a good one. The example of the Dowager Queen, reviving and improving on the example of the late Duke of Sussex, makes the present no unfit occasion for the utterance of a hope that these things are at last progressing, changing, and resolving themselves into harmony with all other things around them. It is particularly important that this should be the case when a new line of Sovereigns is stretching out before us. It is particularly important that this should be the case when the hopes, the happiness, the property, the liberties, the lives of innumerable people may, and in great measure must, depend on Royal Childhood not being too thickly hedged in, or loftily walled round, from a great range of human sympathy, access, and knowledge. Therefore we could desire to have the words of their departed relative, "We are all alike before the throne of God," commended to the earliest understanding of our rising Princes and Princesses. Therefore we could desire to bring the chief of the Court ceremonies a little more into the outer world, and cordially to give him the greeting,

My good Lord Chamberlain

Well are you welcome to this open air! [1849]

THE AGRICULTURAL INTEREST.

THE present Government, having shown itself to be particularly clever in its management of Indictments for Conspiracy, cannot do better, we think (keeping in its administrative eye the pacification of some of its most influential and most unruly supporters), than indict the whole manufacturing interest of the country for a conspiracy against the agricultural interest. As the jury ought to be beyond impeachment, the panel might be chosen from among the Duke of Buckingham's tenants, with the Duke of Buckingham himself as foreman; and, to the end that the country might be quite satisfied with the judge, and have ample security beforehand for his moderation and impartiality, it would be desirable, perhaps, to make such a slight change in the working of the law (a mere nothing to a Conservative Government, bent upon its end), as would enable the question to be tried before an Ecclesiastical Court, with the Bishop of Exeter presiding. The Attorney-General for Ireland, turning his sword into a ploughshare, might conduct the prosecution; and Mr. Cobden and the other traversers might adopt any ground of defence they chose, or prove or disprove anything they pleased, without being embarrassed by the least anxiety or doubt in reference to the verdict.

That the country in general is in a conspiracy against this sacred but unhappy agricultural interest, there can be no doubt. It is not alone within the walls of Covent Garden Theatre, or the Free Trade Hall at Manchester, or the Town Hall at Birmingham, that the cry "Repeal the Corn-laws!" is raised. It may be heard, moaning at night, through the straw-littered wards of Refuges for the Destitute; it may be read in the gaunt and famished faces which make our streets terrible; it is muttered in the thankful grace pronounced by haggard wretches over their felon fare in gaols; it is inscribed in dreadful characters upon the walls of Fever Hospitals; and may be plainly traced in every record of mortality. All of which proves, that there is a vast conspiracy afoot, against the unfortunate agricultural interest.

They who run, even upon railroads, may read of this conspiracy. The old stage-coachman was a farmer's friend. He wore top-boots, understood cattle, fed his horses upon corn, and had a lively personal interest in malt. The engine-driver's garb, and sympathies, and tastes belong to the factory. His fustian dress, besmeared with coal-dust and begrimed with soot; his oily hands, his dirty face, his knowledge of machinery; all point him out as one devoted to the manufacturing interest. Fire and smoke, and red-hot cinders follow in his wake. He has no attachment to the soil, but travels on a road of iron, furnace wrought. His warning is not conveyed in the fine old Saxon dialect of our glorious forefathers, but in a fiendish yell. He never cries "ya-hip", with agricultural lungs; but jerks forth a manufactured shriek from a brazen throat.

Where *is* the agricultural interest represented? From what phase of our social life has it not been driven, to the undue setting up of its false rival?

Are the police agricultural? The watchmen were. They wore woollen nightcaps to a man; they encouraged the growth of timber, by patriotically adhering to staves and rattles of immense size; they slept every night in boxes, which were but another form of the celebrated wooden walls of Old England; they never woke up till it was too late—in which respect you might have thought them very farmers. How is it with the police? Their buttons are made at Birmingham; a dozen of their truncheons would poorly furnish forth a watchman's staff; they have no wooden walls to repose between; and the crowns of their hats are plated with cast-iron.

Are the doctors agricultural? Let Messrs. Morison and Moat, of the Hygeian establishment at King's-Cross, London, reply. Is it not, upon the constant showing of those gentlemen, an ascertained fact that the whole medical profession have united to depreciate the worth of the Universal Vegetable Medicines? And is this opposition to vegetables, and exaltation of steel and iron instead, on the part of the regular practitioners, capable of any interpretation but one? Is it not a distinct renouncement of the agricultural interest, and a setting up of the manufacturing interest instead?

Do the professors of the law at all fail in their truth to the beautiful maid whom they ought to adore? Inquire of the Attorney-General for Ireland. Inquire of that honourable and learned gentleman, whose last public act was to cast aside the grey goose-quill, an article of agricultural produce, and take up the pistol, which, under the system of percussion locks, has not even a flint to connect it with farming. Or put the question to a still higher legal functionary, who, on the same occasion, when he should have been a reed, inclining here and there, as adverse gales of evidence disposed him, was seen to be a manufactured image on the seat of Justice, cast by Power, in most impenetrable brass.

The world is too much with us in this manufacturing interest, early and late; that is the great complaint and the great truth. It is not so with the agricultural interest, or what passes by that name. It never thinks of the suffering world, or sees it, or cares to extend its knowledge of it; or, so long as it remains a world, cares anything about it. All those whom Dante placed in the first pit or circle of the doleful regions, might have represented the agricultural interest in the present Parliament, or at quarter sessions, or at meetings of the farmers' friends, or anywhere else.

But that is not the question now. It is conspired against; and we have given a few proofs of the conspiracy, as they shine out of various classes engaged in it. An indictment against the whole manufacturing interest need not be longer, surely, than the indictment in the case of the Crown against O'Connell and others. Mr. Cobden may be taken as its representative—as indeed he is, by one consent already. There may be no evidence; but that is not required. A judge and jury are all that is needed. And the Government know where to find *them*, or they gain experience to little purpose.   [1844]

THREATENING LETTER TO THOMAS HOOD,
FROM AN ANCIENT GENTLEMAN.

Mr. Hood. Sir,

The Constitution is going at last! You needn't laugh, Mr. Hood. I am aware that it has been going, two or three times before; perhaps four times; but it is on the move now, sir, and no mistake.

I beg.to say, that I use those last expressions advisedly, sir, and not in the sense in which they are now used by Jackanapeses. There were no Jackanapeses when I was a boy, Mr. Hood. England was Old England when I was young. I little thought it would ever come to be Young England when I was old. But everything is going backward.

Ah! governments were governments, and judges were judges, in *my* day, Mr. Hood. There was no nonsense then. Any of your seditious complainings, and we were ready with the military on the shortest notice. We should have charged Covent Garden Theatre, sir, on a Wednesday night: at the point of the bayonet. Then, the judges were full of dignity and firmness, and knew how to administer the law. There is only one judge who knows how to do his duty, now. He tried that revolutionary female the other day, who, though she was in full work (making shirts at three-halfpence a piece), had no pride in her

country, but treasonably took it in her head, in the distraction of having been robbed of her easy earnings, to
attempt to drown herself and her young child; and the
glorious man went out of his way, sir—out of his way—
to call her up for instant sentence of Death; and to tell
her she had no hope of mercy in this world—as you may
see yourself if you look in the papers of Wednesday the
17th of April. He won't be supported, sir, I know he
won't; but it is worth remembering that his words were
carried into every manufacturing town of this kingdom,
and read aloud to crowds in every political parlour, beer-
shop, news-room, and secret or open place of assembly,
frequented by the discontented working-men; and that no
milk-and-water weakness on the part of the executive can
ever blot them out. Great things like that, are caught
up, and stored up, in these times, and are not forgotten,
Mr. Hood. The public at large (especially those who
wish for peace and conciliation) are universally obliged
to him. If it is reserved for any man to set the Thames
on fire, it is reserved for him; and indeed I am told he
very nearly did it, once.

But even he won't save the constitution, sir: it is mauled
beyond the power of preservation. Do you know in what
foul weather it will be sacrificed and shipwrecked, Mr.
Hood? Do you know on what rock it will strike, sir?
You don't, I am certain; for nobody does know as yet
but myself. I will tell you.

The constitution will go down, sir (nautically speaking),
in the degeneration of the human species in England, and
its reduction into a mingled race of savages and pigmies.

That is my proposition. That is my prediction. That
is the event of which I give you warning. I am now
going to prove it, sir.

You are a literary man, Mr. Hood, and have written, I am told, some things worth reading. I say I am told, because I never read what is written in these days. You'll excuse me; but my principle is, that no man ought to know anything about his own time, except that it is the worst time that ever was, or is ever likely to be. That is the only way, sir, to be truly wise and happy.

In your station, as a literary man, Mr. Hood, you are frequently at the Court of Her Gracious Majesty the Queen. God bless her! You have reason to know that the three great keys to the royal palace (after rank and politics) are Science, Literature, Art. I don't approve of this myself. I think it ungenteel and barbarous, and quite un-English; the custom having been a foreign one, ever since the reigns of the uncivilised sultans in the Arabian Nights, who always called the wise men of their time about them. But so it is. And when you don't dine at the royal table, there is always a knife and fork for you at the equerries' table: where, I understand, all gifted men are made particularly welcome.

But all men can't be gifted, Mr. Hood. Neither scientific, literary, nor artistical powers are any more to be inherited than the property arising from scientific, literary, or artistic productions, which the law, with a beautiful imitation of nature, declines to protect in the second generation. Very good, sir. Then, people are naturally very prone to cast about in their minds for other means of getting at Court Favour; and, watching the signs of the times, to hew out for themselves, or their descendants, the likeliest roads to that distinguished goal.

Mr. Hood, it is pretty clear, from recent records in the Court Circular, that if a father wish to train up his son in the way he should go, to go to Court: and cannot in denture him to be a scientific man, an author, or an artist, three causes are open to him. He must endeavour by artificial means to make him a dwarf, a wild man, or a Boy Jones. *

Now, sir, this is the shoal and quicksand on which the constitution will go to pieces.

I have made inquiry, Mr. Hood, and find that in my neighbourhood two families and a fraction out of every four, in the lower and middle classes of society, are study- ing and practising all conceivable arts to keep their infant children down. Understand me. I do not mean down in their numbers, or down in their precocity, but down in their growth, sir. A destructive and subduing drink, compounded of gin and milk in equal quantities, such as is given to puppies to retard their growth: not something short, but something shortening: is administered to these young creatures many times a day. An unnatural and artificial thirst is first awakened in these infants by meals of salt beef, bacon, anchovies, sardines, red herrings, shrimps, olives, pea-soup, and that description of diet; and when they screech for drink, in accents that might melt a heart of stone, which they do constantly (I allude to screeching, not to melting), this liquid is introduced into their too confiding stomachs. At such an early age, and to so great an extent, is this custom of provoking thirst, then quenching it with a stunting drink, observed, that brine pap has already superseded the use of tops- and-bottoms; and wet-nurses, previously free from any kind of reproach, have been seen to stagger in the streets: owing, sir, to the quantity of gin introduced into their

* A reference to the then recent visit of "General" Tom Thumb to Her Majesty the Queen and Court.

systems, with a view to its gradual and natural conversion into the fluid I have already mentioned.

Upon the best calculation I can make, this is going on, as I have said, in the proportion of about two families and a fraction in four. In one more family and a fraction out of the same number, efforts are being made to reduce the children to a state of nature; and to inculcate, at a tender age, the love of raw flesh, train oil, new rum, and the acquisition of scalps. Wild and outlandish dances are also in vogue (you will have observed the prevailing rage for the Polka); and savage cries and whoops are much indulged in (as you may discover, if you doubt it, in the House of Commons any night). Nay, some persons, Mr. Hood; and persons of some figure and distinction too; have already succeeded in breeding wild sons; who have been publicly shown in the Courts of Bankruptcy, and in police-offices, and in other commodious exhibition-rooms, with great effect, but who have not yet found favour at court; in consequence, as I infer, of the impression made by Mr. Rankin's wild men being too fresh and recent, to say nothing of Mr. Rankin's wild men being foreigners.

I need not refer you, sir, to the late instance of the Ojibbeway Bride. But I am credibly informed, that she is on the eve of retiring into a savage fastness, where she may bring forth and educate a wild family, who shall in course of time, by the dexterous use of the popularity they are certain to acquire at Windsor and St. James's, divide with dwarfs the principal offices of state, of patronage, and power, in the United Kingdom.

Consider the deplorable consequences, Mr. Hood, which must result from these proceedings, and the encouragement they receive in the highest quarters.

The dwarf being the favourite, sir, it is certain that the

public mind will run in a great and eminent degree upon the production of dwarfs. Perhaps the failures only will be brought up, wild. The imagination goes a long way in these cases; and all that the imagination *can* do, will be done, and is doing. You may convince yourself of this, by observing the condition of those ladies who take particular notice of General Tom Thumb at the Egyptian Hall, during his hours of performance.

The rapid increase of dwarfs, will be first felt in her Majesty's recruiting department. The standard will, of necessity, be lowered; the dwarfs will grow smaller and smaller; the vulgar expression "a man of his inches" will become a figure of fact, instead of a figure of speech; crack regiments, household-troops especially, will pick the smallest men from all parts of the country; and in the two little porticoes at the Horse Guards, two Tom Thumbs will be daily seen, doing duty, mounted on a pair of Shetland ponies. Each of them will be relieved (as Tom Thumb is, at this moment, in the intervals of his performance) by a wild man; and a British Grenadier will either go into a quart pot, or be an Old Boy, or Blue Gull, or Flying Bull, or some other savage chief of that nature.

I will not expatiate upon the number of dwarfs who will be found representing Grecian statues in all parts of the metropolis; because I am inclined to think that this will be a change for the better; and that the engagement of two or three in Trafalgar Square will tend to the improvement of the public taste.

The various genteel employments at Court being held by dwarfs, sir, it will be necessary to alter, in some respects, the present regulations. It is quite clear that not even General Tom Thumb himself could preserve a becoming dignity on state occasions, if required to walk about with a scaffolding-pole under his arm; therefore the gold and silver sticks at present used, must be cut down into skewers of those precious metals; a twig of the black rod will be quite as much as can be conveniently preserved; the coral and bells of his Royal Highness the Prince of Wales, will be used in lieu of the mace at present in existence; and that bauble (as Oliver Cromwell called it, Mr. Hood), its value being first calculated by Mr. Finlayson, the government actuary, will be placed to the credit of the National Debt.

All this, sir, will be the death of the constitution. But this is not all. The constitution dies hard, perhaps; but there is enough disease impending, Mr. Hood, to kill it three times over.

Wild men will get into the House of Commons. Imagine that, sir! Imagine Strong Wind in the House of Commons! It is not an easy matter to get through a debate now; but I say, imagine Strong Wind, speaking for the benefit of his constituents, upon the floor of the House of Commons! or imagine (which is pregnant with more awful consequences still) the ministry having an interpreter in the House of Commons, to tell the country, in English, what it really means!

Why, sir, that in itself would be blowing the constitution out of the mortar in St. James's Park, and leaving nothing of it to be seen but smoke.

But this, I repeat it, is the state of things to which we are fast tending, Mr. Hood; and I inclose my card for your private eye, that you may be quite certain of it. What the condition of this country will be, when its standing army is composed of dwarfs, with here and there a wild man to throw its ranks into confusion, like the elephants employed in war in former times, I leave you to imagine, sir. It may be objected by some hopeful jackanapeses, that the number of impressments in the navy, consequent upon the seizure of the Boy-Joneses, or remaining portion of the population ambitious of Court Favour, will be in itself sufficient to defend our Island from foreign invasion. But I tell those jackanapeses, sir, that while I admit the wisdom of the Boy Jones precedent, of kidnapping such youths after the expiration of their several terms of imprisonment as vagabonds; hurrying them on board ship; and packing them off to sea again whenever they venture to take the air on shore; I deny the justice of the inference; inasmuch as it appears to me, that the inquiring minds of those young outlaws must naturally lead to their being hanged by the enemy as spies, early in their career; and before they shall have been rated on the books of our fleet as able seamen.

Such, Mr. Hood, sir, is the prospect before us! And unless you, and some of your friends who have influence at Court, can get up a giant as a forlorn hope, it is all over with this ill-fated land.

In reference to your own affairs, sir, you will take whatever course may seem to you most prudent and advisable after this warning. It is not a warning to be slighted: that I happen to know. I am informed by the gentleman who favours this, that you have recently been making some changes and improvements in your Magazine, and are, in point of fact, starting afresh. If I be well informed, and this be really so, rely upon it that you cannot start too small, sir. Come down to the duodecimo size instantly, Mr. Hood. Take time by the forelock; and, reducing the stature of your Magazine every month, bring it at last to the dimensions of the little almanack no longer issued, I regret to say, by the ingenious Mr. Schloss: which was invisible to the naked eye until examined through a little eye-glass.

You project, I am told, the publication of a new novel, by yourself, in the pages of your Magazine. A word in your ear. I am not a young man, sir, and have had some experience. Don't put your own name on the title-page; it would be suicide and madness. Treat with General Tom Thumb, Mr. Hood, for the use of his name on any terms. If the gallant general should decline to treat with you, get Mr. Barnum's name, which is the next best in the market. And when, through this politic course, you shall have received, in presents, a richly jewelled set of tablets from Buckingham Palace, and a gold watch and appendages from Marlborough House; and when those valuable trinkets shall be left under a glass case at your publisher's for inspection by your friends and the public in general;—then, sir, you will do me the justice of remembering this communication.

It is unnecessary for me to add, after what I have observed in the course of this letter, that I am not,

Sir,

Ever

Your

Tuesday, 23rd April, 1844.   CONSTANT READER.

P.S.—Impress it upon your contributors that they cannot be too short; and that if not dwarfish, they must be wild —or at all events not tame.

PREFACE TO "EVENINGS OF A WORKING MAN."

THE indulgent reader of this little book [1]—not called indulgent, I may hope, by courtesy alone, but with some
reference also to its title. and pretensions—may very naturally inquire how it comes to have a preface to which
my name is attached, nor is the reader's right or inclination
to be satisfied on this head, likely to be much diminished,
when I state, in the outset, that I do not recommend it
as a book of surpassing originality or transcendent merit.
That I do not claim to have discovered, in humble life,
an extraordinary and brilliant genius. That I cannot
charge mankind in general, with having entered into a
conspiracy to neglect the author of this volume, or to leave
him pining in obscurity. That I have not the smallest
intention of comparing him with Burns, the exciseman; or
with Bloomfield, the shoemaker; or with Ebenezer Elliott,
the worker in iron; or with James Hogg, the shepherd.
That I see no reason to be hot, or bitter, or lowering,
or sarcastic, or indignant, or fierce, or sour, or sharp, in
his behalf. That I have nothing to rail at; nothing to
exalt; nothing to flourish in the face of a stony-hearted
world; and have but a very short and simple tale to tell.

But, such as it is, it has interested me: and I hope it

---

[1] Preface to "Evenings of a Working Man," by John Overs, 1844.

may interest the reader too, if I state it, unaffectedly and plainly.

John Overs, the writer of the following pages, is, as is set forth in the title-page, a working man. A man who earns his weekly wages (or who did when he was strong enough) by plying of the hammer, plane, and chisel. He became known to me, to the best of my recollection, nearly six years ago, when he sent me some songs, appropriate to the different months of the year, with a letter, stating under what circumstances they had been composed, and in what manner he was occupied from morning until night. I was, just then, relinquishing the conduct of a monthly periodical: or I would gladly have published them. As it was, I returned them to him, with a private expression of the interest I felt in such productions. They were afterwards accepted, with much readiness and consideration, by Mr. Tait, of Edinburgh; and were printed in his Magazine.

Finding, after some further correspondence with my new friend, that his authorship had not ceased with these verses, but that he still occupied his leisure moments in writing, I took occasion to remonstrate with him seriously against his pursuing that course. I pointed out to him a few of the uncertainties, anxieties, and difficulties of such a life, at the best. I entreated him to remember the position of heavy disadvantage in which he stood, by reason of his self education, and imperfect attainments; and I besought him to consider whether, having one or two of his pieces accepted occasionally, here and there, after long suspense and many refusals, it was probable that he would find himself, in the end, a happier or a more contented man. On all these grounds, I told him, his persistence in his new calling made me uneasy; and

I advised him to abandon it, as strongly as I could.

In answer to this dissuasion of mine, he wrote me as manly and straight-forward, but withal, as modest a letter, as ever I read in my life. He explained to me how limited his ambition was : soaring no higher than the establishment of his wife in some light business, and the better education of his children. He set before me, the difference between his evening and holiday studies, such as they were ; and the having no better resource than an alehouse or a skittle-ground. He told me, how every small addition to his stock of knowledge, made his Sunday walks the pleasanter ; the hedge-flowers sweeter ; everything more full of interest and meaning to him. He assured me, that his daily work was not neglected for his self-imposed pursuits ; but was faithfully and honestly performed ; and so, indeed, it was. He hinted to me, that his greater self-respect was some inducement and reward ; supposing every other to elude his grasp ; and showed me, how the fancy that he would turn this or that acquisition from his books to account, by-and-by, in writing, made him more fresh and eager to peruse and profit by them, when his long day's work was done.

I would not, if I could, have offered one solitary objection more, to arguments so unpretending and so true.

From that time to the present, I have seen him frequently. It has been a pleasure to me to put a few books in his way ; to give him a word or two of counsel in his little projects and difficulties ; and to read his compositions with him, when he has had an hour, or so, to spare. I have never altered them, otherwise than by recommending condensation now and then ; nor have I, in looking over these sheets, made any emendation in them, beyond the ordinary corrections of the press ; desiring

them to be his genuine work, as they have been his sober
and rational amusement.

The latter observation brings me to the origin of the
present volume, and of this my slight share in it. The
reader will soon comprehend why I touch the subject
lightly, and with a sorrowful and faltering hand.

In all the knowledge I have had of John Overs, and
in all the many conversations I have held with him, I
have invariably found him, in every essential particular,
but one, the same. I have found him from first to last
a simple, frugal, steady, upright, honourable man; especially to be noted for the unobtrusive independence of
his character, the instinctive propriety of his manner, and
the perfect neatness of his appearance. The extent of his
information: regard being had to his opportunities of
acquiring it: is very remarkable; and the discrimination
with which he has risen superior to the mere prejudices
of the class with which he is associated, without losing
his sympathy for all their real wrongs and grievances—
they have a few—impressed me, in the beginning of our
acquaintance, strongly in his favour.

The one respect in which he is not what he was, is in
his hold on life.

He is very ill; the faintest shadow of the man who
came into my little study for the first time half-a-dozen
years ago, after the correspondence I have mentioned.
He has been very ill for a long, long period; his disease
is a severe and wasting affection of the lungs, which has
incapacitated him, these many months, for every kind of
occupation. "If I could only do a hard day's work,"
he said to me the other day, "how happy I should
be!"

Having these papers by him, amongst others, he bethought

8

himself that if he could get a bookseller to purchase them
for publication in a volume, they would enable him to
make some temporary provision for his sick wife and very
young family. We talked the matter over together, and
that it might be easier of accomplishment, I promised him
that I would write an introduction to his book.

I would to Heaven that I could do him better service!
I would to Heaven it were an introduction to a long, and
vigorous, and useful life! But Hope will not trim her lamp
the less brightly for him and his, because of this impulse
to their struggling fortunes; and trust me, reader, they
deserve her light, and need it sorely.

He has inscribed this book to one whose skill will help
him, under Providence, in all that human skill can do.
To one who never could have recognised in any potentate
on earth, a higher claim to constant kindness and attention, than he has recognised in him.

I have little more to say of it. While I do not commend
it, on the one hand, as a prodigy, I do sincerely believe
it, on the other, to possess some points of real interest,
however considered; but which, if considered with reference
to its title and origin, are of great interest.

If any delicate readers should approach the perusal of
these " Evenings of a Working Man ", with a genteel distaste
to the principle of a working-man turning author at all, I
may perhaps be permitted to suggest that the best protection
against such an offence will be found in the Universal
Education of the people; for the enlightenment of the many
will effectually swamp any interest that may now attach in
vulgar minds, to the few among them who are enabled,
in any degree, to overcome the great difficulties of their
position.

. And if such readers should deny the immense importance of communicating to this class, at this time, every possible means of knowledge, refinement and recreation; or the cause we have to hail with delight the least token. that may arise among them of a desire to be wiser, better, and more gentle; I earnestly entreat them to educate themselves in this neglected branch of their own learning without delay; promising them that it is the easiest in its acquisition of any: requiring only open eyes and ears, and six easy lessons of an hour each in a working town. Which will render them perfect for the rest of their lives.

CHARLES DICKENS.

London, June, 1844.

CRIME AND EDUCATION.

I OFFER no apology for entreating the attention of the readers of *The Daily News* to an effort which has been making for some three years and a half, and which is making now, to introduce among the most miserable and neglected outcasts in London, some knowledge of the commonest principles of morality and religion; to commence their recognition as immortal human creatures, before the Gaol Chaplain becomes their only schoolmaster; to suggest to Society that its duty to this wretched throng, foredoomed to crime and punishment, rightfully begins at some distance from the police office; and that the careless maintenance from year to year, in this the capital city of the world, of a vast hopeless nursery of ignorance, misery, and vice; a breeding place for the hulks and jails: is horrible to contemplate.

This attempt is being made, in certain of the most obscure and squalid parts of the Metropolis; where rooms are opened, at night, for the gratuitous instruction of all comers, children or adults, under the title of RAGGED SCHOOLS. The name implies the purpose. They who are too ragged, wretched, filthy, and forlorn, to enter any other place: who could gain admission into no charity school, and who would be driven from any church door;

are invited to come in here, and find some people not depraved, willing to teach them something, and show them some sympathy, and stretch a hand out, which is not the iron hand of Law, for their correction.

Before I describe a visit of my own to a Ragged School, and urge the readers of this letter for God's sake to visit one themselves, and think of it (which is my main object), let me say, that I know the prisons of London well. That I have visited the largest of them, more times than I could count; and that the children in them are enough to break the heart and hope of any man. I have never taken a foreigner or a stranger of any kind, to one of these establishments, but I have seen him so moved at sight of the child offenders, and so affected by the contemplation of their utter renouncement and desolation outside the prison walls, that he has been as little able to disguise his emotion, as if some great grief had suddenly burst upon him. Mr. Chesterton and Lieutenant Tracey (than whom more intelligent and humane Governors of Prisons it would be hard, if not impossible, to find) know, perfectly well, that these children pass and repass through the prisons all their lives; that they are never taught; that the first distinctions between right and wrong are, from their cradles, perfectly confounded and perverted in their minds; that they come of untaught parents, and will give birth to another untaught generation; that in exact proportion to their natural abilities, is the extent and scope of their depravity; and that there is no escape or chance for them in any ordinary revolution of human affairs. Happily, there are schools in these prisons now. If any readers doubt how ignorant the children are, let them visit those schools and see them at their tasks, and hear how much they knew when they were sent there.

If they would know the produce of this seed, let them see a class of men and boys together, at their books (as I have seen them in the House of Correction for this county of Middlesex), and mark how painfully the full grown felons toil at the very shape and form of letters; their ignorance being so confirmed and solid. The contrast of this labour in the men, with the less blunted quickness of the boys; the latent shame and sense of degradation struggling through their dull attempts at infant lessons; and the universal eagerness to learn; impress me, in this passing retrospect, more painfully than I can tell.

For the instruction, and as a first step in the reformation, of such unhappy beings, the Ragged Schools were founded. I was first attracted to the subject, and indeed was first made conscious of their existence, about two years ago, or more, by seeing an advertisement in the papers dated from West Street, Saffron-hill, stating "That a room had been opened and supported in that wretched neighbourhood for upwards of twelve months, where religious instruction had been imparted to the poor," and explaining in a few words what was meant by Ragged Schools as a generic term, including, then, four or five similar places of instruction. I wrote to the masters of this particular school to make some further inquiries, and went myself soon afterwards.

It was a hot summer night; and the air of Field-lane and Saffron-hill was not improved by such weather, nor were the people in those streets very sober or honest company. Being unacquainted with the exact locality of the school, I was fain to make some inquiries about it. These were very jocosely received in general; but everybody knew where it was, and gave the right direction to it. The prevailing idea among the loungers (the greater part of them the very sweepings of the streets and station houses) seemed to be, that the teachers were quixotic, and the school upon the whole "a lark". But there was certainly a kind of rough respect for the intention, and (as I have said) nobody denied the school or its whereabouts, or refused assistance in directing to it.

It consisted at that time of either two or three—I forget which—miserable rooms, up-stairs in a miserable house. In the best of these, the pupils in the female school were being taught to read and write; and though there were among the number, many wretched creatures steeped in degradation to the lips, they were tolerably quiet, and listened with apparent earnestness and patience to their instructors. The appearance of this room was sad and melancholy, of course—how could it be otherwise!—but, on the whole, encouraging.

The close, low, chamber at the back, in which the boys were crowded, was so foul and stifling as to be, at first, almost insupportable. But its moral aspect was so far worse than its physical, that this was soon forgotten. Huddled together on a bench about the room, and shown out by some flaring candles stuck against the walls, were a crowd of boys, varying from mere infants to young men; sellers of fruit, herbs, lucifer-matches, flints; sleepers under the dry arches of bridges; young thieves and beggars— with nothing natural to youth about them: with nothing frank, ingenuous, or pleasant in their faces; low-browed, vicious, cunning, wicked; abandoned of all help but this; speeding downward to destruction; and UNUTTERABLY IGNORANT.

This, Reader, was one room as full as it could hold; but these were only grains in sample of a Multitude that are perpetually sifting through these schools; in sample of a Multitude who had within them once, and perhaps have now, the elements of men as good as you or I, and maybe infinitely better; in sample of a Multitude among whose doomed and sinful ranks (oh, think of this, and think of them!) the child of any man upon this earth, however, lofty his degree, must, as by Destiny and Fate, be found, if, at its birth, it were consigned to such an infancy and nurture, as these fallen creatures had!

This was the Class I saw at the Ragged School. They could not be trusted with books; they could only be instructed orally; they were difficult of reduction to anything like attention, obedience, or decent behaviour; their benighted ignorance in reference to the Deity, or to any social duty (how could they guess at any social duty, being so discarded by all social teachers but the gaoler and the hangman!) was terrible to see. Yet, even here, and among these, something had been done already. The Ragged School was of recent date and very poor; but it had inculcated some association with the name of the Almighty, which was not an oath, and had taught them to look forward in a hymn (they sang it) to another life, which would correct the miseries and woes of this.

The new exposition I found in this Ragged School, of the frightful neglect by the State of those whom it punishes so constantly, and whom it might, as easily and less expensively, instruct and save; together with the sight I had seen there, in the heart of London; haunted me, and finally impelled me to an endeavour to bring these Institutions under the notice of the Government; with some faint hope that the vastness of the question would supersede the Theology of the schools, and that the Bench of Bishops might adjust the latter question, after some small grant had been conceded. I made the attempt;

and have heard no more of the subject, from that hour.

The perusal of an advertisement in yesterday's paper, announcing a lecture on the Ragged Schools last night, has led me into these remarks. I might easily have given them another form; but I address this letter to you, in the hope that some few readers in whom I have awakened an interest, as a writer of fiction, may be, by that means, attracted to the subject, who might otherwise, unintentionally, pass it over.

I have no desire to praise the system pursued in the Ragged Schools; which is necessarily very imperfect, if indeed there be one. So far as I have any means of judging of what is taught there, I should individually object to it, as not being sufficiently secular, and as presenting too many religious mysteries and difficulties, to minds not sufficiently prepared for their reception. But I should very imperfectly discharge in myself the duty I wish to urge and impress on others, if I allowed any such doubt of mine to interfere with my appreciation of the efforts of these teachers, or my true wish to promote them by any slight means in my power. Irritating topics, of all kinds, are equally far removed from my purpose and intention. But, I adjure those excellent persons who aid, munificently, in the building of New Churches, to think of these Ragged Schools; to reflect whether some portion of their rich endowments might not be spared for such a purpose; to contemplate, calmly, the necessity of beginning at the beginning; to consider for themselves where the Christian Religion most needs and most suggests immediate help and illustration; and not to decide on any theory or hearsay, but to go themselves into the Prisons and the Ragged Schools, and form their own conclusions. They will be shocked, pained, and repelled, by much that they learn there; but nothing they can learn, will be one-thousandth part so shocking, painful, and repulsive, as the continuance for one year more of these things as they have been for too many years already.

Anticipating that some of the more prominent facts connected with the history of the Ragged Schools, may become known to the readers of *The Daily News* through your account of the lecture in question, I abstain (though in possession of some such information) from pursuing the question further, at this time.   But if I should see occasion, I will take leave to return to it.

[Letter to the Editors of *The Daily News*, Feb. 4, 1846].

THESE are not stray crumbs that have fallen from Mr. Punch's well provided table, but a careful reproduction by Mr. Leech, in a very graceful and cheerful manner, of one of his best series of designs. Admirable as the 'Rising Generation' is in Mr. Punch's gallery, it shows to infinitely greater advantage in the present enlarged and separate form of publication. [1]

It is to be remarked of Mr. Leech that he is the very first English caricaturist (we use the word for want of a better) who has considered beauty as being perfectly compatible with his art. He almost always introduces into his graphic sketches, some beautiful faces or agreeable forms; and in striking out this course and setting this example, we really believe he does a great deal to refine and elevate that popular branch of art which the facilities of steam printing and wood-engraving are rendering more popular every day.

If we turn back to a collection of the works of Rowlandson or Gilray, we shall find in spite of the great humour displayed in many of them, that they are rendered wearisome and unpleasant by a vast amount of personal

[1] The Rising Generation, a series of twelve Drawings on Stone. By John Leech. From his Original Designs in the Gallery of Mr. Punch.

ugliness. Now, besides that it is a poor device to represent
what is satirized as being necessarily ugly—which is but
the resource of an angry child or a jealous woman—it
serves no purpose but to produce a disagreeable result.
There is no reason why the farmer's daughter in the old
caricature who is squalling at the harpsichord (to the
intense delight, by the bye, of her worthy father, the
farmer, whom it is her duty to please) should be squab
and hideous. The satire on the manner of her education,
if there be any in the thing at all, would be just as good
if she were pretty. Mr. Leech would have made her so.
The average of farmers' daughters in England are not
impossible lumps of fat. One is quite as likely to find
a pretty girl in a farm-house as to find an ugly one; and
we think, with Mr. Leech, that the business of this style
of art is with the pretty one. She is not only a pleasanter
object in our portfolio, but we have more interest in her.
We care more about what does become her, and does
not become her. In Mr. Punch's *Almanack* for the new
year, there is one illustration by Mr. Leech representing
certain delicate creatures with bewitching countenances,
encased in several varieties of that amazing garment, the
ladies' paletot. Formerly these fair creatures would have
been made as ugly and ungainly as possible, and there
the point would have been lost, and the spectator, with
a laugh at the absurdity of the whole group, would not
have cared one farthing how such uncouth creatures disguised themselves, or how ridiculous they became.

But to represent female beauty as Mr. Leech represents
it, an artist must have a most delicate perception of it,
and the gift of being able to realise it to us with two or
three slight, sure touches of his pencil. This power Mr.
Leech possesses, in an extraordinary degree.

For this reason, we enter our protest against those of the 'rising generation' who are precociously in love, being made the subject of merriment by a pitiless and unsympathising world. We never saw a boy more distinctly in the right than the young gentleman kneeling on the chair to beg a lock of hair from his pretty cousin, to take back to school. Madness is in her apron, and Virgil, dog's-eared and defaced, is in her ringlets. Doubts may suggest themselves of the perfect disinterestedness of this other young gentleman contemplating the fair girl at the piano—doubts engendered by his worldly allusion to "tin" (though even that may arise in his modest consciousness of his own inability to support an establishment); but that he should be "deucedly inclined to go and cut that fellow out," appears to us one of the most natural emotions of the human breast. The young gentleman with the dishevelled hair and clasped hands, who loves the transcendent beauty with the bouquet, and can't be happy without her, is, to us, a withering and desolate spectacle. Who *could* be happy without her?

The growing boys, or the rising generation, are not less happily observed and agreeably depicted than the grown women. The languid little creature who 'hasn't danced since he was quite a boy', is perfect, and the eagerness of the little girl whom he declines to receive for a partner at the hands of the glorious old lady of the house—her feet quite ready for the first position—her whole heart projected into the quadrille—and her glance peeping timidly at him out of her flutter of hope and doubt—is quite delightful to look at. The intellectual juvenile who awakens the tremendous wrath of a Norma of private life, by considering woman an inferior animal, is lecturing, this present Christmas, we understand, on the Concrete in connection

with the Will.   We recognized the legs of the philosopher
who considers Shakespeare an over-rated man, dangling
over the side of an omnibus last Tuesday.   The scowling
young gentleman who is clear that "if his governor don't
like the way he goes on in, why, he must have chambers
and so much a week," is not of our acquaintance; but we
trust he is by this time in Van Dieman's Land, or he will
certainly come to Newgate.   We should be exceedingly
unwilling to stand possessed of personal property in a strong
box, and be in the relation of bachelor-uncle to that youth.
We would on no account reside at that suburb of ill
omen, Camberwell, under such circumstances, remembering
the Barnwell case.

In all his drawings, whatever Mr. Leech desires to do,
he does.   The expression indicated, though indicated by
the simplest means, is exactly the natural expression, and
is recognised as such immediately.   His wit is good-natured,
and always the wit of a true gentleman.   He has a becoming sense of responsibility and self-restraint; he delights in
pleasant things; he imparts some pleasant air of his own to
things not pleasant in themselves; he is suggestive and full
of matter, and he is always improving.   Into the tone, as
well as into the execution of what he does, he has brought
a certain elegance which is altogether new, without involving any compromise of what is true.   He is an acquisition to popular art in England who has already done
great service, and will, we doubt not, do a great deal
more.   Our best wishes for the future, and our cordial
feeling towards him for the past, attend him in his career.

It is eight or ten years ago since a writer in the
Quarterly Review, making mention of Mr. George Cruikshank, commented, in a few words, on the absurdity o
excluding such a man from the Royal Academy, because

his works were not produced in certain materials, and did not occupy a certain space annually on its walls. Will no Members and Associates be found upon its books, one of these days, the labours of whose oils and brushes will have sunk into the profoundest obscurity, when the many pencil-marks of Mr. Cruikshank and of Mr. Leech will still be fresh in half the houses in the land?   [1848]

WHY an honest republican, coming from the United States to England on a mission of inquiry into ploughs, turnips, mangel-wurzel, and live stock, cannot be easy unless he is for ever exhibiting himself to his admiring countrymen, with a countess hanging on each arm, a duke or two walking deferentially behind, and a few old English barons (all his very particular friends) going on before, we cannot, to our satisfaction, comprehend. Neither is his facility of getting into such company quite intelligible; unless something of the spirit which rushes into print with a record of these genteel processions, pervades the aristocratic as well as the republican breast, and tickles the noble fancy with a bird's eye view of some thousands of American readers across the water, poring, with open mouths and goggle-eyes, over descriptions of its owner's domestic magnificence. We are bound to confess, in justice to a stranger with Mr. Colman's opportunities, that we are not altogether free from a suspicion of this kind.

Mr. Colman came here, as we have already intimated, charged with a mission of inquiry into the general agricultural condition of the country. In this capacity he wrote some reports very creditable to his good sense, expressed in plain nervous English, and testifying to his acquaintance with the rural writings of Cobbett. It would have been better for Mr. Colman, and more agreeable, we conceive, to all Americans of good sense and good taste, if he had contented himself with such authorship; but in an evil hour he committed the two volumes before us,[1] in which

> He talks so like a waiting gentlewoman,
> Of napkins, forks, and spoons (God save the mark!)

—that the dedication of his book to Lady Byron is an obvious mistake, and an outrage on the rights of Mr. N. P. Willis.

Mr. Colman's letters have one very remarkable feature which our readers will probably never have observed before in any similar case. They were not intended for publication. Of this unprecedented fact, there is no doubt. He wrote them, without a twinkle of his eye at the public, to some partial friends; who were so delighted with them and talked so much about them, that all his other friends cried out for copies. They *would have* copies. Now these may be excellent friends, but they are bitter bad judges: still they may be turned to good account; for if Mr. Colman should ever, in future, write anything that is particularly agreeable to this audience, he may rely upon it that the nearest fire will be its fittest destination.

We do not say but that there are parts of these letters which exhibit the writer in the character of a good-natured, kind-hearted private individual, though of a somewhat cumbrous and elephantine jocularity, and of a rather startling sentimentality—as when he goes to see the charity children assembled at St. Paul's, and has impulses, on account of their extraordinary beauty, to pitch himself out

[1] European Life and Manners, in Familiar Letters to Friends. By Henry Colman. 2 Vols. Boston.

of the whispering-gallery head foremost into the midst of those young Christians; a homage to youth and innocence necessarily involving the annihilation of the wearers of several undersized pairs of leather-breeches. But what Mr. Colman may choose to write, in this private aspect of himself, to his friends, is a very different thing from what he is justified in calling upon the public to read. A man may play at horses with his children, in his own parlour, and give nobody offence; but if he should hire the Opera House in London, or the Théâtre Français in Paris, for the exhibition of that performance at so much a head, he would challenge criticism, and might very justly be hissed.

The one great impression on our letter writer's mind, of which it does not appear at all probable that he will ever completely relieve himself, is made by the internal economy of an English nobleman's country house.

MR. COLMAN AT A GREAT COUNTRY MANSION.

As soon as you arrive at the house, your name is announced, your portmanteau is immediately taken into your chamber, which the servant shows you, with every requisite convenience and comfort. At Lord Spencer's the watch opens your door in the night to see if all is safe, as his house was once endangered by a gentleman's reading in bed, and if he should find your light burning after you had retired, excepting the night taper, or you reading in bed, without a single word, he would stretch out a long extinguisher, and put it out. In the morning, a servant comes in to let you know the time in season for you to dress for breakfast. At half-past nine you go in to family prayers, if you find out the time. They are happy to have the guests attend, but they are never asked. The servants are all assembled in the room fitted for a chapel. They all kneel, and the master of the house, or a chaplain, reads the morning service. As soon as it is over they all wait until he and his guests retire, and then the breakfast is served. At breakfast there is no ceremony whatever. You are asked by the servant what you will have, tea or coffee, or you get up and help yourself. Dry

toast, boiled eggs, and bread and butter are on the table, and on the
side table you will find cold ham, tongue, beef, etc., to which you carry
your own plate and help yourself, and come back to the breakfast table
and sit as long as you please. All letters or notes addressed to you
are laid by your plate, and letters to be sent by mail are put in the
post box in the entry, and are sure to go. The arrangements for the
day are then made, and parties are formed, horses and carriages for all
the guests are found at the stables, and each one follows the bent of his
inclination. When he returns, if at noon, he finds a side table with an
abundant lunch upon it if he chooses, and when he goes to his chamber
for preparation for dinner, he finds his dress clothes brushed and folded
in the nicest manner, and cold water, and hot water, and clean napkins
in the greatest abundance.

One would think this sufficiently explicit, but here, a few
pages further on, is

MR. COLMAN AGAIN AT A GREAT COUNTRY MANSION.

In most families the hour of breakfast is announced to you before
retiring, and the breakfast is entirely without ceremony. Your letters are
brought to you in the morning, and the mail goes out every day. The
postage of letters is always prepaid by those who write them, who paste
double or single stamps upon them; and it is considered an indecorum
to send a letter unpaid, or sealed with a wafer. Any expense incurred
for you, if it be only a penny upon a letter, is at once mentioned to
you, and you of course pay it. At breakfast the arrangements are made
for the day; you are generally left to choose what you will do, and
horses and carriages are always at the service of the guests, or guns
and implements for sporting, if those are their habits. There is your
chamber, or the library, the billiard room, or the garden, the park, or
the village. You are not looked for again, unless you make one of some
party until dinner time, which is generally in a nobleman's house, seven
o'clock. Breakfast from nine to ten. Lunch, to which you go if you
choose, which in truth is a dinner, though most things are cold, at half-
past one; coffee immediately after dinner, and tea and cake immediately
after coffee. At eleven o'clock there is always a candle for each guest,
placed on the sideboard or in the entry, with allumettes alongside of
them, and at your pleasure you light your own candle, and bid good
night. In a Scotch family you are expected to shake hands on retiring,
with all the party, and on meeting in the morning. The English are a

little more reserved, though, in general, the master of the house shakes
hands with you. On a first introduction, no gentlemen shake hands,
but simply bow to each other. In the morning you come down in
undress, with boots, trousers of any colour, frock coat, etc. At dinner,
you are always expected to be in full dress; straight coat, black satin,
or white waistcoat, silk stockings and pumps, but not gloves; and if you
dine abroad in London, you keep your hat in your hand until you go in
to dinner, when you give it to a servant, or leave it in an ante-room.
The lady of the house generally claims the arm of the principal stranger,
or the gentleman of the highest rank; she then assigns the other ladies
and gentlemen by name, and commonly waits until all her guests precede
her into dinner, though this is not invariable. The gentleman is expected
to sit near the lady whom he hands in. Grace is almost always said by
the master, and it is done in the shortest possible way. Sometimes no
dishes are put upon the table until the soup is done with, but at other
times there are two covers besides the soup. The soup is various; in
Scotland it is usually what they call hodge-podge, a mixture of vegetables
with some meat. After soup, the fish cover is removed, and this is
commonly served round without any vegetables, but certainly not more
than one kind. After fish, come the plain joints, roast or boiled, with
potatoes, peas or beans, and cauliflowers. Then sherry wine is handed
by the servant to everyone. German wine is offered to those who prefer
it; this is always drunk in green glasses; then come the entrées, which
are a variety of French dishes, and hashes; then champagne is offered;
after this remove, come ducks, or partridges, or other game; after this the
bonbons, puddings, tarts, sweetmeats, blancmange; then cheese and
bread, and a glass of strong ale is handed round; then the removal of
the upper cloth, and oftentimes the most delicious fruits and confectionery
follow, such as grapes, peaches, melons, apples, dried fruits, etc., etc.
After this is put upon the table a small bottle of Constantia wine, which
is deemed very precious, and handed round in small wine glasses, or
noyeau, or some other cordial. Finger glasses are always furnished,
though in some cases I have seen a deep silver plate filled with rose
water presented to each guest in which he dips the corner of his napkin,
to wipe his lips or his fingers. No cigars or pipes are ever offered, and
soon after the removal of the cloth, the ladies retire to the drawing room,
the gentlemen close up at the table, and after sitting as long as you please,
you go into the drawing room to have coffee and then tea. The wines
at table are generally of the most expensive quality; port, sherry, claret,
seldom madeira; but I have never heard any discussion about the character

of wines, excepting that I have been repeatedly asked what wine we usually drank in America.

In connection with this same establishment, we have the happiness of learning that the butler "takes care of all the wines, fruit, glasses, candlesticks, lamps, and plate;" also that he has an under-butler "for his adjunct." The ladies, it seems, "never wear a pair of white satin shoes or white gloves more than once." And we have a dim vision of the agitation of the tremendous depths of this social sea which looks so smooth at top, when we are informed that "some of them (the ladies) if they find, on going into society, *another person of inferior rank wearing the same dress as themselves*"—which would certainly appear an inconvenient proceeding—"the dress, upon being taken off, is at once thrown aside, and the lady's maid perfectly understands her perquisite."

Having recovered our breath, impeded in the contemplation of this awful picture, and the mysterious shadow thrown around the lady's maid, we expect to find our American friend in some new scene; and, indeed, we *do* find him, for a little time, in the company of Scotch gentlemen, who keep small ivory spoons in their pockets "to shove their snuff up their noses," and who likewise carry small brushes in their pockets to sweep their noses and upper lips with afterwards—which is well known to be a practice universal with the bench and bar of Scotland, and with the principal members of the Scottish Universities, whose snuff is for the most part carried after them in coal-scuttles by Highlanders, who cannot be made to sneeze by any artificial process whatever. But our traveller's foot is not upon his native heath in this society, and he is back again in no time.

MR. COLMAN AGAIN IN A GREAT COUNTRY MANSION.

The house is one of the most magnificent and ancient in the country, having been long in the possession of the family. It was once the property of the Marquis of Rockingham, one of the most distinguished ministers of the crown in the war of the revolution, and always an ardent friend of America. I think, upon the whole, it is upon the largest scale of anything I have yet seen. The house itself is six hundred and ten feet in length, and the width proportionate. I was forewarned that I should lose my way in it, and so I have done two or three times, until, at last, I have made sure of my own bedroom. The house is elegantly furnished, parts of it superbly, and the style of living is in keeping. I arrived about six, and after a short walk with my noble host, the dressing bell rung, and I was shown at once to my chamber. The chamber is a large and superb room, called the blue-room, because papered with elegant blue satin paper, and the bed and the windows hung with superb blue silk curtains. My portmanteau had already been carried there, and the straps untied for opening; a large coal fire was blazing; candles were burning on the table, and water and everything else necessary for ablution and comfort. There was, likewise, what is always to be found in an English house, a writing table, letter paper, note paper, new pens, ink, sealing wax, and wax-taper, and a letter box is kept in the house, and notice given to the guests always at what time the post will leave.

Nor is his mind yet discharged of the mere froth and foam of that one idea, which must work henceforth with him, while memory lasts; for, after travelling a few pages, we find

MR. COLMAN AGAIN AT A GREAT COUNTRY MANSION.

Imagine an elegant dining-room, the table covered with the richest plate, and this plate filled with the richest viands which the culinary art and the vintage and the fruit-garden can supply; imagine a horse at your disposal, a servant at your command to anticipate every want, imagine an elegant bed-chamber, a bright coal-fire, fresh water in basins, in goblets, in tubs, napkins without stint as white as snow, a double mattress, a French bed, sheets of the finest linen, a canopy of the richest silk, a table portfolio, writing apparatus and stationery, allumettes, a night lamp, candles and silver candlesticks, and beautiful paintings and exquisite statuary, and every kind of chair or sofa but a rocking chair, and then you will have some little notion of the place where I now am.

And yet a few pages more and here is

MR. COLMAN AT THE GREATEST COUNTRY MANSION OF ALL.

I asked, when I retired, what time do you breakfast? The Duke replied, "just what time you please, from nine to twelve." I always came down at nine precisely, and found the Duchess at her breakfast. About half-past nine the Duke would come in, and the ladies, one by one, soon after. At breakfast, the side table would have on it cold ham, cold chicken, cold pheasant or partridge, which you ask for, or to which, as is most common, you get up and help yourself. On the breakfast table were several kinds of the best bread possible, butter always fresh, made that morning, as I have found at all these houses, and if you ask for coffee or chocolate, it would be brought to you in a silver coffee-pot, and you help yourself; if for tea, you would have a silver urn to each guest, heated by alcohol, placed by you, a small teapot, and a small caddie of black and green tea to make for yourself, or the servant for you. The papers of the morning, from London (for a country paper is rarely seen) were then brought to you, and your letters, if any. At breakfast, the arrangements were made for the day, and if you were to ride, choose your mode, and at the minute, the horses and servants would be at the door.

At two o'clock is the lunch, which I was not at home to take, and very rarely do take. A lunch at such houses, is in fact a dinner; the table is set at half-past one, not quite so large as for dinner. Commonly, there is roast meat, warm, birds, warm or cold, cold chicken, cold beef, cold ham, bread, butter, cheese, fruit, beer, ale, and wines, and every one takes it as he pleases, standing, sitting, waiting for the rest, or not, and going away when he pleases; dinner at seven, sometimes at eight, when all are congregated in the drawing room, five minutes before the hour, in full dress. I have already told you the course at dinner, but at many houses, there is always a bill of fare—in this case written, I had almost said engraved, on the most elegant embossed and coloured paper; always in French, and passed round to the guests.

"The Duke" meantime, it is to be presumed, keeping his noble eyes on Mr. Colman's waistcoat, until he satisfies his noble mind that it is not a waistcoat, like his waistcoat; which would render it indispensable for his Grace instantly to depart from table, take it off in desperation, and bestow it on his valet.

But there is one phase of the national character which impresses our good traveller more than any other. It is remarkable that the guests at a gentleman's house do not dash at the dishes, and contend with one another for "the fixings" they contain, but put their trust in Providence, and in the servants, and in the good time coming if they wait a little longer;—it is a grave consideration that they have water to wash in, sheets to sleep in, paper to write letters on, and allumettes to light their sealing-wax by;—it is matter for a philosopher's reflection that at breakfast you find the cold beef on the sideboard, and at night the chamber candlestick in the entry;—but the distinctive mark of the national character, the centre prong in the trident of Britannia, the strong tuft in the mane of the British lion, is the national propensity to perform that humble household service which is familiarly called "emptying the slops." This, and the kindred national propensity to brush a man's clothes and polish his boots, whensoever and wheresoever the clothes and boots can be seized without the man, are the noteworthy things that can never be effaced from an observant traveller's remembrance.

> Princes and lords may flourish or may fade,

—even "the Duke," with his four and twenty silver tea-caddies all of a row, may be made hay of by the inexorable getter-in of human grass—but the ducal housemaid and the ducal bootsboy will flourish in immortal freshness.

"I forgot to say," writes Mr. Colman, and strange it is indeed that any man should forget the having such a thing to say—"I forgot to say, if you leave your chamber twenty times a day, after using your basin, you would find it clean, and the pitcher replenished on your return; and that you cannot take your clothes off, but they are taken away, brushed, folded, pressed, and placed in the bureau; and at the dressing hour, before dinner, you find your candles lighted, your clothes laid out, your shoes cleaned, and everything arranged for use."

Bye and bye he expatiates on the bell-rope being always within reach; on "a worked night-cap" being "not unfrequently" placed ready for you (though we suspect the Duchess of a personal attention to this article); on the unwonted luxury of a bootjack; on the high civilisation of a little copper tea-kettle; on the imposing solemnity of that complicated Institution known as dinner napkins—which, we are told, "are never left upon the table, but either thrown into your chair, or on the floor under the table,"—but faithful to the one great trait of Britain, he falls back on the boots and clothes for ever "brushed and folded and laid out for use."

Again and again we find Mr. Colman again at a great country mansion—those to which we have followed him having numerous successors. And again and again, after simmering in his "copper-kettle of hot water, and floundering in his "tub of cold," he sinks into a gentle trance of admiration at the brushing of his clothes and cleaning of his boots. We could desire to have known whose blacking the Duke uses, and we must regard the maker's name as unaccountably omitted. It is one of the few such things Mr. Colman has "forgotten to say."

Much as we admire Mr. Colman in private life, we must confess to being a little staggered by his appearances in public. They are rare, but marvellous. His singular emotions at St. Paul's we have already referred to, but his experience of another public occasion is still more remarkable.

MR. COLMAN AT THE OLD BAILEY.

The judge, again and again, passed dreadful and heart-rending sentences upon some wretched boy, or some poor, miserable, affrighted woman; and, after telling them, in the harshest manner, that they might congratulate themselves upon escaping so lightly, turned round and laughed heartily at the concern of the compassionate alderman, who sat at his side and did what he could to stay his violence, and at the surprise and anguish of the poor convicts.

Next to our curiosity in respect of the Duke's blacking-maker, and the conflict of our hopes and fears between Warrens blacking 30 Strand, and Day and Martin's 97 High Holborn, we confess to a desire to be favoured with the name of this judge. For we cannot help thinking that it must be Jeffreys, and that Mr. Colman, falling into a magnetic slumber one day, when they had taken away his boots, became clairvoyant as to the Bloody Assize.

With this we think we may conclude. How Mr. Colman could espy no beggars on the roads in France, and how he could find out nothing in Paris, of all the cities upon earth, that had a poverty stricken or vagabond aspect, we will not relate. We hope, and believe, that he writes better about things agricultural than about the topics of the *Court Circular*. We are chiefly sorry for the folly of his letters, because we take him to be a man of better stuff than their contents would indicate; and because, in the still increasing facilities of friendly communication between the two sides of the Atlantic (long may they continue to increase, and to make the inhabitants of each shore better acquainted with the other, to their mutual improvement, forbearance, and advantage!) we feel for the many American gentlemen with an undoubted claim on the hospitality and respect of all classes of English society who stand committed by such very egregious slip-slop. [1849].

CAPITAL PUNISHMENT.

I WILL take for the subject of this letter, the effect of Capital Punishment on the commission of crime, or rather of murder; the only crime with one exception (and that a rare one) to which it is now applied. Its effect in preventing crime, I will reserve for another letter: and a few of the more striking illustrations of each aspect of the subject, for a concluding one.

The effect of Capital Punishment on the commission of Murder.

Some murders are committed in hot blood and furious rage; some, in deliberate revenge; some, in terrible despair; some (but not many) for mere gain; some, for the removal of an object dangerous to the murderer's peace or good name; some, to win a monstrous notoriety.

On murders committed in rage, in the despair of strong affection (as when a starving child is murdered by its parent) or for gain, I believe the punishment of death to have no effect in the least. In the two first cases, the impulse is a blind and wild one, infinitely beyond the reach of any reference to the punishment. In the last, there is little calculation beyond the absorbing greed of the money to be got. Courvoisier, for example, might have robbed his master with greater safety and with fewer chances of detection, if he had not murdered him. But, his calculations going to the gain and not to the loss, he had no balance for the consequences of what he did. So, it would have been more safe and prudent in the woman who was hanged a few weeks since, for the murder in Westminster, to have simply robbed her old companion in an unguarded moment, as in her sleep. But, her calculation going to the gain of what she took to be a Bank note; and the poor old woman living between her and the gain; she murdered her.

On murders committed in deliberate revenge, or to remove a stumbling block in the murderer's path, or in an insatiate craving for notoriety, is there reason to suppose that the punishment of death has the direct effect of an incentive and an impulse?

A murder is committed in deliberate revenge. The murderer is at no trouble to prepare his train of circumstances, takes little or no pains to escape, is quite cool and collected, perfectly content to deliver himself up to the Police, makes no secret of his guilt, but boldly says "I killed him. I'm glad of it. I meant to do it. I am ready to die." There was such a case the other day. There was such another case not long ago. There are such cases frequently. It is the commonest first exclamation on being seized. Now, what is this but a false arguing of the question, announcing a foregone conclusion, expressly leading to the crime, and inseparably arising out of the Punishment of Death? "I took his life. I give up mine to pay for it. Life for life; blood for blood. I have done the crime. I am ready with the atonement. I know all about it; it's a fair bargain between me and the law. Here am I to execute my part of it; and what more is to be said or done?" It is the very essence of the maintenance of this punishment for murder, that it *does* set life against life. It is in the essence of a stupid, weak, or otherwise ill-regulated mind (of such a murderer's mind, in short), to recognise in this set off, a something that diminishes the base and coward character of murder. In a pitched battle, I, a common man, may kill my adversary, but he may kill me. In a duel, a gentleman may shoot his opponent through the head, but the opponent may shoot him too, and this makes it fair. Very well. I take this man's life for a reason I have, or choose to think I have, and the law takes mine. The law says, and the clergyman says, there must be blood for blood and life for life. Here it is. I pay the penalty."

A mind incapable, or confounded in its perceptions— and you must argue with reference to such a mind, or you could not have such a murder—may not only establish on these grounds an idea of strict justice and fair reparation, but a stubborn and dogged fortitude and foresight that satisfy it hugely. Whether the fact be really so, or not, is a question I would be content to rest, alone, on the number of cases of revengeful murder in which this is well known, without dispute, to have been the prevailing demeanour of the criminal: and in which such speeches and such absurd reasoning have been constantly uppermost with him. "Blood for blood," and "life for life," and such like balanced jingles, have passed current in people's mouths, from legislators downwards, until they have been corrupted into "tit for tat," and acted on.

Next, come the murders done, to sweep out of the way a dreaded or detested object. At the bottom of this class of crimes, there is a slow, corroding, growing hate. Violent quarrels are commonly found to have taken place between the murdered person and the murderer: usually of opposite sexes. There are witnesses to old scenes of reproach and recrimination, in which they were the actors; and the murderer has been heard to say, in this or that coarse phrase, "that he wouldn't mind killing her, though he should be hanged for it"—in these cases, the commonest avowal.

It seems to me, that in this well known scrap of evidence, there is a deeper meaning than is usually attached to it. I do not know, but it may be—I have a strong suspicion that it is—a clue to the slow growth of the crime, and its gradual development in the mind. More than this; a clue to the mental connection of the deed, with the punishment to which the doer of that deed is liable, until the two, conjoined, give birth to monstrous and mis-shapen Murder.

The idea of murder, in such a case, like that of self-destruction in the great majority of instances, is not a new one. It may have presented itself to the disturbed mind in a dim shape and afar off; but it has been there. After a quarrel, or with some strong sense upon him of irritation or discomfort arising out of the continuance of this life in his path, the man has brooded over the unformed desire to take it, "Though he should be hanged for it." With the entrance of the Punishment into his thoughts, the shadow of the fatal beam begins to attend —not on himself, but on the object of his hate. At every new temptation, it is there, stronger and blacker yet, trying to terrify him. When she defies or threatens him, the scaffold seems to be her strength and 'vantage ground. Let her not be too sure of that; 'though he should be hanged for it.'

Thus, he begins to raise up, in the contemplation of this death by hanging, a new and violent enemy to brave.

The prospect of a slow and solitary expiation would have no congeniality with his wicked thoughts, but this throttling and strangling has. There is always before him, an ugly, bloody, scarecrow phantom, that champions her, as it were, and yet shows him, in a ghastly way, the example of murder. Is she very weak, or very trustful in him, or infirm, or old? It gives a hideous courage to what would be mere slaughter otherwise; for there it is, a presence always about her, darkly menacing him with that penalty whose murky secret has a fascination for all secret and unwholesome thoughts. And when he struggles with his victim at the last, 'though he should be hanged for it,' it is a merciless wrestle, not with one weak life only, but with that ever-haunting, ever-beckoning shadow of the gallows, too; and with a fierce defiance to it, after their long survey of each other, to come on and do its worst.

Present this black idea of violence to a bad mind contemplating violence; hold up before a man remotely compassing the death of another person, the spectacle of his own ghastly and untimely death by man's hands; and out of the depths of his own nature you shall assuredly raise up that which lures and tempts him on. The laws which regulate those mysteries have not been studied or cared for, by the maintainers of this law; but they are paramount and will always assert their power.

Out of one hundred and sixty seven persons under sentence of Death in England, questioned at different times, in the course of years, by an English clergyman in the performance of his duty, there were only three who had not been spectators of executions.

We come, now, to the consideration of those murders which are committed, or attempted, with no other object than the attainment of an infamous notoriety. That this class of crimes has its origin in the Punishment of Death, we cannot question; because (as we have already seen, and shall presently establish by another proof) great notoriety and interest attach, and are generally understood to attach, only to those criminals who are in danger of being executed.

One of the most remarkable instances of murder originating in mad self-conceit; and of the murderer's part in the repulsive drama, in which the law appears at such great disadvantage to itself and to society, being acted almost to the last with a self-complacency that would be horribly ludicrous if it were not utterly revolting; is presented in the case of Hocker.

Here is an insolent, flippant, dissolute youth: aping the man of intrigue and levity: over-dressed, over-confident, inordinately vain of his personal appearance: distinguished as to his hair, cane, snuff-box, and singing-voice: and unhappily the son of a working shoemaker. Bent on loftier flights than such a poor house-swallow as a teacher in a Sunday-school can take; and having no truth, industry, perseverance or other dull work-a-day quality, to plume his wings withal; he casts about him, in his jaunty way, for some mode of distinguishing himself—some means of getting that head of hair into the print-shops; of having something like justice done to his singing-voice and fine intellect; of making the life and adventures of Thomas Hocker remarkable; and of getting up some excitement in connection with that slighted piece of biography. The Stage? No. Not feasible. There has always been a conspiracy against the Thomas Hockers, in that kind of effort. It has been the same with Authorship in prose and poetry. Is there nothing else? A Murder, now, would make a noise in the papers! There is the gallows to be sure; but without that, it would be nothing. Short of that, it wouldn't be fame. Well! We must all die at one time or other; and to die game, and have it in print, is just the thing for a man of spirit. They always die game at the Minor Theatres and the Saloons, and the people like it very much. Thurtell, too, died very game, and made a capital speech when he was tried. There's all about it in a book at the cigar-shop now. Come, Tom, get your name up! Let it be a dashing murder that shall keep the wood-engravers at it for the next two months. You are the boy to go through with it, and interest the town!

The miserable wretch, inflated by this lunatic conceit, arranges his whole plan for publication and effect. It is quite an epitome of his experience of the domestic melodrama or penny novel. There is the Victim Friend; the mysterious letter of the injured Female to the Victim Friend; the romantic spot for the Death-Struggle by night; the unexpected appearance of Thomas Hocker to the Policeman; the parlour of the Public House, with Thomas Hocker reading the paper to a strange gentleman; the Family Apartment, with a song by Thomas Hocker; the Inquest Room, with Thomas Hocker boldly looking on; the interior of the Marylebone Theatre, with Thomas Hocker taken into custody; the Police Office with Thomas Hocker "affable" to the spectators; the interior of Newgate, with Thomas Hocker preparing his defence; the Court, where Thomas Hocker, with his dancing-master airs, is put upon his trial, and complimented by the Judge; the Prosecution, the Defence, the Verdict, the Black Cap, the Sentence—each of them a line in any Playbill, and how bold a line in Thomas Hocker's life!

It is worthy of remark, that the nearer he approaches to

the gallows—the great last scene to which the whole of these effects have been working up—the more the overweening conceit of the poor wretch shows itself; the more he feels that he is the hero of the hour; the more audaciously and recklessly he lies, in supporting the character. In public—at the condemned sermon—he deports himself as becomes the man whose autographs are precious, whose portraits are innumerable; in memory of whom, whole fences and gates have been borne away, in splinters, from the scene of murder. He knows that the eyes of Europe are upon him; but he is not proud—only graceful. He bows, like the first gentleman in Europe, to the turnkey who brings him a glass of water; and composes his clothes and hassock, as carefully as good Madame Blaize could do. In private—within the walls of the condemned cell—every word and action of his waning life, is a lie. His whole time is divided between telling lies and writing them. If he ever have another thought, it is for his genteel appearance on the scaffold; as when he begs the barber "not to cut his hair too short, or they won't know him when he comes out." His last proceeding but one is to write two romantic love-letters to women who have no existence. His last proceeding of all (but less characteristic, though the only true one) is to swoon away, miserably, in the arms of the attendants, and be hanged up like a craven dog.

Is not such a history, from first to last, a most revolting and disgraceful one; and can the student of it bring himself to believe that it ever could have place in any record of facts, or that the miserable chief-actor in it could have ever had a motive for his arrogant wickedness, but for the comment and the explanation which the Punishment of Death supplies!

It is not a solitary case, nor is it a prodigy, but a mere specimen of a class. The case of Oxford, who fired at Her Majesty in the Park, will be found, on examination, to resemble it very nearly, in the essential feature. There is no proved pretence whatever for regarding him as mad; other than that he was like this malefactor, brimful of conceit, and a desire to become, even at the cost of the gallows (the only cost within his reach) the talk of the town. He had less invention than Hocker, and perhaps was not so deliberately bad; but his attempt was a branch of the same tree and it has its root in the ground where the scaffold is erected.

Oxford had his imitators. Let it never be forgotten in the consideration of this part of the subject, how they were stopped. So long as their attempts invested them with the distinction of being in danger of death at the hangman's hands, so long did they spring up. When the penalty of death was removed, and a mean and humiliating punishment substituted in its place, the race was at an end, and ceased to be.

*   *   *   *   *   *   *   *   *   *

We come, now, to consider the effect of Capital Punishment in the prevention of crime.

Does it prevent crime in those who attend executions?

There never is (and there never was) an execution at the Old Bailey in London, but the spectators include two large classes of thieves—one class who go there as they would go to a dog-fight, or any other brutal sport, for the attraction and excitement of the spectacle; the other who make it a dry matter of business, and mix with the crowd, solely to pick pockets. Add to these, the dissolute, the drunken, the most idle, profligate, and abandoned of both sexes—some moody ill-conditioned minds, drawn thither by a fearful interest—and some impelled by curiosity; of whom the greater part are of an age and temperament rendering the gratification of that curiosity highly dangerous to themselves and to society—and the great elements of the concourse are stated.

Nor is this assemblage peculiar to London. It is the same in country towns, allowing for the different statistics of the population. It is the same in America. I was present at an execution in Rome, for a most treacherous and wicked murder, and not only saw the same kind of assemblage there, but, wearing what is called a shooting-coat, with a great many pockets in it, felt innumerable hands busy in every one of them, close to the scaffold.

I have already mentioned that out of one hundred and sixty seven convicts under sentence of death, questioned at different times in the performance of his duty by an English clergyman, there were only three who had not been spectators of executions. Mr. Wakefield, in his *Facts relating to the Punishment of Death*, goes into the working, as it were, of this sum. His testimony is extremely valuable, because it is the evidence of an educated and observing man, who, before having personal knowledge of the subject and of Newgate, was quite satisfied that the Punishment of Death should continue, but who, when he gained that experience, exerted himself to the utmost for its abolition, even at the pain of constant public reference in his own person to his own imprisonment. "It cannot be egotism," he reasonably observes, "that prompts a man to speak of himself in connection with Newgate."   ·

"Whoever will undergo the pain," says Mr. Wakefield, "of witnessing the public destruction of a fellow creature's life, in London, must be perfectly satisfied that in the great mass of spectators, the effect of the punishment is to excite sympathy for the criminal and hatred of the law. * * * I am inclined to believe that the criminals of London, spoken of as a class and allowing for exceptions, take the same sort of delight in witnessing executions, as the sportsman and soldier find in the dangers of hunting and war. * * * I am confident that few Old Bailey Sessions pass without the trial of a boy, whose first thought of crime occurred whilst he was witnessing an execution. * * * And one grown man, of great mental powers and superior education, who was acquitted of a charge of forgery, assured me that the first idea of committing a forgery occurred to him at the moment when he was accidentally witnessing the execution of Fauntleroy. To which it may be added, that Fauntleroy is said to have made precisely the same declaration in reference to the origin of his own criminality.

But one convict "who was within an ace of being hanged," among the many with whom Mr. Wakefield conversed, seems to me to have unconsciously put a question which the advocates of Capital Punishment would find it very difficult indeed to answer. "Have you often seen an execution?" asked Mr. Wakefield. "Yes, often." "Did it not frighten you?" "No. *Why should it?*"

It is very easy and very natural to turn from this ruffian, shocked by the hardened retort; but answer his question, why should it? Should he be frightened by the sight of a dead man? We are born to die, he says, with a careless triumph. We are not born to the treadmill, or to servitude and slavery, or to banishment; but the executioner has done no more for that criminal than nature may do to-morrow for the judge, and will certainly do, in her own good time, for judge and jury, counsel and witnesses, turnkeys, hangman, and all. Should he be frightened by the manner of the death? It is horrible, truly, so horrible, that the law, afraid or ashamed of its own deed, hides the face of the struggling wretch it slays; but does this fact naturally awaken in such a man, terror—or defiance? Let the same man speak. "What did you think then?" asked Mr. Wakefield. "Think? Why, I thought it was a—shame."

Disgust and indignation, or recklessness and indifference, or a morbid tendency to brood over the sight until temptation is engendered by it, are the inevitable consequences of the spectacle, according to the difference of habit and disposition in those who behold it. Why should it frighten or deter? We know it does not. We know it from the police reports, and from the testimony of those who have experience of prisons and prisoners, and we may know it, on the occasion of an execution, by the evidence of our own senses; if we will be at the misery of using them for such a purpose. But why should it? Who would send his child or his apprentice, or what tutor would send his scholars, or what master would send his servants, to be deterred from vice by the spectacle of an execution? If it be an example to criminals, and to criminals only, why are not the prisoners in Newgate brought out to see the show before the debtors' door? Why, while they are made parties to the condemned sermon, are they rigidly excluded from the improving postscript of the gallows? Because an execution is well known to be an utterly useless, barbarous, and brutalising sight, and because the sympathy of all beholders, who have any sympathy at all, is certain to be always with the criminal, and never with the law.

I learn from the newspaper accounts of every execution, how Mr. So-and-so, and Mr. Somebody else, and Mr.

So-forth shook hands with the culprit, but I never find them shaking hands with the hangman. All kinds of attention and consideration are lavished on the one; but the other is universally avoided, like a pestilence. I want to know why so much sympathy is expended on the man who kills another in the vehemence of his own bad passions, and why the man who kills him in the name of the law is shunned and fled from? Is it because the murderer is going to die? Then by no means put him to death. Is it because the hangman executes a law, which, when they once come near it face to face, all men instinctively revolt from? Then by all means change it. There is, there can be, no prevention in such a law.

It may be urged that Public Executions are not intended for the benefit of those dregs of society who habitually attend them. This is an absurdity, to which the obvious answer is, So much the worse. If they be not considered with reference to that class of persons, comprehending a great host of criminals in various stages of development they ought to be, and must be. To lose sight of that consideration is to be irrational, unjust, and cruel. All other punishments are especially devised, with a reference to the rooted habits, propensities, and antipathies of criminals. And shall it be said, out of Bedlam, that this last punishment of all, is alone to be made an exception from the rule, even where it is shown to be a means of propagating vice and crime?

But there may be people who do not attend executions, to whom the general fame and rumour of such scenes is an example, and a means of deterring from crime.

Who are they? We have seen, that around Capital Punishment there lingers a fascination, urging weak and bad people towards it, and imparting an interest to details

connected with it, and with malefactors awaiting it or
suffering it, which even good and well disposed people
cannot withstand. We know that last-dying speeches,
and Newgate calendars, are the favourite literature of very
low intellects. The gallows is not appealed to, as an example
in the instruction of youth (unless they are training for
it); nor are there condensed accounts of celebrated executions for the use of national schools. There is a story
in an old spelling-book, of a certain Don't Care, who was
hanged at last, but it is not understood to have had any
remarkable effect on crimes or executions in the generation
to which it belonged, and with which it has passed away.
Hogarth's idle apprentice is hanged; but the whole
scene—with the unmistakeable stout lady, drunk and pious,
in the cast; the quarrelling, blasphemy, lewdness, and
uproar; Tiddy Doll vending his gingerbread, and the boys
picking his pocket—is a bitter satire on the great example;
as efficient then, as now.

Is it efficient to prevent crime? The parliamentary
returns demonstrate that it is not. I was engaged in
making some extracts from these documents, when I found
them so well abstracted in one of the papers published
by the committee on this subject established at Aylesbury
last year, by the humane exertions of Lord Nugent, that
I am glad to quote the general results from its pages:

"In 1843, a return was laid on the table of the House
of the commitments and executions for murder in England
and Wales, during the 30 years ending with December
1842; divided into five periods of six years each. It
shows that in the last six years, from 1836 to 1842, during
which there were only 50 executions, the commitments
for murder were fewer by 61 than in the six years preceding with 74 executions; fewer by 63 than in the six

years ending 1830 with 75 executions; fewer by 56 than in the six years ending 1824 with 94 executions; and fewer by 93 than in the six years ending 1818, when there was no less a number of executions than 122. But it may be said perhaps, that, in the inference we draw from this return, we are substituting cause for effect, and that, in each successive cycle, the number of murders decreased in consequence of the example of public executions in the cycle immediately preceding, and that it was for that reason there were fewer commitments. This might be said with some colour of truth, if the example had been taken from *two* successive cycles *only*. But when the comparative examples adduced are of no less than *five* successive cycles, and the result gradually and constantly progressive in the same direction, the relation of facts to each other is determined beyond all ground for dispute, namely, that the number of these crimes has diminished in consequence of the diminution of the number of executions. More especially when it is also remembered that it was *immediately after* the first of these cycles of five years, when there had been the greatest number of executions and the greatest number of murders, that the greatest number of persons were suddenly cast loose upon the country, without employ, by the reduction of the Army and Navy; that then came periods of great distress and great disturbance in the agricultural and manufacturing districts; and *above all*, that it was during the subsequent cycles that the most important mitigations were effected in the law, and that the Punishment of Death was taken away not only for crimes of stealth, such as cattle and horse stealing, and forgery, of which crimes corresponding statistics show likewise a corresponding decrease, but for the crimes of violence too, *tending to murder*, such as are many

of the incendiary offences, and such as are highway robbery
and burglary. But another return, laid before the House
at the same time, bears upon our argument, if possible,
still more conclusively. In table 11, we have *only* the
years which have occurred since 1810, in which *all* persons convicted of murder suffered death ; and, compared
with these an *equal* number of years in which the *smallest*
proportion of persons convicted were executed. In the
first case there were 66 persons convicted, *all* of whom
underwent the penalty of death; in the second 83 were
convicted, of whom 31 only were executed. Now see
how these two very different methods of dealing with the
crime of murder affected the commission of it *in the years
immediately following.* The number of commitments for
murder, in the four years immediately following those in
which all persons convicted were executed, was 270.

"In the four years immediately following those in which
little more than one-third of the persons convicted were
executed, there were but 222, being 48 less. If we compare the commitments in the following years with those
in the first years, we shall find that, immediately after the
examples of unsparing execution, the crime *increased nearly
13 per cent,* and that after commutation was the practice
and capital punishment the exception, it *decreased 17
per cent.*

"In the same parliamentary return is an account of the
commitments and executions in London and Middlesex,
spread over a space of 32 years, ending in 1842, divided
into two cycles of 16 years each. In the first of these,
34 persons were *convicted* of murder, *all of whom were
executed.* In the second, 27 were *convicted,* and only 17
executed. The *commitments* for murder during the latter
long period, with 17 executions, were *more than one half*

fewer than they had been in the former *long* period with *exactly double the number of executions*. This appears to us to be as conclusive upon our argument as any statistical illustration can be upon any argument professing to place successive events in the relation of cause and effect to each other. How justly then is it said in that able and useful periodical work, now in the course of publication at Glasgow, under the name of the 'Magazine of Popular Information on Capital and Secondary Punishment;' 'the greater the number of executions, the greater the number of murders; the smaller the number of executions, the smaller the number of murders. The lives of her Majesty's subjects are less safe with a hundred executions a year than with fifty; less safe with fifty than with twenty-five.'"

Similar results have followed from rendering public executions more and more infrequent, in Tuscany, in Prussia, in France, in Belgium. Wherever capital punishments are diminished in their number, there, crimes diminish in their number too.

But the very same advocates of the Punishment of Death who contend, in the teeth of all facts and figures, that it does prevent crime, contend in the same breath against its abolition because it does not! 'There are so many bad murders,' say they, 'and they follow in such quick succession, that the Punishment must not be repealed.' Why, is not this a reason, among others, *for* repealing it? Does it not go to show that it is ineffective as an example; that it fails to prevent crime; and that it is wholly inefficient to stay that imitation, or contagion, call it what you please, which brings one murder on the heels of another?

One forgery came crowding on another's heels in the same way, when the same punishment attached to that crime. Since it has been removed, forgeries have diminished in a most remarkable degree. Yet within five and thirty years, Lord Eldon, with tearful solemnity, imagined in the House of Lords as a possibility for their Lordships to shudder at, that the time might come when some visionary and morbid person might even propose the abolition of the punishment of Death for forgery. And when it *was* proposed, Lords Lyndhurst, Wynford, Tenterden[*], and Eldon—all Law Lords—opposed it.

The same Lord Tenterden[*] manfully said, on another occasion and another question, that he was glad the subject of the amendment of the laws had been taken up by Mr. Peel, "who had not been bred to the law; for those who were, were rendered dull, by habit, to many of its defects!" I would respectfully submit, in extension of this text, that a criminal judge is an excellent witness against the Punishment of Death, but a bad witness in its favour; and I will reserve this point for a few remarks in the next, concluding, Letter.

＊　＊　＊　＊　＊　＊　＊　＊　＊

The last English Judge, I believe, who gave expression to a public and judicial opinion in favour of the Punishment of Death, is Mr. Justice Coleridge, who, in charging the Grand Jury at Hertford last year, took occasion to lament the presence of serious crimes in the calendar, and to say that he feared that they were referable to the comparative infrequency of Capital Punishment.

It is not incompatible with the utmost deference and respect for an authority so eminent, to say that, in this, Mr. Justice Coleridge was not supported by facts, but quite

* Printed "Tenderden" in *The Daily News*, in error.]

the reverse. He went out of his way to found a general assumption on certain very limited and partial grounds, and even on those grounds was wrong. For among the few crimes which he instanced, murder stood prominently forth. Now persons found guilty of murder are more certainly and unsparingly hanged at this time, as the Parliamentary Returns demonstrate, than such criminals ever were. So how can the decline of public executions affect that class of crimes? As to persons committing murder, and yet not found guilty of it by juries, they escape solely because there *are* many public executions— not because there are none or few.

But when I submit that a criminal judge is an excellent witness against Capital Punishment, but a bad witness in its favour, I do so on more broad and general grounds than apply to this error in fact and deduction (so I presume to consider it) on the part of the distinguished judge in question. And they are grounds which do not apply offensively to judges, as a class; than whom there are no authorities in England so deserving of general respect and confidence, or so possessed of it; but which apply alike to all men in their several degrees and pursuits.

It is certain that men contract a general liking for those things which they have studied at great cost of time and intellect, and their proficiency in which has led to their becoming distinguished and successful. It is certain that out of this feeling arises, not only that passive blindness to their defects of which the example given by my Lord Tenterden was quoted in the last letter, but an active disposition to advocate and defend them. If it were otherwise; if it were not for this spirit of interest and partisanship; no single pursuit could have that attraction for its votaries which most pursuits in course of time establish.

Thus legal authorities are usually jealous of innovations on legal principles. Thus it is described of the lawyer in the Introductory Discourse to the Description of Utopia, that he said of a proposal against Capital Punishment, "'this could never be so established in England but that it must needs bring the weal-public into great jeopardy and hazard,' and as he was thus saying, he shaked his head, and made a wry mouth, and so he held his peace." Thus the Recorder of London, in 1811, objected to "the capital part being taken off" from the offence of picking pockets. Thus the Lord Chancellor, in 1813, objected to the removal of the penalty of death from the offence of stealing to the amount of five shillings from a shop. Thus, Lord Ellenborough, in 1820, anticipated the worst effects from there being no punishment of death for stealing five shillings worth of wet linen from a bleaching ground. Thus the Solicitor General, in 1830, advocated the punishment of death for forgery, and "the satisfaction of thinking" in the teeth of mountains of evidence from bankers and other injured parties (one thousand bankers alone!) "that he was deterring persons from the commission of crime, by the severity of the law." Thus, Mr. Justice Coleridge delivered his charge at Hertford in 1845. Thus there were in the criminal code of England, in 1790, one hundred and sixty crimes punishable with death. Thus the lawyer has said, again and again, in his generation, that any change in such a state of things "must needs bring the weal-public into jeopardy and hazard." And thus he has, all through the dismal history, "shaked his head, and made a wry mouth, and held his peace." Except—a glorious exception!—when such lawyers as Bacon, More, Blackstone, Romilly, and—let us ever gratefully remember—in later times Mr. Basil Montagu, have striven, each in his day, within the utmost limits of the endurance of the mistaken feeling of the people or the legislature of the time, to champion and maintain the truth.

There is another and a stronger reason still, why a criminal judge is a bad witness in favour of the Punishment of Death. He is a chief actor in the terrible drama of a trial, where the life or death of a fellow creature is at issue. No one who has seen such a trial can fail to know, or can ever forget, its intense interest. I care not how painful this interest is, to the good, wise judge upon the bench. I admit its painful nature, and the judge's goodness and wisdom to the fullest extent—but I submit that his prominent share in the excitement of such a trial, and the dread mystery involved, has a tendency to bewilder and confuse the judge upon the general subject of that penalty. I know the solemn pause before the verdict, the hush and stilling of the fever in the court, the solitary figure brought·back to the bar, and standing there, observed of all the outstretched heads and gleaming eyes, to be, next minute, stricken dead, as one may say, among them. I know the thrill that goes round when the black cap is put on, and how there will be shrieks among the women, and a taking out of some one in a swoon; and, when the judge's faltering voice delivers sentence, how awfully the prisoner and he confront each other; two mere men, destined one day, however far removed from one another at this time, to stand alike as suppliants at the bar of God. I know all this; I can imagine what the office of the judge costs, in this execution of it; but I say that in these strong sensations he is lost, and is unable to abstract the penalty as a preventive or example, from an experience of it, and from associations surrounding it, which are and can be, only his, and his alone.

Not to contend that there is no amount of wig or

ermine that can change the nature of the man inside; not to say that the nature of a judge may be, like the dyer's hand, subdued to what it works in, and may become too used to this punishment of death, to consider it quite dispassionately; not to say that it may possibly be inconsistent to have, deciding as calm authorities in favour of death, judges who have been constantly sentencing to death;—I contend that for the reasons I have stated, alone, a judge, and especially a criminal judge, is a bad witness for the punishment but an excellent witness against it, inasmuch as in the latter case his conviction of its inutility has been so strong and paramount as utterly to beat down and conquer these adverse incidents. I have no scruple in stating this position, because, for anything I know, the majority of excellent judges now on the bench may have overcome them, and may be opposed to the Punishment of Death under any circumstances.

I mentioned that I would devote a portion of this letter to a few prominent illustrations of each head of objection to the Punishment of Death. Those on record are so very numerous that selection is extremely difficult; but in reference to the possibility of mistake, and the impossibility of reparation, one case is as good (I should rather say as bad) as a hundred; and if there were none but Eliza Fenning's, that would be sufficient. Nay, if there were none at all, it would be enough to sustain this objection, that men of finite and limited judgment do inflict, on testimony which admits of doubt, an infinite and irreparable punishment. But there are on record numerous instances of mistake; many of them very generally known and immediately recognisable in the following summary, which I copy from the New York Report already referred to.

" There have been cases in which groans have been heard in the apartment of the crime, which have attracted the steps of those on whose testimony the case has turned —when, on proceeding to the spot, they have found a man bending over the murdered body, a lantern in the left hand, and the knife yet dripping with the warm current in the blood-stained right, with horror-stricken countenance, and lips which, in the presence of the dead, seem to refuse to deny the crime in the very act of which he is thus surprised—and yet the man has been, many years after, when his memory alone could be benefited by the discovery, ascertained *not* to have been the real murderer! [*] There have been cases in which, in a house in which were two persons alone, a murder has been committed on one of them—when many additional circumstances have fastened the imputation upon the other—and when, all apparent modes of access from without, being closed inward, the demonstration has seemed complete of the guilt for which that other has suffered the doom of the law—yet suffered *innocently!* There have been cases in which a father has been found murdered in an outhouse, the only person at home being a son, sworn by a sister to have been dissolute and undutiful, and anxious for the death of the father, and succession to the family property—when the track of his shoes in the snow is found from the house to the spot of the murder, and the hammer with which it was committed, (known as his own) found, on a search, in the corner of one of his private drawers, with the bloody evidence of the deed only imperfectly effaced from it—and yet the son has been innocent!—the sister, years after, on her death-bed, confessing herself the fratricide as well as the

[* Printed "murdered" in *The Daily News.*]

11

parricide. There have been cases in which men have been hung on the most positive testimony to identity (aided by many suspicious circumstances), by persons familiar with their appearance, which have afterwards proved grievous mistakes, growing out of remarkable personal resemblance. There have been cases in which two men have been seen fighting in a field—an old enmity existing between them— the one found dead, killed by a stab from a pitch-fork, known as belonging to the other, and which that other had been carrying, the pitch-fork lying by the side of the murdered man—and yet its owner has been afterwards found not to have been the author of the murder of which it had been the instrument, the true murderer sitting on the jury that tried him. There have been cases in which an innkeeper has been charged by one of his servants with the murder of a traveller, the servant deposing to having seen his master on the stranger's bed, strangling him, and afterwards rifling his pockets—another servant deposing that she saw him come down at that time at a very early hour in the morning, steal into the garden, take gold from his pocket, and carefully wrapping it up bury it in a designated spot—on the search of which the ground is found loose and freshly dug, and a sum of thirty pounds in gold found buried according to the description—the master, who confessed the burying of the money, with many evidences of guilt in his hesitation and confusion, has been hung of course, and proved innocent only too late. There have been cases in which a traveller has been robbed on the highway, of twenty guineas which he had taken the precaution to *mark*—one of these is found to have been paid away or changed by one of the servants of the inn which the traveller reaches the same evening—the servant is about the height of the robber, who had been cloaked and disguised—his master deposes to his having been recently unaccountably extravagant and flush of gold—and on his trunk being searched the other nineteen marked guineas and the traveller's purse are found there, the servant being asleep at the time, half-drunk—he is of course convicted and hung, for the crime of which his master was the author! There have been cases in which a father and daughter have been overheard in violent dispute—the words '*barbarity*,' '*cruelty*,' and '*death*' being heard frequently to proceed from the latter—the former goes out, locking the door behind him—groans are overheard, and the words, '*cruel father, thou art the cause of my death!*'—on the room being opened, she is found on the point of death from a wound in her side, and near her the knife with which it had been inflicted—and on being questioned as to her owing her death to her father, her last motion, before expiring is an expression of assent—the father, on returning to the room exhibits the usual evidences of guilt—he, too, is of course hung—and it is not till nearly a year afterwards that, on the discovery of conclusive evidence that it was a suicide, the vain reparation is made to his memory by the public authorities, of—waving a pair of colours over his grave in token of the recognition of his innocence."

More than a hundred such cases are known, it is said in this Report, in English criminal jurisprudence. The same Report contains three striking cases of supposed criminals being unjustly hanged in America; and also five more in which people whose innocence was not afterwards established were put to death on evidence as purely circumstantial and as doubtful, to say the least of it, as any that was held to be sufficient in this general summary of legal murders. Mr. O'Connell defended, in Ireland, within five and twenty years, three brothers who were hanged for a murder of which they were afterwards shown to have been innocent. I cannot find the reference at this moment, but I have seen it stated on good authority, that but for the exertions, I think of the present Lord Chief Baron, six or seven innocent men would certainly have been hanged. Such are the instances of wrong judgment which are known to us. How many more there may be, in which the real murderers never disclosed their guilt, or were never discovered, and where the odium of great crimes still rests on guiltless people long since resolved to dust in their untimely graves, no human power can tell.

The effect of public executions on those who witness them, requires no better illustration, and can have none, than the scene which any execution in itself presents, and the general Police-office knowledge of the offences arising out of them. I have stated my belief that the study of rude scenes leads to the disregard of human life, and to murder. Referring since that expression of opinion to the very last trial for murder in London, I have made inquiry, and am assured that the youth now under sentence of death in Newgate for the murder of his master in Drury-lane, was a vigilant spectator of the three last public executions in this City. What effects a daily increasing familiarity with the scaffold, and with death upon it, wrought in France in the Great Revolution, everybody knows. In reference to this very question of Capital Punishment, Robespierre himself, before he was

"in blood stept in so far,"

warned the National assembly that in taking human life, and in displaying before the eyes of the people scenes of cruelty and the bodies of murdered men, the law awakened ferocious prejudices, which gave birth to a long and growing train of their own kind. With how much reason this was said, let his own detestable name bear witness! If we would know how callous and hardened society, even in a peaceful and settled state, becomes to public executions when they are frequent, let us recollect how few they were who made the last attempt to stay the dreadful Monday-morning spectacles of men and women strung up in a row for crimes as different in their degree as our whole social scheme is different in its component parts, which, within some fifteen years or so, made human shambles of the Old Bailey.

There is no better way of testing the effect of public executions on those who do not actually behold them, but who read of them and know of them, than by inquiring into their efficiency in preventing crime. In this respect they have always, and in all countries, failed. According to all facts and figures, failed. In Russia, in Spain, in France, in Italy, in Belgium, in Sweden, in England, there has been, one result. In Bombay, during the Recorder-ship of Sir James Macintosh, there were fewer crimes in seven years without one execution, than in the preceding seven years with forty-seven executions; notwithstanding that in the seven years without capital punishment, the population had greatly increased, and there had been a large accession to the numbers of the ignorant and licentious soldiery, with whom the more violent offences originated. During the four wickedest years of the Bank of England (from 1814 to 1817, inclusive), when the one-pound note capital prosecutions were most numerous and shocking, the number of forged one-pound notes discovered by the Bank steadily increased, from the gross amount in the first year of £10,342, to the gross amount in the last of £28,412. But in every branch of this part of the subject—the inefficiency of capital punishment to prevent crime, and its efficiency to produce it—the body of evidence (if there were space to quote or analyse it here) is overpowering and resistless.

I have purposely deferred until now any reference to one objection which is urged against the abolition of capital punishment: I mean that objection which claims to rest on Scriptural authority.

It was excellently well said by Lord Melbourne, that no class of persons can be shown to be very miserable and oppressed, but some supporters of things as they are will immediately rise up and assert—not that those persons are moderately well to do, or that their lot in life has a reasonably bright side—but that they are, of all sorts and conditions of men, the happiest. In like manner when a certain proceeding or institution is shown to be very wrong indeed, there is a class of people who rush to the fountain-head at once, and will have no less an authority for it than the Bible, on any terms.

So, we have the Bible appealed to in behalf of Capital Punishment. So, we have the Bible produced as a distinct authority for Slavery. So, American representatives find the title of their country to the Oregon territory distinctly laid down in the Book of Genesis. So, in course of time, we shall find Repudiation, perhaps, expressly commanded in the Sacred Writings.

It is enough for me to be satisfied, on calm inquiry and with reason, that an Institution or Custom is wrong and bad; and thence to feel assured that IT CANNOT BE a part of the law laid down by the Divinity who walked the earth. Though every other man who wields a pen, should turn himself into a commentator on the Scriptures—

not all their united efforts, pursued through our united
lives, could ever persuade me that Slavery is a Christian
law; nor, with one of these objections to an execution
in my certain knowledge, that Executions are a Christian
law, my will is not concerned. I could not, in my venera-
tion for the life and lessons of Our Lord, believe it. If
any text appeared to justify the claim, I would reject that
limited appeal, and rest upon the character of the Redeemer,
and the great scheme of His Religion, where, in its broad
spirit, made so plain—and not this or that disputed letter—
we all put our trust. But, happily, such doubts do not
exist. The case is far too plain. The Rev. Henry Christmas, in a recent pamphlet on this subject, shows clearly
that in five important versions of the Old Testament (to
say nothing of versions of less note) the words, "by man,"
in the often-quoted text, "Whoso sheddeth man's blood,
by man shall his blood be shed," do not appear at all.
We know that the law of Moses was delivered to certain
wandering tribes, in a peculiar and perfectly different
social condition from that which prevails among us at this
time. We know that the Christian Dispensation did distinctly repeal and annul certain portions of that law. We
know that the doctrine of retributive justice or vengeance,
was plainly disavowed by the Saviour. We know that
on the only occasion of an offender, liable by the law to
death, being brought before Him for His judgment, it was
not death. We know that He said, "Thou shalt not kill."
And if we are still to inflict capital punishment because
of the Mosaic law (under which it was not the consequence
of a legal proceeding, but an act of vengeance from
the next of kin, which would surely be discouraged
by our later laws if it were revived among the Jews
just now) it would be equally reasonable to establish

the lawfulness of a plurality of wives on the same authority.

Here I will leave this aspect of the question. I should not have treated of it at all, in the columns of a news-paper, but for the possibility of being unjustly supposed to have given it no consideration in my own mind.

In bringing to a close these letters on a subject, in connection with which there is happily very little that is new to be said or written, I beg to be understood as advocating the total abolition of the Punishment of Death, as a general principle, for the advantage of society, for the prevention of crime, and without the least reference to, or tenderness for any individual malefactor whomsoever. Indeed, in most cases of murder, my feeling towards the culprit is very strongly and violently the reverse. I am the more desirous to be so understood, after reading a speech made by Mr. Macaulay in the House of Commons last Tuesday night, in which that accomplished gentleman hardly seemed to recognise the possibility of anybody entertaining an honest conviction of the inutility and bad effects of Capital Punishment in the abstract, founded on enquiry and reflection, without being the victim of "a kind of effeminate feeling." Without staying to inquire what there may be that is especially manly and heroic in the advocacy of the gallows, or to express my admiration of Mr. Calcraft, the hangman, as doubtless one of the most manly specimens now in existence, I would simply hint a doubt, in all good humour, whether this be the true Macaulay way of meeting a great question? One of the instances of effeminacy of feeling quoted by Mr. Macaulay, I have reason to think was not quite fairly stated. I allude to the petition in Tawell's case. I had neither hand nor part in it myself; but, unless I am greatly mistaken, it did pretty clearly set forth that Tawell was a most abhorred villain, and that the House might conclude how strongly the petitioners were opposed to the Punishment of Death, when they prayed for its non-infliction even in such a case.

[Letters to the Editors of *The Daily News*, 1846].

A PRELIMINARY WORD.

THE name that we have chosen for this publication [1] expresses, generally, the desire we have at heart in originating it.

We aspire to live in the Household affections, and to be numbered among the Household thoughts of our readers. We hope to be the comrade and friend of many thousands of people, of both sexes, and of all ages and conditions, on whose faces we may never look. We seek to bring into innumerable homes, from the stirring world around us, the knowledge of many social wonders, good and evil, that are not calculated to render any of us less ardently persevering in ourselves, less tolerant of one another, less faithful in the progress of mankind, less thankful for the privilege of living in this summer-dawn of time.

No mere utilitarian spirit, no iron binding of the mind to grim realities, will give a harsh tone to our Household Words. In the bosoms of the young and old, of the well-to-do and of the poor, we would tenderly cherish that light of Fancy which is inherent in the human breast; which, according to its nurture, burns with an inspiring flame, or sinks into a sullen glare, but which (or woe betide that day!) can never be extinguished. To show

[1] *Household Words.*

to all, that in all familiar things, even in those which are
repellent on the surface, there is Romance enough, if we
will find it out:—to teach the hardest workers at this
whirling wheel of toil, that their lot is not necessarily a
moody brutal fact, excluded from the sympathies and
graces of imagination, to bring the greater and the lesser
in degree, together, upon that wide field, and mutually
dispose them to a better acquaintance and a kinder understanding—is one main object of our *Household Words*.

The mightier inventions of this age are not, to our
thinking, all material, but have a kind of souls in their
stupendous bodies which may find expression in *Household
Words*. The traveller whom we accompany on his railroad or his steamboat journey, may gain, we hope, some
compensation for incidents which these later generations
have outlived, in new associations with the Power that
bears him onward; with the habitations and the ways of
life of crowds of his fellow creatures among whom he
passes like the wind; even with the towering chimneys he
may see, spirting out fire and smoke upon the prospect.
The swart giants, Slaves of the Lamp of Knowledge, have
their thousand and one tales, no less than the Genii of
the East; and these, in all their wild, grotesque, and
fanciful aspects, in all their many phases of endurance, in
all their many moving lessons of compassion and consideration, we design to tell.

Our *Household Words* will not be echoes of the present
time alone, but of the past too. Neither will they treat
of the hopes, the enterprises, triumphs, joys, and sorrows,
of this country only, but, in some degree, of those of every
nation upon earth. For nothing can be a source of rea
interest in one of them, without concerning all the rest.

We have considered what an ambition it is to be admitted

into many homes with affection and confidence; to be
regarded as a friend by children and old people; to be
thought of in affliction and in happiness; to people the
sick room with airy shapes 'that give delight and hurt not,'
and to be associated with the harmless laughter and the
gentle tears of many hearths.   We know the great responsibility of such a privilege; its vast reward; the pictures
that it conjures up, in hours of solitary labour, of a multitude moved by one sympathy; the solemn hopes which
it awakens in the labourer's breast, that he may be free
from self-reproach in looking back at last upon his work,
and that his name may be remembered in his race in time
to come, and borne by the dear objects of his love with
pride.   The hand that writes these faltering lines, happily
associated with *some Household Words* before to-day, has
known enough of such experiences to enter in an earnest
spirit upon this new task, and with an awakened sense of
all it involves.

Some tillers of the field into which we now come, have
been before us, and some are here whose high usefulness
we readily acknowledge, and whose company it is an honour
to join.   But there are others here—Bastards of the Mountain, draggled fringe on the Red Cap, Panders to the basest
passions of the lowest natures—whose existence is a national
reproach.   And these, we should consider it our highest
service to displace.

Thus, we begin our career!   The adventurer in the old
fairy story, climbing towards the summit of a steep eminence
on which the object of his search was stationed, was
surrounded by a roar of voices, crying to him, from the
stones in the way, to turn back.   All the voices *we* hear,
cry Go on!   The stones that call to us have sermons in
them, as the trees have tongues, as there are books in the

running brooks, as there is good in everything! They, and the Time, cry out to us Go on! With a fresh heart, a light step, and a hopeful courage, we begin the journey. The road is not so rough that it need daunt our feet: the way is not so steep that we need stop for breath, and, looking faintly down, be stricken motionless. Go on, is all we hear, Go on! In a glow already, with the air from yonder height upon us, and the inspiriting voices joining in this acclamation, we echo back the cry, and go on cheerily! [1850]

THE AMUSEMENTS OF THE PEOPLE.

I.

As one half of the world is said not to know how the other half lives, so it may be affirmed that the upper half of the world neither knows nor greatly cares how the lower half amuses itself. Believing that it does not care mainly because it does not know, we purpose occasionally recording a few facts on this subject.

The general character of the lower class of dramatic amusements is a very significant sign of a people, and a very good test of their intellectual condition. We design to make our readers acquainted in the first place with a few of our experiences under this head in the metropolis.

It is probable that nothing will ever root out from among the common people an innate love they have for dramatic entertainment in some form or other. It would be a very doubtful benefit to society, we think, if it could . be rooted out. The Polytechnic Institution in Regent Street, where an infinite variety of ingenious models are exhibited and explained, and where lectures comprising a quantity of useful information on many practical subjects are delivered, is a great public benefit and a wonderful place, but we think a people formed *entirely* in their hours of leisure by Polytechnic Institutions would be an uncomfortable community. We would rather not have to appeal to the generous sympathies of a man of five-and-twenty, in respect of some affliction of which he had had no personal experience, who had passed all his holidays, when a boy, among cranks and cog wheels. We should be more disposed to trust him if he had been brought into occasional contact with a Maid and a Magpie; if he had made one or two diversions into the Forest of Bondy; or had even gone the length of a Christmas Pantomime. There is a range of imagination in most of us, which no amount of steam-engines will satisfy; and which The-great-exhibition-of-the-works-of-industry-of-all-nations, itself, will probably leave unappeased. The lower we go, the more natural it is that the best relished provision for this should be found in dramatic entertainments; as at once the most obvious, the least troublesome, and the most real, of all escapes out of the literal world. Joe Whelks, of the New Cut, Lambeth, is not much of a reader, has no great store of books, no very commodious room to read in, no very decided inclination to read, and no power at all of presenting vividly before his mind's eye what he reads about. But, put Joe in the gallery of the Victoria Theatre; show him doors and windows in the scene that will open and shut, and that people can get in and out of; tell him a story with these aids, and by the help of live men and women dressed up, confiding to him their innermost secrets, in voices audible half a mile off; and Joe will unravel a story through all its entanglements, and sit there as long after midnight as you have anything left to show him. Accordingly, the Theatres to which Mr. Whelks resorts, are always full; and whatever changes of fashion the drama knows elsewhere, it is always fashionable in the New Cut.

The question, then, might not unnaturally arise, one

would suppose, whether Mr. Whelks's education is at all susceptible of improvement, through the agency of his theatrical tastes. How far it is improved at present, our readers shall judge for themselves.

In affording them the means of doing so, we wish to disclaim any grave imputation on those who are concerned in ministering to the dramatic gratification of Mr. Whelks. Heavily taxed, wholly unassisted by the state, deserted by the gentry, and quite unrecognised as a means of public instruction, the higher English Drama has declined. Those who would live to please Mr. Whelks, must please Mr. Whelks to live. It is not the Manager's province to hold the Mirror up to Nature, but to Mr. Whelks——the only person who acknowledges him. If, in like manner, the actor's nature, like the dyer's hand, become subdued to what he works in, the actor can hardly be blamed for it. He grinds hard at his vocation, is often steeped in direful poverty, and lives, at the best, in a little world of mockeries! It is bad enough to give away a great estate six nights a-week, and want a shilling; to preside at imaginary banquets, hungry for a mutton chop; to smack the lips over a tankard of toast and water, and declaim about the mellow produce of the sunny vineyard on the banks of the Rhine; to be a rattling young lover, with the measles at home, and to paint sorrow over, with burnt cork and rouge, without being called upon to despise his vocation too. If he can utter the trash to which he is condemned, with any relish, so much the better for him, Heaven knows; and peace be with him!

A few weeks ago, we went to one of Mr. Whelks's favourite Theatres, to see an attractive Melo-Drama called MAY MORNING, OR THE MYSTERY OF 1715, AND THE MURDER! We had an idea that the former of these

titles might refer to the month in which either the Mystery or
the Murder happened, but we found it to be the name of
the heroine, the pride of Keswick Vale; who was called 'May
Morning' (after a common custom among the English Peas-
antry) ' from her bright eyes and merry laugh'. Of this young
lady, it may be observed, in passing, that she subsequently
sustained every possible calamity of human existence in a
white muslin gown with blue tucks; and that she did every
conceivable and inconceivable thing with a pistol, that could
anyhow be effected by that description of fire-arms.

The Theatre was extremely full.   The prices of admission
were, to the boxes, a shilling; to the pit, sixpence; to
the gallery, threepence.   The gallery was of enormous
dimensions (among the company, in the front row, we
observed Mr. Whelks); and overflowing with occupants.
It required no close observation of the attentive faces
rising one above another, to the very door in the roof, and
squeezed and jammed in, regardless of all discomforts,
even there, to impress a stranger with a sense of its being
highly desirable to lose no possible chance of effecting
any mental improvement in that great audience.

The company in the pit were not very clean or sweet-
savoured, but there were some good-humoured young
mechanics among them, with their wives.   These were
generally accompanied by 'the baby,' insomuch that the
pit was a perfect nursery.   No effect made on the stage
was so curious, as the looking down on the quiet faces
of these babies fast asleep, after looking up at the staring
sea of heads in the gallery.   There were a good many
cold fried soles in the pit, besides; and a variety of flat
stone bottles, of all portable sizes.

The audience in the boxes was of much the same
character (babies and fish excepted) as the audience in

the pit. A private in the Foot Guards sat in the next box; and a personage who wore pins on his coat instead of buttons, and was in such a damp habit of living as to be quite mouldy, was our nearest neighbour. In several parts of the house we noticed some young pickpockets of our acquaintance; but as they were evidently there as private individuals, and not in their public capacity, we were little disturbed by their presence. For we consider the hours of idleness passed by this class of society as so much gain to society at large; and we do not join in a whimsical sort of lamentation that is generally made over them, when they are found to be unoccupied.

As we made these observations the curtain rose, and we were presently in possession of the following particulars.

Sir George Elmore, a melancholy Baronet with every appearance of being in that advanced stage of indigestion in which Mr. Morrison's patients usually are, when they happen to hear, through Mr. Moat, of the surprising effect of his Vegetable Pills, was found to be living in a very large castle, in the society of one round table, two chairs, and Captain George Elmore 'his supposed son, the Child of Mystery, and the Man of Crime.' The Captain, in addition to an undutiful habit of bullying his father on all occasions, was a prey to many vices; foremost among which may be mentioned his desertion of his wife, 'Estella de Neva, a Spanish lady,' and his determination unlawfully to possess himself of May Morning; M. M. being then on the eve of marriage to Will Stanmore, a cheerful sailor, with very loose legs.

The strongest evidence, at first, of the Captain's being the Child of Mystery and the Man of Crime was deducible from his boots, which, being very high and wide, and

apparently made of sticking-plaister, justified the worst
theatrical suspicions to his disadvantage. And indeed he
presently turned out as ill as could be desired: getting
into May Morning's Cottage by the window after dark,
refusing to 'unhand' May Morning when required to do
so by that lady; waking May Morning's only surviving
parent, a blind old gentleman with a black ribbon over his
eyes, whom we shall call Mr. Stars, as his name was stated
in the bill thus * * * * * *; and showing himself desperately
bent on carrying off May Morning by force of arms. Even
this was not the worst of the Captain; for, being foiled
in his diabolical purpose—temporarily by means of knives
and pistols, providentially caught up and directed at him
by May Morning, and finally, for the time being, by the
advent of Will Stanmore—he caused one Slink, his adherent,
to denounce Will Stanmore as a rebel, and got that cheerful
mariner carried off, and shut up in prison. At about the
same period of the Captain's career, there suddenly
appeared in his father's castle, a dark complexioned lady
of the name of Manuella, 'a Zingara Woman from the
Pyrenean mountains; the wild wanderer of the heath, and
the pronouncer of the prophecy,' who threw the melancholy
baronet, his supposed father, into the greatest confusion
by asking him what he had upon his conscience, and by
pronouncing mysterious rhymes concerning the Child of
Mystery and the Man of Crime to a low trembling of
fiddles. Matters were in this state when the Theatre
resounded with applause, and Mr. Whelks fell into a fit
of unbounded enthusiasm, consequent on the entrance
of 'Michael the Mendicant.'

At first we referred something of the cordiality with
which Michael the Mendicant was greeted, to the fact of
his being 'made up' with an excessively dirty face, which

might create a bond of union between himself and a large
majority of the audience. But it soon came out that
Michael the Mendicant had been hired in old time by
Sir George Elmore, to murder his (Sir George Elmore's)
elder brother—which he had done; notwithstanding which
little affair of honour, Michael was in reality a very good
fellow; quite a tender-hearted man; who, on hearing of
the Captain's determination to settle Will Stanmore, cried
out, 'What! more bel—ood!' and fell flat—overpowered
by his nice sense of humanity. In like manner, in describing that small error of judgment into which he had
allowed himself to be tempted by money, this gentleman
exclaimed, 'I ster-ruck him down, and fel-ed in er-orror!'
and further he remarked, with honest pride, 'I have
liveder as a beggar—a roadersider vaigerant, but no cer-
rime since then has stained these hands!' All these
sentiments of the worthy man were hailed with showers
of applause; and when, in the excitement of his feelings on one occasion, after a soliloquy, he 'went off'
on his back, kicking and shuffling along the ground,
after the manner of bold spirits in trouble, who object
to be taken to the station-house, the cheering was
tremendous.

And to see how little harm he had done, after all!
Sir George Elmore's elder brother was NOT dead. Not
he! He recovered, after this sensitive creature had 'fel-ed
in er-orror,' and, putting a black ribbon over his eyes to
disguise himself, went and lived in a modest retirement
with his only child. In short, Mr. Stars was the identical
individual! When Will Stanmore turned out to be the
wrongful Sir George Elmore's son, instead of the Child of
Mystery and Man of Crime, who turned out to be Michael's
son (a change having been effected, in revenge, by the

lady from the Pyrenean Mountains, who became the Wild Wanderer of the Heath, in consequence of the wrongful Sir George Elmore's perfidy to her and desertion of her), Mr. Stars went up to the Castle, and mentioned to his murdering brother how it was.   Mr. Stars said it was all right; he bore no malice; he had kept out of the way, in order that his murdering brother (to whose numerous virtues he was no stranger) might enjoy the property; and now he would propose that they should make it up and dine together.   The murdering brother immediately consented, embraced the Wild Wanderer, and it is supposed sent instructions to Doctors' Commons for a license to marry her.   After which, they were all very comfortable indeed.   For it is not much to try to murder your brother for the sake of his property, if you only suborn such a delicate assassin as Michael the Mendicant!

All this did not tend to the satisfaction of the Child of Mystery and Man of Crime, who was so little pleased by the general happiness, that he shot Will Stanmore, now joyfully out of prison and going to be married directly to May Morning, and carried off the body, and May Morning to boot, to a lone hut.   Here, Will Stanmore, laid out for dead at fifteen minutes past twelve, P.M., arose at seventeen minutes past, infinitely fresher than most daisies, and fought two strong men single-handed.   However, the Wild Wanderer, arriving with a party of male wild wanderers, who were always at her disposal—and the murdering brother arriving arm-in-arm with Mr. Stars—stopped the combat, confounded the Child of Mystery and Man of Crime, and blessed the lovers.

The adventures of 'Red Riven the Bandit' concluded the moral lesson of the evening.   But, feeling by this time a little fatigued, and believing that we already discerned in the countenance of Mr. Whelks a sufficient confusion between right and wrong to last him for one night, we retired; the rather as we intended to meet him, shortly, at another place of dramatic entertainment for the people.   [1850]

THE AMUSEMENTS OF THE PEOPLE.

II.

MR. WHELKS being much in the habit of recreating himself at a class of theatres called 'Saloons', we repaired to one of these, not long ago, on a Monday evening; Monday being a great holiday-night with Mr. Whelks and his friends.

The Saloon in question is the largest in London (that which is known as The Eagle, in the City Road, should be excepted from the generic term, as not presenting by any means the same class of entertainment), and is situate not far from Shoreditch Church. It announces 'The People's Theatre', as its second name. The prices of admission are, to the boxes, a shilling; to the pit, sixpence; to the lower gallery, fourpence; to the upper gallery and back seats, threepence. There is no half-price. The opening piece on this occasion was described in the bills as 'the greatest hit of the season, the grand new legendary and traditionary drama, combining supernatural agencies with historical facts, and identifying extraordinary superhuman causes with material, terrific, and powerful effects.' All the queen's horses and all the queen's men could not have drawn Mr. Whelks into the place like . this description. Strengthened by lithographic representations of the principal superhuman causes, combined with the most popular of the material, terrific, and powerful effects, it became irresistible. Consequently, we had already failed, once, in finding six square inches of room within the walls, to stand upon; and when we now paid our money for a little stage box, like a dry shower-bath, we did so in the midst of a stream of people who persisted in paying their's for other parts of the house in despite of the representations of the Money-taker that it was ' very full, everywhere '.

The outer avenues and passages of the People's Theatre bore abundant testimony to the fact of its being frequented by very dirty people. Within, the atmosphere was far from odoriferous. The place was crammed to excess in all parts. Among the audience were a large number of boys and youths, and a great many very young girls grown into bold women before they had well ceased to be children. These last were the worst features of the whole crowd, and were more prominent there than in any other sort of public assembly that we know of, except at a public execution. There was no drink supplied, beyond the contents of the porter-can (magnified in its dimensions, perhaps), which may be usually seen traversing the galleries of the largest Theatres as well as the least, and which was seen here everywhere. Huge ham-sandwiches, piled on trays like deals in a timber-yard, were handed about for sale to the hungry; and there was no stint of oranges, cakes, brandy-balls, or other similar refreshments. The Theatre was capacious with a very large capable stage, well lighted, well appointed, and managed in a business-like, orderly manner in all respects; the performances had begun so early as a quarter past six, and had been then in progress for three-quarters of an hour.

It was apparent here, as in the theatre we had previously visited, that one of the reasons of its great attraction was its being directly addressed to the common people, in the provision made for their seeing and hearing. Instead of being put away in a dark gap in the roof of an immense building, as in our once National Theatres, they were here in possession of eligible points of view, and thoroughly able to take in the whole performance. Instead of being at a great disadvantage in comparison with the mass of the audience, they were *the* audience, for whose accommodation the place was made. We believe this to be one great cause of the success of these speculations. In whatever way the common people are addressed, whether in churches, chapels, schools, lecture-rooms, or theatres, to be successfully addressed they must be directly appealed to. No matter how good the feast, they will not come to it on mere sufferance. If, on looking round us, we find that the only things plainly and personally addressed to them, from quack medicines upwards, be bad or very defective things, — so much the worse for them and for all of us, and so much the more unjust and absurd the system which has haughtily abandoned a strong ground to such occupation.

We will add that we believe these people have a right to be amused. A great deal that we consider to be unreasonable, is written and talked about not licensing these places of entertainment. We have already intimated that we believe a love of dramatic representations to be an inherent principle in human nature. In most conditions of human life of which we have any knowledge, from the Greeks to the Bosjesmen, some form of dramatic representation has always obtained. [1]

---

[1] In the remote interior of Africa, and among the North American Indians, this truth is exemplified in an equally striking manner. Who

We have a vast respect for county magistrates, and for the lord chamberlain; but we render greater deference to such extensive and immutable experience, and think it will outlive the whole existing court and commission. We would assuredly not bear harder on the fourpenny theatre, than on the four shilling theatre, or the four guinea theatre; but we would decidedly interpose to turn to some wholesome account the means of instruction which it has at command, and we would make that office of Dramatic Licenser, which, like many other offices, has become a mere piece of Court favour and dandy conventionality, a real, responsible, educational trust. We would have it exercise a sound supervision over the lower drama, instead of stopping the career of a real work of art, as it did in the case of Mr. Chorley's play at the Surrey Theatre, but a few weeks since, for a sickly point of form.

To return to Mr. Whelks. The audience being able to see and hear were very attentive. They were so closely packed, that they took a little time in settling down after any pause; but otherwise the general disposition was to lose nothing, and to check (in no choice language) any disturber of the business of the scene.

On our arrival, Mr. Whelks had already followed Lady Hatton the Heroine (whom we faintly recognised as a mutilated theme of the late Thomas Ingoldsby) to the 'Gloomy Dell and Suicide's Tree,' where Lady H. had encountered the 'apparition of the dark man of doom', that saw the four grim, stunted, abject Bush-people at the Egyptian Hall — with two natural actors among them out of that number, one a male and the other a female—can forget how something human and imaginative gradually broke out in the little ugly man, when he was roused from crouching over the charcoal fire, into giving a dramatic representation of the tracking of a beast, the shooting of it with poisoned arrows, and the creature's death?

and heard the 'fearful story of the Suicide.' She had also 'signed the compact in her own Blood,' beheld 'the Tombs rent asunder;' seen 'skeletons start from their graves, and gibber Mine, mine, for ever!' and undergone all these little experiences, (each set forth in a separate line in the bill) in the compass of one act. It was not yet over, indeed, for we found a remote king of England of the name of 'Enerry', refreshing himself with the spectacle of a dance in a Garden, which was interrupted by the 'thrilling appearance of the Demon.' This 'superhuman cause' (with black eyebrows slanting up into his temples, and red-foil cheekbones,) brought the Drop-Curtain down as we took possession of our Shower-Bath.

It seemed, on the curtain's going up again, that Lady Hatton had sold herself to the Powers of Darkness, on very high terms, and was now overtaken by remorse, and by jealousy too; the latter passion being excited by the beautiful Lady Rodolpha, ward to the King. It was to urge Lady Hatton on to the murder of this young female (as well as we could make out, but both we and Mr. Whelks found the incidents complicated) that the Demon appeared 'once again in all his terrors'. Lady Hatton had been leading a life of piety, but the Demon was not to have his bargain declared off, in right of any such artifices, and now offered a dagger for the destruction of Rodolpha. Lady Hatton hesitating to accept this trifle from Tartarus, the Demon, for certain subtle reasons of his own, proceeded to entertain her with a view of the 'gloomy court-yard of a convent,' and the apparitions of the "Skeleton Monk', and the 'King of Terrors'. Against these superhuman causes, another superhuman cause, to wit, the ghost of Lady H's mother, came into play, and greatly confounded the Powers of Darkness,

by waving the 'sacred emblem' over the head of the else
devoted Rodolpha, and causing her to sink into the earth.
Upon this the Demon, losing his temper, fiercely invited
Lady Hatton to 'Be-old the tortures of the damned!'
and straightway conveyed her to a 'grand and awful view
of Pandemonium, and Lake of Transparent Rolling Fire,'
whereof, and also of 'Prometheus chained, and the Vulture gnawing at his liver,' Mr. Whelks was exceedingly
derisive.

The Demon still failing, even there, and still finding
the ghost of the old lady greatly in his way, exclaimed
that these vexations had such a remarkable effect upon
his spirit as to 'sear his eyeballs', and that he must go
'deeper down', which he accordingly did. Hereupon it
appeared that it was all a dream on Lady Hatton's part,
and that she was newly married and uncommonly happy.
This put an end to the incongruous heap of nonsense,
and set Mr. Whelks applauding mightily; for, except
with the lake of transparent rolling fire (which was not
half infernal enough for him), Mr. Whelks was infinitely
contented with the whole of the proceedings.

Ten thousand people, every week, all the year round,
are estimated to attend this place of amusement. If it
were closed to-morrow—if there were fifty such, and they
were all closed to-morrow—the only result would be to
cause that to be privately and evasively done, which is
now publicly done; to render the harm of it much greater,
and to exhibit the suppressive power of the law in an
oppressive and partial light. The people who now resort
here, *will be* amused somewhere. It is of no use to blink
that fact, or to make pretences to the contrary. We had
far better apply ourselves to improving the character of their
amusement. It would not be exacting much, or exacting

anything very difficult, to require that the pieces represented in these Theatres should have, at least, a good,
plain, healthy purpose in them.

To the end that our experiences might not be supposed
to be partial or unfortunate, we went, the very next night,
to the Theatre where we saw May Morning, and found
Mr. Whelks engaged in the study of an 'Original old
English Domestic and Romantic Drama', called ' Eva the
Betrayed, or The Ladye of Lambythe'. We proceed to
develope the incidents which gradually unfolded themselves
to Mr. Whelks's understanding.

One Geoffrey Thornley the younger, on a certain fine
morning, married his father's ward, Eva the Betrayed, the
Ladye of Lambythe. She had become the betrayed, in
right—or in wrong—of designing Geoffrey's machinations;
for that corrupt individual, knowing her to be under promise
of marriage to Walter More, a young mariner (of whom
he was accustomed to make slighting mention, as a 'minion'),
represented the said More to be no more, and obtained
the consent of the too trusting Eva to their immediate union.

Now, it came to pass, by a singular coincidence, that
on the identical morning of the marriage, More came home,
and was taking a walk about the scenes of his boyhood—
a little faded since that time—when he rescued 'Wilbert
the Hunchback' from some very rough treatment. This
misguided person, in return, immediately fell to abusing
his preserver in round terms, giving him to understand
that he (the preserved) hated 'manerkind, wither two
eckerceptions', one of them being the deceiving Geoffrey,
whose retainer he was, and for whom he felt an uncon-
querable attachment; the other, a relative, whom, in a
similar redundancy of emphasis, adapted to the require-
ments of Mr. Whelks, he called his 'assister'. This

misanthrope also made the cold-blooded declaration, 'There was a timer when I loved my fellow keretures till they deserpised me. Now, I live only to witness man's disergherace and woman's misery!' In furtherance of this amiable purpose of existence, he directed More to where the bridal procession was coming home from church, and Eva recognised More, and More reproached Eva, and there was a great to-do, and a violent struggling, before certain social villagers who were celebrating the event with morris-dances. Eva was borne off in a tearing condition, and the bill very truly observed that the end of that part of the business was 'despair and madness'.

Geoffrey, Geoffrey, why were you already married to another! Why could you not be true to your lawful wife Katherine, instead of deserting her, and leaving her to come tumbling into public-houses (on account of weakness) in search of you! You might have known what it would end in, Geoffrey Thornley! You might have known that she would come up to your house on your wedding day with her marriage-certificate in her pocket, determined to expose you. You might have known beforehand, as you now very composedly observe, that you would have 'but one course to pursue.' That course clearly is to wind your right hand in Katherine's long hair, wrestle with her, stab her, throw down the body behind the door (Cheers from Mr. Whelks), and tell the devoted Hunchback to get rid of it. On the devoted Hunchback's finding that it is the body of his 'assister,' and taking her marriage-certificate from her pocket and denouncing you, of course you have still but one course to pursue, and that is to charge the crime upon him, and have him carried off with all speed into the 'deep and massive dungeons beneath Thornley Hall.'

More having, as he was rather given to boast, 'a goodly vessel on the lordly Thames,' had better have gone with it, weather permitting, than gone after Eva. Naturally, he got carried down to the dungeons too, for lurking about, and got put into the next dungeon to the Hunchback, then expiring from poison. And there they were, hard and fast, like two wild beasts in dens, trying to get glimpses of each other through the bars, to the unutterable interest of Mr. Whelks.

But when the Hunchback made himself known, and when More did the same; and when the Hunchback said he had got the certificate which rendered Eva's marriage illegal; and when More raved to have it given to him, and when the Hunchback (as having some grains of misanthropy in him to the last) persisted in going into his dying agonies in a remote corner of his cage, and took unheard-of trouble not to die anywhere near the bars that were within More's reach; Mr. Whelks applauded to the echo. At last the Hunchback was persuaded to stick the certificate on the point of a dagger, and hand it in; and that done, died extremely hard, knocking himself violently about, to the very last gasp, and certainly making the most of all the life that was in him.

Still More had yet to get out of his den before he could turn his certificate to any account. His first step was to make such a violent uproar as to bring into his presence a certain 'Norman Free Sauce' who kept watch and ward over him. His second, to inform this warrior, in the style of the Polite Letter-Writer, that 'circumstances had occurred' rendering it necessary that he should be immediately let out. The warrior declining to submit himself to the force of these circumstances, Mr. More proposed to him, as a gentleman and a man of honour, to allow

him to step out into the gallery, and there adjust an old
feud subsisting between them, by single combat. The
unwary Free Lance, consenting to this reasonable proposal,
was shot from behind by the comic man, whom he bitterly
designated as 'a snipe' for that action, and then died
exceedingly game.

All this occurred in one day—the bridal day of the
Ladye of Lambythe; and now Mr. Whelks concentrated
all his energies into a focus, bent forward, looked straight
in front of him, and held his breath. For, the night of
the eventful day being come, Mr. Whelks was admitted
to the 'bridal chamber of the Ladye of Lambythe', where
he beheld a toilet table, and a particularly large and
desolate four-post bedstead. Here the Ladye, having
dismissed her bridesmaids, was interrupted in deploring
her unhappy fate, by the entrance of her husband; and
matters, under these circumstances, were proceeding to
very desperate extremities, when the Ladye (by this time
aware of the existence of the certificate) found a dagger
on the dressing-table, and said, 'Attempt to enfold me in
thy pernicious embrace, and this poignard—!' etc. He
did attempt it, however, for all that, and he and the
Ladye were dragging one another about like wrestlers,
when Mr. More broke open the door, and entering with
the whole domestic establishment and a Middlesex magistrate, took him into custody and claimed his bride.

It is but fair to Mr. Whelks to remark on one curious
fact in this entertainment. When the situations were very
strong indeed, they were very like what some favourite
situations in the Italian Opera would be to a profoundly
deaf spectator. The despair and madness at the end of
the first act, the business of the long hair, and the struggle
in the bridal chamber, were as like the conventional pas-

sion of the Italian singers, as the orchestra was unlike the opera band, or its 'hurries' unlike the music of the great composers. So do extremes meet; and so is there some hopeful congeniality between what will excite Mr. Whelks, and what will rouse a Duchess. [1850]

THE GUILD OF LITERATURE AND ART.

THERE are reasons, sufficiently obvious to our readers without explanation, which render the present a fitting place for a few words of remark on the proposed Institution bearing this name.

Its objects, as stated in the public advertisement, are, " to encourage life assurance and other provident habits among authors and artists; to render such assistance to both, as shall never compromise their independence; and to found a new Institution where honorable rest from arduous labour shall still be associated with the discharge of congenial duties."

The authors and artists associated in this endeavour would be but indifferent students of human nature, and would be but poorly qualified for the pursuit of their art, if they supposed it possible to originate any scheme that would be free from objection. They have neither the right, nor the desire, to take offence at any discussion of the details of their plan. All that they claim, is, such consideration for it as their character and position may justly demand, and such moderate restraint in regard of misconception or misrepresentation as is due to any body of gentlemen disinterestedly associated for an honorable purpose.

It is proposed to form a Society of Authors and Artists by profession, who shall all effect some kind of Insurance on their lives;—whether for a hundred pounds or a thousand pounds—whether on high premiums terminable at a certain age, or on premiums payable through the whole of life—whether for deferred annuities, or for pensions to widows, or for the accumulation of sums destined to the education or portioning of children—is in this, as in all other cases, at the discretion of the individual insuring. The foundation of a New Life Insurance Office, expressly for these purposes, would be, obviously, a rash proceeding, wholly unjustifiable in the infancy of such a design. Therefore its proposers recommend one existing Insurance Office—firstly, because its constitution appears to secure to its insurers better terms than they can meet with elsewhere; secondly, because in Life Insurance, as in most other things, a body of persons can obtain advantages which individuals cannot. The chief advantage thus obtained in this instance, is stated in the printed Prospectus as a deduction of five per cent from all the premiums paid by Members of the Society to that particular office. It is needless to add, that if an author or an artist be already insured in another office, or if he have any peculiar liking, in effecting a new insurance, for paying five per cent more than he need, he is at perfect liberty to insure where he pleases, and in right of any insurance whatever to become a Member of the Society if he will.

But, there may be cases in which, on account of impaired health or of advanced age at the present time, individuals desirous of joining the Society, may be quite unable to obtain acceptance at any Life Office. In such instances the required qualification of Life Insurance will be dispensed with. In cases of proved temporary inability to meet a periodical payment due on an Insurance, the Society proposes to assist the insurer from its funds.

" In connexion with this Society," the Prospectus proceeds, " by which it is intended to commend and enforce the duties of prudence and foresight, especially incumbent on those whose income is wholly, or mainly, derived from the precarious profit of a profession, it is proposed to establish and endow an Institute, having at its disposal certain salaries, to which certain duties will be attached; together with a limited number of free residences, which, though sufficiently small to be adapted to a very moderate income, will be completed with due regard to the ordinary habits and necessary comforts of gentlemen. The offices of Endowment will consist:

" First,—Of a Warden, with a house and a salary of two hundred pounds a year;

" Second,—Of Members, with a house and one hundred and seventy pounds, or, without a house, two hundred pounds a year;

" Third,—Of Associates, with a salary of one hundred pounds a year.

" For these offices all who are Insurers in the Society above mentioned are qualified to offer themselves as Candidates. Such Insurance is to be considered an indispensable qualification, saving in exceptional cases (should any such arise) where an individual can prove that he has made every effort to insure his life, but cannot find acceptance at any Life Office, by reason of impaired health, or of advanced age, at the date of this prospectus.

" Each Member will be required to give, either personally or by a proxy selected from the Associates, with the approval of the Warden, three lectures in each year—one in London, the others at the Mechanics' Institutes, or some public building suited for the purpose, in the principal provincial towns. Considering the many duties exacting time and attention that will devolve on the Warden, he will not be required to give more than one lecture annually (which, if delivered by a proxy, he will, health permitting, be expected to compose himself), and that in the Metropolis.

"These lectures will be subject to the direction and control of the managing body of the Endowment. They will usually relate to Letters or Art, and will invariably avoid all debateable ground of Politics or Theology. It will be the endeavour of the Committee to address them to points on which the public may be presumed to be interested, and to require dispassionate and reliable information—to make them, in short, an educational and improving feature of the time.

"The duties of Associates will be defined and fixed by the Council (consisting of the Warden, the Members, and a certain number of the Associates themselves), according to the previous studies and peculiar talent of each—whether in gratuitous assistance to any learned bodies, societies for the diffusion of knowledge, etc., or, as funds increase, and the utilities of the Institution develope themselves, in co-operating towards works of national interest and importance, but on subjects of a nature more popular, and at a price more accessible, than those which usually emanate from professed academies. It is well to add, that while, on every account, it is deemed desirable to annex to the receipt of a salary the performance of a duty, it is not intended that such duty should make so great a demand upon the time and labour, either of Member or Associate, as to deprive the public of their services in those departments in which they have gained distinction, or to divert their own efforts for independence from their accustomed professional pursuits.

"The design of the Institution proposed, is, to select for the appointment of Members (who will be elected for life) those Writers and Artists of established reputation, and generally of mature years (or, if young, in failing health), to whom the income attached to the appointment may be an object of honorable desire; while the office of Associate is intended partly for those whose toils or merits are less known to the general public than their professional brethren, and partly for those, in earlier life, who give promise of future eminence, and to whom a temporary income of one hundred pounds a year may be of essential and permanent service. There are few men professionally engaged in Art or Letters, even though their labours may have raised them into comparative wealth, who cannot look back to some period of struggle in which an income so humble would have saved them from many a pang, and, perhaps, from the necessity of stooping their ambition to occupations at variance with the higher aims of their career.

"An Associate may, therefore, be chosen for life, or for one or more years, according to the nature of his claims, and the discretion of the Electors."

With the view of bringing this project into general notice, Sir Edward Bulwer Lytton (besides a gift of land) has written a new comedy, and presented it to the friends associated with him in the origination of the scheme. They will act it, first, before Her Majesty at Devonshire House, and afterwards publicly. Over and above the profits that may arise from these dramatic representations, the copyright of the comedy, both for acting and publishing, being unconditionally given to the Association, has already enabled it to realise a handsome sum of money.

Many of our readers are aware that this company of amateur actors has been for some time in existence. Its public existence was accidental. It was originally formed for the private amusement of a leisure hour. Yielding to urgent entreaty, it then had the good fortune to render service to the Sanatorium, one of the most useful and most necessary Institutions ever founded in this country. It was subsequently enabled to yield timely assistance to three distinguished literary men, all of whom Her Majesty has since placed on the Pension List, and entirely to support one of them for nearly three years. It is now about to renew its exertions for the cause we have set forth. To say that its members do not merely seek their own entertainment and display (easily attainable by far less troublesome and responsible means) is to award them the not very exalted praise of being neither fools nor impostors.

The Guild of Literature and Art may be a good name or a bad name; the details of this endowment—mere suggestions at present, and not to be proceeded with, until much work shall have been patiently done—may be perfect or most imperfect; the retirement proposed, may be taken for granted to be everything that it is not intended to be; and still we conceive the real question to remain untouched. It is, whether Literature shall continue to be an exception from all other professions and pursuits, in having no resource for its distressed and divided followers but in eleemosynary aid; or, whether it is good that they should be provident, united, helpful of one another, and independent.

No child can suppose that the profits of the comedy alone will be sufficient for such an Endowment as is sought

to be established.   It is expressly stated in the Prospectus
that " for farther support to the Endowment by subscription,
and especially by annual subscription, it is intended to
appeal to the Public."   If the Public will disembarras the
question of any little cobwebs that may be spun about it,
and will confine it to this, it will be faithful to its ever
generous and honest nature.

    There is no reason for affecting to conceal that the writer
of these few remarks is active in the project, and is impelled
by a zealous desire to advance what he knows to be a
worthy object.   He would be false to the trust placed in
him, by the friends with whom he is associated, and to
the secret experience of his daily life, and of the calling
to which he belongs, if he had any dainty reserve in such
a matter.   He is one of an order beyond which he affects
to be nothing, and aspires to be nothing.   He knows—
few men can know, he thinks, with better reason—that
he does his duty to it in taking this part; and he wishes
his personal testimony to tell for what it is worth.

                                                    [1851]

WHOLE HOGS.

THE public market has been of late more than usually remarkable for transactions on the American principle in Whole and indivisible Hogs. The market has been heavy— not the least approach to briskness having been observed in any part of it; but, the transactions, such as they have been, have been exclusively for Whole Hogs. Those who may only have had a retail inclination for sides, ribs, limbs, cheeks, face, trotters, snout, ears, or tail, have been required to take the Whole Hog, sinking none of the offal, but consenting to it all—and a good deal of it too.

It has been discovered that mankind at large can only be regenerated by a Tee-total Society, or by a Peace Society, or by always dining on Vegetables. It is to be particularly remarked that either of these certain means of regeneration is utterly defeated, if so much as a hair's-breadth of the tip of either ear of that particular Pig be left out of the bargain. Qualify your water with a tea-spoonful of wine or brandy—we beg pardon—alcohol—and there is no virtue in Temperance. Maintain a single sentry at the gate of the Queen's Palace, and it is utterly impossible that you can be peaceful. Stew so much as the bone of a mutton chop in the pot with your vegetables, and you will never make another Eden out of a Kitchen Garden. You must

take the Whole Hog, Sir, and every bristle on him, or you
and the rest of mankind will never be regenerated.

Now, without enquiring at present whether means of
regeneration that are so easily spoiled, may not a little
resemble the pair of dancing-shoes in the story, which
the lady destroyed by walking across a room in them,
we will consider the Whole Hog question from another
point of view.

First, stand aside to see the great Tee-total Procession
come by. It is called a Temperance Procession—which
is not an honest use of a plain word, but never mind
that. Hurrah! hurrah! The flags are blue and the letters
golden. Hurrah! hurrah! Here are a great many excellent,
straight-forward, thoroughly well-meaning, and exemplary
people, four and four, or two and two. Hurrah! hurrah!
Here are a great many children, also four and four, or
two and two. Who are they?—They, Sir, are the Juvenile
Temperance Bands of Hope.—Lord bless me! What are
the Juvenile Temperance Bands of Hope?—They are the
Infantine Brigade of Regenerators of Mankind.—Indeed?
Hurrah! hurrah! These young citizens being pledged to
total abstinence, and being fully competent to pledge
themselves to anything for life; and it being the custom
of such young citizens' parents, in the existing state of
unregenerated society, to bring them up on ardent spirits
and strong beer (both of which are commonly kept in
barrels, behind the door, on tap, in all large families,
expressly for persons of tender years, of whom it is calculated that seven-eighths always go to bed drunk); this
is a grand show. So, again, Hurrah! hurrah!

Who are these gentlemen walking two and two, with
medals on their stomachs and bows in their button-
holes?—These, Sir, are the Committee.—Are they? Hur-

rah! hurrah! One cheer more for the Committee! Hoo-
o-o-o-rah! A cheer for the Reverend Jabez Fireworks—
fond of speaking; a cheer for the gentleman with the
stand-up collar, Mr. Gloss—fond of speaking; a cheer for
the gentleman with the massive watch-chain, who smiles
so sweetly on the surrounding Fair, Mr. Glib—fond of
speaking; a cheer for the rather dirty little gentleman who
looks like a converted Hyæna, Mr. Scradger—fond of
speaking; a cheer for the dark-eyed, brown gentleman,
the Dove Delegate from America—fond of speaking; a
cheer for the swarm who follow, blackening the procession,—
Regenerators from everywhere in general—all good men—
all fond of speaking; and all going to speak.

I have no right to object, I am sure. Hurrah, hurrah!

The Reverend Jabez Fireworks, and the great Mr. Gloss,
and the popular Mr. Glib, and the eminent Mr. Scradger,
and the Dove Delegate from America, and the distinguished
swarm from everywhere, have ample opportunity (and
profit by it, too,) for speaking to their heart's content.
For, is there not, to-day, a Grand Demonstration Meeting;
and to-morrow, another Grand Demonstration Meeting;
and, the day after to-morrow, a Grand United Regenerative Zoological Visitation; and, the day after that, a Grand
Aggregate General Demonstration; and, the day after that,
a Grand Associated Regenerative Breakfast; and, the day
after that, a Grand Associated Regenerative Tea; and, the
day after that, a Final Grand Aggregate Compounded
United and Associated Steam-boat River Demonstration;
and do the Regenerators go anywhere without speaking, by
the bushel? Still, what offence to me? None. Still, I am
content to cry, Hurrah! hurrah! If the Regenerators,
though estimable men, be the most tiresome men (as
speakers) under Heaven; if their sincerest and best follow-

ers cannot, in the infirmity of human nature, bear the
infliction of such oratory, but occupy themselves in preference with tea and rolls, or resort for comfort to the
less terrible society of Lions, Elephants, and Bears, or
drown the Regenerative eloquence in the clash of brazen
Bands; I think it sensible and right, and still exclaim,
Hurrah!

But how, if with the matter of such eloquence, when
any of it happens to be heard, and also happens not to
be a singular compound of references to the Bible, and
selections from Joe Miller, I find, on drawing nearer, that
I *have* some business? How, if I find that the distinguished swarm are not of that quiet class of gentlemen
whom Mr. Carlyle describes as consuming their own
smoke; but that they emit a vast amount of smoke and
blacken their neighbours very considerably? Then, as a
neighbour myself, I have perhaps a right to speak?

In Bedlam, and in all other madhouses, Society is
denounced as being wrongfully combined against the patient.
In Newgate, and in all other prisons, Society is denounced
as being wrongfully combined against the criminal. In
the speeches of the Reverend Jabez, and the other Regenerators, Society is denounced as being wrongfully and
wickedly combined against their own particular Whole
Hog—who must be swallowed, every bristle, or there is no
Pork in him.

The proof? Society won't come in and sign the pledge;
Society won't come in and recruit the Juvenile Temperance
bands of hope. Therefore, Society is fond of drunkenness,
sees no harm in it, favors it very much, *is* a drunkard—
a base, worthless, sensual, profligate brute. Fathers and
mothers, sons and daughters, brothers and sisters, divines,
physicians, lawyers, editors, authors, painters, poets, musi-

cians, Queen, lords, ladies, and commons, are all in league against the Regenerators, are all violently attached to drunkenness, are all the more dangerous if by any chance they be personal examples of temperance, in the real meaning of the word!—which last powerful steam-hammer of logic has become a pet one, and is constantly to be observed in action.

Against this sweeping misrepresentation, I take the liberty of entering my feeble protest. With all respect for Jabez, for Gloss, for Glib, for Dove Delegate, and for Scradger, I must make so bold as to observe that when a Malay runs a-muck he cannot be considered in a temperate state of mind; also, that when a thermometer stands at Fever Heat, it cannot claim to indicate Temperate weather. A man, to be truly temperate, must be temperate in many respects—in the rejection of strong words no less than of strong drinks—and I crave leave to assert against my good friends the Regenerators, that, in such gross statements, they set a most intemperate example. I even doubt whether an equal number of drunkards, under the excitement of the strongest liquors, could set a worse example.

And I would beg to put it seriously to the consideration of those who have sufficient powers of endurance to stand about the platform, listening, whether they think of this sufficiently? Whether they ever knew the like of this before? Whether they have any experience or knowledge of a good cause that was ever promoted by such bad means? Whether they ever heard of an association of people, deliberately, by their chosen vessels, throwing overboard every effort but their own, made for the amelioration of the condition of men; unscrupulously vilifying all other laborers in the vineyard; calumniously setting down as aiders and abettors of an odious vice which they know to be held in general abhorrence, and consigned to general shame, the great compact mass of the community—of its intelligence, of its morality, of its earnest endeavour after better things? If, upon consideration, they know of no such other case, then the enquiry will perhaps occur to them, whether, in supporting a so-conducted cause, they really be upholders of Temperance, dealing with words, which should be the signs for Truth, according to the truth that is in them?

Mankind can only be regenerated, proclaim the fatteners of the Whole Hog Number Two, by means of a Peace Society. Well! I call out of the nearest Peace Society my worthy friend John Bates—an excellent workman and a sound man, lineally descended from that sturdy soldier of the same name who spake with King Henry the Fifth, on the night before the battle of Agincourt. "Bates," says I, "how about this Regeneration? *Why* can it only be effected by means of a Peace Society?" Says Bates in answer, "Because War is frightful, ruinous, and unchristian. Because the details of one battle, because the horrors of one siege, would so appal you, if you knew them, that probably you never could be happy afterwards. Because man was not created in the image of his Maker to be blasted with gunpowder, or pierced with bayonets, or gashed with swords, or trampled under iron hoofs of horses into a puddle of mire and blood. Because War is a wickedness that always costs us dear. Because it wastes our treasure, hardens our hearts, paralyses our industry, cripples our commerce, occasions losses, ills, and devilish crimes, unspeakable and out of number." Says I, sadly, " But have I not, O Bates, known all this for this many a year?" "It may be so," says Bates; "then come into the Peace Society." Says I, "Why come in there, Bates?"

Says Bates, "Because we declare we won't have War or show of War. We won't have armies, navies, camps, or ships. England shall be disarmed, we say, and all these horrors ended." Says I, "How ended, Bates?" Says Bates, "By arbitration. We have a Dove Delegate from America, and a Mouse Delegate from France; and we are establishing a Bond of brotherhood, and that'll do it." Alas! It will NOT do it, Bates. I, too, have thought upon the horrors of war, of the blessings of peace, and of the fatal distraction of men's minds from seeking them, by the roll of the drum and the thunder of the inexorable cannon. However, Bates, the world is not so far upon its course, yet, but that there are tyrants and oppressors left upon it, watchful to find Freedom weak that they may strike, and backed by great armies. O John Bates, look out towards Austria, look out towards Russia, look out towards Germany, look out towards the purple Sea, that lies so beautiful and calm beyond the filthy jails of Naples! Do you see nothing there?" Says Bates (like the sister in Blue Beard, but much more triumphantly), "I see nothing there, but dust;"—and this is one of the inconveniences of a fattened Whole and indivisible Hog, that it fills up the doorway, and its breeders cannot see beyond it. "Dust!" says Bates. I tell Bates that it is because there are, behind that dust, oppressors and op-pressed, arrayed against each other—that it is because there are, beyond his Dove Delegate and his Mouse Delegate, the wild beasts of the Forest—that it is because I dread and hate the miseries of tyranny and war—that it is because I would not be soldier-ridden, nor have other men so—that I am not for the disarming of England, and cannot be a member of his Peace Society; admitting all his premises, but denying his conclusion. Whereupon

Bates, otherwise just and sensible, insinuates that not being for his Whole and indivisible Hog, I can be for no part of his Hog; and that I have never felt or thought what his Society now tells me it, and only it, feels and thinks as a new discovery; and that when I am told of the new discovery I don't care for it!

Mankind can only be regenerated by dining on Vegetables. Why? Certain worthy gentlemen have dined, it seems, on vegetables for ever so many years, and are none the worse for it. Straightway, these excellent men, excited to the highest pitch, announce themselves by public advertisement as "DISTINGUISHED VEGETARIANS," vault upon a platform, hold a vegetable festival, and proceed to show, not without prolixity and weak jokes, that a vegetable diet is the only true faith, and that, in eating meat, mankind is wholly mistaken and partially corrupt. Distinguished Vegetarians. As the men who wear Nankeen trousers might hold a similar meeting, and become Distinguished Nankeenarians! But am I to have NO meat? If I take a pledge to eat three cauliflowers daily in the cauliflower season, a peck of peas daily in the pea time, a gallon of broad Windsor beans daily when beans are "in", and a young cabbage or so every morning before breakfast, with perhaps a little ginger between meals (as a vegetable substance, corrective of that windy diet), may I not be allowed half an ounce of gravy-beef to flavour my potatoes? Not a shred! Distinguished Vegetarians can acknowledge no imperfect animal. Their Hog must be a Whole Hog, according to the fashion of the time.

Now, we would so far renew the custom of sacrificing animals, as to recommend that an altar be erected to Our Country, at present sheltering so many of these very inconvenient and unwieldy Hogs, on which their grosser portions should be "burnt and purged away." The Whole Hog of the Temperance Movement divested of its intemperate assumption of infallibility and of its intemperate determination to run grunting at the legs of the general population of this empire, would be a far less unclean and a far more serviceable creature than at present. The Whole Hog of the Peace Society, acquiring the recognition of a community of feeling between itself and many who hold war in no less abhorrence, but who yet believe, that, in the present era of the world, some preparation against it is a preservative of peace and a restraint upon despotism, would become as much enlightened as its learned predecessor Toby of Immortal Memory. And if distinguished Vegetarians, of all kinds, would only allow a little meat, and if distinguished Fleshmeatarians, of all kinds, would only yield a little vegetable; if the former, quietly devouring the fruits of the earth to any extent, would admit the possible morality of mashed potatoes with beef—and if the latter would concede a little spinach with gammon; and if both could manage to get on with a little less platforming—there being at present rather an undue preponderance of cry over wool —if all of us, in short, were to yield up something of our whole and entire animals, it might be very much the better in the end, both for us and for them.

After all, my friends and brothers, even the best Whole and indivisible Hog may be but a small fragment of the higher and greater work, called Education? [1851]

ROCHESTER AND CHATHAM.

[FROM "ONE MAN IN A DOCKYARD"]

I AM a man of good average size and strength; John Strongitharm by name; five feet eight, in my shoes; and able to lift a hundred-weight and a half, without turning purple in the face. The last time I had a tussle with Peter Briggs, I sent him clean into the back parlour, from the front dining-room (all in an amicable way), and my weight is barely eleven stone, while Peter weighs at least fourteen. I consider myself, therefore, as neither weak nor helpless.

But of what use on earth, is a single man? I mean—of how small an amount of practical labour is an individual capable, when he compares his powers, not only with the entire magnitude of great public works, but with one of the countless number of subordinate parts, nay, one of the mere temporary details and preliminaries. I stand in the evening looking up at St. Paul's—a small dark object in the broad shade of its huge sombre walls. My eye ascends the darkness, and wanders round the great black dome, and then slowly returns by way of the roof of one of its great porticoes, and finds its way down one of the large dark pillars. What are my strength and weight compared with that one pillar? Could I have set it up there—could I have moved one tenth part of it, or a twentieth part of it, as it lay upon the ground? I can throw Peter Briggs, who weighs fourteen stone, but there is a cornice up there which I could not stir if I had it before my feet, but which, if it fell upon me, would exterminate me.

I often have this feeling in gazing at large edifices. I took a stroll about the town of Chatham, the other day, and almost everything I looked at there, engendered it in an unusual degree.

There was Rochester Castle, to begin with. I surveyed that massive ruin from the Bridge, and thought what a brief little practical joke I seemed to be, in comparison with its solidity, stature, strength, and length of life. I went inside; and, standing in the solemn shadow of its walls, looking up at the blue sky, its only remaining roof (to the disturbance of the crows and jackdaws, who garrison the venerable fortress now) calculated how much wall of that thickness I, or any other mere man, could build in his whole life—say from eight years old, to eighty—and what a ridiculous result would be produced. I climbed the rugged staircase, stopping now and then to peep at great holes where the rafters of floors were once—bare as toothless gums now—or to enjoy glimpses of the Medway through dreary apertures like eye-sockets without eyes; and, looking down from the Castle ramparts on the Old Cathedral, and on the crumbling remains of the old Priory, and on the row of staid old red brick houses where the Cathedral dignitaries live, and on the shrunken fragments of one of the old City gates, and on the old trees with their high tops below me, felt quite apologetic to the scene in general for my own juvenility and insignificance. One of the river-boatmen had told me, on the Bridge, (as country folks usually do tell of such places) that in the old times when those buildings were in progress, a labourer's wages were "a penny a day, and enough too." Even as a solitary penny was to their whole cost, it appeared to me was the utmost strength and exertion of one man towards the labour of their erection.

As I sauntered along the old High Street on my way towards Chatham, I seemed to dwindle more and more. Here, was another old gate; here, were very old houses, with the strangest gables; here, was a queer, queer, little old House, founded by Richard Watts, Esquire, for the nightly shelter and entertainment of so many poor travellers, "not being rogues or proctors," who were to be dismissed in the morning with a Godspeed and fourpence each. It was all very well my being able to throw Peter Briggs into the next room, but what could I throw into the next century? If I, John Strongitharm, were to go at it (as the saying is) with all my might and main, what object could *I* set up, that should be on earth to be wondered at, a few generations hence? Unassisted, probably not so much as a mile-stone.

Coming into Chatham, it appeared to me as if the feeble absurdity of an individual were made more and more manifest at every step I took. Men were only noticeable here by scores, by hundreds, by thousands, rank and file, companies, regiments, detachments, vessels full for exportation. They walked about the streets in rows or bodies, carrying their heads in exactly the same way, and doing exactly the same thing with their limbs. Nothing in the shape of clothing was made for an individual; everything was contracted for, by the million. The children of Israel were established in Chatham, as salesmen, outfitters, tailors, old clothesmen, army and navy accoutrement makers, bill discounters, and general despoilers of the Christian world, in tribes, rather than in families. The cannon, and pyramidal piles of cannon-balls, renounced the insignificance of individuality, and combined by the score. In the town-barracks, if I saw one soldier pipe-claying a belt, I was sure to see twenty: nineteen of whom might have been compound reflections of the first one in a combination of looking-glasses. No man cooked his dinner in a saucepan; the whole regiment's dinner came out of a copper. The muskets stood in ranks, and even the drums were gregarious. Up in the airy Artillery Barracks, Private Jones or Brown lived in a mansion labelled "120 men," or "160 men,"—that was his door-plate—he had no separate existence. The only fact that made the least approach to the recognition of an individual was a sentry box; but that, after all, was for the accommodation of all the rank and file in the barracks, as their turns came.

I took a walk upon the Lines, and mused among the fortifications; grassy and innocent enough on the surface, at present, but tough subjects at the core. Here I saw the artfullest pits and drawbridges, the slyest batteries, the most unexpected angles and turnings; the loneliest, deep-set, beetle-browed little windows, down among the stinging-nettles at the bottoms of trenches, indicative of subterranean passages and bombproof rooms. Here, I saw forts, and citadels, and great-guns hiding their muzzles deceitfully behind mounds of earth; and the low flat tops of inner buildings crouching out of the range of telescopes and aim of shells; and mysterious gateways and archways, honey-combed with loopholes for small arms; and tokens of undermined communication between place and place; and narrow passages beset by dark vaults with gratings to fire through, that one would like to see the inside of, they are so mysterious, and smell so chill and earthy. Steeped in these mysteries, I wandered round the trenches of Fort Pitt, and away to Fort Clarence—a dismal military prison now, like an old Giant's Castle "new-hatched to the woeful time;"—and looking down upon the river from the sloping bank, I saw even there, upon the shore, a stranded little fort, with its blank, weather-beaten brick face staring at the mud; which fort, I settled in my own mind, somehow communicated with all the other forts, and had unknown means of blowing them up into the air if need should be. Then, I went back to the Lines, and strolled away to the low stagnant level of the river in that direction, by other solitary trenches, forts, drawbridges, and posts of guard. Everywhere, I found some fragments of a comprehensive engineering scheme for cutting off, cutting down, blowing up, alluring on to his own destruction, or driving back to his defeat, "the enemy"—all these contrivances having reference to men by the hundred, and the thousand, and the ten thousand, without the least offence to any individual. [1851]

TRADING IN DEATH.

SEVERAL years have now elapsed since it began to be clear to the comprehension of most rational men, that the English people had fallen into a ·condition much to be regretted, in respect of their Funeral customs. A system of barbarous show and expense was found to have gradually erected itself above the grave, which, while it could possibly do no honor to the memory of the dead, did great dishonor to the living, as inducing them to associate the most solemn of human occasions with unmeaning mummeries, dishonest debt, profuse waste, and bad example in an utter oblivion of responsibility. The more the subject was examined, and the lower the investigation was carried, the more monstrous (as was natural) these usages appeared to be, both in themselves and in their consequences. No class of society escaped. The competition among the middle classes for superior gentility in Funerals—the gentility being estimated by the amount of ghastly folly in which the undertaker was permitted to run riot—descended even to the very poor: to whom the cost of funeral customs was so ruinous and so disproportionate to their means, that they formed Clubs among themselves to defray such charges. Many of these Clubs, conducted by designing villains who preyed upon the general infirmity,

cheated and wronged the poor, most cruelly; others, by
presenting a new class of temptations to the wickedest
natures among them, let to a new class of mercenary
murders, so abominable in their iniquity, that language
cannot stigmatize them with sufficient severity. That
nothing might be wanting to complete the general depravity, hollowness, and falsehood, of this state of things, the
absurd fact came to light, that innumerable harpies assumed
the titles of furnishers of Funerals, who possessed no Funeral furniture whatever, but who formed a long file of
middlemen between the chief mourner and the real tradesman, and who hired out the trappings from one to another
—passing them on like water-buckets at a fire—every one
of them charging his enormous percentage on his share of
the "black job." Add to all this, the demonstration, by
the simplest and plainest practical science, of the terrible
consequences to the living, inevitably resulting from the
practice of burying the dead in the midst of crowded
towns; and the exposition of a system of indecent horror,
revolting to our nature and disgraceful to our age and
nation, arising out of the confined limits of such burial-
grounds, and the avarice of their proprietors; and the
culminating point of this gigantic mockery is at last
arrived at.

Out of such almost incredible degradation, saving that
the proof of it is too easy, we are still very slowly and
feebly emerging. There are now, we confidently hope,
among the middle classes, many, who having made themselves acquainted with these evils through the parliamentary
papers in which they are described, would be moved by
no human consideration to perpetuate the old bad example;
but who will leave it as their solemn injunction on their
nearest and dearest survivors, that they shall not, in their

death, be made the instruments of infecting, either the minds or the bodies of their fellow-creatures. Among persons of note, such examples have not been wanting. The late Duke of Sussex did a national service when he desired to be laid, in the equality of death, in the cemetery of Kensal Green, and not with the pageantry of a State Funeral in the Royal vault at Windsor. Sir Robert Peel requested to be buried at Drayton. The late Queen Dowager left a pattern to every rank in these touching and admirable words. "I die in all humility, knowing well that we are all alike before the Throne of God; and I request, therefore, that my mortal remains be conveyed to the grave without any pomp or state. They are to be removed to St. George's Chapel, Windsor, where I request to have as private and quiet a funeral as possible. I particularly desire not to be laid out in state. I die in peace and wish to be carried to the tomb in peace, and free from the vanities and pomp of this world. I request not to be dissected or embalmed, and desire to give as little trouble as possible."

With such precedents and such facts fresh in the general knowledge, and at this transition-time in so serious a chapter of our social history, the obsolete custom of a State Funeral has been revived, in miscalled "honor" of the late Duke of Wellington. To whose glorious memory be all true honor while England lasts!

We earnestly submit to our readers that there is, and that there can be, no kind of honor in such a revival; that the more truly great the man, the more truly little the ceremony; and that it has been, from first to last, a pernicious instance and encouragement of the demoralising practice of trading in Death.

It is within the knowledge of the whole public, of all

diversities of political opinion, whether or no any of the Powers that be, have traded in this Death—have saved it up, and petted it, and made the most of it, and reluctantly let it go. On that aspect of the question we offer no further remark.

But, of the general trading spirit which, in its inherent emptiness and want of consistency and reality, the long-deferred State Funeral has appropriately awakened, we will proceed to furnish a few instances all faithfully copied from the advertising columns of The Times.

First, of seats and refreshments. Passing over that desirable first-floor where a party could be accommodated with "the use of a piano"; and merely glancing at the decorous daily announcement of "The Duke of Wellington Funeral Wine," which was in such high demand that immediate orders were necessary; and also "The Duke of Wellington Funeral Cake," which "delicious article" could only be had of such a baker; and likewise "The Funeral Life Preserver," which could only be had of such a tailor; and further "the celebrated lemon biscuits," at one and fourpence per pound, which were considered by the manufacturer as the only infallible assuagers of the national grief; let us pass in review some dozen of the more eligible opportunities the public had of profiting by the occasion.

LUDGATE HILL.—The fittings and arrangements for viewing this grand and solemnly imposing procession are now completed at this establishment, and those who are desirous of obtaining a fine and extensive view, combined with every personal convenience and comfort, will do well to make immediate inspection of the SEATS now remaining on hand.

FUNERAL, including Beds the night previous.—To be LET, a SECOND FLOOR, of three rooms, two windows, having a good view of the procession. Terms, including refreshment, 10 guineas. Single places, including bed and breakfast, from 15s.

THE DUKE'S FUNERAL.—A first-rate VIEW for 15 persons, also good clean beds and a sitting-room on reasonable terms.

But above all let us not forget the

NOTICE TO CLERGYMEN.—T. C. Fleet-street, has reserved for clergy-men exclusively, *upon condition only that they appear in their surplices*, FOUR FRONT SEATS, at £1 each; four second tier, at 15s. each; four third tier, at 12s. 6d.; four fourth tier, at 10s.; four fifth tier, at 7s. 6d.; and four sixth tier, at 5s. All the other seats are respectively 40s., 30s., 20s., 15s., 10s.

The anxiety of this enterprising tradesman to get up a reverend tableau in his shop-window of four-and-twenty clergymen all on six rows, is particularly commendable, and appears to us to shed a remarkable grace on the solemnity.

These few specimens are collected at random from scores upon scores of such advertisements, mingled with descriptions of non-existent ranges of view, and with invi-tations to a few agreeable gentlemen who are wanted to complete a little assembly of kindred souls, who have laid in abundance of "refreshments, wines, spirits, provisions, fruit, plate, glass, china," and other light matters too numerous to mention, and who keep "good fires." On looking over them we are constantly startled by the words in large capitals, "WOULD TO GOD NIGHT OR BLUCHER WERE COME!" which, referring to a work of art, are relieved by a legend setting forth how the lamented hero observed of it, "in his characteristic manner, 'Very good; very good indeed.'" O Art! *You* too trading in Death!

Then, autographs fall into their place in the State Funeral train. The sanctity of a seal, or the confidence of a letter, is a meaningless phrase that has no place in the vocabulary of the Traders in Death. Stop, trumpets, in the Dead March, and blow to the world how characteristic we autographs are!

To be SOLD, SIX AUTOGRAPH LETTERS from F. M. the Duke of WELLINGTON, with Envelopes and Seals, which have been most generously given to aid a lady in distressed circumstances.

A CLERGYMAN has TWO LETTERS, with Envelopes, addressed to him by the late DUKE, and bearing striking testimony to the extent of his Grace's private charities, to be DISPOSED OF at the highest offer (for one or both), received by the 18th instant. The offers may be contingent on further particulars being satisfactory.

ONE of the last LETTERS of the DUKE of WELLINGTON for DISPOSAL, dated from Walmer Castle within a day or two of his death, highly characteristic, with seal and post-marks distinct. This being probably the last letter written by the late Duke its interest as a relic must be greatly enhanced. The highest offer accepted. May be seen on application.

THE GREAT DUKE.—A LETTER of the GREAT HERO, dated March 27, 1851, to be SOLD. Also a beautiful Letter from Jenny Lind, dated June 30, 1852. The highest offer will be accepted. Address with offers of price.

Miss Lind's autograph would appear to have lingered in the shade until the Funeral Train came by, when it modestly stepped into the procession and took a conspicuous place. We are in doubt which to admire most; the ingenuity of this little stroke of business; or the affecting delicacy that sells "probably the last letter written by the late Duke" before the aged hand that wrote it under some manly sense of duty, is yet withered in its grave; or the piety of that excellent clergyman—did he appear in his surplice in the front row of T. C.'s shop-window? —who is so anxious to sell "striking testimony to the extent of His Grace's private charities;" or the generosity of that Good Samaritan who poured "six letters with envelopes and seals" into the wounds of the lady in distressed circumstances.

Lastly come the relics—precious remembrances worn next to the bereaved heart, like Hardy's miniature of Nelson, and never to be wrested from the advertisers but with ready money.

MEMENTO of the late DUKE of WELLINGTON.—To be DISPOSED OF, a LOCK of the late illustrious DUKE'S HAIR. Can be guaranteed. The highest offer will be accepted. Apply by letter pre-paid.

VALUABLE RELIC of the late DUKE of WELLINGTON.—A lady, having in her possession a quantity of the late illustrious DUKE'S HAIR, cut in 1841, is willing to PART WITH a portion of the same for £25. Satisfactory proof will be given of its identity, and of how it came into the owner's possession, on application by letter, pre-paid.

RELIC of the DUKE of WELLINGTON for SALE.—The son of the late well-known haircutter to his Grace the late Duke of Wellington, at Strathfieldsaye, has a small quantity of HAIR, that his father cut from the Duke's head, which he is willing to DISPOSE OF. Any one desirous of possessing such a relic of England's hero are requested to make their offer for the same, by letter.

RELICS of the late DUKE of WELLINGTON.—For SALE, a WAISTCOAT, in good preservation, worn by his Grace some years back, which can be well authenticated as such.

Next, a very choice article—quite unique—the value of which may be presumed to be considerably enhanced by the conclusive impossibility of its being doubted in the least degree by the most suspicious mind.

A MEMENTO of the DUKE of WELLINGTON.—La Mort de Napoleon, Ode d'Alexandre Manzoni, avec la Traduction en Français, par Edmond Angelini, de Venise.—A book, of which the above is the title, was torn up by the Duke and thrown by him from the carriage, in which he was riding, as he was passing through Kent: the pieces of the book were collected and put together by a person who saw the Duke tear it and

throw the same away. Any person desirous of obtaining the above
memento will be communicated with.

Finally, a literary production of astonishing brilliancy
and spirit; without which, we are authorized to state, no
nobleman's or gentleman's library can be considered
complete.

DUKE of WELLINGTON and SIR R. PEEL.—A talented, interesting, and
valuable WORK, on Political Economy and Free Trade, was published
in 1830, and immediately bought up by the above statesmen, except
one copy, which is now for DISPOSAL. Apply by letter only.

Here, for the reader's sake, we terminate our quotations.
They might easily have been extended through the whole
of the present number of this Journal.

We believe that a State Funeral at this time of day—
apart from the mischievously confusing effect it has on the
general mind, as to the necessary union of funeral expense
and pomp with funeral respect, and the consequent injury
it may do to the cause of a great reform most necessary
for the benefit of all classes of society—is, in itself, so
plainly a pretence of being what it is not: is so unreal,
such a substitution of the form for the substance: is so cut
and dried, and stale: is such a palpably got up theatrical
trick: that it puts the dread solemnity of death to flight,
and encourages these shameless traders in their dealings
on the very coffin-lid of departed greatness. That private
letters and other memorials of the great Duke of Wellington
would still have been advertised and sold, though he had
been laid in his grave amid the silent respect of the whole
country with the simple honors of a military commander,
we do not doubt; but that, in that case, the traders would
have been discouraged from holding anything like this
Public Fair and Great Undertakers' Jubilee over his remains,

we doubt as little. It is idle to attempt to connect the
frippery of the Lord Chamberlain's Office and the Herald's
College, with the awful passing away of that vain shadow
in which man walketh and disquieteth himself in vain.
There is a great gulf set between the two which is set
there by no mortal hands, and cannot by mortal hands
be bridged across. Does any one believe that, otherwise,
" the Senate" would have been "mourning its hero" (in
the likeness of a French Field-Marshal) on Tuesday evening,
and that the same Senate would have been in fits of laughter
with Mr. Hume on Wednesday afternoon when the same
hero was still in question and unburied?

The mechanical exigencies of this journal render it
necessary for these remarks to be written on the evening
of the State Funeral. We have already indicated in these
pages that we consider the State Funeral a mistake, and
we hope temperately to leave the question here for temperate
consideration. It is easy to imagine how it may have
done much harm, and it is hard to imagine how it can
have done any good. It is only harder to suppose that
it can have afforded a grain of satisfaction to the immediate
descendants of the great Duke of Wellington, or that it
can reflect the faintest ray of lustre on so bright a name.
If it were assumed that such a ceremonial was the general
desire of the English people, we would reply that that
assumption was founded on a misconception of the popular
character, and on a low estimate of the general sense;
and that the sooner both were better appreciated in high
places, the better it could not fail to be for us all. Taking
for granted at this writing, what we hope may be assumed
without any violence to the truth; namely, that the ceremonial was in all respects well conducted, and that the
English people sustained throughout, the high character

they have nobly earned, to the shame of their silly detractors among their own countrymen; we must yet express our hope that State Funerals in this land went down to their tomb, most fitly, in the tasteless and tawdry Car that nodded and shook through the streets of London on the eighteenth of November, eighteen hundred and fifty-two. And sure we are, with large consideration for opposite opinions, that when History shall rescue that very ugly machine—worthy to pass under decorated Temple Bar, as decorated Temple Bar was worthy to receive it—from the merciful shadows of obscurity, she will reflect with amazement—remembering his true, manly, modest, self-contained, and genuine character—that the man who, in making it the last monster of its race, rendered his last enduring service to the country he had loved and served so faithfully, was Arthur Duke of Wellington.   [1852]

THAT OTHER PUBLIC.

In our ninth volume, [1] it fell naturally in our way to make a few inquiries as to the abiding place of that vague noun of multitude signifying many, The Public. We reminded our readers that it is never forthcoming when it is the subject of a joke at the theatre: which is always perceived to be a hit at some other Public richly deserving it but not present. The circumstances of this time considered, we cannot better commence our eleventh volume, than by gently jogging the memory of that other Public: which is often culpably oblivious of its own duties, rights, and interests, and to which it is perfectly clear that neither we nor our readers are in the least degree related. We are the sensible, reflecting, prompt Public, always up to the mark—wheras that other Public persists in supinely lagging behind, and behaving in an inconsiderate manner.

To begin with a small example lately revived by our friend, *The Examiner* newspaper. What can that other Public mean, by allowing itself to be fleeced every night of its life, by responsible persons whom it accepts for its servants? The case stands thus. Bribes and fees to small officials, had become quite insupportable at the time when the great Railway Companies sprang into existence. All

[1] *Household Words*, volume IX, page 156.

15

such abuses they immediately, and very much to their
credit, struck out of their system of management; the
keepers of hotels were soon generally obliged to follow in
this rational direction; the Public (meaning always, that
other one, of course) were relieved from a most annoying
and exasperating addition to the hurry and worry of travel;
and the reform, as is in the nature of every reform
that is necessary and sensible, extended in many smaller
directions, and was beneficially felt in many smaller ways.
The one persistent and unabashed defyer of it, at this
moment, is the Theatre—which pursues its old obsolete
course of refusing to fulfil its contract with that other
Public, unless that other Public, after paying for its box-
seats or stalls, will also pay the wages of theatre servants
who buy their places that they may prey upon that other
Public. As if we should sell our publisher's post to the
highest bidder, leaving him to charge an additional penny
or twopence, or as much as he could·get, on every number
of *Household Words* with which he should graciously favour
that other Public! Within a week or two of this present
writing, we paid five shillings, at nine o'clock in the evening,
for our one seat at a pantomime; after our cheerful compliance with which demand, a hungry footpad clapped a
rolled-up playbill to our breast, like the muzzle of a pistol,
and positively stood before the door of which he was the
keeper, to prevent our access (without forfeiture of another
shilling for his benefit) to the seat we had purchased.
Now, that other Public still submits to the gross imposition,
notwithstanding that its most popular entertainer has
abandoned all the profit derivable from it, and has plainly
pointed out its manifest absurdity and extortion. And
although to be sure it is universally known that the Theatre,
as an Institution, is in a highly thriving and promising

state, and although we have only to see a play, hap-hazard, to perceive that the great body of ladies and gentlemen representing it, have educated themselves with infinite labour and expense in a variety of accomplishments, and have really qualified for their calling in the true spirit of students of the Fine Arts; yet, we take leave to suggest to that other Public with which, our readers and we are wholly unconnected, that these are no reasons for its being so egregiously gulled.

We just now mentioned Railway Companies. That other Public is very jealous of Railway Companies. It is not unreasonable in being so, for, it is quite at their mercy; we merely observe that it is not usually slow to complain of them when it has any cause. It has remonstrated, in its time, about rates of Fares, and has adduced instances of their being undoubtedly too high. But, has that other Public ever heard of a preliminary system from which the Railway Companies have no escape, and which runs riot in squandering treasure to an incredible amount, before they have excavated one foot of earth or laid a bar of iron on the ground? Why does that other Public never begin at the beginning, and raise its voice against the monstrous charges of soliciting private bills in Parliament, and conducting inquiries before Committees of the House of Commons—allowed on all hands to be the very worst tribunals conceivable by the mind of man? Has that other Public any adequate idea of the corruption, profusion, and waste, occasioned by this process of misgovernment? Supposing it were informed that, ten years ago, the average Parliamentary and law expenses of all the then existing Railway Companies amounted to a charge of seven hundred pounds a mile on every mile of railway made in the United Kingdom, would it be startled? But,

supposing it were told in the next breath, that this charge
was really—not seven, but SEVENTEEN HUNDRED POUNDS
A MILE, what would that other Public (on whom, of course,
every farthing of it falls), say then? Yet this is the
statement, in so many words and figures, of a document
issued by the Board of Trade, and which is now rather
scarce—as well it may be, being a perilous curiosity.
That other Public may learn from the same pages, that
on the Law and Parliamentary expenses of a certain
Stone and Rugby Line, the Bill for which was lost (and
the Line consequently not made after all), there was
expended the modest little preliminary total of one hundred
and forty-six thousand pounds! That was in the joyful
days when counsel learned in Parliamentary Law, refused
briefs marked with one hundred guinea fees, and accepted
the same briefs marked with one thousand guinea fees;
the attorney making the neat addition of a third cipher,
on the spot, with a presence of mind suggestive of his own
little bill against that other Public (quite dissociated from
us as aforesaid), at whom our readers and we are now
bitterly smiling. That was also in the blessed times when,
there being no Public Health Act, Whitechapel paid to the
tutelary deities, Law and Parliament, six thousand five
hundred pounds, to be graciously allowed to pull down,
for the public good, a dozen odious streets inhabited by
Vice and Fever.

Our Public know all about these things, and *our* Public
are not blind to their enormity. It is that other Public,
somewhere or other—where can it be?—which is always
getting itself humbugged and talked over. It has been in
a maze of doubt and confusion, for the last three or four
years, on that vexed question, the Liberty of the Press.
It has been told by Noble Lords that the said Liberty is

vastly inconvenient. No doubt it is. No doubt all Liberty is—to some people. Light is highly inconvenient to such as have their sufficient reasons for preferring darkness; and soap and water is observed to be a particular inconvenience to those who would rather be dirty than clean. But, that other Public finding the Noble Lords much given to harping between whiles, in a sly dull way, on this string, became uneasy about it, and wanted to know what the harpers would have—wanted to know, for instance, how they would direct and guide this dangerous Press. Well, now they may know. If that other Public will ever learn, their instruction-book, very lately published, is open before them. Chapter one is a High Court of Justice; chapter two is a history of personal adventure, whereof they may hear more, perhaps, one of these days. The Queen's Representative in a most important part of the United Kingdom—a thorough gentleman, and a man of unimpeachable honour beyond all kind of doubt—knows so little of this Press, that he is seen in secret personal communication with tainted and vile instruments which it rejects, buying their praise with the public money, overlooking their dirty work, and setting them their disgraceful tasks. One of the great national departments in Downing Street is exhibited under strong suspicion of like ignorant and disreputable dealing, to purchase remote puffery among the most puff-ridden people ever propagated on the face of this earth. *Our* Public know this very well, and have, of course, taken it thoroughly to heart, in its many suggestive aspects; but, when will that other Public—always lagging behindhand in some out of the way place—become informed about it, and consider it, and act upon it?

It is impossible to over-state the completeness with which *our* Public have got to the marrow of the true question arising out of the condition of the British Army before Sebastopol. *Our* Public knew perfectly, that, making every deduction for haste, obstruction, and natural strength of feeling in the midst of goading experiences, the correspondence of *The Times* has revealed a confused heap of mismanagement, imbecility, and disorder, under which the nation's bravery lies crushed and withered. *Our* Public is profoundly acquainted with the fact that this is not a new kind of disclosure, but, that similar defection and incapacity have before prevailed at similar periods until the labouring age has heaved up a man strong enough to wrestle with the Misgovernment of England and throw it on its back. Wellington and Nelson both did this, and the next great General and Admiral—for whom we now impatiently wait, but may wait some time, content (if we can be) to know that it is not the tendency of our service, by sea or land, to help the greatest Merit to rise—must do the same, and will assuredly do it, and by that sign ye shall know them. *Our* Public reflecting deeply on these materials for cogitation, will henceforth hold fast by the truth, that the system of administering their affairs is innately bad; that classes and families and interests, have brought them to a very low pass; that the intelligence, steadfastness, foresight, and wonderful power of resource, which in private undertakings distinguish England from all other countries, have no vitality in its public business; that while every merchant and trader has enlarged his grasp and quickened his faculties, the Public Departments have been drearily lying in state, a mere stupid pageant of gorgeous coffins and feebly-burning lights; and that the windows must now be opened wide, and the candles put out, and the coffins buried, and the daylight freely admitted, and the

furniture made firewood, and the dirt clean swept away.
This is the lesson from which *our* Public is nevermore to
be distracted by any artifice, we all know. But, that
other Public. What will *they* do? They are a humane,
generous, ardent Public; but, will they hold like grim
Death to the flower Warning, we have plucked from
this nettle War? Will they steadily reply to all cajolers,
that though every flannel waistcoat in the civilized, and
every bearskin and buffalo-skin in the uncivilized, world,
had been sent out in these days to our ill-clad countrymen
(and never reached them), they would not in the least
affect the lasting question, or dispense with a single item
of the amendment proved to be needful, and, until made,
to be severely demanded, in the whole household and
system of Britannia? When the war is over, and that
other Public, always ready for a demonstration, shall be
busy throwing up caps, lighting up houses, beating drums,
blowing trumpets, and making hundreds of miles of printed
columns of speeches, will they be flattered and wordily-
pumped dry of the one plain issue left, or will they
remember it? O that other Public! If we—you, and I,
and all the rest of us—could only make sure of that other
Public!

Would it not be a most extraordinary remissness on
the part of that other Public, if it were content, in a crisis
of uncommon difficulty, to laugh at a Ministry without a
Head, and leave it alone? Would it not be a wonderful
instance of the shortcomings of that other Public, if it
were never seen to stand aghast at the supernatural imbecility of that authority to which, in a dangerous hour,
it confided the body and soul of the nation? *We* know
what a sight it would be to behold that miserable patient,
Mr. Cabinet, specially calling his relations and friends

together before Christmas, tottering on his emaciated legs
in the last stage of paralysis, and feebly piping that if
such and such powers were not entrusted to him for instant use, he would certainly go raving mad of defeated
patriotism, and pluck his poor old wretched eyes out in
despair; *we* know with what disdainful emotions we should
see him gratified and then shuffle away and go to sleep:
to make no use of what he had got, and be heard of no
more until one of his nurses, more irritable than the rest,
should pull his weazen nose and make him whine—*we*
know, what these experiences would be to us, and Bless
us! *we* should act upon them in round earnest—but, where
is that other Public, whose indifference is the life of such
scarecrows, and whom it would seem that not even plague
pestilence and famine, battle murder and sudden death,
can rouse?

There is one comfort in all this. We English are not
the only victims of that other Public. It is to be heard
of, elsewhere. It got across the Atlantic, in the train of the
Pilgrim Fathers, and has frequently been achieving wonders in
America. Ten or eleven years ago, one Chuzzlewit was heard
to say, that he had found it on that side of the water, doing
the strangest things. The assertion made all sorts of
Publics angry, and there was quite a cordial combination
of Publics to resent it and disprove it. But there *is* a
little book of Memoirs to be heard of at the present time,
which looks as if young Chuzzlewit had reason in him
too. Does the "smart" Showman, who makes such a
Mermaid, and makes such a Washington's Nurse, and
makes such a Dwarf, and makes such a Singing Angel
upon earth, and makes such a fortune, and, above all,
makes such a book—does *he* address the free and enlightened Public of the great United States, the Public of

State Schools, Liberal Tickets, First-chop Intelligence, and Universal Education? No, no. That other Public is the sharks'-prey. It is that other Public, down somewhere or other, whose bright particular star and stripe are not yet ascertained, which is so transparently cheated and so hardily outfaced. For that other Public, the hatter of New York outbid Creation at the auction of the first Lind seat. For that other Public, the Lind speeches were made, the tears shed, the serenades given. It is that other Public, always on the boil and ferment about anything or nothing, whom the travelling companion shone down upon from the high Hotel-Balconies. It is that other Public who will read, and even buy, the smart book in which they have so proud a share, and who will fly into raptures about its being circulated from the old Ocean Cliffs of the Old Granite State to the Rocky Mountains. It is indubitably in reference to that other Public that we find the following passage in a book called American Notes.

"Another prominent feature is the love of 'smart' dealing, which gilds over many a swindle and gross breach of trust, many a defalcation, public and private; and enables many a knave to hold his head up with the best, who well deserves a halter—though it has not been without its retributive operation; for, this smartness has done more in a few years to impair the public credit and to cripple the public resources, than dull honesty, however rash, could have effected in a century. The merits of a broken speculation, or a bankruptcy, or of a successful scoundrel, are not gauged by its or his observance of the golden rule, 'Do as you would be done by', but are considered with reference to their smartness. The following dialogue I have held a hundred times:—'Is it not a very disgraceful circumstance that such a man as So and So should be acquiring a large property by the most infamous and odious means; and, notwithstanding all the crimes of which he has been guilty, should be tolerated and abetted by your Citizens? He is a public nuisance, is he not?'—'Yes, sir'—'A convicted liar?'—'Yes, sir.'—'He has been kicked and cuffed and caned?'—'Yes, sir.'—'And he is utterly dishonourable, debased, and profligate?'—'Yes, sir.'—'In the name of wonder, then, what is his merit?'—'Well, sir, he is a smart man.'"

That other Public of our own bore their full share, and more, of bowing down before the Dwarf aforesaid, in despite of his obviously being too young a child to speak plainly: and *we*, the Public who are never taken in, will not excuse their folly. So, if John on this shore, and Jonathan over there, could each only get at that troublesome other Public of his, and brighten them up a little, it would be very much the better for both brothers.

[1855

I AM a poor clerk, who, being out of employment, was on that morning travelling to Southampton to present myself to the firm of Heavahoy Brothers, in some little hope of procuring occupation in their counting-house. To my eyes things were dreary down below, for I am thirty-five years old, and do not see my way yet to a marriage with poor Lucy Jane whose first love-letter to me was dated in the year one thousand eight hundred and thirty-nine. I have been earning my own living for seventeen years, and have saved up to this date eighty-one pounds two shillings and ninepence. Nevertheless, Lucy Jane's friends, who are exceedingly respectable, consider me unable to keep myself, and still less able to keep a wife. What does the great world care about that? Nothing at all, to be sure, and yet it is to my purpose to say so much, for I desire it to be seen whether I had not full reason to be dismal on that morning of which I speak. Hopes and fears as to the success of my application to the Heavahoys had kept me awake all night. There are foreign agencies connected with their house for which my ambition was, if I once entered the service of the firm, to become qualified. With a view to some such opening I had been learning Spanish. My hope had come to be that I might some day carry Lucy Jane to Buenos Ayres, or some other distant place. No matter. I lay awake all night and rose, unrefreshed, at an uncomfortable hour. I left a half eaten breakfast to hurry to the Waterloo Road, running through rain in close May weather, with a great coat on my back, a carpet-bag in one hand and an umbrella in the other. I arrived at the station hot, damp, weary, wretched, and took my place in a third-class carriage with a discontented man close at my elbow and a crowd of noisy market people round about. I looked forward to the journey with dread. I was eager to be at the other end, and we were bound to lag on the road, stopping at every station.

The first bell had rung. Suddenly it occurred to me that I would have a book. It was long since I had added one to the small stock from which I got solace of evenings in my lodgings. I had saved two shillings in cab-hire, and I was saving more than five shillings by travelling third-class. For my run through the wet and my discomfort on the road I would repay myself by spending on a book half of what I had saved in travelling expense. That would be three shillings and sixpence. I had only time to jump upon the platform, hurry to the railway-stall and take—partly for the name's sake of its author, partly because the price was fitted to my notion—a volume of Leigh Hunt's Stories in Verse. With that in my hand I regained my seat; the door was beaten in after me; the second bell rang, and the engine heaved us out into the misty weather.

For a time my sad thoughts were my only company. I paid no attention to the chimneys among which we passed, or to the meaning of the noise made by my companions, or to the talisman against dullness that reposed

upon my lap. A stench aroused me suddenly. The train
was passing near the Thames at Lambeth, and getting
among the pest manufactories. I looked out of window,
and saw them through the rain. Close by the line of rail
were miserable garret windows; back yards choked with
enormous dust-heaps; tumble-down sheds and despondent
poultry.

"Call this May, sir?" cried my neighbour, shivering
uncomfortably. "I hope you don't object to tobacco?"

I smiled faintly. Nothing disgusts me more than the
addition of the smoke of bad tobacco to an atmosphere
already loaded with the smoke out of the damp bodies
and clothes of dirty men. But I am bound to love my
fellow-creatures, and be courteous to them. I smiled
faintly and opened my book, to begin Leigh Hunt's Story
of Rimini:

"The sun is up, and 'tis a morn of May round old
Ravenna's clear-shown towers and bay—a morn the love-
liest which the year has seen, last of the spring, yet fresh
with all its green. For a warm eve and gentle rains at
night have left a sparkling welcome for the light. And
there's a crystal clearness all about—the leaves are sharp,
the distant hills look out. A balmy briskness comes upon
the breeze, the smoke goes dancing from the cottage trees;
and when you listen you may hear a coil of bubbling
springs about the grassier soil; and all the scene, in short—
earth, sky, and sea, breathes like a bright-eyed face, that
laughs out openly."

Thereat I was myself almost ready to laugh out openly
with ease and pleasure; for my heavens and my earth
were changed. I did not raise my eye from the page of
the poet to look freely out upon the broad horizon whence
my heart was gladly stirred to see "the far ships, lifting

their sails of white like joyful hands, come up with scattered light—come gleaming up, true to the wished-for day, and chase the whistling brine and swirl into the bay."

Those words stand in the book line under line because they are poetry; but they speak quite as well to the heart written like prose, straight on together—also because they are poetry. Never mind that. What do the ships bring?—Why are the people who make holiday all crowding to Ravenna? It is because there "peace returning and processions rare, princes and donatives and faces fair, and, to crown all, a marriage in May weather, are summonses to bring blithe souls together. For on this great glad day, Ravenna's pride, the daughter of their prince, becomes a bride, a bride to ransom an exhausted land; and he whose victories have obtained her hand has taken with the dawn—so flies report—his promised journey to the expecting court, with hasting pomp and squires of high degree, the bold Giovanni, lord of Rimini." And having told me this, the poet took me down into the streets of the gay city, filled my ears with the stir of feet, the hum, the talk, the laugh, callings and clapping doors; filled my eyes with the spectacle of arméd bands making important way, gallant and grave, the lords of holiday; caused me to note the greetings of the neighbours; to pass through the crowds of pilgrims chanting in the morning sun; to see the tapestry spread in the windows, and the fair dames who took their seats with upward gaze admired—some looking down, some forwards or aside; some re-adjusting tresses newly tied: some turning a trim waist, or o'er the flow of crimson cloths hanging a hand of snow; but all with smiles prepared and garlands green, and all in fluttering talk impatient for the scene. Glorious fortune for a poor fellow like me to chance to be at Ravenna on a day like that!

The train stopped. "Clapham! Clapham!" shouted a far distant voice. Strange that I should have been able to hear at Ravenna the voice of a man shouting at Clapham!

I paid not much heed to the marvel; for there was Duke Guido seated with his fair daughter over the marble gate of his palace; there was the square before them kept with guards; there were knights and ladies on a grass plot sitting under boughs of rose and laurel, and in the midst, fresh whistling through the scene, a lightsome fountain starts from out the green, clear and compact, till at its height o'errun, it shakes its loosening silver in the sun. The courtly knights are bending down in talk over the ladies, and the people are all looking up with love and wonder at the princely maid, the daughter of Duke Guido, the bride sought with so much pomp by a bridegroom whom she never saw, the sad and fair Francesca.

Now the procession comes with noise of cavalry and trumpets clear, a princely music unbedinned with drums; the mighty brass seems opening as it comes; and now it fills and now it shakes the air, and now it bursts into the sounding square. I saw the whole of it. In magic verse the story-teller caused trumpeter and heralds, squires and knights, to prance before me. Mine was a front place for looking at the show. I noted the dresses and the jewels, and the ladies' favours of the knights; the action of the horses and the faces of the riders; the life, the carelessness, the sudden heed; the body curving to the rearing steed; the patting hand, that best persuades the check, makes the quarrel up with a proud neck—the thigh broad-pressed, the spanning palm upon it, and the jerk'd feather flowing on the bonnet. Then came, after an interval of stately length, a troop of steeds, milk-white and unattired, Arabian bred, each by a blooming boy lightsomely led. What next? The pages of the court, in rows of three—of white and crimson is their livery. Space after space, and still the trains appear—a fervid whisper fills the general ear. Ah! yes—no—'tis not he, but 'tis the squires who go before him when his pomp requires. And now his huntsman shows the lessening train—now the squire carver and the chamberlain. And now his banner comes, and now his shield, borne by the squire that waits him to the field. And then an interval—a lordly space—a pin-drop's silence strikes o'er all the place. The princess from a distance scarcely knows which way to look; her colour comes and goes, and with an impulse and affection free, she lays her hand upon her father's knee, who looks upon her with a labour'd smile, gathering it up into his own the while. When some one's voice, as if it knew not how to check itself, exclaims, "The Prince! Now—now!" And on a milk-white courser, like the air, a glorious figure springs into the square. Up with a burst of thunder goes the shout—["Wimbledon and Malden! Wimbledon and Malden! Passengers for Wimbledon and Malden!"]—and rolls the echoing walls and peopled roofs about.

The noble youth, at sight of whom surprise, relief, a joy scarce understood, something, perhaps, of very gratitude, and fifty feelings, undefined and new, danced through the bride and flushed her faded hue, was Paulo. And, alas for a fair maiden's love, he was to be no more to her than the brother of the bridegroom, by whom he had been sent as proxy to be wedded in his name and to convey the bride to Rimini. To Paulo poor Francesca gave her hand in mockery, her heart in truth. And as I read more of her tale the rainy weather found its way into my eyes, so that I even murmured to myself after Giovanni when he stood over the dead youth, "And, Paulo, thou wert the completest knight that ever rode with banner to the fight; and thou wert the most beautiful to see that ever came in press of chivalry; and of a sinful man thou wert the best that ever for his friend put spear in rest; and thou wert the most meek and cordial that ever among ladies ate in hall; and thou wert still, for all that bosom gor'd, the kindest man that ever struck with sword."

"I could walk faster than this train is going," said my discontented neighbour; "we shall never see our journey's end—it's shameful!"

I had the end to see of Francesca, and I did not answer him. How could I? I knew nothing about the journey—it was his journey, not mine—why should he talk to me about it? But I had not remained much longer absorbed in my book before my discontented neighbour put his head, pipe and all, into my face to say,—

"Esher, sir! We have been twenty minutes coming from Kingston Junction—twen-ty minutes! I ask you, sir, is it not shameful?"

"Doubtless; I have not noticed."

"Not noticed, sir! Perhaps you've an objection to fast travelling?"

"I—I don't think we've been sitting in the same train. I was just thinking how agreeable it was to be carried in one minute from Rimini to the Hellespont, only to see Hero and Leander."

"O! where next?"

"Why, sir," I said, turning a leaf or two, "my next station, I see, is in Sherwood Forest; I am to stop there to make friends with Robin Hood."

"The writer of that book drives a long excursion-train. I wouldn't mind a word with Robin Hood myself, God

16

bless him! but, as for your poets, I hate them all: they tie their English into knots, and want a mile of it—knots and all—to say 'fine weather for the ducks,' as, truly, it is this morning—Ugh!"

"I say nothing of that, sir; I have nothing just now in my mind except this book of stories—which is just a book of stories, all of them good ones, written in such verse as may be read by rich and poor with almost equal pleasure. They are only told in verse in order that the music may give force and beauty to the sense; read them or print them how you will, you cannot destroy their music or convict them of being by a syllable too wordy; they discharge their burden in plain sentences, without even going out of their way to avoid expressions common in the mouths of the people. Every picture in them is poetical in its conception, and in its expression musical. There is nothing far-fetched—there is no mystification; these are just stories in verse which may be enjoyed by the entire mass of the people. There is even as little as possible of simple meditation in them, though that would have been welcome from the mind of a pure-hearted man, beloved of poets in his youth and in his prime, now worthy to be loved of all mankind. Of him there are fewer to speak ill than even of Robin Hood, when not a soul in Locksley town would speak him an ill-word; the friars raged; but no man's tongue nor even feature stirred; except among a very few, who dined in the abbey halls; and then with a sigh bold Robin knew his true friends from his false." I was not talking or reading to my neighbour with the pipe. I do not know at what stage of my discourse or meditation I had left my hold upon his ear. I had been thinking about Leigh Hunt to myself, and went on reading to myself of those unfaithful comrades, Roger the monk, and Midge, on whom Robin had never turned his face but tenderly; with one or two, they say, besides— Lord! that in this life's dream men should abandon one true thing, that would abide with them.

> We cannot bid our strength remain,
> Our cheeks continue round;
> We cannot say to an aged back,
> Stoop not towards the ground:
>
> We cannot bid our dim eyes see,
> Things as bright as ever,
> Nor tell our friends, though friends from youth,
> That they'll forsake us never:
>
> But we can say, I never will,
> False world, be false for thee:
> And oh, Sound Truth and Old Regard,
> Nothing shall part us three.

"Woking Junction! Woking! Passengers for Guildford, Godalming, and Alton, change here!"

I did not change there, but sat reading the brave legend of the knight who cured a lady of disdain by doing battle in a shift against three warriors in steel—a story with a pure and tender moral for the innocent, the noble, and the wise. And when the train was off again I was not travelling by train at all, but humming to myself—"The palfrey goes, the palfrey goes, merrily well the palfrey goes; he carrieth laughter, he carrieth woes, yet merrily ever the palfrey goes." For I was reading then of Sir Grey and Sir Guy, the proper old boys, who met with a world of coughing, and noise, to mar young love like mine and Lucy Jane's. O! if we had but a horse that could in our behalf take, like the palfrey, vigorous courses! Well, but never mind that. The palfrey carried me merrily well to Farnborough, where there was a great tournament with lions in the presence of King Francis, and a knight taught vanity a lesson. The rest of the journey was a feast of little stories. I was shown what passed between Abou-ben-Adhem and the Angel, told how the brave Mondeer, in spite of the Sultan's order that no man should praise the dead Jaffàr, stood forth in Bagdad daily in the square where once had stood a happy house, and there harangued the tremblers at the scimetar on all they owed to the divine Jaffàr. "Bring me this man," the caliph cried. The man was brought—was gazed upon—the mutes began to bind his arms. "Welcome, brave cords!" cried he; "from bonds far worse Jaffàr delivered me; from wants, from shames, from loveless household fears; made a man's eyes friends with delicious tears; restored me—loved me —put me on a par with his great self. How can I pay Jaffàr?" Hàroun, who felt that on a soul like this, the mightiest vengeance could but fall amiss, now deigned to smile, as one great lord of fate might smile upon another half as great. He said, "Let worth grow frenzied if it will; the caliph's judgment shall be master still. Go: and since gifts thus move thee, take this gem, the richest in the Tartar's diadem, and hold the giver as thou deemest fit"—"Gifts!" cried the friend. He took; and holding it high tow'rds the heavens, as though to meet his star, exclaimed, "This, too, I owe to thee, Jaffàr."

More stories, as full of pleasant wit and noble feeling, were told me after this; and when we got to Basingstoke, where my neighbour swore a good deal at a crowd of market people who had blocked him (and I suppose me) up with huge baskets and wet umbrellas, I had been introduced to Chaucer, and was riding on the brazen horse of Cambus Khan. The brazen horse which in a day and night, through the dark half as safely as the light, o'er sea and land, and with your perfect ease, can bear your body wheresoe'er you please. (It matters not if skies be foul or fair; the thing is like a thought, and cuts the air so smoothly, and so well observes the track, the man that will may sleep upon his back). This brazen horse, I say, suddenly dropped me at Southampton. There were some stories told by the Italian poets told again in English waiting to be heard, Dante's own Paulo and Francesca; his story of Ugolino; Ariosto's Medora and Cloridano. I was vexed that I had reached my journey's end, and must in that day read no more; began to observe with surprise that it was raining; to look for the first time at some of my departing fellow-passengers; to resent the smell of my neighbour's bad tobacco, that impregnated my clothes; to think about my carpet bag, and all my troubles; not resenting them, because my book had tuned me to a brave endurance of the troubles of this world, with, I believe, the sole exception of the smell of stale tobacco. I had made two journeys at one time, by packing off my body as a parcel to Southampton, while all the rest of me, having paid a trifling sum for a perpetual ticket (which I shall take heed to keep by me) set out in company with a right genial and noble story-teller to Parnassus. Nevertheless, there was the whole of me at Heavahoy's when wanted, and I am happy to say that from the counting house of that substantial firm I date the present communication. I have told a plain traveller's tale about travellers' tales, which, as the teller of them hopes, will be read and shown to one another by travellers who are descendants of those travellers about whom Chaucer discoursed: men who beguiled each other's way with tales as they rode side by side on horseback, while yet all horses in existence were of flesh and blood.   [1855]

THE disclosures in reference to the adulteration of Food, Drinks, and Drugs, for which the public are indebted to the vigor and spirit of our contemporary *The Lancet*, lately inspired us with the idea of originating a Commission to inquire into the extensive adulteration of certain other articles which it is of the last importance that the country should possess in a genuine state. Every class of the general public was included in this large Commission; and the whole of the analyses, tests, observations, and experiments, were made by that accomplished practical chemist, Mr. Bull.

The first subject of inquiry was that article of universal consumption familiarly known in England as "Government." Mr. Bull produced a sample of this commodity, purchased about the middle of July in the present year, at a wholesale establishment in Downing Street. The first remark to be made on the sample before the Commission, Mr. Bull observed, was its excessive dearness. There was little doubt that the genuine article could be furnished to the public, at a fairer profit to the real producers, for about fifty per cent. less than the cost price of the specimen under consideration. In quality, the specimen was of an exceedingly poor and low description; being deficient in flavor, character, clearness, brightness, and almost every other requisite. It was what would be popularly termed wishy-washy, muddled, and flat. Mr. Bull pointed out to the Commission, floating on the top of this sample, a volatile ingredient, which he considered had no business there. It might be harmless enough, taken into the system at a debating-society, or after a public dinner, or a comic song; but in its present connection, it was dangerous. It had not improved with ceeping. It had come into use as a ready means of making froth, but froth was exactly what ought not to be found at the top of this article, or indeed in any part of it. The sample before the Commission, was frightfully adulterated with immense infusions of the common weed called Talk. Talk, in such combination, was a rank Poison. He had obtained a precipitate of Corruption from this purchase. He did not mean metallic corruption, as deposits of gold, silver or copper; but, that species of corruption which, on the proper tests being applied, turned white into black, and black into white, and likewise engendered quantities of parasite vermin. He had tested the strength of the sample, and found it not nearly up to the mark. He had detected the presence of a Grey deposit in one large Department, which produced vacillation and weakness; indisposition to action to-day, and action upon compulsion to-morrow. He considered the sample, on the whole, decidedly unfit for use. Mr. Bull went on to say, that he had purchased another specimen of the same commodity at an opposition establishment over the way, which bore the sign of the British Lion, and proclaimed itself, with the aid of a Brass Band, as "The only genuine and patriotic shop;" but, that he had found it equally deleterious; and that he had not succeeded in discovering any dealer in the commodity under consideration who sold it in a genuine or wholesome state.

The bitter drug called Public Offices, formed the next subject of inquiry. Mr. Bull produced an immense number of samples of this drug, obtained from shops in Downing Street, Whitehall, Palace Yard, the Strand, and elsewhere. Analysis had detected in every one of them, from seventy-five to ninety-eight per cent. of Noodledom. Noodledom was a deadly poison. An over-dose of it would destroy a whole nation, and he had known a recent case where it had caused the death of many thousand men. It was sometimes called Routine, sometimes Gentlemanly Business, sometimes The Best Intentions, and sometimes Amiable Incapacity; but, call it what you would, analysis always resolved it into Noodledom. There was nothing in the whole united domains of the animal, vegetable, and mineral kingdoms, so incompatible with all the functions of life as Noodledom. It was producible with most unfortunate ease. Transplant anything from soil and conditions it was fit for, to soil and conditions it was not fit for, and you immediately had Noodledom. The germs of self-propagation contained within this baleful poison, were incalculable: Noodledom uniformly and constantly engendering Noodledom, until every available inch of space was over-run by it. The history of the adulteration of the drug now before the Commission, he conceived to be this:—Every wholesale dealer in that drug was sure to have on hand, in beginning business, a large stock of Noodledom; which was extremely cheap, and lamentably abundant. He immediately mixed the drug with the poison. Now, it was the peculiarity of the Public-Office trade that the wholesale dealers were constantly retiring from business, and having successors. A new dealer came into possession of the already adulterated stock, and he, in his turn, infused into it a fresh quantity of Noodledom

from his own private store. Then, on his retirement,
came another dealer who did the same; then, on *his*
retirement, another dealer who did the same; and so on.
Thus, many of the samples before the Commission,
positively contained nothing but Noodledom—enough, in
short, to paralyze the whole country. To the question,
whether the useful properties of the drug before the
Commission were not of necessity impaired by these
malpractices, Mr. Bull replied, that all the samples were
perniciously weakened, and that half of them were good
for nothing. To the question, how he would remedy a
state of things so much to be deplored, Mr. Bull replied,
that he would take the drug out of the hands of mercenary
dealers altogether.

Mr. Bull next exhibited three or four samples of
Lawn-sleeves, warranted at the various establishments
from which they had been procured, to be fine and
spotless, but evidently soiled and composed of inferior
materials ill made up. On one pair, he pointed out
extensive stains of printer's-ink, of a very foul kind; also
a coarse interweaving, which on examination clearly betrayed,
without the aid of the microscope, the fibres of the thistle,
Old Bailey Attorneyism. A third pair of these sleeves,
though sold as white, were really nothing but the ordinary
Mammon pattern, chalked over—a fact which Mr. Bull
showed to be beyond dispute, by merely holding them up
to the light. He represented this branch of industry as
over-stocked, and in an unhealthy condition.

There were then placed upon the table, several samples
of British Peasant, to which Mr. Bull expressed himself
as particularly solicitous to draw the attention of the
Commission, with one plain object: the good of his beloved
country. He remarked that with that object before him,

he would not inquire into the general condition, whether perfectly healthy or otherwise, of any of the samples now produced. He would not ask, whether this specimen or that specimen might have been stronger, larger, better fitted for wear and tear, and less liable to early decay, if the human creature were reared with a little more of such care, study, and attention, as were rightfully bestowed on the vegetable world around it. But, the samples before the Commission had been obtained from every county in England, and, though brought from opposite parts of the kingdom, were alike deficient in the ability to defend their country by handling a gun or a sword, or by uniting in any mode of action, as a disciplined body. It was said in a breath, that the English were not a military people, and that they made (equally on the testimony of their friends and enemies), the best soldiers in the world. He hoped that in a time of war and common danger he might take the liberty of putting those opposite assertions into the crucible of Common Sense, consuming the Humbug, and producing the Truth—at any rate he would, whether or no. Now, he begged to inform the Commission that, in the samples before them and thousands of others, he had carefully analysed and tested the British Peasant, and had found him to hold in combination just the same qualities that he always had possessed. Analysing and testing, however, as a part of the inquiry, certain other matters not fairly to be separated from it, he (Mr. Bull) had found the said Peasant to have been some time ago disarmed by lords and gentlemen who were jealous of their game, and by administrations—hirers of spies and suborners of false witnesses—who were jealous of their power. "So, if you wish to restore to these samples," said Mr. Bull, "the serviceable quality that I find to be wanting in them, and the absence of which so much surprises you, be a little more patriotic and a little less timorously selfish; trust your Peasant a little more; instruct him a little better, in a freeman's knowledge—not in a good child's merely; and you will soon have your Saxon Bowmen with percussion rifles, and may save the charges of your Foreign Legion. "

Having withdrawn the samples to which his observations referred—the production whereof, in connection with Mr. Bull's remarks, had powerfully impressed the assembled Commission, some of whom even went so far as to register vows on the spot that they would look into this matter some day—Mr. Bull laid before the Commission a great variety of extremely fine specimens of genuine British Job. He expressed his opinion that these thriving Plants upon the public property, were absolutely immortal: so surprisingly did . they flourish, and so perseveringly were they cultivated. Job was the only article he had found in England, in a perfectly unadulterated state. He congratulated the Commission on there being at least one commodity enjoyed by Great Britain, with which nobody successfully meddled, and of which the Public always had an ample supply, unattended by the smallest prospect of failure in the perennial crop.

On the subsidence of the sensation of pleasure with which this gratifying announcement was received, Mr. Bull informed the Commission, that he now approached the most serious and the most discouraging part of his task. He would not shrink from a faithful description of the laborious and painful analysis which formed the crown of his labors, but he would prepare the Commission to be shocked by it. With these introductory words, he laid before them a specimen of Representative Chamber.

When the Commission had examined, obviously with emotions of the most poignant and painful nature, the miserable sample produced, Mr. Bull proceeded with his description. The specimen of Representative Chamber to which he invited their anxious attention, was brought from Westminster Market. It had been collected there in the month of July in the present year. No particular counter had been resorted to more than another, but the whole market had been laid under contribution to furnish the sample. Its diseased condition would be apparent, without any scientific aids, to the most short-sighted individual. It was fearfully adulterated with Talk, stained with Job, and diluted with large quantities of coloring matter of a false and deceptive nature. It was thickly overlaid with a varnish which he had resolved into its component parts, and had found to be made of Trash (both maudlin and defiant), boiled up with large quantities of Party Turpitude, and a heap of Cant. Cant, he need not tell the Commission, was the worst of poisons. It was almost inconceivable to him how an article in itself so wholesome as Representative Chamber, could have been got into this disgraceful state. It was mere Carrion, wholly unfit for human consumption, and calculated to produce nausea and vomiting.

On being questioned by the Commission, whether, in addition to the deleterious substances already mentioned, he had detected the presence of Humbug in the sample before them, Mr. Bull replied, "Humbug? Rank Humbug, in one form or another, pervades the entire mass." He went on to say, that he thought it scarcely in human nature to endure, for any length of time, the close contemplation of this specimen: so revolting was it to all the senses. Mr. Bull was asked, whether he could account;

first, for this alarming degeneracy in an article so important to the Public; and secondly, for its acceptance by the Public? The Commission observing that however the stomachs of the people might revolt at it—and justly— still they did endure it, and did look on at the Market in which it was exposed. In answer to these inquiries, Mr. Bull offered the following explanation.

In respect of the wretched condition of the article itself (he said), he attributed that result, chiefly, to its being in the hands of those unprincipled wholesale dealers, to whom he had already referred. When one of those dealers succeeded to a business—or "came in," according to the slang of the trade—his first proceeding, after the adultera- tion of Public Office with Noodledom, was to consider how he could adulterate and lower his Representative Chamber. This he did by a variety of arts, recklessly employing the dirtiest agents. Now, the trade had been so long in the hands of these men, and one of them had so uniformly imitated another (however violent their trade-opposition might be among themselves), in adulterating this commodity, that respectable persons who wished to do business fairly, had been prevented from investing their capital, whatever it might be, in this branch of commerce, and had indeed been heard to declare in many instances that they would prefer the calling of an honest scavenger. Again, it was to be observed, that the before— mentioned dealers, being for the most part in a large way, had numbers of retainers, tenants, tradesmen, and workpeople, upon whom they put off their bad Represent- ative Chamber, by compelling them to take it whether they liked it or not. In respect of the acceptance of this dreadful commodity by the Public, Mr. Bull observed, that it was not to be denied that the Public had been much too prone to accept the coloring matter in preference to the genuine article. Sometimes it was Blood, and sometimes it was Beer; sometimes it was Talk, and sometimes it was Cant; but, mere coloring-matter they certainly had too often looked for, when they should have looked for bone and sinew. They suffered heavily for it now, and he believed were penitent; there was no doubt whatever in his mind that they had arrived at the mute stage of indignation, and had thoroughly found this article out.

One further question was put by the Commission: namely, what hope had the witness of seeing this necessary of English life, restored to a genuine and wholesome state? Mr. Bull returned, that his sole hope was in the Public's resolutely rejecting all coloring matter whatsoever—in their being equally inexorable with the dealers, whether they threatened or cajoled—and in their steadily insisting on being provided with the commodity in a pure and useful form. The Commission then adjourned, in exceedingly low spirits, *sine die.*   [1855]

THE WORTHY MAGISTRATE.

UNDER this stereotyped title expressive of deference to the police-bench, we take the earliest opportunity afforded us by our manner of preparing this publication, of calling upon every Englishman who reads these pages to take notice what he is. The circulation of this journal comprising a wide diversity of classes, we use it to disseminate the information that every Englishman is a drunkard. Drunkenness is the national characteristic. Whereas the German people (when uncontaminated by the English), are always sober, the English, setting at nought the bright example of the pure Germans domiciled among them, are always drunk. The authority for this polite and faithful exposition of the English character, is a modern Solomon, whose temple rears its head near Drury Lane; the wise Mr. Hall, Chief Police Magistrate, sitting at Bow Street, Covent Garden, in the County of Middlesex, Barrister at Law.

As we hope to keep this household word of Drunkard, affixed to the Englishman by the awful Mr. Hall from whom there is no appeal, pretty steadily before our readers, we present the very pearl discovered in that magisterial oyster. On Thursday, the ninth of this present month of August, the following sublime passage evoked the virtuous laughter of the thieftakers of Bow Street:

MR. HALL.—Were you sober, Sir?

Prosecutor.—Yes, certainly.

MR. HALL.—You must be a foreigner, then?

Prosecutor.—I am a German.

MR. HALL.—Ah, that accounts for it. If you had been an English-man, you would have been drunk, for a certainty.

Prosecutor (smiling).—The Germans get drunk sometimes, I fear.

MR. HALL.—Yes, after they have resided any time in this country. They acquire our English habits.

In reproducing these noble expressions, equally honourable to the Sage who uttered them, and to the Country that endures them, we will correct half-a-dozen vulgar errors which, within our observation, have been rather prevalent since the great occasion on which the Oracle at Bow Street, spake.

1. It is altogether a mistake to suppose that if a magistrate wilfully deliver himself of a slanderous aspersion, knowing it to be unjust, he is unfit for his post.

2. It is altogether a mistake, to suppose that if a magistrate, in a fit of bile brought on by recent disregard of some very absurd evidence of his, so yield to his ill-temper as to deliver himself, in a sort of mad exasperation, of such slanderous aspersion as aforesaid, he is unfit for his post.

3. It is altogether a mistake to suppose it to be very questionable whether, even in degraded Naples at this time, a magistrate could from the official bench insult and traduce the whole people, without being made to suffer for it.

4. It is altogether a mistake to suppose that it would be becoming in some one individual out of between six and seven hundred national representatives, to be so far jealous of the honour of his country, as indignantly to protest against its being thus grossly stigmatised.

5.   It is altogether a mistake to suppose that the Home Office has any association whatever with the general credit, the general self-respect, the general feeling in behalf of decent utterance, or the general resentment when the same is most discreditably violated.   The Home Office is merely an ornamental institution supported out of the general pocket.

6.   It is altogether a mistake to suppose that Mr. Hall is anybody's business, or that we, the mere bone and sinew, tag rag and bobtail of England, have anything to do with him, but to pay him his salary, accept his Justice, and meekly bow our heads to his high and mighty reproof.

[1855]

OLD LAMPS FOR NEW ONES.

THE Magician in "Aladdin" may possibly have neglected the study of men, for the study of alchemical books; but it is certain that in spite of his profession he was no conjuror. He knew nothing of human nature, or the everlasting set of the current of human affairs. If, when he fraudulently sought to obtain possession of the wonderful Lamp, and went up and down, disguised, before the flying-palace, crying New Lamps for Old Ones, he had reversed his cry, and made it Old Lamps for New Ones, he would have been so far before his time as to have projected himself into the nineteenth century of our Christian Era.

This age is so perverse, and is so very short of faith—in consequence, as some suppose, of there having been a run on that bank for a few generations—that a parallel and beautiful idea, generally known among the ignorant as the Young England hallucination, unhappily expired before it could run alone, to the great grief of a small but a very select circle of mourners. There is something so fascinating, to a mind capable of any serious reflection, in the notion of ignoring all that has been done for the happiness and elevation of mankind during three or four centuries of slow and dearly-bought amelioration, that we have always thought it would tend soundly to the improvement of the general public, if any tangible symbol, any outward and visible sign, expressive of that admirable conception, could be held up before them.   We are happy to have found such a sign at last; and although it would make a very indifferent sign, indeed, in the Licensed Victualling sense of the word, and would probably be rejected with contempt and horror by any Christian publication, it has our warmest philosophical appreciation.

In the fifteenth century, a certain feeble lamp of art arose in the Italian town of Urbino. This poor light, Raphael Sanzio by name, better known to a few miserably mistaken wretches in these later days, as Raphael (another burned at the same time, called Titian), was fed with a preposterous idea of Beauty—with a ridiculous power of etherealising, and exalting to the very Heaven of Heavens, what was most sublime and lovely in the expression of the human face divine on Earth—with the truly contemptible conceit of finding in poor humanity the fallen likeness of the angels of God, and raising it up again to their pure spiritual condition. This very fantastic whim effected a low revolution in Art, in this wise, that Beauty came to be regarded as one of its indispensable elements.   In this very poor delusion, Artists have continued until this present nineteenth century, when it was reserved for some bold aspirants to "put it down."

The Pre-Raphael Brotherhood, Ladies and Gentlemen, is the dread Tribunal which is to set this matter right. Walk up, walk up; and here, conspicuous on the wall of the Royal Academy of Art in England, in the eighty-second year of their annual exhibition, you shall see what this new Holy Brotherhood, this terrible Police that is to disperse all Post-Raphael offenders, has "been and done!"

You come—in this Royal Academy Exhibition, which
is familiar with the works of Wilkie, Collins, Etty,
Eastlake, Mulready, Leslie, Maclise, Turner, Stanfield,
Landseer, Roberts, Danby, Creswick, Lee, Webster,
Herbert, Dyce, Cope, and others who would have been
renowned as great masters in any age or country—you
come, in this place, to the contemplation of a Holy
Family. You will have the goodness to discharge from
your minds all Post-Raphael ideas, all religious aspirations,
all elevating thoughts; all tender, awful, sorrowful, ennobling,
sacred, graceful, or beautiful associations; and to prepare
yourselves, as   befits   such   a   subject—Pre-Raphaelly
considered—for the lowest depths of what is mean, odious,
repulsive, and revolting.

You behold the interior of a carpenter's shop. In the
foreground of that carpenter's shop is a hideous, wry-
necked, blubbering, red-headed boy, in a bed-gown; who
appears to have received a poke in the hand, from the
stick of another boy with whom he has been playing in
an adjacent gutter, and to be holding it up for the contemplation of a kneeling woman, so horrible in her ugliness,
that (supposing it were possible for any human creature
to exist for a moment with that dislocated throat) she
would stand out from the rest of the company as a
Monster, in the vilest cabaret in France, or the lowest
gin-shop in England. Two almost naked carpenters, master
and journeyman, worthy companions of this agreeable
female, are working at their trade; a boy, with some small
flavor of humanity in him, is entering with a vessel of
water; and nobody is paying any attention to a snuffy
old woman who seems to have mistaken that shop for the
tobacconist's next door, and to be hopelessly waiting at
the counter to be served with half an ounce of her

favourite mixture. Wherever it is possible to express ugliness of feature, limb, or attitude, you have it expressed. Such men as the carpenters might be undressed in any hospital where dirty drunkards, in a high state of varicose veins, are received. Their very toes have walked out of Saint Giles's.

This, in the nineteenth century, and in the eighty-second year of the annual exhibition of the National Academy of Art, is the Pre-Raphael representation to us, Ladies and Gentlemen, of the most solemn passage which our minds can ever approach. This, in the nineteenth century, and in the eighty-second year of the annual exhibition of the National Academy of Art, is what Pre-Raphael Art can do to render reverence and homage to the faith in which we live and die! Consider this picture well. Consider the pleasure we should have in a similar Pre-Raphael rendering of a favourite horse, or dog, or cat; and, coming fresh from a pretty considerable turmoil about "desecration" in connexion with the National Post-Office, let us extol this great achievement, and commend the National Academy!

In further considering this symbol of the great retrogressive principle, it is particularly gratifying to observe that such objects as the shavings which are strewn on the carpenter's floor are admirably painted; and that the Pre-Raphael Brother is indisputably accomplished in the manipulation of his art. It is gratifying to observe this, because the fact involves no low effort at notoriety; everybody knowing that it is by no means easier to call attention to a very indifferent pig with five legs, than to a symmetrical pig with four. Also, because it is good to know that the National Academy thoroughly feels and comprehends the high range and exalted purposes of Art; distinctly per-

ceives that Art includes something more than the faithful
portraiture of shavings, or the skilful colouring of drapery—
imperatively requires, in short, that it shall be informed
with mind and sentiment; will on no account reduce it
to a narrow question of trade-juggling with a palette,
palette-knife, and paint-box. It is likewise pleasing to
reflect that the great educational establishment foresees
the difficulty into which it would be led, by attaching
greater weight to mere handicraft, than to any other
consideration—even to considerations of common reverence
or decency; which absurd principle, in the event of a
skilful painter of the figure becoming a very little more
perverted in his taste, than certain skilful painters are just
now, might place Her Gracious Majesty in a very painful
position, one of these fine Private View Days.

Would it were in our power to congratulate our readers
on the hopeful prospects of the great retrogressive principle,
of which this thoughtful picture is the sign and emblem!
Would that we could give our readers encouraging assurance
of a healthy demand for Old Lamps in exchange for New
ones, and a steady improvement in the Old Lamp Market!
The perversity of mankind is such, and the untoward
arrangements of Providence are such, that we cannot lay
that flattering unction to their souls. We can only report
what Brotherhoods, stimulated by this sign, are forming;
and what opportunities will be presented to the people,
if the people will but accept them.

In the first place, the Pre-Perspective Brotherhood
will be presently incorporated, for the subversion of all
known rules and principles of perspective. It is intended
to swear every P.P.B. to a solemn renunciation of the
art of perspective on a soup-plate of the willow pattern;
and we may expect, on the occasion of the eighty-third

Annual Exhibition of the Royal Academy of Art in England, to see some pictures by this pious Brotherhood, realising Hogarth's idea of a man on a mountain several miles off, lighting his pipe at the upper window of a house in the foreground. But we are informed that every brick in the house will be a portrait; that the man's boots will be copied with the utmost fidelity from a pair of Bluchers, sent up out of Northamptonshire for the purpose; and that the texture of his hands (including four chilblains, a whitlow, and ten dirty nails) will be a triumph of the Painter's art.

A Society, to be called the Pre-Newtonian Brotherhood, was lately projected by a young gentleman, under articles to a Civil Engineer, who objected to being considered bound to conduct himself according to the laws of gravitation. But this young gentleman, being reproached by some aspiring companions with the timidity of his conception, has abrogated that idea in favour of a Pre-Galileo Brotherhood now flourishing, who distinctly refuse to perform any annual revolution round the Sun, and have arranged that the world shall not do so any more. The course to be taken by the Royal Academy of Art in reference to this Brotherhood is not yet decided upon; but it is whispered that some other large Educational Institutions in the neighbourhood of Oxford are nearly ready to pronounce in favour of it.

Several promising Students connected with the Royal College of Surgeons have held a meeting, to protest against the circulation of the blood, and to pledge themselves to treat all the patients they can get, on principles condemnatory of that innovation. A Pre-Harvey-Brotherhood is the result, from which a great deal may be expected — by the undertakers.

In literature, a very spirited effort has been made, which is no less than the formation of a P.G.A.P.C.B., or Pre-Gower and Pre-Chaucer Brotherhood, for the restora - tion of the ancient English style of spelling, and the weeding out from all libraries, public and private, of those and all later pretenders, particularly a person of loose character named Shakespeare. It having been suggested, however, that this happy idea could scarcely be considered complete while the art of printing was permitted to remain unmolested, another society, under the name of the Pre- Laurentius Brotherhood, has been established in connexion with it, for the abolition of all but manuscript books. These Mr. Pugin has engaged to supply, in characters that nobody on earth shall be able to read. And it is confidently expected by those who have seen the House of Lords, that he will faithfully redeem his pledge.

In Music, a retrogressive step, in which there is much hope, has been taken. The P.A.B., or Pre-Agincourt Brotherhood has arisen, nobly devoted to consign to oblivion Mozart, Beethoven, Handel, and every other such ridiculous reputation, and to fix its Millenium (as its name implies) before the date of the first regular musical com- position known to have been achieved in England. As this Institution has not yet commenced active operations, it remains to be seen whether the Royal Academy of Music will be a worthy sister of the Royal Academy of Art, and admit this enterprising body to its orchestra. We have it on the best authority, that its compositions will be quite as rough and discordant as the real old original—that it will be, in a word, exactly suited to the pictorial Art we have endeavoured to describe. We have strong hopes, therefore, that the Royal Academy of Music, not wanting an example, may not want courage.

The regulation of social matters, as separated from the Fine Arts, has been undertaken by the Pre-Henry-the-Seventh Brotherhood, who date from the same period as the Pre-Raphael Brotherhood. This Society, as cancelling all the advances of nearly four hundred years and reverting to one of the most disagreeable periods of English History, when the Nation was yet very slowly emerging from barbarism, and when gentle female foreigners, come over to be the wives of Scottish Kings, wept bitterly (as well they might) at being left alone among the savage Court, must be regarded with peculiar favour. As the time of ugly religious caricatures (called mysteries), it is thoroughly Pre-Raphael in its spirit; and may be deemed the twin brother to that great society. We should be certain of the Plague among many other advantages, if this Brotherhood were properly encouraged.

All these Brotherhoods, and any other society of the like kind, now in being or yet to be, have at once a guiding star, and a reduction of their great ideas to something palpable and obvious to the senses, in the sign to which we take the liberty of directing their attention. We understand that it is in the contemplation of each Society to become possessed, with all convenient speed, of a collection of such pictures; and that once, every year, to wit upon the first of April, the whole intend to amalgamate in a high festival, to be called the Convocation of Eternal Boobies.

1850]

THE SUNDAY SCREW.

THIS little instrument, remarkable for its curious twist, has been at work again. A small portion of the collective wisdom of the nation has affirmed the principle that there must be no collection or delivery of posted letters on a Sunday. The principle was discussed by something less than a fourth of the House of Commons, and affirmed by something less than a seventh.

Having no doubt whatever, that this brilliant victory is, in effect, the affirmation of the principle that there ought to be No Anything but churches and chapels on a Sunday; or that it is the beginning of a Sabbatarian Crusade, outrageous to the spirit of Christianity, irreconcilable with the health, the rational enjoyments, and the true religious feeling, of the community; and certain to result, if successful, in a violent re-action, threatening contempt and hatred of that seventh day which it is a great religious and social object to maintain in the popular affection; it would ill become us to be deterred from speaking out upon the subject, by any fear of being misunderstood, or by any certainty of being misrepresented.

Confident in the sense of the country, and not unacquainted with the habits and exigencies of the people, we approach the Sunday question, quite undiscomposed by the late storm of mad mis-statement and all uncharitableness which cleared the way for Lord Ashley's motion. The preparation may be likened to that which is usually described in the case of the Egyptian Sorcerer and the boy who has some dark liquid poured into the palm of his hand, which is presently to become a magic mirror. " Look for Lord Ashley. What do you see?" "Oh, here's some one with a broom!" "Well! what is he doing?" "Oh, he's sweeping away Mr. Rowland Hill! Now, there is a great crowd of people all sweeping Mr. Rowland Hill away; and now, there is a red flag with Intolerance on it; and now, they are pitching a great many Tents called Meetings. Now, the tents are all upset, and Mr. Rowland Hill has swept everybody else away. And oh! *now*, here's Lord Ashley, with a Resolution in his hand!"

One Christian sentence is all-sufficient with us, on the theological part of this subject. " The Sabbath was made for man, and not man for the Sabbath." No amount of signatures to petitions can ever sign away the meaning of those words; no end of volumes of Hansard's Parliamentary Debates can ever affect them in the least. Move and carry resolutions, bring in bills, have committees, upstairs, downstairs, and in my lady's chamber; read a first time, read a second time, read a third time, read thirty thousand times; the declared authority of the Christian dispensation over the letter of the Jewish Law, particularly in this especial instance, cannot be petitioned, resolved, read, or committee'd away.

It is important in such a case as this affirmation of a principle, to know what amount of practical sense and logic entered into its assertion. We will inquire.

Lord Ashley (who has done much good, and whom we mention with every sentiment of sincere respect, though we believe him to be most mischievously deluded on this question,) speaks of the people employed in the Country Post-Offices on Sunday, as though they were continually at work, all the livelong day. He asks whether they are to be "a Pariah race, excluded from the enjoyments of the rest of the community?" He presents to our mind's eye, rows of Post-Office clerks, sitting, with dishevelled hair and dirty linen, behind small shutters, all Sunday long, keeping time with their sighs to the ringing of the church bells, and watering bushels of letters, incessantly passing through their hands, with their tears. Is this exactly the reality? The Upas tree is a figure of speech almost as ancient as our lachrymose friend the Pariah, in whom most of us recognise a respectable old acquaintance. Supposing we were to take it into our heads to declare in these Household Words, that every Post-Office clerk employed on Sunday in the country, is compelled to sit under his own particular sprig of Upas, planted in a flower-pot beside him for the express purpose of blighting him with its baneful shade, should we be much more beyond the mark than Lord Ashley himself? Did any of our readers ever happen to post letters in the Country on a Sunday? Did they ever see a notice outside a provincial Post-Office, to the effect that the presiding Pariah would be in attendance at such an hour on Sunday, and not before? Did they ever wait for the Pariah, at some inconvenience, until the hour arrived, and observe him come to the office in an extremely spruce condition as to his shirt collar, and do a little sprinkling of business in a very easy off-hand manner? We have such recollections ourselves. We have posted and received letters in most parts of this kingdom on a Sunday, and we never yet observed the Pariah to be quite crushed. On the con-

trary, we have seen him at church, apparently in the best
health and spirits (notwithstanding an hour or so of sorting,
earlier in the morning), and we have met him out a-walk-
ing with the young lady to whom he is engaged, and we
have known him meet her again with her cousin, after the
dispatch of the Mails, and really conduct himself as if he
were not particularly exhausted or afflicted. Indeed, how
could he be so, on Lord Ashley's own showing? There
is a Saturday before the Sunday. We are a people
indisposed, he says, to business on a Sunday. More than
a million of people are known, from their petitions, to be
too scrupulous to hear of such a thing. Few counting-
houses or offices are ever opened on a Sunday. The
Merchants and Bankers write by Saturday night's post.
The Sunday night's post may be presumed to be chiefly
limited to letters of necessity and emergency. Lord Ashley's whole case would break down, if it were probable
that the Post-Office Pariah had half as much confinement
on Sunday, as the He-Pariah who opens my Lord's street-
door when any body knocks, or the She-Pariah who nurses
my Lady's baby.

If the London Post-Office be not opened on a Sunday,
says Lord Ashley, why should the Post-Offices of provincial towns be opened on a Sunday? Precisely because
the provincial towns are NOT London, we apprehend.
Because London is the great capital, mart, and business-
centre of the world; because in London there are hundreds of thousands of people, young and old, away from
their families and friends; because the stoppage of the
Monday's Post Delivery in London would stop, for many
precious hours, the natural flow of the blood from every
vein and artery in the world to the heart of the world,
and its return from the heart through all those tributary

channels.   Because the broad difference between London
and every other place in England, necessitated this distinction, and has perpetuated it.

But, to say nothing of petitioners elsewhere, it seems
that two hundred merchants and bankers in Liverpool
"formed themselves into a committee, to forward the
object of this motion." In the name of all the Pharisees
of Jerusalem, could not the two hundred merchants and
bankers form themselves into a committee to write or
read no business-letters themselves on a Sunday—and let
the Post-Office alone? The Government establishes a
monopoly in the Post-Office, and makes it not only difficult
and expensive for me to send a letter by any other means,
but illegal. What right has any merchant or banker to
stop the course of any letter that I may have sore necessity to post, or may choose to post? If any one of the
two hundred merchants and bankers lay at the point of
death, on Sunday, would he desire his absent child to
be written to—the Sunday Post being yet in existence?
And how do they take upon themselves to tell us that
the Sunday Post is not a "necessity," when they know,
every man of them, every Sunday morning, that before the
clock strikes next, they and theirs may be visited by any
one of incalculable millions of accidents, to make it a
dire need? Not a necessity? Is it possible that these
merchants and bankers suppose there is any Sunday Post,
from any large town, which is not a very agony of necessity
to some one? I might as well say, in my pride of strength,
that a knowledge of bone-setting in surgeons is not a
necessity, because I have not broken my leg.

There is a Sage of this sort in the House of Commons.
He is of opinion that the Sunday Police is a necessity,
but the Sunday Post is not. That is to say, in a certain

house in London or Westminster, there are certain silver spoons, engraved with the family crest—a Bigot rampant—which would be pretty sure to disappear, on an early Sunday, if there were no Policemen on duty; whereas the Sage sees no present probability of his requiring to write a letter into the country on a Saturday night—and, if it should arise, he can use the Electric Telegraph. Such is the sordid balance some professing Heathens hold of their own pounds against other men's pennies, and their own selfish wants against those of the community at large! Even the Member for Birmingham, of all the towns in England, is afflicted by this selfish blindness, and, because *he* is "tired of reading and answering letters on a Sunday," cannot conceive the possibility of there being other people not so situated, to whom the Sunday Post may, under many circumstances, be an unspeakable blessing.

The inconsequential nature of Lord Ashley's positions, cannot be better shown, than by one brief passage from his speech. "When he said the transmission of the Mail, he meant the Mail-bags; he did not propose to interfere with the passengers." No? Think again Lord Ashley.

When the Honorable Member for Whitened Sepulchres moves his resolution for the stoppage of Mail Trains—in a word, of all Railway travelling—on Sunday; and when that Honorable Gentleman talks about the Pariah clerks who take the money and give the tickets, the Pariah engine-drivers, the Pariah stokers, the Pariah porters, the Pariah police along the line, and the Pariah flys waiting at the Pariah stations to take the Pariah passengers, to be attended by Pariah servants at the Pariah Arms and other Pariah Hotels; what will Lord Ashley do then? Envy insinuated that Tom Thumb made his giants first, and then killed them, but you cannot do the like by your

Pariahs. You cannot get an exclusive patent for the manufacture and destruction of Pariah dolls. Other Honorable Gentlemen are certain to engage in the trade; and when the Honorable Member for Whitened Sepulchres makes *his* Pariahs of all these people, you cannot refuse to recognise them as being of the genuine sort, Lord Ashley. Railway and all other Sunday Travelling, suppressed, by the Honorable Member for Whitened Sepulchres, the same Honorable Gentleman, who will not have been particularly complimented in the course of that achievement by the Times Newspaper, will discover that a good deal is done towards the Times of Monday, on a Sunday night, and will Pariah the whole of that immense establishment. For, this is the great inconvenience of Pariah-making, that when you begin, they spring up like mushrooms: insomuch, that it is very doubtful whether we shall have a house in all this land, from the Queen's Palace downward, which will not be found, on inspection, to be swarming with Pariahs. Not touch the Mails, and yet abolish the Mail-bags? Stop all those silent messengers of affection and anxiety, yet let the talking traveller, who is the cause of infinitely more employment, go? Why, this were to suppose all men Fools, and the Honorable Member for Whitened Sepulchres even a greater Noodle than he is!

Lord Ashley supports his motion by reading some perilous bombast, said to be written by a working man— of whom the intelligent body of working men have no great reason, to our thinking, to be proud,—in which there is much about not being robbed of the boon of the day of rest; but, with all Lord Ashley's indisputably humane and benevolent impulses, we grieve to say we know no robber whom the working man, really desirous to preserve

his Sunday, has so much to dread, as Lord Ashley himself. He is weakly lending the influence of his good intention to a movement which would make that day no
day of rest—rest to those who are overwrought, includes
recreation, fresh air, change—but a day of mortification
and gloom. And this not to one class only, be it understood. This is not a class question. If there be no
gentleman of spirit in the House of Commons to remind
Lord Ashley that the highflown nonsense he quoted, concerning labour, is but another form of the stupidest socialist
dogma, which seeks to represent that there is only one
class of laborers on earth, it is well that the truth should
be stated somewhere. And it is, indisputably, that three-
fourths of us are laborers who work hard for our living;
and that the condition of what we call the working-man
has its parallel, at a remove of certain degrees, in almost
all professions and pursuits. Running through the middle
classes, is a broad deep vein of constant, compulsory, indispensable work. There are innumerable gentlemen, and
sons and daughters of gentlemen, constantly at work, who
have no more hope of making fortunes in their vocation,
than the working man has in his. There are innumerable
families in which the day of rest is the only day out of
the seven, where innocent domestic recreations and enjoyments are very feasible. In our mean gentility, which
is the cause of so much social mischief, we may try to
separate ourselves, as to this question, from the working-
man; and may very complacently resolve that there is no
occasion for his excursion-trains and tea-gardens, because
we don't use them; but we had better not deceive ourselves. It is impossible that we can cramp his means of
needful recreation and refreshment, without cramping our
own, or basely cheating him. We cannot leave him to

the Christian patronage of the Honorable Member for Whitened Sepulchres, and take ourselves off. We cannot restrain him and leave ourselves free. Our Sunday wants are pretty much the same as his, though his are far more easily satisfied; our inclinations and our feelings are pretty much the same; and it will be no less wise than honest in us, the middle classes, not to be Janus-faced about the matter.

What is it that the Honorable Member for Whitened Sepulchres, for whom Lord Ashley clears the way, wants to do? He sees on a Sunday morning, in the large towns of England, when the bells are ringing for church and chapel, certain unwashed, dim-eyed, dissipated loungers, hanging about the doors of public-houses, and loitering at the street corners, to whom the day of rest appeals in much the same degree as a sunny summer-day does to so many pigs. Does he believe that any weight of hand-cuffs on the Post-Office, or any amount of restriction imposed on decent people, will bring Sunday home to these? Let him go, any Sunday morning, from the new Town of Edinburgh where the sound of a piano would be profanation, to the old Town, and see what Sunday is in the Canongate. Or let him get up some statistics of the drunken people in Glasgow, while the churches are full—and work out the amount of Sabbath observance which is carried downward, by rigid shows and sad-colored forms.

But, there is another class of people, those who take little jaunts, and mingle in social little assemblages, on a Sunday, concerning whom the whole constituency of Whitened Sepulchres, with their Honorable Member in the chair, find their lank hair standing on end with horror, and pointing, as if they were all electrified straight up to the skylights of Exeter Hall. In reference to this class, we would whisper in the ears of the disturbed assemblage, three short words, "Let well alone!"

The English people have long been remarkable for their domestic habits, and their household virtues and affections. They are, now, beginning to be universally respected by intelligent foreigners who visit this country, for their unobtrusive politeness, their good-humour, and their cheerful recognition of all restraints that really originate in consideration for the general good. They deserve this testimony (which we have often heard, of late, with pride) most honorably. Long maligned and mistrusted, they proved their case from the very first moment of having it in their power to do so; and have never, on any single occasion within our knowledge, abused any public confidence that has been reposed in them. It is an extraordinary thing to know of a people, systematically excluded from galleries and museums for years, that their respect for such places, and for themselves as visitors to them, dates, without any period of transition, from the very day when their doors were freely opened. The national vices are surprisingly few. The people in general are not gluttons, nor drunkards, nor gamblers, nor addicted to cruel sports, nor to the pushing of any amusement to furious and wild extremes. They are moderate, and easily pleased, and very sensible to all affectionate influences. Any knot of holiday-makers, without a large proportion of women and children among them, would be a perfect phenomenon. Let us go into any place of Sunday enjoyment where any fair representation of the people resort, and we shall find them decent, orderly, quiet, sociable among their families and neighbours. There is a general feeling of respect for religion, and for religious observances. The churches and chapels are well filled. Very few people who keep servants or apprentices, leave out of consideration their opportunities of attending church or chapel; the general demeanour within those edifices, is particularly grave and decorous; and the general recreations without, are of a harmless and simple kind. Lord Brougham never did Henry Brougham more justice, than in declaring to the House of Lords, after the success of this motion in the House of Commons, that there is no country where the Sabbath is, on the whole, better observed than in England. Let the constituency of Whitened Sepulchres ponder, in a Christian spirit, on these things; take care of their own consciences; leave their Honorable Member to take care of his; and let well alone.

For it is in nations as in families. Too tight a hand in these respects, is certain to engender a disposition to break loose, and to run riot. If the private experience of any reader, pausing on this sentence, cannot furnish many unhappy illustrations of its truth, it is a very fortunate experience indeed. Our most notable example of it, in England, is just two hundred years old.

Lord Ashley had better merge his Pariahs into the body politic; and the Honorable Member for Whitened Sepulchres had better accustom his jaundiced eyes to the Sunday sight of dwellers in towns, roaming in green fields, and gazing upon country prospects. If he will look a little beyond them, and lift up the eyes of his mind, perhaps he may observe a mild, majestic figure in the distance, going through a field of corn, attended by some common men who pluck the grain as they pass along, and whom their Divine Master teaches that he is the Lord, even of the Sabbath-Day.   [1850]

A FEW CONVENTIONALITIES.

A CHILD enquired of us, the other day, why a gentleman always said his first prayer in.church, in the crown of his hat. We were reduced to the ignominious necessity of replying that we didn't know—but it was the custom.

Having dismissed our young friend with a severe countenance (which we always assume under the like circumstances of discomfiture) we began to ask ourself a few questions.

Our first list had a Parliamentary reference.

Why must an honorable gentleman always "come down" to this house? Why can't he sometimes "come up"— like a horse—or "come in" like a man? What does he mean by invariably coming down? Is it indispensable that he should "come down" to get into the House of Commons—say for instance, from Saint Albans? Or is that house on a lower level than most other houses? Why is he always "free to confess"? It is well known that Britons never never never will be slaves; then why can't he say what he has to say, without this superfluous assertion of his freedom? Why must an Irish Member always "taunt" the noble Lord with this, that, or the other? Can't he tell him of it civilly, or accuse him of it plainly? *Must* he so ruthlessly taunt him? Why does the Honorable Member for Groginhole call upon the Secretary of State for the Home Department to "lay his hand upon his heart," and proclaim to the country such and such a thing? The Home Secretary is not in the habit of laying his hand upon his heart. When he has anything to proclaim to the country, he generally puts his hands under his coat-tails. Why is he thus personally and solemnly adjured to lay one of them on the left side of his waistcoat for any Honorable Member's gratification? What makes my Honorable friend, the Member for Gammonrife, feel so acutely that he is required to "pin his faith" upon the measures of Her Majesty's Government? Is he always required to attach it in that particular manner only; and are needle and thread, hooks and eyes, buttons, wafers, sealing-wax, paste, bird-lime, gum, and glue, utterly prohibited to him? Who invested the unfortunate Speaker with all the wealth and poverty of the Empire, that he should be told "Sir, when you look around you, and behold your seas swarming with ships of every variety of tonnage and construction—when you behold your flag waving over the forts of a territory so vast that the Sun never sets upon it—when you consider that your storehouses are teeming with the valuable products of the earth—and when you reflect that millions of your poor are held in the bonds of pauperism and ignorance,—can you, I ask, reconcile it to yourself; can you, I demand, justify it to your conscience; can you, I enquire, Sir, stifle the voice within you, by these selfish, these time-serving, these shallow, hollow mockeries of legislation?" It is really dreadful to have an innocent and worthy gentleman bullied in this manner. Again, why do "I hold in my hand" all sorts of things? Can I never lay them down, or carry them under my arm? There was a Fairy in the Arabian Nights who could hold in her hand a pavilion large enough to shelter the Sultan's army, but she could never have held half the petitions, blue books, bills, reports, returns, volumes of Hansard, and other miscellaneous papers, that a very ordinary Member for a very ordinary place will hold in his hand now-a-days. Then, again, how did it come to be necessary to the Constitution that I should be such a very circuitous and prolix peer as to "take leave to remind you, my Lords, of what fell from the noble and learned lord on the opposite side of your Lordships' house, who preceded my noble and learned friend on the cross Benches when he addressed himself with so much ability to the observations of the Right Reverend Prelate near me, in reference to the measure now brought forward by the Noble Baron"—when, all this time, I mean, and only want to say, Lord Brougham? Is it impossible for my honorable friend the Member for Drowsyshire, to wander through his few dreary sentences immediately before the division, without premising that "at this late hour of the night and in this stage of the debate," etc.? Because if it be not impossible why does he never do it? And why, why, above all, in either house of Parliament must the English language be set to music—bad and conventional beyond any parallel on earth—and delivered, in a manner barely expressible to the eye, as follows:

Is Parliament included in the Common Prayer-book under the denomination of "quires and places where they sing"? And if so, wouldn't it be worth a small grant to make a national arrangement for instruction in the art by Mr. Hullah?

Then consider the theatrical and operatic questions that arise, likewise admitting of no solution whatever.

No man ever knew yet, no man ever will know, why a stage-nobleman is bound to go to execution with a stride and a stop alternately, and cannot proceed to the scaffold on any other terms. It is not within the range of the loftiest intellect to explain why a stage-letter, before it can be read by the recipient, must be smartly rapped back, after being opened, with the knuckles of one hand. It is utterly unknown why choleric old gentlemen always have a trick of carrying their canes behind them, between the waist-buttons of their coat. Several persons are understood to be in Bedlam at the present time, who went distracted in endeavouring to reconcile the bran-new appearance of Mr. Cooper, in John Bull, bearing a highly polished surgical instrument-case under his arm, with the fact of his having been just fished out of the deep deep sea, in company with the case in question. Inexplicable phenomena continually arise at the Italian Opera, where we have ourself beheld (it was in the time of Robert of Normandy) Nuns buried in garments of that perplexing nature that the very last thing one could possibly suppose they had taken, was a veil of any order. Who knows how it came about that the young Swiss maiden in the ballet should, as an established custom, revolve, on her nuptial morning, so airily and often, that at length she stands before us, for some seconds, like a beautiful white muslin pen-wiper? Why is her bed chamber always imme-

diately over the cottage-door? Why is she always awakened
by three taps of her lover's hands? Why does her mother always spin? Why is her residence invariably near a bridge? In
what Swiss canton do the hardy mountaineers pursue the cha-
mois, in silk stockings, pumps, blue breeches, cherry-coloured
bows, and their shirt-sleeves? When the Tenor Prince is
made more tenor by the near approach of death from steel
or poison; when the Bass enemy growls glutted vengeance,
and the Heroine (who was so glad in the beginning of
her story to see the villagers that she had an irrepressible
impulse to be always shaking hands with them) is rushing
to and fro among the living and disturbing the wig of the
dead; why do we always murmur our Bra-a-avo! or our
Bra-a-ava! as the case may be, in exactly the same tone,
at exactly the same places, and execute our little audience
conventionalities with the punctuality and mechanism of
the stage itself? Why does the Primo Buffo always rub
his hands and tap his nose? When did mankind enter
into articles of agreement that a most uncompromising and
uncomfortable box, with the lid at a certain angle, should
be called a mossy bank? Who first established an indis-
soluble connexion between the Demon and the brass
instruments? When the sailors become Bacchanalian, how
do they do it out of such little mugs, replenished from
pitchers that have always been turned upside down?
Granted that the Count must go a-hunting, why must he
therefore wear fur round the tops of his boots, and never
follow the chase with any other weapon than a spear with
a large round knob at the blunt end?

Then, at public dinners and meetings, why must Mr.
Wilson refer to Mr. Jackson as "my honorable friend, if
he will permit me to call him so?" Has Wilson any
doubt about it? Why does Mr. Smithers say that he is

sensible he has already detained you too long, and why
do *you* say, "No, no; go on!" when you know you are
sorry for it directly afterwards? You are not taken by
surprise when the Toastmaster cries, in giving the Army
and Navy, "Upstanding, gentlemen, *and* good fires"—then
what do you laugh for? No man could ever say why he
was greatly refreshed and fortified by forms of words, as
"Resolved.   That this meeting respectfully but firmly views
with sorrow and apprehension, not unmixed with abhorrence
and dismay"—but they *do* invigorate the patient, in most
cases, like a cordial.   It is a strange thing that the chairman
is obliged to refer to "the present occasion";—that there
is a horrible fascination in the phrase which he can't
elude.   Also, that there should be an unctuous smack and
relish in the enunciation of titles, as "And I may be
permitted to inform this company that when I had the
honor of waiting on His Royal Highness, to ask His
Royal Highness to be pleased to bestow his gracious
patronage on our excellent Institution, His Royal Highness
did me the honor to reply, with that condescension which is
ever His Royal Highness's most distinguishing characteristic"
—and so forth.   As to the singular circumstance that
such and such a duty should not have been entrusted to
abler hands than mine, everybody is familiar with that
phenomenon, but, it's very strange that it *must* be so!

Again, in social matters.   It is all very well to wonder
who invents slang phrases, referential to Mr. Ferguson or
any such mythological personage, but the wonder does
not stop there.   It extends into Belgravia.   Saint James's
has its slang, and a great deal of it.   Nobody knows who
first drawled, languidly, that so and so, or such and such
a thing, was "good fun," or "capital fun," or "a—the
best fun in the world, I'm told"— but some fine gentleman

or lady did so, and accordingly a thousand do. They don't know why. We have the same mysterious authority for enquiring, in our faint way, if Cawberry is a nice person—if he is a superior person—for a romance being so charmingly horrible, or a woman so charmingly ugly— for the Hippopotamus being quite charming in his bath, and the little Elephant so charmingly like its mother—for the glass palace being (do you know) so charming to me that I absolutely bore every creature with it—for those horrid sparrows not having built in the dear gutters, which are so charmingly ingenious—for a great deal more, to the same very charming purpose.

When the old stage-coaches ran, and overturns took place in which all the passengers were killed or crippled, why was it invariably understood that no blame whatever was attributable to the coachman? In railway accidents of the present day, why is the coroner always convinced that a searching enquiry must be made, and the Railway authorities are affording every possible facility in aid of the elucidation of this unhappy disaster? When a new building tumbles into a heap of ruin, why are architect, contractor, and materials, always the best that could be got for money, with additional precautions—as if that splendid termination were the triumph of construction, and all buildings that don't tumble down were failures? When a boiler bursts, why was it the very best of boilers; and why, when somebody thinks that if the accident were not the boiler's fault it is likely to have been the engineer's, is the engineer then morally certain to have been the steadiest and skilfullest of men? If a public servant be impeached, how does it happen that there never was such an excellent public servant as he will be shown to be by Red-Tape-osophy? If an abuse be brought to light, how does it come to pass that it is sure to be, in fact, (if rightly viewed) a blessing? How can it be that we have gone on, for so many years, surrounding the grave with ghastly, ruinous, incongruous, and inexplicable mummeries, and curtaining the cradle with a thousand ridiculous and prejudicial customs?

All these things are conventionalities. It would be well for us if there were no more and no worse in common use. But, having run the gauntlet of so many, in a breath, we must yield to the unconventional necessity of taking breath, and stop here.

[1851]

I HAVE a comfortable property. What I spend, I spend upon myself; and what I don't spend I save. Those are my principles. I am warmly attached to my principles, and stick to them on all occasions.

I am not, as some people have represented, a mean man. I never denied myself anything that I thought I should like to have. I may have said to myself, "Snoady" —that is my name—"you will get those peaches cheaper if you wait till next week;" or, I may have said to myself, "Snoady, you will get that wine for nothing, if you wait till you are asked out to dine;" but I never deny myself anything. If I can't get what I want without buying it, and paying its price for it, I *do* buy it and pay its price for it. I have an appetite bestowed upon me; and, if I baulked it, I should consider that I was flying in the face of Providence.

I have no near relation but a brother. If he wants anything of me, he don't get it. All men are my brothers; and I see no reason why I should make his an exceptional case.

I live at a cathedral town where there is an old corporation. I am not in the Church, but it may be that I hold a little place of some sort. Never mind. It may be profitable. Perhaps yes, perhaps no. It may, or it may

not be a sinecure. I don't choose to say. I never enlightened my brother on these subjects, and I consider all
men my brothers. The Negro is a man and a brother—
should I hold myself accountable for my position in life,
to him? Certainly not.

I often run up to London. I like London. The way
I look at it, is this. London is not a cheap place, but,
on the whole, you can get more of the real thing for
your money there—I mean the best thing, whatever it is—
than you can get in most places. Therefore, I say to the
man who has got the money, and wants the thing, "Go
to London for it, and treat yourself."

When *I* go, I do it in this manner. I go to Mrs.
Skim's Private Hotel and Commercial Lodging House, near
Aldersgate Street, City (it is advertised in "Bradshaw's
Railway Guide," where I first found it), and there I pay,
"for bed and breakfast, with meat, two and ninepence
per day, including servants." Now, I have made a
calculation, and I am satisfied that Mrs. Skim cannot
possibly make much profit out of *me*. In fact, if all her
patrons were like me, my opinion is, the woman would
be in the Gazette next month.

Why do I go to Mrs. Skim's when I could go to the
Clarendon, you may ask? Let us argue that point. If I
went to the Clarendon I could get nothing in bed but
sleep; could I? No. Now, sleep at the Clarendon is an
expensive article; whereas sleep, at Mrs. Skim's, is decidedly cheap. I have made a calculation, and I don't
hesitate to say, all things considered, that it's cheap. Is
it an inferior article, as compared with the Clarendon
sleep, or is it of the same quality? I am a heavy sleeper,
and it is of the same quality. Then why should I go
to the Clarendon?

But as to breakfast? you may say.—Very well. As to breakfast. I could get a variety of delicacies for breakfast at the Clarendon, that are out of the question at Mrs. Skim's. Granted. But I don't want to have them! My opinion is, that we are not entirely animal and sensual. Man has an intellect bestowed upon him. If he clogs that intellect by too good a breakfast, how can he properly exert that intellect in meditation, during the day, upon his dinner? That's the point. We are not to enchain the soul. We are to let it soar. It is expected of us.

At Mrs. Skim's, I get enough for breakfast (there is no limitation to the bread and butter, though there is to the meat) and not too much. I have all my faculties about me, to concentrate upon the object I have mentioned, and I can say to myself besides, "Snoady, you have saved six, eight, ten, fifteen, shillings, already to-day. If there is anything you fancy for your dinner, have it. Snoady, you have earned your reward."

My objection to London, is, that it is the head-quarters of the worst radical sentiments that are broached in England. I consider that it has a great many dangerous people in it. I consider the present publication (if it's "Household Words") very dangerous, and I write this with the view of neutralising some of its bad effects. My political creed is, let us be comfortable. We are all very comfortable as we are—*I* am very comfortable as I am—leave us alone!

All mankind are my brothers, and I don't think it Christian—if you come to that—to tell my brother that he is ignorant, or degraded, or dirty, or anything of the kind. I think it's abusive and low. You meet me with the observation that I am required to love my brother.

I reply, "I do." I am sure I am always willing to say to my brother, "My good fellow, I love you very much; go along with you; keep to your own road; leave me to mine; whatever is, is right; whatever isn't, is wrong; don't make a disturbance!" It seems to me, that this is at once the whole duty of man, and the only temper to go to dinner in.

Going to dinner in this temper in the City of London, one day not long ago, after a bed at Mrs. Skim's, with meat-breakfast and servants included, I was reminded of the observation which, if my memory does not deceive me, was formerly made by somebody on some occasion, that man may learn wisdom from the lower animals. It is a beautiful fact, in my opinion, that great wisdom is to be learnt from that noble animal, the Turtle.

I had made up my mind, in the course of the day I speak of, to have a Turtle dinner. I mean a dinner mainly composed of Turtle. Just a comfortable tureen of soup, with a pint of punch, and nothing solid to follow, but a tender juicy steak. I like a tender juicy steak. I generally say to myself when I order one, "Snoady, you have done right."

When I make up my mind to have a delicacy, expense is no consideration. The question resolves itself, then, into a question of the very best. I went to a friend of mine who is a Member of the Common Council, and with that friend I held the following conversation.

Said I to him, "Mr. Groggles, the best Turtle is where?"

Says he, "If you want a basin for lunch, my opinion is, you can't do better than drop into Birch's."

Said I, "Mr. Groggles, I thought you had known me better, than to suppose me capable of a basin. My intention is to dine. A tureen."

Says Mr. Groggles, without a moment's consideration, and in a determined voice, " Right opposite the India House, Leadenhall Street."

We parted. My mind was not inactive during the day, and at six in the afternoon I repaired to the house of Mr. Groggles's recommendation. At the end of the passage, leading from the street into the coffee-room, I observed a vast and solid chest, in which I then supposed that a Turtle of unusual size might be deposited. But, the correspondence between its bulk and that of the charge made for my dinner, afterwards satisfied me that it must be the till of the establishment.

I stated to the waiter what had brought me there, and I mentioned Mr. Groggles's name. He feelingly repeated after me, " A tureen of Turtle, and a tender juicy steak." His manner, added to the manner of Mr. Groggles in the morning, satisfied me that all was well. The atmosphere of the coffee-room was odoriferous with Turtle and the steams of thousands of gallons, consumed within its walls, hung, in savoury grease, upon their surface. I could have inscribed my name with a pen-knife, if I had been so disposed, in the essence of innumerable Turtles. I preferred to fall into a hungry reverie, brought on by the warm breath of the place, and to think of the West Indies and the Island of Ascension.

My dinner came—and went. I will draw a veil over the meal, I will put the cover on the empty tureen, and merely say that it was wonderful—and that I paid for it.

I sat meditating, when all was over, on the imperfect nature of our present existence, in which we can eat only for a limited time, when the waiter roused me with these words.

Said he to me, as he brushed the crumbs off the table, "Would you like to see the Turtle, Sir?"

"To see what Turtle, waiter?" said I (calmly) to him.

"The tanks of Turtle below, Sir," said he to me.

Tanks of Turtle! Good Gracious! "Yes!"

The waiter lighted a candle, and conducted me down stairs to a range of vaulted apartments, cleanly whitewashed and illuminated with gas, where I saw a sight of the most astonishing and gratifying description; illustrative of the greatness of my native country. "Snoady," was my first observation to myself, "Rule Britannia, Britannia rules the waves!"

There were two or three hundred Turtle in the vaulted apartments—all alive. Some in tanks, and some taking the air in long dry walks littered down with straw. They were of all sizes; many of them enormous. Some of the enormous ones had entangled themselves with the smaller ones, and pushed and squeezed themselves into corners, with their fins over water-pipes, and their heads downwards, where they were apoplectically struggling and splashing, apparently in the last extremity. Others were calm at the bottom of the tanks; others languidly rising to the surface. The Turtle in the walks littered down with straw, were calm and motionless. It was a thrilling sight. I admire such a sight. It rouses my imagination. If you wish to try its effect on yours, make a call right opposite the India House any day you please—dine—pay—and ask to be taken below.

Two athletic young men, without coats, and with the sleeves of their shirts tucked up to the shoulders, were in attendance on these noble animals. One of them, wrestling with the most enormous Turtle in company, and dragging him up to the edge of the tank, for me to look

at, presented an idea to me which I never had before.
I ought to observe that I like an idea. I say, when I get
a new one, "Snoady, book that!"

My idea on the present occasion, was, Mr. Groggles!
It was not a Turtle that I saw, but Mr. Groggles. It was
the dead image of Mr. Groggles. He was dragged up to
confront me, with his waistcoat—if I may be allowed the
expression—towards me; and it was identically the waistcoat of Mr. Groggles. It was the same shape, very nearly
the same colour, only wanted a gold watch-chain and a
bunch of seals, to BE the waistcoat of Mr. Groggles.
There was what I should call a bursting expression about
him in general, which was accurately the expression of
Mr. Groggles. I had never closely observed a Turtle's
throat before. The folds of his loose cravat, I found to
be precisely those of Mr. Groggles's cravat. Even the
intelligent eye—I mean to say, intelligent enough for a
person of correct principles, and not dangerously so—was
the eye of Mr. Groggles. When the athletic young man
let him go, and, with a roll of his head, he flopped
heavily down into the tank, it was exactly the manner
of Mr. Groggles as I have seen him ooze away into his
seat, after opposing a sanitary motion in the Court of
Common Council!

"Snoady," I couldn't help saying to myself, "you
have done it. You have got an idea, Snoady, in which
a great principle is involved. I congratulate you!"
I followed the young man, who dragged up several Turtle
to the brinks of the various tanks. I found them all the
same—all varieties of Mr. Groggles—all extraordinarily like
the gentlemen who usually eat them. "Now, Snoady,"
was my next remark, "what do you deduce from this?"

"Sir," said I, "what I deduce from this, is, confusion

to those Radicals and other Revolutionists who talk about improvement. Sir," said I, "what I deduce from this, is, that there isn't this resemblance between the Turtles and the Groggleses for nothing. It's meant to show mankind that the proper model for a Groggles, is a Turtle; and that the liveliness we want in a Groggles, is the liveliness of a Turtle, and no more." "Snoady," was my reply to this, "you have hit it. You are right!"

I admired the idea very much, because, if I hate anything in the world, it's change. Change has evidently no business in the world, has nothing to do with it, and isn't intended. What we want is (as I think I have mentioned) to be comfortable. I look at it that way. Let us be comfortable, and leave us alone. Now, when the young man dragged a Groggles—I mean a Turtle—out of his tank, this was exactly what the noble animal expressed as he floundered back again.

I have several friends besides Mr. Groggles in the Common Council, and it might be a week after this, when I said, "Snoady, if I was you, I would go to that court, and hear the debate to-day." I went. A good deal of it was what I call a sound, old English discussion. One eloquent speaker objected to the French as wearing wooden shoes; and a friend of his reminded him of another objection to that foreign people, namely, that they eat frogs. I had feared, for many years, I am sorry to say, that these wholesome principles were gone out. How delightful to find them still remaining among the great men of the City of London, in the year one thousand eight hundred and fifty! It made me think of the Lively Turtle.

But, I soon thought more of the Lively Turtle. Some Radicals and Revolutionists have penetrated even to the

Common Council—which otherwise I regard as one of the last strongholds of our afflicted constitution; and speeches were made, about removing Smithfield Market—which I consider to be a part of that Constitution—and about appointing a Medical Officer for the City, and about preserving the public health; and other treasonable practices, opposed to Church and State. These proposals Mr. Groggles, as might have been expected of such a man, resisted; so warmly, that, as I afterwards understood from Mrs. Groggles, he had rather a sharp attack of blood to the head that night. All the Groggles party resisted them too, and it was a fine constitutional sight to see waistcoat after waistcoat rise up in resistance of them and subside. But what struck me in the sight was this. "Snoady," said I, "here is your idea carried out, Sir! These Radicals and Revolutionists are the athletic young men in shirt sleeves, dragging the Lively Turtle to the edges of the tank. The Groggleses are the Turtle, looking out for a moment, and flopping down again. Honour to the Groggleses! Honour to the Court of Lively Turtle! The wisdom of the Turtle is the hope of England!"

There are three heads in the moral of what I had to say. First, Turtle and Groggles are identical; wonderfully alike externally, wonderfully alike mentally. Secondly, Turtle is a good thing every way, and the liveliness of the Turtle is intended as an example for the liveliness of man; you are not to go beyond that. Thirdly, we are all quite comfortable. Leave us alone!　　　[1850]

A DECEMBER VISION.

I SAW a mighty Spirit, traversing the world without any rest or pause. It was omnipresent, it was all-powerful, it had no compunction, no pity, no relenting sense that any appeal from any of the race of men could reach. It was invisible to every creature born upon the earth, save once to each. It turned its shaded face on whatsoever living thing, one time; and straight the end of that thing was come. It passed through the forest, and the vigorous tree it looked on shrunk away; through the garden, and the leaves perished and the flowers withered; through the air, and the eagles flagged upon the wing and dropped; through the sea, and the monsters of the deep floated, great wrecks, upon the waters. It met the eyes of lions in their lairs, and they were dust; its shadow darkened the faces of young children lying asleep, and they awoke no more.

It had its work appointed it; it inexorably did what was appointed to it to do, and neither sped nor slackened. Called to, it went on unmoved, and did not come. Besought, by some who felt that it was drawing near, to change its course, it turned its shaded face upon them, even while they cried, and they were dumb. It passed into the midst of palace chambers, where there were lights and music, pictures, diamonds, gold and silver; crossed the wrinkled and the grey, regardless of them, looked into the eyes of a bright bride; and vanished. It revealed itself to the baby on the old crone's knee, and left the old crone wailing by the fire. But, whether the beholder of its face were, now a King, or now a labourer, now a Queen, or now a seamstress; let the hand it palsied, be on the sceptre, or the plough, or yet too small and nerveless to grasp anything: the Spirit never paused in its appointed work, and, sooner or later, turned its impartial face on all.

I saw a Minister of State, sitting in his Closet; and, round about him, rising from the country which he governed, up to the Eternal Heavens, was a low dull howl of Ignorance. It was a wild, inexplicable mutter, confused, but full of threatening, and it made all hearers' hearts to quake within them. But, few heard. In the single city where this Minister of State was seated, I saw Thirty Thousand children, hunted, flogged, imprisoned, but not taught—who might have been nurtured by the wolf or bear, so little of humanity had they, within them or without —all joining in this doleful cry. And, ever among them, as among all ranks and grades of mortals, in all parts of the globe, the Spirit went; and ever by thousands, in their brutish state, with all the gifts of God perverted in their breasts or trampled out, they died.

The Minister of State, whose heart was pierced by even the little he could hear of these terrible voices, day and night rising to Heaven, went among the Priests and Teachers of all denominations, and faintly said :

"Hearken to this dreadful cry! What shall we do to stay it ? "

One body of respondents answered, "Teach this!"

Another said, "Teach that!"

Another said, "Teach neither this nor that, but t'other!"

Another quarrelled with all the three; twenty others quarrelled with all the four, and quarrelled no less bitterly among themselves. The voices, not stayed by this, cried out day and night; and still, among those many thousands, as among all mankind, went the Spirit, who never rested from its labour; and still, in brutish sort, they died.

Then, a whisper murmured to the Minister of State: ·

"Correct this for thyself. Be bold! Silence these voices, or virtuously lose thy power in the attempt to do it. Thou canst not sow a grain of good seed in vain. Thou knowest it well. Be bold, and do thy duty!"

The Minister shrugged his shoulders, and replied, "It is a great wrong—BUT IT WILL LAST MY TIME." And so he put it from him.

Then, the whisper went among the Priests and Teachers, saying to each, "In thy soul thou knowest it is a truth, O, man, that there are good things to be taught, on which all men may agree. Teach those, and stay this cry."

To which, each answered in like manner, "It is a great wrong—BUT IT WILL LAST MY TIME." And so *he* put it from him.

I saw a poisoned air, in which Life drooped. I saw Disease, arrayed in all its store of hideous aspects and appalling shapes, triumphant in every alley, by-way, court, back-street, and poor abode, in every place where human beings congregated—in the proudest and most boastful places, most of all. I saw innumerable hosts, fore-doomed to darkness, dirt, pestilence obscenity, misery, and early death. I saw, wheresoever I looked, cunning preparations made for defacing the Creator's Image, from the moment of its appearance here on earth, and stamping over it the

image of the Devil. I saw, from those reeking and pernicious stews, the avenging consequences of such Sin
issuing forth, and penetrating to the highest places. I saw
the rich struck down in their strength, their darling children
weakened and withered, their marriageable sons and
daughters perish in their prime. I saw that not one
miserable wretch breathed out his poisoned life in the
deepest cellar of the most neglected town, but, from the
surrounding atmosphere, some particles of his infection
were borne away, charged with heavy retribution on the
general guilt.

There were many attentive and alarmed persons looking
on, who saw these things too. They were well clothed,
and had purses in their pockets; they were educated, full
of kindness, and loved mercy. They said to one another,
"This is horrible, and shall not be!" and there was a
stir among them to set it right. But, opposed to these,
came a small multitude of noisy fools and greedy knaves,
whose harvest was in such horrors; and they, with impudence
and turmoil, and with scurrilous jests at misery and death,
repelled the better lookers-on, who soon fell back, and
stood aloof.

There, the whisper went among those better lookers-on,
saying, "Over the bodies of those fellows, to the remedy!"

But, each of them moodily shrugged his shoulders, and
replied, "It is a great wrong—BUT IT WILL LAST MY
TIME!" And so *they* put it from them.

I saw a great library of laws and law-proceedings, so
complicated, costly, and unintelligible, that, although
numbers of lawyers united in a public fiction that these
were wonderfully just and equal, there was scarcely an
honest man among them, but who said to his friend,
privately consulting him, "Better put up with a fraud or

other injury than grope for redress through the manifold blind turnings and strange chances of this system."

I saw a portion of the system, called (of all things) EQUITY, which was ruin to suitors, ruin to property, a shield for wrong-doers having money, a rack for right-doers having none; a by-word for delay, slow agony of mind, despair, impoverishment, trickery, confusion, insupportable injustice. A main part of it, I saw prisoners wasting in jail; mad people babbling in hospitals; suicides chronicled in the yearly records, orphans robbed of their inheritance; infants righted (perhaps) when they were grey.

Certain lawyers and laymen came together, and said to one another, "In only one of these our Courts of Equity, there are years of this dark perspective before us at the present moment. We must change this."

Uprose, immediately, a throng of others, Secretaries, Petty Bags, Hanapers, Chaff-waxes, and what not, singing (in answer) "Rule Britannia," and "God save the Queen," making flourishing speeches, pronouncing hard names, demanding committees, commissions, commissioners, and other scarecrows, and terrifying the little band of innovators out of their five wits.

Then, the whisper went among the latter, as they shrunk back, saying, "If there is any wrong within the universal knowledge, this wrong is. Go on! Set it right!"

Whereon, each of them sorrowfully thrust his hands in his pockets, and replied, "It is indeed a great wrong;— BUT IT WILL LAST MY TIME!" and so *they* put it from them.

The Spirit with its face concealed, summoned all the people who had used this phrase about their Time, into its presence. Then, it said, beginning with the Minister of State:

"Of what duration is *your* Time?"

The Minister of State replied, "My ancient family has always been long-lived. My father died at eighty-four; my grandfather, at ninety-two. We have the gout, but bear it (like our honors) many years."

"And you," said the Spirit to the Priests and Teachers, "what may *your* time be?"

Some, believed that they were so strong, as that they should number many more years than threescore and ten; others, were the sons of old incumbents who had long outlived youthful expectants. Others, for any means they had of calculating, might be long-lived or short-lived—generally (they had a strong persuasion) long. So, among the well-clothed lookers-on. So, among the lawyers and laymen.

"But, every man, as I understand you, one and all," said the Spirit, "has his time?"

"Yes!" they exclaimed together.

"Yes," said the Spirit; "and it is—ETERNITY! Whosoever is a consenting party to a wrong, comforting himself with the base reflection that it will last his time, shall bear his portion of that wrong throughout ALL TIME. And, in that hour when he and I stand face to face, he shall surely know it, as my name is Death!"

It departed, turning its shaded face hither and thither as it passed along upon its ceaseless work, and blighting all on whom it looked.

Then went among many trembling hearers the whisper, saying, "See, each of you, before you take your ease, O wicked, selfish men, that what will 'last your time,' be just enough to last for ever!"

[1850]

PERFECT FELICITY.

IN A BIRD'S-EYE VIEW.

I AM the Raven in the Happy Family—and nobody knows what a life of misery I lead!

The dog informs me (he was a puppy about town before he joined us; which was lately) that there is more than one Happy Family on view in London. Mine, I beg to say, may be known by being the Family which contains a splendid Raven.

I want to know why I am to be called upon to accommodate myself to a cat, a mouse, a pigeon, a ringdove, an owl (who is the greatest ass I have ever known), a guinea-pig, a sparrow, and a variety of other creatures with whom I have no opinion in common. Is this national education? Because, if it is, I object to it. Is our cage what they call neutral ground, on which all parties may agree? If so, war to the beak I consider preferable.

What right has any man to require me to look complacently at a cat on a shelf all day? It may be all very well for the owl. My opinion of *him* is that he blinks and stares himself into a state of such dense stupidity that he has no idea what company he is in. I have seen him, with my own eyes, blink himself, for hours, into the conviction that he was alone in a belfry. But *I* am not the owl. It would have been better for me, if I had been born in that station of life.

300

I am a Raven. I am, by nature, a sort of collector, or antiquarian. If I contributed, in my natural state, to any Periodical, it would be *The Gentleman's Magazine*. I have a passion for amassing things that are of no use to me, and burying them. Supposing such a thing—I don't wish it to be known to our proprietor that I put this case, but I say, supposing such a thing—-as that I took out one of the Guinea-Pig's eyes; how could I bury it here? The floor of the cage is not an inch thick. To be sure, I could dig through it with my bill (if I dared), but what would be the comfort of dropping a Guinea-Pig's eye into Regent Street?

What I want is privacy. I want to make a collection. I desire to get a little property together. How can I do it here? Mr. Hudson couldn't have done it, under corresponding circumstances.

I want to live by my own abilities, instead of being provided for in this way. I am stuck in a cage with these incongruous companions, and called a member of the Happy Family; but suppose you took a Queen's Counsel out of Westminster Hall, and settled him board and lodging free, in Utopia, where there would be no excuse for 'his quiddits, his quillets, his cases, his tenures, and his tricks,' how do you think *he'd* like it? Not at all. Then why do you expect *me* to like it, and add insult to injury by calling me a 'Happy' Raven!

This is what *I* say: I want to see men do it. I should like to get up a Happy Family of men, and show 'em, I should like to put the Rajah Brooke, the Peace Society, Captain Aaron Smith, several Malay Pirates, Doctor Wiseman, the Reverend Hugh Stowell, Mr. Fox of Oldham, the Board of Health, all the London undertakers, some of the Common (very common *I* think) Council and all the vested interests in the filth and misery of the poor, into a good-sized cage, and see how *they'd* get on. I should like to look at 'em through the bars, after they had undergone the training I have undergone. You wouldn't find Sir Peter Laurie 'putting down' Sanitary Reform then, or getting up in *that* vestry, and pledging his word and honour to the non-existence of Saint Paul's Cathedral, I expect! And very happy *he'd* be, wouldn't he, when he couldn't do that sort of thing?

I have no idea of you lords of the creation coming staring at me in this false position. Why don't you look at home? If you think I'm fond of the dove, you're very much mistaken. If you imagine there is the least good will between me and the pigeon, you never were more deceived in your lives. If you suppose I wouldn't demolish the whole Family (myself excepted), and the cage too, if I had my own way, you don't know what a real Raven is. But if you *do* know this, why am *I* to be picked out as a curiosity? Why don't you go and stare at the Bishop of Exeter? Ecod, he's one of our breed, if any body is!

Do you make me lead this public life because I seem to be what I ain't? Why, I don't make half the pretences that are common among you men! You never heard *me* call the sparrow my noble friend. When did *I* ever tell the Guinea Pig that he was my Christian brother? Name the occasion of my making myself a party to the 'sham' (my friend Mr. Carlyle will lend me his favourite word for the occasion) that the cat hadn't really her eye upon the mouse! Can you say as much? What about the last Court Ball, the next Debate in the Lords, the last great Ecclesiastical Suit, the next long assembly in the Court Circular? I wonder you are not ashamed to look me in the eye! I am an independent Member—of the Happy Family; and I ought to be let out.

I have only one consolation in my inability to damage anything, and that is that I hope I am instrumental in propagating a delusion as to the character of Ravens. I have a strong impression that the sparrows on our beat are beginning to think they may trust a Raven. Let 'em try! There's an uncle of mine, in a stable-yard down in Yorkshire, who will very soon undeceive any small bird that may favour him with a call.

The dogs too. Ha ha! As they go by they look at me and this dog, in quite a friendly way. They never suspect how I should hold on to the tip of his tail, if I consulted my own feelings instead of our proprietor's. It's almost worth being here, to think of some confiding dog who has seen me, going too near a friend of mine who lives at a hackney-coach stand in Oxford Street. You wouldn't stop *his* squeaking in a hurry, if my friend got a chance at him.

It's the same with the children. There's a young gentleman with a hat and feathers, resident in Portland Place, who brings a penny to our proprietor, twice a week. He wears very short white drawers, and has mottled legs above his socks. He hasn't the least idea what I should do to his legs, if I consulted my own inclinations. He never imagines what I am thinking of, when we look at one another. May he only take those legs, in their present juicy state, close to the cage of my brother-in-law of the Zoological Gardens, Regent's Park!

Call yourselves rational beings, and talk about our being reclaimed? Why, there isn't one of us who wouldn't astonish you, if we could only get out! Let *me* out, and see whether *I* should be meek or not. But this is the

way you always go on in—you know you do. Up at
Pentonville, the sparrow says—and he ought to know, for
he was born in a stack of chimneys in that prison—you
are spending I am afraid to say how much every year
out of the rates, to keep men in solitude, where they
CAN'T do any harm (that you know of), and then you
sing all sorts of choruses about their being good. So am
I what you call good—here. Why? Because I can't help
it. Try me outside!

You ought to be ashamed of yourselves, the Magpie
says; and I agree with him. If you are determined to
pet only those who take things and hide them, why don't·
you pet the Magpie and me? We are interesting enough
for you, ain't we? The Mouse says you are not half so
particular about the honest people. He is not a bad
authority. He was almost starved when he lived in a
workhouse, wasn't he? He didn't get much fatter, I
suppose, when he moved to a labourer's cottage? He
was thin enough when he came from that place, here—I
know that. And what does the Mouse (whose word is his
bond) declare? He declares that you don't take half the
care you ought of your own young, and don't teach 'em
half enough. Why don't you then? You might give our
proprietor something to do, I should think, in twisting
miserable boys and girls *into* their proper nature, instead
of twisting us out of ours. You are a nice set of fellows,
certainly, to come and look at Happy Families, as if you
had nothing else to look after!

I take the opportunity of our proprietor's pen and ink
in the evening, to write this. I shall put it away in a
corner—quite sure, as it's intended for the Post Office, of
Mr. Rowland Hill's getting hold of it somehow, and sending
it to somebody. I understand he can do anything with

a letter. Though the Owl says (but I don't believe him), that the present prevalence of measles and chicken-pox among infants in all parts of this country, has been caused by Mr. Rowland Hill. I hope I needn't add that we Ravens are all good scholars, but that we keep our secret (as the Indians believe the Monkeys do, according to a Parrot of my acquaintance) lest our abilities should be imposed upon. As nothing worse than my present degradation as a member of the Happy Family can happen to me, however, I desert the General Freemason's Lodge of Ravens, and express my disgust in writing.

[1850]

FROM THE RAVEN IN THE HAPPY FAMILY.

I won't bear it, and I don't see why I should.

Having begun to commit my grievances to writing, I have made up my mind to go on. You men have a saying, 'I may as well be hung for a sheep as a lamb'. Very good. *I* may as well get into a false position with our proprietor for a ream of manuscript as a quire. Here goes!

I want to know who Buffon was. I'll take my oath he wasn't a bird. Then what did *he* know about birds—especially about Ravens? He pretends to know all about Ravens. Who told him? Was his authority a Raven? I should think not. There never was a Raven yet who committed himself, you'll find, if you look into the precedents.

There's a schoolmaster in dusty black knee-breeches and stockings, who comes and stares at our establishment every Saturday, and brings a lot of boys with him. He is always bothering the boys about Buffon. That's the way I know what Buffon says. He is a nice man, Buffon; and you're all nice men together, ain't you?

What do you mean by saying that I am inquisitive and impudent, that I go everywhere, that I affront and drive off the dogs, that I play pranks on the poultry, and that I am particularly assiduous in cultivating the good-will of the cook? That's what your friend Buffon says, and you adopt him it appears. And what do you mean by calling me 'a glutton by nature, and a thief by habit?' Why, the identical boy who was being told this, on the strength of Buffon, as he looked through our wires last Saturday, was almost out of his mind with pudding, and had got another boy's top in his pocket.

I tell you what. I like the idea of you men, writing histories of *us*, and settling what we are, and what we are not, and calling us any names you like best. What colors do you think you would show in, yourselves, if some of us were to take it into our heads to write histories of *you?* I know something of Astley's Theatre, I hope; I was about the stables there a few years. Ecod! if you heard the observations of the Horses after the performance, you'd have some of the conceit taken out of you!

I don't mean to say that I admire the Cat. I don't admire her. On the whole, I have a personal animosity towards her. But, being obliged to lead this life, I condescend to hold communication with her, and I have asked her what *her* opinion is. She lived with an old lady of property before she came here, who had a number of nephews and nieces. She says she could show you up to that extent, after her experience in that situation, that even you would be hardly brazen enough to talk of cats being sly and selfish any more.

I am particularly assiduous in cultivating the good-will of the cook, am I? Oh! I suppose you never do anything of this sort, yourselves? No politician among you was ever particularly assiduous in cultivating the good-will of a minister, eh? No clergyman in cultivating the good-will

of a bishop, humph? No fortune-seeker in cultivating the
good-will of a patron, hah? You have no toad-eating,
no time-serving, no place-hunting, no lacqueyship of gold
and silver sticks, or anything of that sort, I suppose?
You haven't too many cooks, in short, whom you are all
assiduously cultivating, till you spoil the general broth?
Not you. You leave that to the Ravens.

Your friend Buffon, and some more of you, are
mighty ready, it seems, to give *us* characters. Would you
like to hear about your own temper and forbearance?
Ask the Dog. About your never overloading or ill-using
a willing creature? Ask my brother-in-law's friend, the
Camel, up in the Zoological. About your gratitude to,
and your provision for, old servants? I wish I could refer
you to the last Horse I dined off (he was very tough),
up at a knacker's yard in Battle Bridge. About your
mildness, and your abstinence from blows and cudgels?
Wait till the Donkey's book comes out!

You are very fond of laughing at the parrot, I observe.
Now, I don't care for the parrot. I don't admire the
parrot's voice—it wants hoarseness. And I despise the
parrot's livery—considering black the only true wear. I
would as soon stick my bill into the parrot's breast as
look at him. Sooner. But if you come to that, and you
laugh at the parrot because the parrot says the same
thing over and over again, don't you think you could get
up a laugh at yourselves? Did you ever know a Cabinet
Minister say of a flagrant job or great abuse, perfectly
notorious to the whole country, that he had never heard
a word of it himself, but could assure the honourable
gentleman that every enquiry should be made? Did you
ever hear a Justice remark, of any extreme example of
ignorance, that it was a most extraordinary case, and he

couldn't have believed in the possibility of such a case—
when there had been, all through his life, ten thousand
such within sight of his chimney-pots? Did you ever hear,
among yourselves, anything approaching to a parrot repetition of the words, Constitution, Country, Public Service,
Self-Government, Centralisation, Un-English, Capital, Balance of Power, Vested Interests, Corn, Rights of Labor,
Wages, or so forth? *Did* you ever? No! Of course you
never!

But to come back to that fellow Buffon. He finds
us Ravens to be most extraordinary creatures. We have
properties so remarkable, that you'd hardly believe it. 'A
piece of money, a teaspoon, or a ring,' he says, 'are always tempting baits to our avarice. These we will slily
seize upon; and, if not watched, carry to our favorite
hole.' How odd!

Did you ever hear of a place called California? *I* have.
I understand there are a number of animals over there,
from all parts of the world, turning up the ground with
their bills, grubbing under the water, sickening, moulting,
living in want and fear, starving, dying, tumbling over on
their backs, murdering one another, and all for what?
Pieces of money that they want to carry to their favourite
holes. Ravens every one of 'em! Not a man among 'em,
bless you!

Did you ever hear of Railway Scrip? *I* have. We made
a pretty exhibition of ourselves about that, we feathered
creatures! Lord, how we went on about that Railway Scrip!
How we fell down, to a bird, from the Eagle to the
Sparrow, before a scarecrow, and worshipped it for the
love of the bits of rag and paper fluttering from its dirty
pockets! If it hadn't tumbled down in its rottenness, we
should have clapped a title on it within ten years, I'll be·

sworn!—Go along with you, and your Buffon, and don't talk to me!

'The Raven don't confine himself to petty depradations on the pantry or the larder'—here you are with your Buffon again—'but he soars at more magnificent plunder, that he can neither exhibit nor enjoy.'   This must be very strange to you men—more than it is to the Cat who lived with that old lady, though!

Now, I am not going to stand this.   You shall not have it all your own way.   I am resolved that I won't have Ravens written about by men, without having men written about by Ravens—at all events by one Raven, and that's me.   I shall put down my opinions about you. As leisure and opportunity serve, I shall collect a natural history of you.   You are a good deal given to talk about *your* missions.   That's my mission.   How do you like it?

I am open to contributions from any animal except one of your set; bird, beast, or fish, may assist me in my mission, if he will.   I have mentioned it to the Cat, intimated it to the Mouse, and proposed it to the Dog.

The Owl shakes his head when I confide it to him, and says he doubts.   He always did shake his head, and doubt.   Whenever he brings himself before the public, he never does anything except shake his head and doubt. I should have thought he had got himself into a sufficient mess by doing that, when he roosted for a long time in the Court of Chancery.   But he can't leave off.   He's always at it.

Talking of missions, here's our Proprietor's Wife with a mission now!   She has found out that she ought to go and vote at elections; ought to be competent to sit in Parliament; ought to be able to enter the learned professions— the army and navy, too, I believe.   She has

made the discovery that she has no business to be the
comfort of our Proprietor's life, and to have the hold upon
him of not being mixed up in all the janglings and
wranglings of men, but is quite ill-used in being the
solace of his home, and wants to go out speechifying.
That's our Proprietor's Wife's new mission. Why, you
never heard the Dove go on in that ridiculous way. She
knows her true strength better.

You are mighty proud about your language; but it
seems to me that you don't deserve to have words, if you
can't make a better use of 'em. You know you are
always fighting about 'em. Do you never mean to leave
that off, and come to things a little? I thought you had
high authority for *not* tearing each other's eyes out about
words. You respect it, don't you?

. I declare I am stunned with words, on my perch in
the Happy Family. I used to think the cry of a Peacock
bad enough, when I was on sale in a menagerie, but I
had rather live in the midst of twenty peacocks, than one
Gorham and a Privy Council. In the midst of your
wordy squabbling, you don't think of the lookers-on. But
if you heard what *I* hear in my public thoroughfare,
you'd stop a little of that noise, and leave the great bulk
of the people something to believe in place. You are
overdoing it, I assure you.

I don't wonder at the Parrot picking words up and
occupying herself with them. She has nothing else to do.
There are no destitute parrots, no uneducated parrots, no
foreign parrots in a contagious state of distraction, no
parrots in danger of pestilence, no festering heaps of
miserable parrots, no parrots crying to be sent away
beyond the sea for dear life. But among you!—

Well! I repeat, I am not going to stand it. Tame submission to injustice is unworthy of a Raven. I croak the croak of revolt, and call upon the Happy Family to rally round me. You men have had it all your own way for a long time. *Now*, you shall hear a sentiment or two about yourselves.

I find my last communication gone from the corner where I hid it. I rather suspect the magpie, but he says, 'Upon his honor.' If Mr. Rowland Hill has got it, he will do me justice—more justice than you have done him lately, or I am mistaken in my man.

* * * * * * * * * * *

Halloa!

You *won't* let me begin that Natural History of you, eh? You *will* always be doing something or other, to take off my attention? Now, you have begun to argue with the Undertakers, have you? What next!

Ugh! you are a nice set of fellows to be discussing, at this time of day, whether you shall countenance that humbug any longer. "Performing" funerals, indeed! I have heard of performing dogs and cats, performing goats and monkeys, performing ponies, white-mice, and canary-birds; but, performing drunkards at so much a day, guzzling over your dead, and throwing half of you into debt for a twelvemonth, beats all I ever heard of. Ha, ha!

The other day there was a person "went and died" (as our Proprietor's wife says) close to our establishment. Upon my beak I thought I should have fallen off my perch, you made me laugh so, at the funeral!

Oh my crop and feathers, what a scene it was! *I* never saw the Owl so charmed. It was just the thing for him.

First of all, two dressed-up fellows came—trying to look

sober, but they couldn't do it—and stuck themselves outside the door. There they stood, for hours, with a couple
of crutches covered over with drapery: cutting their jokes
on the company as they went in, and breathing such
strong rum and water into our establishment over the
way, that the Guinea Pig (who has a poor little head)
was drunk in ten minutes. You are so proud of your
humanity. Ha, ha! As if a pair of respectable crows
wouldn't have done it much better?

By-and-bye, there came a hearse and four, and then
two carriages and four; and on the tops of 'em, and on
all the horses' heads, were plumes of feathers, hired at so
much per plume; and everything, horses and all, was
covered over with black velvet, till you couldn't see it.
Because there were not feathers enough yet, there was a
fellow in the procession carrying a board of 'em on his
head, like Italian images; and there were about five-and-
twenty or thirty other fellows (all hot and red in the face
with eating and drinking) dressed up in scarves and hat-
bands, and carrying—shut-up fishing-rods, I believe—who
went draggling through the mud, in a manner that I thought
would be the death of me; while the "Black Jobmaster"—
that's what he calls himself—who had let the coaches and
horses to a furnishing undertaker, who had let 'em to a
haberdasher, who had let 'em to a carpenter, who had
let 'em to the parish-clerk, who had let 'em to the sexton,
who had let 'em to the plumber, painter and glazier who
had got the funeral to do, looked out of the public-house
window at the corner, with his pipe in his mouth, and
said—for I heard him—"that was the sort of turn-out to
do a gen-teel party credit." That! As if any two-and-
sixpenny masquerade, tumbled into a vat of blacking,
wouldn't be quite as solemn, and immeasurably cheaper!

Do you think I don't know you? You're mistaken :f
you think so. But perhaps you do. Well! Shall I tell
you what I know? Can you bear it? Here it is then.
The Black Jobmaster is right. The root of all this, is the
gen-teel party.

You don't mean to deny it, I hope? You don't mean
to tell me that this nonsensical mockery isn't owing to
your gentility. Don't I know a Raven in a Cathedral
Tower, who has often heard your service for the Dead?
Don't I know that you almost begin it with the words,
"We brought nothing into this world, and it is certain that
we can carry nothing out"? Don't I know that in a
monstrous satire on those words, you carry your hired
velvets, and feathers, and scarves, and all the rest of it,
to the edge of the grave, and get plundered (and serve
you right!) in every article, because you WILL be gen-teel
parties to the last?

Eh? Think a little! Here's the plumber, painter and
glazier come to take the funeral order which he is going
to give to the sexton, who is going to give it to the clerk,
who is going to give it to the carpenter, who is going to
give it to the haberdasher, who is going to give it to the
furnishing undertaker, who is going to divide it with the
Black Jobmaster. "Hearse and four, Sir?" says he.
"No, a pair will be sufficient." "I beg your pardon, Sir,
but when we buried Mr. Grundy at number twenty, there
was four on 'em, Sir; I think it right to mention it."
"Well, perhaps there had better be four." "Thank you,
Sir. Two coaches and four, Sir, shall we say?" "No.
Coaches and pair." "You'll excuse my mentioning it,
Sir, but pairs to the coaches, and four to the hearse,
would have a singular appearance to the neighbours. When
we put four to anything, we always carry four right

through." "Well! say four!" "Thank you, Sir. Feathers of course?" "No. No feathers. They're absurd." "Very good, Sir. *No* feathers?" "No." "*Very* good, Sir. We *can* do fours without feathers, Sir, but it's what we never do. When we buried Mr. Grundy, there was feathers, and—I only throw it out, Sir—Mrs. Grundy might think it strange." "Very well! Feathers!" "Thank you, Sir,"—and so on.

Is it and so on, or not through the whole black job of jobs, because of Mrs. Grundy and the gen-teel party?

I suppose you've thought about this? I suppose you've reflected on what you're doing, and on what you've done? When you read about those poisonings for the burial money, do you consider how it is that burial Societies ever came to be, at all? You perfectly understand—you who are not the poor, and ought to set 'em an example—that besides making the whole thing costly, you've confused their minds about this burying, and have taught 'em to confound expense and show, with respect and affection. You know all you've got to answer for, you gen-teel parties? I'm glad of it.

I believe it's only the monkeys who are servile imitators, is it? You reflect! To be sure you do. So does Mrs. Grundy—and she casts reflections—don't she?

What animals are those who scratch shallow holes in the ground in crowded places, scarcely hide their dead in 'em, and become unnaturally infected by their dead, and die by thousands? Vultures, I suppose. I think you call the Vulture an obscene bird? I don't consider him agreeable, but I never caught him misconducting himself in that way.

My honourable friend, the dog—I call him my honourable friend in your Parliamentary sense, because I hate him—

turns round three times before he goes to sleep. I ask
him why? He says he don't know; but he always does
it. Do *you* know how you ever came to have that board
of feathers carried on a fellow's head? Come. You're a
boastful race. Show yourselves superior to the dog, and
tell me!

Now, I don't love many people: but I do love the
undertakers. I except them from the censure I pass upon
you in general. They know you so well, that I look upon
'em as a sort of Ravens. They are so certain of your
being gen-teel parties, that they stick at nothing. They
are sure they've got the upper hand of you. Our proprietor
was reading the paper, only last night, and there was an
advertisement in it from a sensitive and libelled undertaker,
to wit, that the allegation " that funerals were unnecessarily
expensive, was an insult to his professional brethren."
Ha! ha! Why, he knows he has you on the hip. It's
nothing to him that their being unnecessarily expensive is
a fact within the experience of all of you as glaring as
the sun when there's not a cloud. He is certain that
when you want a funeral "performed," he has only to be
down upon you with Mrs. Grundy to do what he likes
with you—and then he'll go home, and laugh like a
Hyæna.

I declare (supposing I wasn't detained against my will
by our Proprietor) that, if I had any arms, I'd take the
undertakers to 'em! There's another, in the same paper,
who says they're libelled, in the accusation of having
disgracefully disturbed the meeting in favour of what you
call your General Interment Bill. Our establishment was
in the Strand, that night. There was no crowd of undertakers' men there, with circulars in their pockets, calling
on 'em to come in coloured clothes to make an uproar;

it wasn't undertakers' men who got in with forged orders
to yell and screech; it wasn't undertakers' men who made
a brutal charge at the platform, and overturned the ladies
like a troop of horse. Of course not. *I* know all about it.

But—and lay this well to heart, you Lords of the
creation, as you call yourselves!—it *is* these undertakers'
men to whom, in the last trying, bitter grief of life, you
confide the loved and honoured forms of your sisters,
mothers, daughters, wives. It *is* to these delicate gentry,
and to their solemn remarks, and decorous behaviour, that
you entrust the sacred ashes of all that has been the
purest to you, and the dearest to you, in this world.
Don't improve the breed! Don't change the custom! Be
true to my opinion of you, and to Mrs. Grundy!

I nail the black flag of the black Jobmaster to our cage
—figuratively speaking—and I stand up for the gen-teel
parties. So (but from different motives) does the Owl.
You've got a chance, by means of that bill I've mentioned
—by the bye, I call my own a General Interment Bill,
for it buries everything it gets hold of—to alter the whole
system; to avail yourselves of the results of all improved
European experience; to separate death from life; to
surround it with everything that is sacred and solemn, and
to dissever it from everything that is shocking and sordid.
You won't read the bill? You won't dream of helping it?
You won't think of looking at the evidence on which it's
founded—Will you? No. That's right!

Gen-teel parties, step forward, if you please, to the
rescue of the black Jobmaster! The rats are with you.
I am informed that they have unanimously passed a
resolution that the closing of the London churchyards will
be an insult to their professional brethren, and will oblige
'em " to fight for it. " The Parrots are with you. The

Owl is with you. The Raven is with you. No General Interments. Carrion for ever! Ha, ha! Halloa!

*　*　*　*　*　*　*　*.　*　*　*

I suppose you thought I was dead? No such thing. Don't flatter yourselves that I haven't got my eye upon you. I am wide awake, and you give me plenty to look at.

I have begun my great work upon you. I have been collecting materials from the Horse, to begin with. You are glad to hear it, ain't you? Very likely. Oh, he gives you a nice character! He makes you out a charming set of fellows.

He informs me, by the bye, that he is a distant relation of the pony that was taken up in a balloon, a few weeks ago; and that the pony's account of your going to see him at Vauxhall Gardens, is an amazing thing. The pony says, that when he looked round on the assembled crowd, come to see the realisation of the wood-cut in the bill, he found it impossible to discover which was the real Mister Green—there were so many Mister Greens—and they were all so very green!

But, that's the way with you. You know it is. Don't tell me! You'd go to see anything that other people went to see. And don't flatter yourselves that I am referring to "the vulgar curiosity," as you choose to call it, when you mean some curiosity in which you don't participate yourselves. The polite curiosity in this country, is as vulgar as any curiosity in the world.

Of course you'll tell me, no it isn't, but I say yes it is. What have you got to say for yourselves about the Nepaulese Princes, I should like to know? Why, there has been more crowding, and pressing, and pushing, and jostling, and struggling, and striving, in genteel houses this last season, on account of those Nepaulèse Princes, than would take place in vulgar Cremorne Gardens and Green-wich Park, at Easter time and Whitsuntide! And what for? Do you know anything about 'em? Have you any idea why they came here? Can you put your finger on their country in the map? Have you ever asked yourselves a dozen common questions about its climate, natural his-tory, government, productions, customs, religion, manners? Not you! Here are a couple of swarthy Princes very much out of their element, walking about in wide muslin trousers, and sprinkled all over with gems (like the clock-work figure on the old round platform in the street, grown up), and they're fashionable outlandish monsters, and it's a new excitement for you to get a stare at 'em. As to asking 'em to dinner, and seeing 'em sit at table without eating in your company (unclean animals as you are!) you fall into raptures at that. Quite delicious, isn't it? Ugh, you dunder-headed boobies!   .

I wonder what there is, new and strange, that you *wouldn't* lionise, as you call it. Can you suggest anything? It's not a hippopotamus, I suppose. I hear from my brother-in-law in the Zoological Gardens, that you are always pelting away into the Regent's Park, by thousands, to see the hippopotamus. Oh, you're very fond of hippo-potami, ain't you? You study one attentively, when you *do* see one, don't you? You come away, so much wiser than you went, reflecting so profoundly on the wonders of creation—eh?

Bah! You follow one another like wild geese, but you are not so good to eat!

These, however, are not the observations of my friend

the Horse. *He* takes you, in another point of view. Would you like to read his contribution to my Natural History of you? No? You shall then.

He is a Cab-horse now. He wasn't always, but he is now, and his usual stand is close to our Proprietor's usual stand. That's the way we have come into communication, we "dumb animals." Ha, ha! Dumb, too! Oh, the conceit of you men, because you can bother the community out of their five wits, by making speeches!

Well, I mentioned to this Horse that I should be glad to have his opinions and experiences of you. Here they are:

"At the request of my honourable friend the Raven, I proceed to offer a few remarks in reference to the animal called Man. I have had varied experiences of this strange creature for fifteen years, and am now driven by a Man, in the hackney cabriolet, number twelve thousand four hundred and fifty-two.

"The sense Man entertains of his own inferiority to the nobler animals—and I am now more particularly referring to the Horse—has impressed me forcibly, in the course of my career. If a Man knows a Horse well, he is prouder of it than of any knowledge of himself, within the range of his limited capacity. He regards it, as the sum of all human acquisition. If he is learned in a Horse, he has nothing else to learn. And the same remark applies, with some little abatement, to his acquaintance with Dogs. I have seen a good deal of Man in my time, but I think I have never met a Man who didn't feel it necessary to his reputation to pretend, on occasion, that he knew something of Horses and Dogs, though he really knew nothing. As to making us a subject of conversation, my opinion is that we are more talked about, than history, philosophy,

literature, art, and science, all put together. I have encountered innumerable gentlemen in the country who were
totally incapable of interest in anything but Horses and
Dogs—except Cattle. And I have always been given to
understand that they were the flower of the civilised world.

"It is very doubtful, to me, whether there is, upon the
whole, anything Man is so ambitious to imitate, as an
ostler, a jockey, a stage coachman, a horse-dealer, or a
dog-fancier. There may be some other character which
I do not immediately remember, that fires him with
emulation; but, if there be, I am sure it is connected with
Horses, or Dogs, or both. This is an unconscious com-
pliment, on the part of the tyrant, to the nobler animals,
which I consider to be very remarkable. I have known
Lords, and Baronets, and Members of Parliament, out of
number, who have deserted every other calling, to become
but indifferent stablemen, or kennelmen, and be cheated
on all hands, by the real aristocracy of those pursuits who
were regularly born to the business.

"All this, I say, is a tribute to our superiority which
I consider to be very remarkable. Yet, still, I can't quite
understand it. Man can hardly devote himself to us, in
admiration of our virtues, because he never imitates them.
We Horses are as honest, though I say it, as animals can
be. If, under the pressure of circumstances, we submit
to act at a Circus, for instance, we always show that we
are acting. We never deceive anybody. We would scorn
to do it. If we are called upon to do anything in earnest,
we do our best. If we are required to run a race falsely,
and to lose when we could win, we are not to be relied
upon, to commit a fraud; Man must come in at that
point, and force us to it. And the extraordinary circumstance to me, is, that Man (whom I take to be a

21

powerful species of Monkey) is always making us nobler
animals the instruments of his meanness and cupidity.
The very name of our kind has become a byword for
all sorts of trickery and cheating. We are as innocent as
counters at a game—and yet this creature WILL play
falsely with us!

"Man's opinion, good or bad, is not worth much, as
any rational Horse knows. But, justice is justice; and
what I complain of, is, that Mankind talks of us as if We
had something to do with all this. They say that such
a man was 'ruined by Horses.' Ruined by Horses!
They can't be open, even in that, and say he was ruined
by Men; but they lay it at *our* stable-door! As if we
ever ruined anybody, or were ever doing anything but
being ruined ourselves, in our generous desire to fulfil the
useful purposes of our existence!

"In the same way, we get a bad name as if we were
profligate company. 'So and so got among Horses, and
it was all up with him.' Why, *we* would have reclaimed
him—*we* would have made him temperate, industrious,
steady, sensible—what harm would he ever have got from
us, I should wish to ask?

"Upon the whole, speaking of him as I have found
him, I should describe Man as an unmeaning and con-
ceited creature, very seldom to be trusted, and not likely
to make advances towards the honesty of the nobler
animals. I should say that his power of warping the
nobler animals to bad purposes, and damaging their reputation by his companionship, is, next to the art of growing
oats, hay, carrots, and clover, one of his principal attributes.
He is very unintelligible in his caprices; seldom expressing
with distinctness what he wants of us; and relying greatly
on our better judgment to find out. He is cruel, and

fond of blood—particularly at a steeple-chase—and is very ungrateful.

"And yet, so far as I can understand, he worships us too. He sets up images of us (not particularly like, but meant to be) in the streets, and calls upon his fellows to admire them, and believe in them. As well as I can make out, it is not of the least importance what images of Man are put astride upon these images of Horses, for I don't find any famous personage among them—except one, and *his* image seems to have been contracted for, by the gross. The jockeys who ride our statues are very queer jockeys, it appears to me, but it is something to find Man even posthumously sensible of what he owes to us. I believe that when he has done any great wrong to any very distinguished Horse, deceased, he gets up a subscription to have an awkward likeness of him made, and erects it in a public place, to be generally venerated. I can find no other reason for the statues of us that abound.

"It must be regarded as a part of the inconsistency of Man, that he erects no statues to the Donkeys—who, though far inferior animals to ourselves, have great claims upon him. I should think a Donkey opposite the Horse at Hyde Park, another in Trafalgar Square, and a group of Donkeys, in brass, outside the Guildhall of the City of London (for I believe the Common Council Chamber is inside that building) would be pleasant and appropriate memorials.

"I am not aware that I can suggest anything more, to my honourable friend the Raven, which will not already have occurred to his fine intellect. Like myself, he is the victim of brute force, and must bear it until the present state of things is changed—as it possibly may be in the good time which I understand is coming, if I wait a little longer."

There! How do you like that? That's the Horse! You shall have another animal's sentiments soon.   I have communicated with plenty of 'em, and they are all down upon you.   It's not I alone who have found you out.   You are generally detected, I am happy to say, and shall be covered with confusion.

Talking about the horse, are you going to set up any more horses? Eh! Think a bit. Come! You haven't got horses enough yet, surely? Couldn't you put somebody else on horseback, and stick him up, at the cost of a few thousands? You have already statues to most of the "benefactors of mankind," (SEE ADVERTISEMENT) in your principal cities. You walk through groves of great inventors, instructors, discoverers, assuagers of pain, preventers of disease, suggesters of purifying thoughts, doers of noble deeds.   Finish the list.   Come!

Whom will you hoist into the saddle? Let's have a cardinal virtue! Shall it be · Faith? Hope? Charity? Aye, Charity's the virtue to ride on horseback! Let's have Charity!

How shall we represent it?   Eh?   What do you think? Royal? Certainly. Duke? Of course. Charity always was typified in that way, from the time of a certain widow, downwards. And there's nothing less left to put up; all the commoners who were " benefactors of mankind " having had their statues in the public places, long ago.

How shall we dress it? Rags? Low. Drapery? Commonplace. Field-Marshal's uniform? The very thing! Charity in a Field-Marshal's uniform (none the worse for wear) with thirty thousand pounds a-year, public money, in its pocket, and fifteen thousand more, public money, up behind, will be a piece of plain uncompromising truth in the highways, and an honor to the country and the time.

Ha, ha, ha! You can't leave the memory of an un-assuming, honest, good-natured, amiable old Duke alone, without bespattering it with your flunkeyism, can't you? That's right—and like you! Here are three brass buttons in my crop. I'll subscribe 'em all. One, to the statue of Charity; one, to a statue of Hope; one, to a statue of Faith. For Faith, we'll have the Nepaulese Ambassador on horseback—being a prince. And for Hope, we'll put the Hippopotamus on horseback, and so make a group.

Let's have a meeting about it!

[1850]

FRAUDS ON THE FAIRIES.

WE may assume that we are not singular in entertaining a very great tenderness for the fairy literature of our childhood. What enchanted us then, and is captivating a million of young fancies now, has, at the same blessed time of life, enchanted vast hosts of men and women who have done their long day's work, and laid their grey heads down to rest. It would be hard to estimate the amount of gentleness and mercy that has made its way among us through these slight channels. Forbearance, courtesy, consideration for the poor and aged, kind treatment of animals, the love of nature, abhorrence of tyranny and brute force—many such good things have been first nourished in the child's heart by this powerful aid. It has greatly helped to keep us, in some sense, ever young, by preserving through our wordly [*] ways one slender track not overgrown with weeds, where we may walk with children, sharing their delights.

In an utilitarian age, of all other times, it is a matter of grave importance that Fairy tales should be respected. Our English red tape is too magnificently red ever to be employed in the tying up of such trifles, but every one who has considered the subject knows full well that a nation without fancy, without some romance, never did,

[* Obviously a misprint for "worldly."]

326

never can, never will, hold a great place under the sun. The theatre, having done its worst to destroy these admirable fictions—and having in a most exemplary manner destroyed itself, its artists, and its audiences, in that perversion of its duty—it becomes doubly important that the little books themselves, nurseries of fancy as they are, should be preserved. To preserve them in their usefulness, they must be as much preserved in their simplicity, and purity, and innocent extravagance, as if they were actual fact. Whosoever alters them to suit his own opinions, whatever they are, is guilty, to our thinking, of an act of presumption, and appropriates to himself what does not belong to him.

We have lately observed, with pain, the intrusion of a Whole Hog of unwieldy dimensions into the fairy flower garden. The rooting of the animal among the roses would in itself have awakened in us nothing but indignation; our pain arises from his being violently driven in by a man of genius, our own beloved friend, Mr. George Cruikshank. That incomparable artist is, of all men, the last who should lay his exquisite hand on fairy text. In his own art he understands it so perfectly, and illustrates it so beautifully, so humorously, so wisely, that he should never lay down his etching needle to "edit" the Ogre, to whom with that little instrument he can render such extraordinary justice. But, to "editing" Ogres, and Hop-o'-my-thumbs, and their families, our dear moralist has in a rash moment taken, as a means of propagating the doctrines of Total Abstinence, Prohibition of the sale of spirituous liquors, Free Trade, and Popular Education. For the introduction of these topics, he has altered the text of a fairy story; and against his right to do any such thing we protest with all our might and main. Of his likewise altering it to advertise that excellent series of plates, "The Bottle," we say nothing more than that we foresee a new and improved edition of "Goody Two Shoes," edited by E. Moses and Son; of the Dervish with the box of ointment, edited by Professor Holloway; and of "Jack and the Beanstalk," edited by Mary Wedlake, the popular authoress of "Do you bruise your oats yet."

Now, it makes not the least difference to our objection whether we agree or disagree with our worthy friend, Mr. Cruikshank, in the opinions he interpolates upon an old fairy story. Whether good or bad in themselves, they are, in that relation, like the famous definition of a weed; a thing growing up in a wrong place. He has no greater moral justification in altering the harmless little books than we should have in altering his best etchings. If such a precedent were followed we must soon become disgusted with the old stories into which modern personages so obtruded themselves, and the stories themselves must soon be lost. With seven Blue Beards in the field, each coming at a gallop from his own platform mounted on a foaming hobby, a generation or two hence would not know which was which, and the great original Blue Beard would be confounded with the counterfeits. Imagine a Total abstinence edition of Robinson Crusoe, with the rum left out. Imagine a Peace edition, with the gunpowder left out, and the rum left in. Imagine a Vegetarian edition, with the goat's flesh left out. Imagine a Kentucky edition, to introduce a flogging of that 'tarnal ole nigger Friday, twice a week. Imagine an Aborigines Protection Society edition, to deny the cannibalism and make Robinson embrace the amiable savages whenever they landed. Robinson Crusoe would be "edited" out of his island in a hundred years, and the island would be swallowed up in the editorial ocean.

Among the other learned professions we have now the
Platform profession, chiefly exercised by a new and
meritorious class of commercial travellers who go about to
take the sense of meetings on various articles: some, of a
very superior description: some, not quite so good. Let
us write the story of Cinderella, "edited" by one of these
gentlemen, doing a good stroke of business, and having a
rather extensive mission.

Once upon a time, a rich man and his wife were the
parents of a lovely daughter. She was a beautiful child,
and became, at her own desire, a member of the Juvenile
Band of Hope when she was only four years of age.
When this child was only nine years of age her mother
died, and all the Juvenile Bands of Hope in her district
—the Central district, number five hundred and twenty-
seven—formed in a procession of two and two, amounting
to fifteen hundred, and followed her to the grave, singing
chorus Number forty-two, "O come," etc. This grave was
outside the town, and under the direction of the Local
Board of Health, which reported at certain stated intervals
to the General Board of Health, Whitehall.

The motherless little girl was very sorrowful for the
loss of her mother, and so was her father too, at first;
but, after a year was over, he married again—a very cross
widow lady, with two proud tyrannical daughters as cross
as herself. He was aware that he could have made his
marriage with this lady a civil process by simply making
a declaration before a Registrar; but he was averse to this
course on religious grounds, and, being a member of the
Montgolfian persuasion, was married according to the
ceremonies of that respectable church by the Reverend
Jared Jocks, who improved the occasion.

He did not live long with his disagreeable wife. Having

been shamefully accustomed to shave with warm water
instead of cold, which he ought to have used (see Medical
Appendix B. and C.), his undermined constitution could
not bear up against her temper, and he soon died.   Then,
this orphan was cruelly treated by her stepmother and the
two daughters, and was forced to do the dirtiest of the
kitchen work; to scour the saucepans, wash the dishes,
and light the fires—which did not consume their own
smoke, but emitted a dark vapour prejudicial to the
bronchial tubes.   The only warm place in the house where
she was free from ill-treatment was the kitchen chimney-
corner, and as she used to sit down there, among the
cinders, when her work was done, the proud fine sisters
gave her the name of Cinderella.

About this time, the King of the land, who never made
war against anybody, and allowed everybody to make war
against him—which was the reason why his subjects were
the greatest manufacturers on earth, and always lived in
security and peace—gave a great feast, which was to last
two days.   This splendid banquet was to consist entirely
of artichokes and gruel; and from among those who were
invited to it, and to hear the delightful speeches after
dinner, the King's son was to choose a bride for himself.
The proud fine sisters were invited, but nobody knew
anything about poor Cinderella, and she was to stay
at home.

She was so sweet-tempered, however, that she assisted
the haughty creatures to dress, and bestowed her admirable
taste upon them as freely as if they had been kind to her.
Neither did she laugh when they broke seventeen stay-
laces in dressing; for, although she wore no stays herself,
being sufficiently acquainted with the anatomy of the
human figure to be aware of the destructive effects of

tight-lacing, she always reserved her opinions on that subject for the Regenerative Record (price three halfpence in a neat wrapper), which all good people take in, and to which she was a Contributor.

At length the wished for moment arrived, and the proud fine sisters swept away to the feast and speeches, leaving Cinderella in the chimney-corner. But, she could always occupy her mind with the general question of the Ocean Penny Postage, and she had in her pocket an unread Oration on that subject, made by the well known Orator, Nehemiah Nicks. She was lost in the fervid eloquence of that talented Apostle when she became aware of the presence of one of those female relatives which (it may not be generally known) it is not lawful for a man to marry. I allude to her grandmother.

"Why so solitary, my child?" said the old lady to Cinderella.

"Alas, grandmother," returned the poor girl, "my sisters have gone to the feast and speeches, and here sit I in the ashes, Cinderella!"

"Never," cried the old lady with animation, "shall one of the Band of Hope despair! Run into the garden, my dear, and fetch me an American Pumpkin! American, because in some parts of that independent country, there are prohibitory laws against the sale of alcoholic drinks in any form. Also; because America produced (among many great Pumpkins) the glory of her sex, Mrs. Colonel Bloomer. None but an American Pumpkin will do, my child."

Cinderella ran into the garden, and brought the largest American Pumpkin she could find. This virtuously democratic vegetable her grandmother immediately changed into a splendid coach. Then, she sent her for six mice from the mouse-trap, which she changed into prancing horses, free from the obnoxious and oppressive post-horse duty. Then, to the rat-trap in the stable for a rat, which she changed to a state-coachman, not amenable to the iniquitous assessed taxes. Then, to look behind a watering-pot for six lizards, which she changed into six footmen, each with a petition in his hand ready to present to the Prince, signed by fifty thousand persons, in favour of the early closing movement.

"But, grandmother," said Cinderella, stopping in the midst of her delight, and looking at her clothes, "how can I go to the palace in these miserable rags?"

"Be not uneasy about that, my dear," returned her grandmother.

Upon which the old lady touched her with her wand, her rags disappeared, and she was beautifully dressed. Not in the present costume of the female sex, which has been proved to be at once grossly immodest and absurdly inconvenient, but in rich sky-blue satin pantaloons gathered at the ankle, a puce-colored satin pelisse, sprinkled with silver flowers, and a very broad Leghorn hat. The hat was chastely ornamented with a rainbow-coloured ribbon hanging in two bell-pulls down the back; the pantaloons were ornamented with a golden stripe; and the effect of the whole was unspeakably sensible, feminine, and retiring. Lastly, the old lady put on Cinderella's feet a pair of shoes made of glass: observing that but for the abolition of the duty on that article, it never could have been devoted to such a purpose; the effect of all such taxes being to cramp invention, and embarrass the producer, to the manifest injury of the consumer. When the old lady had made these wise remarks, she dismissed Cinderella to the feast and speeches, charging her by no means to remain after twelve o'clock at night.

The arrival of Cinderella at the Monster Gathering produced a great excitement. As a delegate from the United States had just moved that the King do take the chair, and as the motion had been seconded and carried unanimously, the King himself could not go forth to receive her. But His Royal Highness the Prince (who was to move the second resolution), went to the door to hand her from her carriage. This virtuous Prince, being completely covered from head to foot with Total Abstinence Medals, shone as if he were attired in complete armour; while the inspiring strains of the Peace Brass Band in the gallery (composed of the Lambkin Family, eighteen in number, who cannot be too much encouraged) awakened additional enthusiasm.

The King's son handed Cinderella to one of the reserved seats for pink tickets, on the platform, and fell in love with her immediately. His appetite deserted him; he scarcely tasted his artichokes, and merely trifled with his gruel. When the speeches began, and Cinderella, wrapped in the eloquence of the two inspired delegates who occupied the entire evening in speaking to the first Resolution, occasionally cried, "Hear, hear!" the sweetness of her voice completed her conquest of the Prince's heart. But, indeed the whole male portion of the assembly loved her —and doubtless would have done so, even if she had been less beautiful, in consequence of the contrast which her dress presented to the bold and ridiculous garments of the other ladies.

At a quarter before twelve the second inspired delegate having drunk all the water in the decanter, and fainted away, the King put the question, "That this Meeting do now adjourn until to-morrow." Those who were of that opinion holding up their hands, and then those who were

of the contrary, theirs, there appeared an immense majority
in favour of the resolution, which was consequently carried.
Cinderella got home in safety, and heard nothing all that
night, or all next day, but the praises of the unknown
lady with the sky-blue satin pantaloons.

When the time for the feast and speeches came round
again, the cross stepmother and the proud fine daughters
went out in good time to secure their places. As soon
as they were gone, Cinderella's grandmother returned and
changed her as before. Amid a blast of welcome from
the Lambkin family, she was again handed to the pink
seat on the platform by His Royal Highness.

This gifted Prince was a powerful speaker, and had the
evening before him. He rose at precisely ten minutes
before eight, and was greeted with tumultuous cheers and
waving of handkerchiefs. When the excitement had in
some degree subsided, he proceeded to address the meeting:
who were never tired of listening to speeches, as no good
people ever are. He held them enthralled for four hours
and a quarter. Cinderella forgot the time, and hurried
away so when she heard the first stroke of twelve, that
her beautiful dress changed back to her old rags at the
door, and she left one of her glass shoes behind. The
Prince took it up, and vowed—that is, made a declaration
before a magistrate; for he objected on principle to the
multiplying of oaths—that he would only marry the charming
creature to whom that shoe belonged.

He accordingly caused an advertisement to that effect
to be inserted in all the newspapers; for, the advertisement duty, an impost most unjust in principle and most
unfair in operation, did not exist in that country; neither
was the stamp on newspapers known in that land—which
had as many newspapers as the United States, and got

as much good out of them. Innumerable ladies answered
the advertisement and pretended that the shoe was theirs;
but, every one of them was unable to get her foot into
it. The proud fine sisters answered it, and tried their feet
with no greater success. Then, Cinderella, who had
answered it too, came forward amidst their scornful jeers,
and the shoe slipped on in a moment. It is a remarkable tribute to the improved and sensible fashion of the
dress her grandmother had given her, that if she had not worn
it the Prince would probably never have seen her feet.

The marriage was solemnized with great rejoicing. When
the honeymoon was over, the King retired from public
life, and was succeeded by the Prince. Cinderella, being
now a queen, applied herself to the government of the
country on enlightened, liberal, and free principles. All
the people who ate anything she did not eat, or who
drank anything she did not drink, were imprisoned for
life. All the newspaper offices from which any doctrine
proceeded that was not her doctrine, were burnt down.
All the public speakers proved to demonstration that if
there were any individual on the face of the earth who
differed from them in anything, that individual was a
designing ruffian and an abandoned monster. She also
threw open the right of voting, and of being elected to
public offices, and of making the laws, to the whole of her
sex; who thus came to be always gloriously occupied with
public life and whom nobody dared to love. And they
all lived happily ever afterwards.

Frauds on the Fairies once permitted, we see little reason
why they may not come to this, and great reason why they
may. The Vicar of Wakefield was wisest when he was tired of
being always wise. The world is too much with us, early and
late. Leave this precious old escape from it, alone. [1853]

THE LATE MR. JUSTICE TALFOURD.

THE readers of these pages will have known, many days before the present number [*] can come into their hands, that on Monday the thirteenth of March, this upright judge and good man died suddenly at Stafford in the discharge of his duties. Mercifully spared protracted pain and mental decay, he passed away in a moment, with words of Christian eloquence, of brotherly tenderness and kindness towards all men, yet unfinished on his lips.

As he died, he had always lived. So amiable a man, so gentle, so sweet-tempered, of such a noble simplicity, so perfectly unspoiled by his labors and their rewards, is very rare indeed upon this earth. These lines are traced by the faltering hand of a friend; but none can so fully know how true they are, as those who knew him under all circumstances, and found him ever the same.

In his public aspects; in his poems, in his speeches, on the bench, at the bar, in Parliament; he was widely appreciated, honoured, and beloved. Inseparable as his great and varied abilities were from himself in life, it is yet to himself and not to them, that affection in its first grief naturally turns. They remain, but he is lost.

The chief delight of his life was to give delight to others. His nature was so exquisitely kind, that to be

[* *Household Words*, March 25th, 1854.]

336

kind was its highest happiness. Those who had the privilege of seeing him in his own home when his public successes were greatest,—so modest, so contented with little things, so interested in humble persons and humble efforts, so surrounded by children and young people, so adored in remembrance of a domestic generosity and greatness of heart too sacred to be unveiled here, can never forget the pleasure of that sight.

If ever there were a house, in England, justly celebrated for the reverse of the picture, where every art was honoured for its own sake, and where every visitor was received for his own claims and merits, that house was his. It was in this respect a great example, as sorely needed as it will be sorely missed. Rendering all legitimate deference to rank and riches, there never was a man more composedly, unaffectedly, quietly, immovable by such considerations than the subject of this sorrowing remembrance. On the other hand, nothing would have astonished him so much as the suggestion that he was anybody's patron or protector. His dignity was ever of that highest and purest sort which has no occasion to proclaim itself, and which is not in the least afraid of losing itself.

In the first joy of his appointment to the judicial bench, he made a summer-visit to the sea-shore, "to share his exultation in the gratification of his long-cherished ambition, with the friend"—now among the many friends who mourn his death and lovingly recall his virtues. Lingering in the bright moonlight at the close of a happy day, he spoke of his new functions, of his sense of the great responsibility he undertook, and of his placid belief that the habits of his professional life rendered him equal to their efficient discharge; but, above all, he spoke, with an earnestness never more to be separated in his friend's mind from the murmur of the sea upon a moonlight night, of his reliance on the strength of his desire to do right before God and man. He spoke with his own singleness of heart, and his solitary hearer knew how deep and true his purpose was. They passed, before parting for the night, into a playful dispute at what age he should retire, and what he would do at three-score years and ten. And ah! within five short years, it is all ended like a dream!

But, by the strength of his desire to do right, he was animated to the last moment of his existence. Who, knowing England at this time, would wish to utter with his last breath a more righteous warning than that its curse is ignorance, or a miscalled education which is as bad or worse, and a want of the exchange of innumerable graces and sympathies among the various orders of society, each hardened unto each and holding itself aloof? Well will it be for us and for our children, if those dying words be never henceforth forgotten on the Judgment Seat.

An example in his social intercourse to those who are born to station, an example to those who win it for themselves; teaching the one class to abate its stupid pride: the other, to stand upon its eminence, not forgetting the road by which it got there, and fawning upon no one; the conscientious judge, the charming writer and accomplished speaker, the gentle-hearted, guileless, affectionate man, has entered on a brighter world. Very, very many have lost a friend; nothing in Creation has lost an enemy.

The hand that lays this poor flower on his grave, was a mere boy's when he first clasped it—newly come from the work in which he himself began life—little used to the plough it has followed since—obscure enough, with much to correct and learn. Each of its successive tasks through many intervening years has been cheered by his warmest interest, and the friendship then begun has ripened to maturity in the passage of time; but there was no more self-assertion or condescension in his winning goodness at first, than at last. The success of other men made as little change in him as his own.

[1854]

THE THOUSAND AND ONE HUMBUGS.

EVERYBODY is acquainted with that enchanting collection of stories, the Thousand and One Nights, better known in England as the Arabian Nights' Entertainments. Most people know that these wonderful fancies are unquestionably of genuine Eastern origin, and are to be found in Arabic manuscripts now existing in the Vatican, in Paris, in London, and in Oxford; the last-named city being particularly distinguished in this connection, as possessing, in the library of Christchurch, a manuscript of the never to be forgotten Voyages of Sinbad the Sailor.

The civilised world is indebted to France for a vast amount of its possessions, and among the rest for the first opening to Europe of this gorgeous storehouse of Eastern riches. So well did M. Galland, the original translator, perform his task, that when Mr. Wortley Montague brought home the manuscript now in the Bodleian Library, there was found (poetical quotations excepted), to be very little, and that of a very inferior kind, to add to what M. Galland had already made perfectly familiar to France and England.

Thus much as to the Thousand and One Nights, we recall, by way of introduction to the discovery we are about to announce.

There has lately fallen into our hands, a manuscript in the Arabic Character (with which we are perfectly acquainted), containing a variety of stories extremely similar in structure and incident to the Thousand and One Nights; but presenting the strange feature that although they are evidently of ancient origin, they have a curious accidental bearing on the present time. Allowing for the difference of manners and customs, it would often seem—were it not for the manifest impossibility of such prophetic knowledge in any mere man or men—that they were written expressly with an eye to events of the current age. We have referred the manuscript (which may be seen at our office on the first day of April in every year, at precisely four o'clock in the morning), to the profoundest Oriental Scholars of England and France, who are no less sensible than we are ourselves of this remarkable coincidence, and are equally at a loss to account for it. They are agreed, we may observe, on the propriety of our rendering the title in the words, The Thousand and One Humbugs. For, although the Eastern story-tellers do not appear to have possessed any word, or combination of parts of words, precisely answering to the modern English Humbug (which, indeed, they expressed by the figurative phrase, A Camel made of sand), there is no doubt that they were conversant with so common a thing, and further that the thing was expressly meant to be designated in the general title of the Arabic manuscript now before us. Dispensing with further explanation, we at once commence the specimens we shall occasionally present, of this literary curiosity.

INTRODUCTORY CHAPTER.

Among the ancient Kings of Persia who extended their glorious conquests into the Indies, and far beyond the famous River Ganges, even to the limits of China, Taxed-taurus (or Fleeced Bull) was incomparably the most re-nowned. He was so rich that he scorned to undertake the humblest enterprise without inaugurating it by ordering his Treasurers to throw several millions of pieces of gold into the dirt. For the same reason he attached no value to his foreign possessions, but merely used them as play-things for a little while, and then always threw them away or lost them.

This wise Sultan, though blessed with innumerable sources of happiness, was afflicted with one fruitful cause of dis-content. He had been married many scores of times, yet had never found a wife to suit him. Although he had raised to the dignity of Howsa Kummauns[1] (or Peerless Chatterer), a great variety of beautiful creatures, not only of the lineage of the high nobles of his court, but also selected from other classes of his subjects, the result had uniformly been the same. They proved unfaithful, brazen, talkative, idle, extravagant, inefficient, and boastful. Thus it naturally happened that a Howsa Kummauns very rarely died a natural death, but was generally cut short in some violent manner.

At length, the young and lovely Reefawm (that is to say Light of Reason), the youngest and fairest of all the Sultan's wives, and to whom he had looked with hope to recompense him for his many disappointments, made as bad a Howsa Kummauns as any of the rest. The un-fortunate Taxedtaurus took this so much to heart that he fell into a profound melancholy, secluded himself from observation, and for some time was so seldom seen or heard of that many of his great officers of state supposed him to be dead.

---

[1] Sounded like House o' Commons.

Shall I never, said the unhappy Monarch, beating his breast in his retirement in the Pavilion of Failure, and giving vent to his tears, find a Howsa Kummauns, who will be true to me! He then quoted from the Poet, certain verses importing, Every Howsa Kummauns has deceived me, Every Howsa Kummauns is a Humbug, I must slay the present Howsa Kummauns as I have slain so many others, I am brought to shame and mortification, I am despised by the world. After which his grief so overpowered him, that he fainted away.

It happened that on recovering his senses he heard the voice of the last-made Howsa Kummauns, in the Divan adjoining. Applying his ear to the lattice, and finding that that shameless Princess was vaunting her loyalty and virtue, and denying a host of facts—which she always did, all night—the Sultan drew his scimitar in a fury, resolved to put an end to her existence.

But, the Grand Vizier Parmarstoon (or Twirling Weathercock), who was at that moment watching his incensed master from behind the silken curtains of the Pavilion of Failure, hurried forward and prostrated himself, trembling, on the ground. This Vizier had newly succeeded to Abaddeen (or the Addled), who had for his misdeeds been strangled with a garter.

The breath of the slave, said the Vizier, is in the hands of his Lord, but the Lion will sometimes deign to listen to the croaking of the frog. I swear to thee, Vizier, replied the Sultan, that I have borne too much already and will bear no more. Thou and the Howsa Kummauns are in one story, and by the might of Allah and the beard of the Prophet, I have a mind to destroy ye both!

When the Vizier heard the Sultan thus menace him with destruction, his heart drooped within him. But, being a brisk and ready man, though stricken in years, he quoted certain lines from the Poet, implying that the thunder-cloud often spares the leaf or there would be no fruit, and touched the ground with his forehead in token of submission. What wouldst thou say? demanded the generous Prince, I give thee leave to speak. Thou art not unaccustomed to public speaking; speak glibly! Sire, returned the Vizier, but for the dread of the might of my Lord, I would reply in the words addressed by the ignorant man to the Genie. And what were those words? demanded the Sultan. Repeat them! Parmarstoon replied, To hear is to obey:

THE STORY OF THE IGNORANT MAN AND THE GENIE.

Sire, on the barbarous confines of the kingdom of the Tartars, there dwelt an ignorant man, who was obliged to make a journey through the Great Desert of Desolation; which, as your Majesty knows, is sometimes a journey of upwards of three score and ten years. He bade adieu to his mother very early in the morning, and departed without a guide, ragged, barefoot, and alone. He found the way surprisingly steep and rugged, and beset by vile serpents and strange unintelligible creatures of horrible shapes. It was likewise full of black bogs and pits, into which he not only fell himself, but often had the misfortune to drag other travellers whom he encountered, and who got out no more, but were miserably stifled.

Sire, on the fourteenth day of the journey of the ignorant man of the kingdom of the Tartars, he sat down to rest by the side of a foul well (being unable to find a better), and there cracked for a repast, as he best could, a very hard nut, which was all he had about him. He threw the shell anywhere as he stripped it off, and having made an end of his meal arose to wander on again, when suddenly the air was darkened, he heard a frightful cry, and saw a monstrous Genie, of gigantic stature, who brandished a mighty scimetar in a hand of iron, advancing towards him. Rise, ignorant beast, said the monster, as he drew nigh, that I, Law, may kill thee for having affronted my ward. Alas, my lord, returned the ignorant man, how can I have affronted thy ward whom I never saw? He is invisible to thee, returned the Genie, because thou art a benighted barbarian; but if thou hadst ever learnt any good thing thou wouldst have seen him plainly, and wouldst have respected him. Lord of my life, pleaded the traveller, how could I learn where there were none to teach me, and how affront thy ward whom I have not the power to see? I tell thee, returned the Genie, that with thy pernicious refuse thou hast struck my ward, Prince Socieetee, in the apple of the eye; and because thou hast done this, I will be thy ruin. I maim and kill the like of thee by thousands every year, for no other crime. And shall I spare *thee?* Kneel and receive the blow.

Your Majesty will believe (continued the Grand Vizier) that the ignorant man of the kingdom of the Tartars, gave himself up for lost when he heard those cruel words. Without so much as repeating the formula of our faith— There is but one Allah, from him we come, to him we must return, and who shall resist his will (for he was too ignorant even to have heard it), he bent his neck to receive the fatal stroke. His head rolled off as he finished saying these words: Dread Law, if thou hadst taken half the pains to teach me to discern thy ward that thou hast taken to avenge him, thou hadst been spared the great account to which I summon thee!

Taxedtaurus the Sultan of Persia listened attentively to
this recital on the part of his Grand Vizier, and when it
was concluded said, with a threatening brow, Expound to
me, O, nephew of a dog! the points of resemblance
between the Tiger and the Nightingale, and what thy
ignorant man of the accursed kingdom of the Tartars has
to do with the false Howsa Kummauns and the glib
Vizier Parmarstoon? While speaking he again raised his
glittering scimetar. Let not my master sully the sole of
his foot by crushing an insect, returned the Vizier, kissing
the ground seven times, I meant but to offer up a petition
from the dust, that the Light of the eyes of the Faithful
would, before striking, deign to hear my daughter. What
of thy daughter? said the Sultan impatiently, and why
should I hear thy daughter any more than the daughter
of the dirtiest of the dustmen? Sire, returned the Vizier,
I am dirtier than the dirtiest of the dustmen in your
Majesty's sight, but my daughter is deeply read in the
history of every Howsa Kummauns who has aspired to
your Majesty's favour during many years, and if your
Majesty would condescend to hear some of the Legends
she has to relate, they might——What dost thou call thy
daughter? demanded the Sultan, interrupting. Hansardadade, replied the Vizier. Go, said the Sultan, bring her
hither. I spare thy life until thou shalt return.

The Grand Vizier Parmarstoon, on receiving the injunction
to bring his daughter Hansardadade into the royal presence,
lost no time in repairing to his palace which was but
across the Sultan's gardens, and going straight to the
women's apartments, found Hansardadade surrounded by
a number of old women who were all consulting her at
once. In truth, this affable Princess was perpetually being
referred to, by all manner of old women. Hastily causing

her attendants, when she heard her father's errand, to attire her in her finest dress which outsparkled the sun; and bidding her young sister, Brothartoon (or Chamber Candlestick), to make similar preparations and accompany her; the daughter of the Grand Vizier soon covered herself with a rich veil, and said to her father, with a low obeisance, Sir, I am ready to attend you, to my Lord, the Commander of the Faithful.

The Grand Vizier, and his daughter Hansardadade, and her young sister Brothartoon, preceded by Mistaspeeka, a black mute, the Chief of the officers of the royal Seraglio, went across the Sultan's gardens by the way the Vizier had come, and arriving at the Sultan's palace, found that monarch on his throne surrounded by his principal counsellors and officers of state. They all four prostrated themselves at a distance, and waited the Sultan's pleasure. That gracious prince was troubled in his mind when he commanded the fair Hansardadade (who, on the whole, was very fair indeed), to approach, for he had sworn an oath in the Vizier's absence from which he could not depart. Nevertheless, as it must be kept, he proceeded to announce it before the assembly. Vizier, said he, thou hast brought thy daughter here, as possessing a large stock of Howsa Kummauns experience, in the hope of her relating something that may soften me under my accumulated wrongs. Know that I have solemnly sworn that if her stories fail—as I believe they will—to mitigate my wrath, I will have her burned and her ashes cast to the winds! Also, I will strangle thee and the present Howsa Kummauns, and will take a new one every day and strangle her as soon as taken, until I find a good and true one. Parmanstoon replied, To hear is to obey.

Hansardadade then took a one-stringed lute, and sang

a lengthened song in prose. Its purport was, I am the recorder of brilliant eloquence, I am the chronicler of patriotism, I am the pride of sages, and the joy of nations. The continued salvation of the country is owing to what I preserve, and without it there would be no business done. Sweet are the voices of the crow and chough, and Persia never never never can have words enough. At the conclusion of this delightful strain, the Sultan and the whole divan were so faint with rapture that they remained n a comatose state for seven hours.

Would your Majesty, said Hansardadade, when all were at length recovered, prefer first to hear the story of the Wonderful Camp, or the story of the Talkative Barber, or the story of Scarli Tapa and the Forty Thieves? I would have thee commence, replied the Sultan, with the story of the Forty Thieves.

Hansardadade began, Sire, there was once a poor relation—when Brothartoon interposed. Dear sister, cried Brothartoon, it is now past midnight, it will be shortly daybreak, and if you are not asleep, you ought to be. I pray you, dear sister, by all means to hold your tongue to-night, and if my Lord the Sultan will suffer you to live another day, you can talk to-morrow. The sultan arose with a clouded face, but went out without giving any orders for the execution.

THE STORY OF SCARLI TAPA AND THE FORTY THIEVES.

Accompanied by the Grand Vizier Parmarstoon, and the black mute Mistaspecka the chief of the Seraglio, Hansardadade again repaired next day to the august presence, and, after making the usual prostrations before the Sultan, began thus:

Sire, there was once a poor relation who lived in a town in the dominions of the Sultan of the Indies, and whose name was Scarli Tapa. He was the youngest son of a Dowajah—which, as your Majesty knows, is a female spirit of voracious appetites, and generally with a wig and a carmine complexion, who prowls about old houses and preys upon mankind. This Dowajah had attained an immense age, in consequence of having been put by an evil Genie on the Penshunlist, or talisman to secure long life; but, at length she very reluctantly died towards the close of a quarter, after making the most affecting struggles to live into the half-year.

Scarli Tapa had a rich elder brother named Cashim, who had married the daughter of a prosperous merchant, and lived magnificently. Scarli Tapa, on the other hand, could barely support his wife and family by lounging about the town and going out to dinner with his utmost powers of perseverance, betting on horse-races, playing at billiards, and running into debt with everybody who would trust him—the last being his principal means of obtaining an honest livelihood.

One day, when Scarli Tapa had strolled for some time along the banks of a great river of liquid filth which ornamented that agreeable country and rendered it salubrious, he found himself in the neighbourhood of the Woods and Forests. Lifting up his eyes, he observed in the distance a great cloud of dust. He was not surprised to see it, knowing those parts to be famous for casting prodigious quantities of dust into the eyes of the Faithful; but, as it rapidly advanced towards him, he climbed into a tree, the better to observe it without being seen himself.

As the cloud of dust approached, Scarli Tapa perceived it from his hiding-place to be occasioned by forty mounted robbers, each bestriding a severely-goaded and heavily-laden Bull. The whole troop came to a halt at the foot of the tree, and all the robbers dismounted. Every robber then tethered his hack to the most convenient shrub, gave it a full meal of very bad chaff, and hung over his arm the empty sack which had contained the same. Then the Captain of the Robbers, advancing to a door in an antediluvian rock, which Scarli Tapa had not observed before, and on which were the enchanted letters O. F. F. I. C. E., said, Debrett's Peerage. Open Sesame! As soon as the Captain of the Robbers had uttered these words, the door, obedient to the charm, flew open, and all the robbers went in. The captain went in last, and the door shut of itself.

The robbers stayed so long within the rock that Scarli Tapa more than once felt tempted to descend the tree and make off. Fearful, however, that they might reappear and catch him before he could escape, he remained hidden by the leaves, as patiently as he could. At last the door opened, and the forty robbers came out. As the captain had gone in last, he came out first, and stood to see the whole troop pass him. When they had all done so, he said, Debrett's Peerage. Shut Sesame! The door immediately closed again as before. Every robber then mounted his Bull, adjusting before him his sack well filled with gold, silver, and jewels. When the captain saw that they were all ready, he put himself at their head, and they rode off by the way they had come.

Scarli Tapa remained in the tree until the receding cloud of dust occasioned by the troop of robbers with their captain at their head, was no longer visible, and then came softly down and approached the door. Making use of the words that he had heard pronounced by the Captain of the Robbers, he said, after first piously strengthening himself with the remembrance of his deceased mother the Dowajah, Debrett's Peerage. Open Sesame! The door instantly flew wide open.

Scarli Tapa, who had expected to see a dull place, was surprised to find himself in an exceedingly agreeable vista of rooms, where everything was as light as possible, and where vast quantities of the finest wheaten loaves, and the richest gold and silver fishes, and all kinds of valuable possessions, were to be got for the laying hold of. Quickly loading himself with as much spoil as he could move under, he opened and closed the door as the Captain of the Robbers had done, and hurried away with his treasure to his poor home.

When the wife of Scarli Tapa saw her husband enter their dwelling after it was dark, and proceed to pile upon the floor a heap of wealth, she cried, Alas! husband, whom have you taken in, now? Be not alarmed, wife, returned Scarli Tapa, no one suffers but the public. And then told her how he, a poor relation, had made his way into Office by the magic words and had enriched himself.

There being more money and more loaves and fishes than they knew what to do with at the moment, the wife of Scarli Tapa, transported with joy, ran off to her sister-in-law, the wife of Cashim Tapa, who lived hard by, to borrow a Measure by means of which their property could be got into some order. The wife of Cashim Tapa looking into the measure when it was brought back, found at the bottom of it, several of the crumbs of fine loaves and of the scales of gold and silver fishes; upon which, flying into an envious rage, she thus addressed her husband: Wretched Cashim, you know you are of high birth as the eldest son of a Dowajah, and you think you are rich, but your despised younger brother, Scarli Tapa, is infinitely richer and more powerful than you. Judge of his wealth from these tokens. At the same time she showed him the measure.

Cashim, who since his marriage to the merchant's widow, had treated his brother coolly and held him at a distance, was at once fired with a burning desire to know how he had become rich. He was unable to sleep all night, and at the first streak of day, before the summons to morning prayers was heard from the minarets of the mosques, arose and went to his brother's house. Dear Scarli Tapa, said he, pretending to be very fraternal, what loaves and fishes are these that thou hast in thy possession ! Scarli Tapa perceiving from this discourse that he could no longer keep his secret, communicated his discovery to his brother, who lost no time in providing all things necessary for the stowage of riches, and in repairing alone to the mysterious door near the Woods and Forests.

When night came, and Cashim Tapa did not return, his relatives became uneasy. His absence being prolonged for several days and nights, Scarli Tapa at length proceeded to the enchanted door in search of him. Opening it by the infallible means, what were his emotions to find that the robbers had encountered his brother within, and had quartered him upon the spot for ever !

Commander of the Faithful, when Scarli Tapa beheld the dismal spectacle of his brother everlastingly quartered upon Office for having merely uttered the magic words, Debrett's Peerage. Open Sesame! he was greatly troubled in his mind. Feeling the necessity of hushing the matter up, and putting the best face upon it for the family credit, he at once devised a plan to attain that object.

There was, in the House where his brother had sat

himself down on his marriage with the merchant's daughter, a discreet slave whose name was Jobbiana. Though a kind of under secretary in the treasury department, she was very useful in the dirty work of the establishment, and had also some knowledge of the stables, and could assist the whippers-in at a pinch. Scarli Tapa, going home and taking the discreet slave aside, related to her how her master was quartered, and how it was now their business to disguise the fact, and deceive the neighbours. Jobbiana replied, To hear is to obey.

Accordingly, before day—for she always avoided daylight —the discreet slave went to a certain cobbler whom she knew, and found him sitting in his stall in the public street. Good morrow, friend, said she, putting a bribe into his hand, will you bring the tools of your trade and come to a House with me? Willingly, but what to do? replied the cobbler, who was a merry fellow. Nothing against my patriotism and conscience, I hope? (at which he laughed heartily). Not in the least, returned Jobbiana, giving him another bribe. But, you must go into the House blindfold and with your hands tied; you don't mind that for a job? I don't mind anything for a job, returned the cobbler with vivacity; I like a job. It is my business to job; only make it worth my while, and I am ready for any job you may please to name. At the same time he arose briskly. Jobbiana then imparted to him the quartering that had taken place, and that he was wanted to cobble the subject up and hide what had been done. Is that all? If it is no more than that, returned the cobbler, blind my eyes and tie my hands, and let us cobble away as long as you like!

Sire, the discreet slave blindfolded the cobbler, and tied his hands, and took him to the House; where he cobbled the subject up with so much skill, that she rewarded him munificently. We must now return to the Captain of the Robbers, whose name was Yawyawah, and whose soul was filled with perplexities and anxieties, when he visited the cave and found, from the state of the wheaten loaves and the gold and silver fishes, that there was yet another person who possessed the secret of the magic door.

Your majesty must know that Yawyawah, Captain of the Robbers (most of whose forefathers had been rebellious Genii, who never had had anything whatever to do with Solomon), sauntering through the city, in a highly disconsolate and languid state, chanced to come before daylight upon the cobbler working in his stall. Good morrow, honourable friend, said he, you job early. My Lord, returned the cobbler, I job early and late. You do well, observed the Captain of the Robbers; but, have you light enough? The less light the better, said the cobbler, for *my* work. Ay! returned Yawyawah; why so? Why so! repeated the cobbler, winking, because I can cobble certain businesses, best, in the dark. When the Captain of the Robbers heard him say this, he quickly understood the hint. He blindfolded him, and tied his hands, as the discreet slave had done, turned his coat, and led him away until he stopped at the House. This is the House that was concerned in the quartering and cobbling, said he. The captain set a mark upon it. But, Jobbiana coming by soon afterwards, and seeing what had been done, set exactly the same mark upon twenty other Houses in the same row. So that in truth they were all precisely alike, and one was marked by Jobbiana exactly as another was, and there was not a pin to choose between them.

Thus discomfited, the Captain of the Robbers called his troop together and addressed them. My noble, right honourable, honourable and gallant, honourable and learned, and simply honourable, friends, said he, it is apparent that we, the old band who for so many years have possessed the command of the magic door, are in danger of being superseded. In a word, it is clear that there are now two bands of robbers, and that we must overcome the opposition, or be ourselves vanquished. All the robbers applauded this sentiment. Therefore, said the captain, I will disguise myself as a trader—in the patriotic line of business—and will endeavour to prevail by stratagem. The robbers as with one voice approved of this design.

The Captain of the Robbers accordingly disguised himself as a trader of that sort which is called at the bazaars a patriot, and, having again had recourse to the cobbler, and having carefully observed the House, arranged his plans without delay. Feigning to be a dealer in soft-soap, he concealed his men in nine-and-thirty jars of that commodity, a man in every jar; and, loading a number of mules with this pretended merchandise, appeared at the head of his caravan one evening at the House, where Scarli Tapa was sitting on a bench in his usual place, taking it (as he generally did in the House) very coolly. My Lord, said the pretended trader, I am a stranger here, and know not where to bestow my merchandise for the night. Suffer me then, I beseech you, to warehouse it here. Scarli Tapa rose up, showed the pretended merchant where to put his goods, and instructed Jobbiana to prepare an entertainment for his guest. Also a bath for himself; his hands being very far from clean.

The discreet slave, in obedience to her orders, proceeded to prepare the entertainment and the bath; but was vexed to discover, when it was late and the shops of the dealers were all shut, that there was no soft-soap in the

House—which was the more unexpected, as there was generally more than enough. Remembering however, that the pretended trader had brought a large stock with him, she went to one of the jars to get a little. As she drew near to it, the impatient robber within, supposing it to be his leader, said in a low voice,—Is it time for our party to come in? Jobbiana, instantly comprehending the danger, replied, Not yet, but presently. She went in this manner to all the jars, receiving the same question, and giving the same answer.

The discreet slave returned into the kitchen, with her presence of mind not at all disturbed, and there prepared a lukewarm mess of soothing syrup, worn-out wigs, weak milk and water, poppy-heads, empty nutshells, froth, and other similar ingredients. When it was sufficiently mawkish, she returned to the jars, bearing a large kettle filled with this mixture, poured some of it upon every robber, and threw the whole troop into a state of insensibility or submission. She then returned to the House, served up the entertainment, cleared away the fragments, and attired herself in a rich dress to dance before her master and his disguised visitor.

In the course of her dances, which were performed in the slowest time, and during which she blew both her own and the family trumpet with extraordinary pertinacity, Jobbiana took care always to approach nearer and still nearer to the Captain of the Robbers. At length she seized him by the sleeve of his disguise, disclosed him in his own dress to her master, and related where his men were, and how they had asked Was it time to come in? Scarli Tapa, so far from being angry with the pretended trader, fell upon his neck and addressed him in these friendly expressions: Since our object is the same and no great difference exists between us, O my brother, let us form a

Coalition. Debrett's Peerage will open Sesame to the Scarli Tapas and the Yawyawahs equally, and will shut out the rest of mankind. Let it be so. There is plunder enough in the cave. So that it is never restored to the original owners and never gets into other hands but ours, why should we quarrel overmuch! The Captain made a suitable reply and embraced his entertainer. Jobbiana, shedding tears of joy, embraced them both.

Shortly afterwards, Scarli Tapa in gratitude to the wise Jobbiana, caused her to be invested with the freedom of the City—where she had been very much beloved for many years—and gave her in marriage to his own son. They had a large family and a powerful number of relations, who all inherited, by right of relationship, the power of opening Sesame and shutting it tight. The Yawyawahs became a very numerous tribe also, and exercised the same privilege. This, Commander of the Faithful, is the reason why, in that distant part of the dominions of the Sultan of the Indies, all true believers kiss the ground seven hundred and seventy-seven times on hearing the magic words, Debrett's Peerage—why the talisman of Office is always possessed in common by the three great races of the Scarli Tapas, the Yawyawahs, and the Jobbianas—why the public affairs, great and small, and all the national enterprises both by land and sea are conducted on a system which is the highest peak of the mountain of justice, and which always succeeds—why the people of that country are serenely satisfied with themselves and things in general, are unquestionably the envy of surrounding nations, and cannot fail in the inevitable order of events to flourish to the end of the world—why all these great truths are incontrovertible, and why all who dispute them receive the bastinado as atheists and rebels.

Here, Hansardadade concluded the story of the Forty Thieves, and said, If my Lord the Sultan will deign to hear another narrative from the lips of the lowest of his servants, I have adventures yet more surprising than these to relate: adventures that are worthy to be written in letters of gold. By Allah! exclaimed the Sultan, whose hand had been upon his scimetar several times during the previous recital, and whose eyes had menaced Parmarstoon until the soul of that Vizier had turned to water, what thou hast told but now, deserves to be recorded in letters of Brass!

Hansardadade was proceeding, Sire, in the great plain at the feet of the mountains of Casgar, which is seven weeks' journey across—when Brothartoon interrupted her: Sister, it is nearly daybreak, and if you are not asleep you ought to be. I pray you dear sister, tell us at present no more of those stories that you know so well, but hold your tongue and go to bed. Hansardadade was silent, and the Sultan arose in a very indifferent humour and gloomily walked out—in great doubt whether he would let her live, on any consideration, over another day.

On the following night, Hansardadade proceeded with:

THE STORY OF THE TALKATIVE BARBER.

In the great plain which lies at the feet of the mountains of Casgar, and which is seven weeks' journey across, there is a city where a lame young man was once invited, with other guests, to an entertainment. Upon his entrance, the company already assembled rose up to do him honour, and the host taking him by the hand invited him to sit down with the rest upon the estrade. At the same time the master of the house greeted his visitor with the salutation, Allah is Allah, there is no Allah but Allah, may his name be praised, and may Allah be with you!

Sire, the lame young man, who had the appearance of one that had suffered much, was about to comply with the invitation of the master of the house to seat himself upon the estrade with the rest of the company, when he suddenly perceived among them, a Barber. He instantly flew back with every token of abhorrence, and made towards the door. The master of the house, amazed at this behaviour, stopped him. Sir, exclaimed the young man, I adjure you by Mecca, do not stop me, let me go. I cannot without horror look upon that abominable Barber. Upon him and upon the whole of his relations be the curse of Allah, in return for all I have endured from his intolerable levity, and from his talk never being to the point or purpose! With these words, the lame young man again made violently towards the door. The guests were astonished at this behaviour, and began to have a very bad opinion of the Barber.

The master of the house so courteously entreated the lame young man to recount to the company the causes of this strong dislike, that at length he could not refuse. Averting his head so that he might not see the Barber, he proceeded. Gentlemen, you must know that this accursed Barber is the cause of my being crippled, and is the occasion of all my misfortunes. I became acquainted with him in the following manner.

I am called Publeek, or The Many Headed. I am one of a large family, who have undergone an infinite variety of adventures and afflictions. One day, I chanced to sit down to rest on a seat in a narrow lane, when a lattice over against me opened, and I obtained a glimpse of the most ravishing Beauty in the world. After watering a pot of

budding flowers which stood in the window, she perceived
me and modestly withdrew; but, not before she had
directed towards me a glance so full of charms, that I
screamed aloud with love and became insensible for a
considerable time.

When I came to myself, I directed a favourite slave
to make enquiries among the neighbours, and, on pain of
death, to bring me an exact account of the young lady's
family and condition. The slave acquitted himself so well,
that he informed me within an hour that the young lady's
name was Fair Guvawnment, and that she was the
daughter of the chief Cadi. The violence of my passion
became so great that I took to my bed that evening, fell
into a fever, and was reduced to the brink of death, when
an old lady of my acquaintance came to see me. Son,
said she, after observing me attentively, I perceive that
your disease is love. Inform me who is the object of your
affections, and rely upon me to bring you together. This
address of the good old lady's had such an effect upon
me, that I immediately arose quite restored in health, and
began to dress myself.

In a word (continued the lame young man, addressing
the company assembled in the house of the citizen of the
plain at the feet of the mountains of Casgar, and always
keeping his head in such a position as that he could not
see the Barber), the old lady exerted herself in my behalf
with such effect, that on the very next day she returned,
commissioned by the enchantress of my soul to appoint a
meeting between us. I arranged to attire myself in my
richest clothes, and dispatched the same favourite slave
with instructions to fetch a Barber, who knew his business, and who could skilfully prepare me for the interview
I was to have, for the first time in all my life, with Fair

Guvawnment. Gentlemen, the slave returned with the wretch whom you see here.

Sir, began this accursed Barber whom a malignant destiny thus inflicted on me, how do you do, I hope you are pretty well. I do not wish to praise myself, but you are lucky to have sent for me. My name is Praymiah. In me you behold an accomplished diplomatist, a first-rate statesman, a frisky speaker, an easy shaver, a touch-and-go joker, a giver of the go-by to all complainers, and above all a member of the aristocracy of Barbers. Sir, I am a lineal descendant of the Prophet, and consequently a born Barber. All my relations, friends, acquaintances, connexions, and associates, are likewise lineal descendants of the Prophet, and consequently born Barbers every one. As I said, but the other day, to Layardeen, or the Troublesome, the aristocracy—May Allah confound thy aristocracy and thee! cried I, will you begin to shave me?

Gentlemen (proceeded the lame young man), the Barber had brought a showy case with him, and he consumed such an immense time in pretending to open it, that I was well nigh fretted to death. I will not be shaved at all, said I. Sir, returned the unabashed Barber, you sent for me to shave you, and with your pardon I will do it, whether you like it or not. Ah, Sir! you have not so good an opinion of me as your father had. I knew your father, and he appreciated me. I said a thousand pleasant things to him, and rendered him a thousand services, and he adored me. Just Heaven, he would exclaim, you are an inexhaustible fountain of wisdom, no man can plumb the depth of your profundity! My dear Sir, I would reply, you do me more honour than I deserve. Still, as a lineal descendant of the Prophet, and one of the aristocracy of born Barbers, I will, with the help of Allah, shave you pretty close before I have done with you.

You may guess, gentlemen, in my state of expectancy, with my heart set on Fair Guvawnment, and the precious time running by, how I cursed this impertinent chattering on the part of the Barber. Barber of mischief, Barber of sin, Barber of false pretence, Barber of froth and bubble, said I, stamping my foot upon the ground, will you begin to do your work? Fair and softly, Sir, said he, let me count you out first. With that, he counted from one up to thirty-eight with great deliberation, and then laughed heartily and went out to look at the weather.

When the Barber returned, he went on prattling as before. You are in high feather, Sir, said he. I am glad to see you look so well. But, how can you be otherwise than flourishing, after having sent' for *me!* I am called the Careless. I am not like Dizzee, who draws blood; nor like Darbee, who claps on blisters; nor like Johnnee, who works with the square and rule; I am the easy shaver, and I care for nobody, I can do anything. Shall I dance the dance of Mistapit to please you, or shall I sing the song of Mistafoks, or joke the joke of Jomillah? Honor me with your attention while I do all three.

The Barber (continued the lame young man, with a groan), danced the dance of Mistapit, and sang the song of Mistafoks, and joked the joke of Jomillah, and then began with fresh impertinences. Sir, said he, with a lofty flourish, when Britteen first at Heaven's command, arose from out the azure main, this was the charter of the land, and guardian angels sang this strain: Singing, as First Lord was a wallerking the Office-garding around, no end of born Barbers he picked up and found, Says he I will load them with silvier and gold, for the country's a donkey,

and as such is sold.—At this point I could bear his
insolence no longer, but starting up, cried, Barber of
hollowness, by what consideration am I restrained from
falling upon and strangling thee? Calmly, Sir, said he, let
me count you out first. He then played his former game
of counting from one to under forty, and again laughed
heartily, and went out to take the height of the sun, and
make a calculation of the state of the wind, that he might
know whether it was an auspicious time to begin to
shave me.

I took the opportunity (said the young man) of flying
from my house so darkened by the fatal presence of this
detestable Barber, and of repairing with my utmost speed
to the house of the Cadi. But, the appointed hour was
long past, and Fair Guvawnment had withdrawn no one
knew whither. As I stood in the street cursing my evil
destiny and execrating this intolerable Barber, I heard a
hue and cry. Looking in the direction whence it came,
I saw the diabolical Barber, attended by an immense troop
of his relations and friends, the lineal descendants of the
Prophet and aristocracy of born Barbers, all offering a
reward to any one who would stop me, and all proclaiming
the unhappy Publeek to be their natural prey and rightful
property. I turned and fled. They jostled and bruised
me cruelly among them, and I became maimed, as you
see. I utterly detest, abominate, and abjure this Barber,
and ever since and evermore I totally renounce him. With
these concluding words, the lame young man arose in a
sullen way that had something very threatening in it, and
left the company.

Commander of the Faithful, when the lame young man
was gone, the guests, turning to the Barber, who wore his
turban very much on one side and smiled complacently,

asked him what he had to say for himself? The Barber immediately danced the dance of Mistapit, and sang the song of Mistafoks, and joked the joke of Jomillah. Gentlemen, said he, not at all out of breath after these performances, it is true that I am called the Careless; permit me to recount to you, as a lively diversion, what happened to a twin-brother of that young man who has so undeservedly abused me, in connexion with a near relation of mine. No one objecting, the Barber related:

THE STORY OF THE BARMECIDE FEAST.

The young man's twin-brother, Guld Publeek, was in very poor circumstances and hardly knew how to live. In his reduced condition he was fain to go about to great men, begging them to take him in—and to do them justice, they did it extensively.

One day in the course of his poverty-stricken wanderings, he came to a large house with two high towers, a spacious hall, and abundance of fine gilding, statuary, and painting. Although the house was far from finished, he could see enough to assure him that enormous sums of money must be lavished upon it. He inquired who was the master of this wealthy mansion, and received for information that he was a certain Barmecide. (The Barmecide, gentlemen, is my near relation, and, like myself, a lineal descendant of the Prophet, and a born Barber.)

The young man's twin-brother passed through the gateway, and crept submissively onward, until he came into a spacious apartment, where he descried the Barmecide sitting at the upper end in the post of honour. The Barmecide asked the young man's brother what he wanted? My Lord, replied he, in a pitiful tone, I am sore distressed, and have none but high and mighty nobles like yourself, to help me. That much at least is true, returned the Barmecide, there is no help save in high and mighty nobles, it is the appointment of Allah. But, what is your distress? My Lord, said the young man's brother, I am fasting from all the nourishment I want, and—whatever you may please to think—am in a dangerous extremity. A very little more at any moment, and you would be astonished at the figure I should make. Is it so, indeed? inquired the Barmecide. Sir, returned the young man's brother, I swear by Heaven and Earth that it is so, and Heaven and Earth are every hour drawing nearer to the discovery that it is so. Alas, poor man! replied the Barmecide, pretending to have an interest in him. Ho, boy! Bring us of the best here, and let us not spare our liberal measures. The poor man shall make good cheer without delay.

Though no boy appeared, gentlemen, and though there was no sign of the liberal measures of which the Barmecide spoke so ostentatiously, the young man's brother, Guld Publeek, endeavoured to fall in with the Barmecide's humour. Come! cried the Barmecide, feigning to pour water on his hands, let us begin fair and fresh. How do you like this purity? Ah, my Lord, returned Guld Publeek, imitating the Barmecide's action, this is indeed purity:' this is in truth a delicious beginning. Then let us proceed, said the Barmecide, seeming to dry his hands, with this smoking dish of Reefawm. How do you like it? Fat? At the same time he pretended to hand choice morsels to the young man's brother. Take you fill of it, exclaimed the Barmecide, there is plenty here, do not spare it, it was cooked for you. May Allah prolong your life, my Lord, said Guld Publeek, you are liberal indeed!

The Barmecide having boasted in this pleasant way of

his smoking dish of Reefawm, which had no existence, affected to call for another dish. Ho! cried he, clapping his hands, bring in those Educational Kabobs. Then, he imitated the action of putting some upon the plate of the young man's brother, and went on. How do you like these Educational Kabobs? The cook who made them is a treasure. Are they not justly seasoned? Are they not so honestly made, as to be adapted to all digestions? You want them very much, I know, and have wanted them this long time. Do you enjoy them? And here is a delicious mess, called Foreen Leejun. Eat of it also, for I pride myself upon it, and expect it to bring me great respect and much friendship from distant lands. And this pillau of Church-endowments-and-duties, which you see so beautifully divided, pray how do you approve of this pillau? It was invented on your account, and no expense has been spared to render it to your taste. Ho, boy, bring in that ragout! Now here, my friend, is a ragout, called Law-of-Partnership. It is expressly made for poor men's eating, and I particularly pride myself upon it. This is indeed a dish at which you may cut and come again. And, boy! hasten to set before my good friend, Guld Publeek, the rare stew of colonial spices, minced crime, hashed poverty, swollen liver of ignorance, stale confusion, rotten tape, and chopped-up bombast, steeped in official sauce, and garnished with a great deal of tongue and a very little brains—the crowning dish, of which my dear friend never can have enough, and upon which he thrives so well! But, you don't eat with an appetite, my brother, said the Barmecide. I fear the repast is hardly to your liking? Pardon me, my benefactor, returned the guest, whose jaws ached with pretending to eat, I am full almost to the throat.

Well then, said the Barmecide, since you have dined so well, try the dessert. Here are apples of discord from the Horse Guards and Admiralty, here is abundance of the famous fruit from the Dead Sea that turns to ashes on the lips, here are dates from the Peninsula in great profusion, and here is a fig for the nation. Eat and be happy! My Lord, replied the object of his merriment, I am quite worn out by your liberality, and can bear no more.

Gentlemen (continued the loquacious Barber), when the humourous Barmecide, my near relation lineally descended from the Prophet, had brought his guest to this pass, he clapped his hands three times to summon around him his slaves, and instructed them to force in reality the vile stew of which he had spoken down the throat of the hungry Guld Publeek, together with a nauseous mess called Dublincumtax, and to put bitters in his drink, strew dust on his head, blacken his face, shave his eyebrows, pluck away his beard, insult him and make merry with him. He then caused him to be attired in a shameful dress and set upon an ass with his face to the tail, and in this state to be publicly exposed with the inscription round his neck, This is the punishment of Guld Publeek who asked for nourishment and said he wanted it. Such is the present droll condition of this person; while my near relation, the Barmecide, sits in the post of honour with his turban very much on one side, enjoying the joke. Which I think you will all admit is an excellent one.

Hansardadade having made an end of the discourse of the loquacious Barber, would have instantly begun another story, had not Brothartoon shut her up with, Dear Sister, it will be shortly daybreak. Get to bed and be quiet. [1855]

SMUGGLED RELATIONS.

WHEN I was a child, I remember to have had my ears boxed for informing a lady-visitor who made a morning call at our house, that a certain ornamental object on the table, which was covered with marbled-paper, "wasn't marble." Years of reflection upon this injury have fully satisfied me that the honest object in question never imposed upon anybody; further, that my honoured parents, though both of a sanguine temperament, never can have conceived it possible that it might, could, should, would, or did, impose upon anybody. Yet, I have no doubt that I had my ears boxed for violating a tacit compact in the family and among the family visitors, to blink the stubborn fact of the marbled paper, and agree upon a fiction of real marble.

Long after this, when my ears had been past boxing for a quarter of a century, I knew a man with a cork leg. That he had a cork leg—or, at all events, that he was at immense pains to take about with him a leg which was not his own leg, or a real leg—was so plain and obvious a circumstance, that the whole universe might have made affidavit of it. Still, it was always understood that this cork leg was to be regarded as a leg of flesh and blood, and even that the very subject of cork in the abstract was to be avoided in the wearer's society.

I have had my share of going about the world; wherever I have been, I have found the marbled paper and the cork leg. I have found them in many forms; but, of all their Protean shapes, at once the commonest and strangest has been — Smuggled Relations.

I was on intimate terms for many, many years, with my late lamented friend, Cogsford, of the great Greek house of Cogsford Brothers and Cogsford. I was his executor. I believe he had no secrets from me but one —his mother. That the agreeable old lady who kept his house for him *was* his mother, must be his mother, couldn't possibly be anybody but his mother, was evident: not to me alone, but to everybody who knew him. She was not a refugee, she was not proscribed, she was not in hiding, there was no price put upon her venerable head; she was invariably liked and respected as a good-humoured, sensible, cheerful old soul. Then why did Cogsford smuggle his mother all the days of his life? I have not the slightest idea why. I cannot so much as say whether she had ever contracted a second marriage, and her name was really Mrs. Bean: or whether that name was bestowed upon her as a part of the smuggling transaction. I only know that there she used to sit at one end of the hospitable table, the living image in a cap of Cogsford at the other end, and that Cogsford knew that I knew who she was. Yet, if I had been a Custom-house officer at Folkestone, and Mrs. Bean a French clock that Cogsford was furtively bringing from Paris in a hat-box, he could not have made her the subject of a more determined and deliberate pretence. It was prolonged for years upon years. It survived the good old lady herself. One day, I received an agitated note from Cogsford, entreating me to go to him immediately; I went, and found him weeping, and

24

in the greatest affliction. "My dear friend," said he, pressing my hand, "I have lost Mrs. Bean. She is no more." I went to the funeral with him. He was in the deepest grief. He spoke of Mrs. Bean, on the way back, as the best of women. But even then he never hinted that Mrs. Bean was his mother; and the first and last acknowledgment of the fact that I ever had from him was in his last will, wherein he entreated "his said dear friend and executor" to observe that he requested to be buried beside his mother—whom he didn't even name, he was so perfectly confident that I had detected Mrs. Bean.

I was once acquainted with another man who smuggled a brother. This contraband relative made mysterious appearances and disappearances, and knew strange things. He was called John—simply John. I have got into a habit of believing that he must have been under a penalty to forfeit some weekly allowance if he ever claimed a surname. He came to light in this way;—I wanted some information respecting the remotest of the Himalaya range of mountains, and I applied to my friend Benting (a member of the Geographical Society, and learned on such points), to advise me. After some consideration, Benting said, in a half reluctant and constrained way, very unlike his usual frank manner, that he "thought he knew a man" who could tell me, of his own experience, what I wanted to learn. An appointment was made for a certain evening at Benting's house. I arrived first, and had not observed for more than five minutes that Benting was under a curious cloud, when his servant announced—in a hushed, and I may say unearthly manner—"Mr. John." A rather stiff and shabby person appeared, who called Benting by no name whatever (a singularity that I always observed whenever I saw them together afterwards), and whose manner was curiously divided between familiarity and distance. I found this man to have been all over the Indies, and to possess an extraordinary fund of traveller's experience. It came from him drily at first; but he warmed, and it flowed freely until he happened to meet Benting's eye. Then, he subsided again, and (it appeared to me) felt himself, for some unknown reason, in danger of losing that weekly allowance. This happened a dozen times in a couple of hours, and not the least curious part of the matter was, that Benting himself was always as much disconcerted as the other man. It did not occur to me that night, that this was Benting's brother, for I had known him very well indeed for years, and had always understood him to have none. Neither can I now recall, nor, if I could, would it matter, by what degrees and stages I arrived at the knowledge. However this may be, I knew it, and Benting knew that I knew it. But we always preserved the fiction that I could have no suspicion that there was any sort of kindred or affinity between them. He went to Mexico, this John—and he went to Australia—and he went to China—and he died somewhere in Persia—and one day, when we went down to dinner at Benting's, I would find him in the dining-room, already seated (as if he had just been counting the allowance on the table-cloth), and another day I would hear of him as being among scarlet parrots in the tropics; but I never knew whether he had ever done anything wrong, or whether he had ever done anything right, or why he went about the world, or how. As I have already signified, I get into habits of believing; and I have got into a habit of believing that Mr. John had something to do with the dip of the magnetic needle—he is all vague and shadowy to me, however, and I only know him for certain to have been a smuggled relation.

Other people, again, put these contraband commodities entirely away from the light, as smugglers of wine and brandy bury tubs. I have heard of a man who never imparted, to his most intimate friend, the terrific secret that he had a relation in the world, except when he lost one by death; and then he would be weighed down by the greatness of the calamity, and would refer to his bereavement as if he had lost the very shadow of himself, from whom he had never been separated since the days of infancy. Within my own experience, I have observed smuggled relations to possess a wonderful quality of coming out when they die. My own dear Tom, who married my fourth sister, and who is a great Smuggler, never fails to speak to me of one of his relations newly deceased, as though, instead of never having in the remotest way alluded to that relative's existence before, he had been perpetually discoursing of it. "My poor, dear, darling Emmy," he said to me, within these six months, "she is gone—I have lost her." Never until that moment had Tom breathed one syllable to me of the existence of any Emmy whomsoever on the face of this earth, in whom he had the smallest interest. He had scarcely allowed me to understand, very distantly and generally, that he had some relations—"my people," he called them —down in Yorkshire. "My own dear, darling Emmy," says Tom, notwithstanding, "she has left me for a better world." (Tom must have left her for his own world, at least fifteen years). I repeated, feeling my way, "Emmy, Tom?" "My favourite niece," said Tom, in a reproachful tone, "Emmy, you know. I was her godfather, you remember. Darling, fair-haired Emmy! Precious, blue-eyed child!" Tom burst into tears, and we both understood that henceforth the fiction was established between us that I had been quite familiar with Emmy by reputation, through a series of years.

Occasionally, smuggled relations are discovered by accident: just as those tubs may be, to which I have referred. My other half—I mean, of course, my wife—once discovered a large cargo in this way, which had been long concealed. In the next street to us lived an acquaintance of ours, who was a Commissioner of something or other, and kept a handsome establishment. We used to exchange dinners, and I have frequently heard him at his own table mention his father as a " poor dear good old boy," who had been dead for any indefinite period. He was rather fond of telling anecdotes of his very early days, and from them it appeared that he had been an only child. One summer afternoon, my other half, walking in our immediate neighbourhood, happened to perceive Mrs. Commissioner's last year's bonnet (to every inch of which, it is unnecessary to add, she could have sworn), going along before her on somebody else's head. Having heard generally of the swell mob, my good lady's first impression was, that the wearer of this bonnet belonged to that fraternity, had just abstracted the bonnet from its place of repose, was in every sense of the term walking off with it, and ought to be given into the custody of the nearest policeman. Fortunately, however, my Susannah, who is not distinguished by closeness of reasoning or presence of mind, reflected, as it were by a flash of inspiration, that the bonnet might have been given away. Curious to see to whom, she quickened her steps, and descried beneath it, an ancient lady of an iron-bound presence, in whom (for my Susannah has an eye), she instantly recognised the lineaments of the Commissioner! Eagerly pursuing this discovery, she, that very afternoon, tracked down an ancient gentleman in one of the Com-

missioner's hats. Next day she came upon the trail of
four stony maidens, decorated with artificial flowers out of
the Commissioner's epergne; and thus we dug up the
Commissioner's father and mother and four sisters, who
had been for some years secreted in lodgings 'round the
corner and never entered the Commissioner's house save
in the dawn of morning and the shades of evening. From
that time forth, whenever my Susannah made a call at
the Commissioner's, she always listened on the doorstep
for any slight preliminary scuffling in the hall, and, hearing
it, was delighted to remark, "The family are here, and
they are hiding them!"

I have never been personally acquainted with any gentleman who kept his mother-in-law in the kitchen, in the
useful capacity of Cook; but I have heard of such a case
on good authority. I once lodged in the house of a
genteel lady claiming to be a widow, who had four pretty
children, and might be occasionally overheard coercing an
obscure man in a sleeved waistcoat, who appeared to be
confined in some Pit below the foundations of the house,
where he was condemned to be always cleaning knives.
One day, the smallest of the children crept into my room,
said, pointing downward with a little chubby finger, "Don't
tell! It's Pa!" and vanished on tiptoe.

One other branch of the smuggling trade demands a
word of mention before I conclude. My friend of friends
in my bachelor days, became the friend of the house when
I got married. He is our Amelia's godfather; Amelia
being the eldest of our cherubs. Through upwards of ten
years he was backwards and forwards at our house three
or four times a week, and always found his knife and
fork ready for him. What was my astonishment on coming
home one day to find Susannah sunk upon the oil-cloth

in the hall, holding her brow with both hands, and meeting my gaze, when I admitted myself with my latch-key,
in a distracted manner! "Susannah," I exclaimed, "what
has happened?" She merely ejaculated, "Larver"—that
being the name of the friend in question. "Susannah!"
said I, "what of Larver? Speak! Has he met with any
accident? Is he ill?" Susannah replied faintly, "Married
—married before we were!" and would have gone into
hysterics but that I make a rule of never permitting that
disorder under my roof.

For upwards of ten years, my bosom friend Larver, in
close communication with me every day, had smuggled a
wife! ·He had at last confided the truth to Susannah, and
had presented Mrs. Larver. There was no kind of reason
for this, that we could ever find out. Even Susannah
had not a doubt of things being all correct. He had
"run" Mrs. Larver into a little cottage in Hertfordshire,
and nobody ever knew why, or ever will know. In fact,
I believe there was no why in it.

The most astonishing part of the matter is, that I have
known other men do exactly the same thing. I could give
the names of a dozen in a footnote, if I thought it right.

[1855]

THE GREAT BABY.

HAS it occurred to any of our readers that that is surely
an unsatisfactory state of society which presents, in the
year eighteen hundred and fifty-five, the spectacle of a
committee of the People's representatives, pompously and
publicly inquiring how the People shall be trusted with the
liberty of refreshing themselves in humble taverns and
tea-gardens on their day of rest ? Does it appear to any
one whom we now address, and who will pause here to
reflect for a moment on the question we put, that there
is anything at all humiliating and incongruous in the
existence of such a body, and pursuit of such an enquiry,
in this country, at this time of day ?

For ourselves, we will answer the question without
hesitation. We feel indignantly ashamed of the thing as
a national scandal. It would be merely contemptible, if it
were not raised into importance by its slanderous aspersions
of a hard-worked, heavily-taxed, but good-humoured and
most patient people, who have long deserved far better
treatment. In this green midsummer, here is a committee
virtually enquiring whether the English can be regarded
in any other light, and domestically ruled in any other
manner, than as a gang of drunkards and disorderlies on
a Police charge-sheet! O my Lords and Gentlemen, my

Lords and Gentlemen, have we got so very near Utopia after our long travelling together over the dark and murderous road of English history, that we have nothing else left to say and do to the people but this? Is there nothing abroad, nothing at home, nothing seen by us, nothing hidden from us, which points to higher and more generous things?

There are two public bodies remarkable for knowing nothing of the people, and for perpetually interfering to put them right. The one is the House of Commons; the other the Monomaniacs. Between the Members and the Monomaniacs, the devoted People, quite unheard, get harried and worried to the last extremity. Everybody of ordinary sense, possessing common sympathies with necessities not their own, and common means of observation—Members and Monomaniacs are of course excepted—has perceived for months past, that it was manifestly impossible that the People could or would endure the inconveniences and deprivations, sought to be imposed upon them by the latest Sunday restrictions. We who write this, have again and again by word of mouth forewarned many scores both of Members and Monomaniacs, as we have heard others forewarn them, that what they were in the densest ignorance allowing to be done, could not be borne. Members and Monomaniacs knew better, or cared nothing about it; and we all know the rest—to this time.

Now, the Monomaniacs, being by their disease impelled to clamber upon platforms, and there squint horribly under the strong possession of an unbalanced idea, will of course be out of reason and go wrong. But, why the Members should yield to the Monomaniacs is another question. And why do they? Is it because the People is altogether an abstraction to them; a Great Baby, to be coaxed and chucked under the chin at elections, and frowned upon at quarter sessions, and stood in the corner on Sundays, and taken out to stare at the Queen's coach on holidays, and kept in school under the rod, generally speaking, from Monday morning to Saturday night? Is it because they have no other idea of the People than a big-headed Baby, now to be flattered and now to be scolded, now to be sung to and now to be denounced to old Boguey, now to be kissed and now to be whipped, but always to be kept in long clothes, and never under any circumstances to feel its legs and go about of itself? We take the liberty of replying, Yes.

And do the Members and Monomaniacs suppose that this is *our* discovery? Do they live in the shady belief that the object of their capricious dandling and punishing does not resentfully perceive that it is made a Great Baby of, and may not begin to kick thereat with legs that may do mischief?

In the first month of the existence of this Journal, [*] we called attention to a detachment of the Monomaniacs, who under the name of jail-chaplains, had taken possession of the prisons, and were clearly offering premiums to vice, promoting hypocrisy, and making models of dangerous scoundrels. They had their way, and the Members backed them; and now their Pets recruit the very worst class of criminals known. The Great Baby, to whom this copy was set as a moral lesson, is supposed to be perfectly unimpressed by the real facts, and to be entirely ignorant of them. So, down at Westminster, night after night, the Right Honourable Gentleman the Member for Somewhere, and the Honourable Gentleman the Member for Somewherelse, badger one another, to the infinite delight of their adherents in the cockpit; and when the Prime Min-

[* *Household Words.*]

ister has released his noble bosom of its personal injuries, and has made his jokes and retorts for the evening, and has said little and done less, he winds up with a standard form of words respecting the vigorous prosecution of the war, and a just and honourable peace, which are especially let off upon the Great Baby; which Baby is always supposed never to have heard before; and which it is understood to be a part of Baby's catechism to be powerfully affected by. And the Member for Somewhere, and the Member for Somewherelse, and the Noble Lord, and all the rest of that Honourable House, go home to bed, really persuaded that the Great Baby has been talked to sleep!

Let us see how the unfortunate Baby is addressed and dealt with, in the inquiry concerning his Sunday eatings and drinkings—as wild as a nursery rhyme, and as inconclusive as Bedlam.

The Great Baby is put upon his trial. A mighty noise of creaking boots is heard in an outer passage. O good gracious, here's an official personage! Here's a solemn witness! Mr. Gamp, we believe you have been a dry-nurse to the Great Baby for some years? Yes, I have.—Intimately acquainted with his character? Intimately acquainted.—As a police magistrate, Mr. Gamp? As a police magistrate. (Sensation.)—Pray, Mr. Gamp, would you allow a working man, a small tradesman, clerk, or the like, to go to Hampstead or to Hampton Court at his own convenience on a Sunday, with his family, and there to be at liberty to regale himself and them, in a tavern where he could buy a pot of beer and a glass of gin-and-water? I would on no account concede that permission to any person.—Will you be so kind as to state why, Mr. Gamp? Willingly. Because I have presided for many years at the Bo-Peep police office, and have seen a

great deal of drunkenness there. A large majority of the
Bo-Peep charges are charges against persons of the lowest
class, of having been found drunk and incapable of taking
care of themselves.—Will you instance a case, Mr. Gamp?
I will instance the case of Sloggins.—Was that a man with
a broken nose, a black eye, and a bull-dog? Precisely
so.—Was Sloggins frequently the subject of such a charge?
Continually. I may say, constantly.—Especially on Monday? Just so. Especially on Monday.—And therefore
you would shut the public-houses, and particularly the
suburban public-houses, against the free access of working-
people on Sunday? Most decidedly so. (Mr. Gamp retires,
much complimented.)

Naughty Baby, attend to the Reverend Single Swallow!
Mr. Swallow, you have been much in the confidence of
thieves and miscellaneous miscreants? I have the happiness to believe that they have made me the unworthy
depository of their unbounded confidence.—Have they
usually confessed to you that they have been in the habit
of getting drunk? Not drunk; upon that point I wish to
explain. Their ingenuous expression has generally been,
"lushy."—But those are convertible terms? I apprehend
they are; still, as gushing freely from a penitent breast,
I am weak enough to wish to stipulate for lushy; I pray
you bear with me.—Have you reason, Mr. Swallow,
to believe that excessive indulgence in "lush" has been
the cause of these men's crimes? O yes indeed. O yes!
—Do you trace their offences to nothing else? They
have always told me, that they themselves traced them to
nothing else worth mentioning.—Are you acquainted with
a man named Sloggins? O yes! I have the truest affection
for Sloggins.—Has he made any confidence to you that
you feel justified in disclosing, bearing on this subject of

becoming lushy? Sloggins, when in solitary confinement, informed me, every morning for eight months, always with tears in his eyes, and uniformly at five minutes past eleven o'clock, that he attributed his imprisonment to his having partaken of rum-and-water at a licensed house of entertainment, called (I use his own words) "The Wiry Tarrier." He never ceased to recommend that the landlord, landlady, young family, potboy, and the whole of the frequenters of that establishment, should be taken up.—Did you recommend Sloggins for a commutation of his term, on a ticket of leave? I did.—Where is he now? I believe he is in Newgate now.—Do you know what for? Not of my own knowledge, but I have heard that he got into trouble through having been weakly tempted into the folly of garotting a market gardener.—Where was he taken for this last offence? At "The Wiry Tarrier," on a Sunday.— It is unnecessary to ask you, Mr. Single Swallow, whether you therefore recommend the closing of all public-houses on a Sunday? Quite unnecessary.

Bad Baby, fold your hands and listen to the Reverend Temple Pharisee, who will step out of his carriage at the Committee Door, to give you a character that will rather astonish you. Mr. Temple Pharisee, you are the incumbent of the extensive rectory of Camel-cum-Needle's eye? I am.—Will you be so good as to state your experience of that district on a Sunday? Nothing can be worse. That part of the Rectory of Camel-cum-Needle's-eye in which my principal church is situated, abuts upon the fields. As I stand in the pulpit, I can actually see the people, through the side windows of the building (when the heat of the weather renders it necessary to have them open), walking. I have, on some occasions, heard them laughing. Whistling has reached my curate's ears (he is an industrious and well-meaning young man); but I cannot say I have heard it myself.—Is your church well frequented? No. I have no reason to complain of the Pew-portion of my flock, who are eminently respectable; but, the Free Seats are comparatively deserted: which is the more emphatically deplorable, as there are not many of them.—Is there a Railway near the church? I regret to state that there is, and that I hear the rush of the trains, even while I am preaching.—Do you mean to say that they do not slacken speed for your preaching? Not in the least.—Is there anything else near the church, to which you would call the Committee's attention? At the distance of a mile and a half and three rods (for my clerk has measured it by my direction), there is a common public house with tea-gardens, called "The Glimpse of Green." In fine weather these gardens are filled with people on a Sunday evening. Frightful scenes take place there. Pipes are smoked; liquors mixed with hot water are drunk; shrimps are eaten; cockles are consumed; tea is swilled; ginger-beer is loudly exploded. Young women with their young men; young men with their young women; married people with their children; baskets, bundles, little chaises, wicker-work perambulators, every species of low abomination, is to be observed there. As the evening closes in, they all come straggling home together through the fields; and the vague sounds of merry conversation which then strike upon the ear, even at the further end of my dining-room (eight-and-thirty feet by twenty-seven), are most distressing. I consider "The Glimpse of Green" irreconcilable with public morality.—Have you heard of pick-pockets resorting to this place? I have. My clerk informed me that his uncle's brother-in-law, a marine store-dealer who went there to observe the depravity of the people, missed his pockethandkerchief when he

reached home. Local ribaldry has represented him to be
one of the persons who had their pockets picked at St.
Paul's Cathedral on the last occasion when the Bishop of
London preached there. I beg to deny this; I know
those individuals very well, and they were people of
condition.—Do the mass of the inhabitants of your district
work hard all the week? I believe they do.—Early and
late? My curate reports so.—Are their houses close and
crowded? I believe they are.—Abolishing "The Glimpse
of Green," where would you recommend them to go on a
Sunday? I should say to church.—Where after church?
Really, that is their affair; not mine.

Adamantine-hearted Baby, dissolve into scalding tears
at sight of the next witness, hanging his head and beating
his breast. He was one of the greatest drunkards in the
world, he tells you. When he was drunk, he was a very
demon—and he never was sober. He never takes any
strong drink now, and is as an angel of light. And because this man never could use without abuse; and because he imitated the Hyæna or other obscene animal, in
not knowing, in the ferocity of his appetites, what Moderation was; therefore, O Big-headed Baby, you perceive
that he must become as a standard for you; and for his
backslidings you shall be put in the corner evermore.

Ghost of John Bunyan, it is surely thou who usherest
into the Committee Room, the volunteer testifier, Mr.
Monomaniacal Patriarch! Baby, a finger in each eye, and
ashes from the nearest dustbin on your wretched head,
for it is all over with you now. Mr. Monomaniacal
Patriarch, have you paid great attention to drunkenness?
Immense attention, unspeakable attention.—For how many
years? Seventy years.—Mr. Monomaniacal Patriarch, have
you ever been in Whitechapel? Millions of times.—Did

you ever shed tears over the scenes you have witnessed
there? Oceans of tears.—Mr. Monomaniacal Patriarch,
will you proceed with your testimony? Yes; I am the
only man to be heard on the subject; I am the only man
who knows anything about it. No connexion with any
other establishment; all others are impostors; I am the
real original. Other men are said to have looked into
these places, and to have worked to raise them out of
the Slough of Despond. Don't believe it. Nothing is
genuine unless signed by me. I am the original fly with
the little eye. Nobody ever mourned over the miseries
and vices of the lowest of the low, but I. Nobody has
ever been haunted by them, waking and sleeping, but I.
Nobody would raise up the sunken wretches, but I. Nobody understands how to do it, but I.—Do you think the
People ever really want any beer or liquor to drink?
Certainly not. I know all about it, and I know they
don't.—Do you think they ever ought to have any beer
or liquor to drink? Certainly not. I know all about it,
and I know they oughtn't.—Do you think they could
suffer any inconvenience from having their beer and liquor
entirely denied them? Certainly not. I know all about
it, and I know they couldn't.

Thus, the Great Baby is dealt with from the beginning
to the end of the chapter. It is supposed equally by the
Members and by the Monomaniacs to be incapable of
putting This and That together, and of detecting the
arbitrary nonsense of these monstrous deductions. That
a whole people,—a domestic, reasonable, considerate people,
whose good-nature and good sense are the admiration of
intelligent foreigners, and who are no less certain to secure
the affectionate esteem of such of their own countrymen
as will have the manhood to be open with them, and to

trust them,—that a whole people should be judged by, and made to answer and suffer for, the most degraded and most miserable among them, is a principle so shocking in its injustice, and so lunatic in its absurdity, that to entertain it for a moment is to exhibit profound ignorance of the English mind and character. In Monomaniacs this may be of no great significance, but in Members it is alarming; for, if they cannot be brought to understand the People for whom they make laws, and if they so grievously under-rate them, how is it to be hoped that they, and the laws, and the People, being such a bundle of anomalies, can possibly thrive together?

It is not necessary for us, or for any decent person, to go to Westminster, or anywhere else, to make a flourish against intemperance. We abhor it; would have no drunkard about us, on any consideration; would thankfully see the child of our heart, dead in his baby beauty, rather than he should live and grow with the shadow of such a horror upon him. In the name of Heaven, let drunkards and ruffians restrain themselves and be restrained by all conceivable means—but not govern, bind, and defame, the temperance, the industry, the rational wants and decent enjoyments of a whole toiling nation!. We oppose those virtuous Malays who run a-muck out of the House of Peers or Exeter Hall, as much as those vicious Malays who run a-muck out of Sailors' lodging-houses in Rother-hithe. We have a constitutional objection in both cases to being stabbed in the back, and we claim that the one kind of Monomaniac has no more right than the other to gash and disfigure honest people going their peaceable way. Lastly, we humbly beg to assert and protest with all the vigour that is in us, that the People is, in sober truth and reality, something very considerably more than a Great Baby; that it has come to an age when it can distinguish sound from sense; that mere jingle, will not do for it; in a word, that the Great Baby is growing up, and had best be measured accordingly.

[1855]

ON MR. FECHTER'S ACTING.

THE distinguished artist whose name is prefixed to these remarks purposes to leave England for a professional tour in the United States. A few words from me, in reference to his merits as an actor, I hope may not be uninteresting to some readers, in advance of his publicly proving them before an American audience, and I know will not be unacceptable to my intimate friend. I state at once that Mr. Fechter holds that relation towards me; not only because it is the fact, but also because our friendship originated in my public appreciation of him. I had studied his acting closely, and had admired it highly, both in Paris and in London, years before we exchanged a word. Consequently, my appreciation is not the result of personal regard, but personal regard has sprung out of my appreciation.

The first quality observable in Mr. Fechter's acting is, that it is in the highest degree romantic. However elaborated in minute details, there is always a peculiar dash and vigour in it, like the fresh atmosphere of the story whereof it is a part. When he is on the stage, it seems to me as though the story were transpiring before me for the first and last time. Thus there is a fervor in his love-making—a suffusion of his whole being with the rapture of his passion—that sheds a glory on its object, and raises her, before the eyes of the audience, into the light in which he sees her. It was this remarkable power that took Paris by storm when he became famous in the lover's part in the *Dame aux Camélias*. It is a short part, really comprised in two scenes, but, as he acted it (he was its original representative), it left its poetic and exalting influence on the heroine throughout the play. A woman who could be so loved—who could be so devotedly and romantically adored—had a hold upon the general sympathy with which nothing less absorbing and complete could have invested her. When I first saw this play and this actor, I could not, in forming my lenient judgment of the heroine, forget that she had been the inspiration of a passion of which I had beheld such profound and affecting marks. I said to myself, as a child might have said: "A bad woman could not have been the object of that wonderful tenderness, could not have so subdued that worshipping heart, could not have drawn such tears from such a lover." I am persuaded that the same effect was wrought upon the Parisian audiences, both consciously and unconsciously, to a very great extent, and that what was morally disagreeable in the *Dame aux Camélias* first got lost in this brilliant halo of romance. I have seen the same play with the same part otherwise acted, and in exact degree as the love became dull and earthy, the heroine descended from her pedestal.

In Ruy Blas, in the Master of Ravenswood, and in the Lady of Lyons,—three dramas in which Mr. Fechter especially shines as a lover, but notably in the first,—this remarkable power of surrounding the beloved creature, in the eyes of the audience, with the fascination that she has for him, is strikingly displayed. That observer must

be cold indeed who does not feel, when Ruy Blas stands
in the presence of the young unwedded Queen of Spain,
that the air is enchanted; or, when she bends over him,
laying her tender touch upon his bloody breast, that it is
better so to die than to live apart from her, and that she
is worthy to be so died for.   When the Master of Ravenswood declares his love to Lucy Ashton, and she hers to
him, and when, in a burst of rapture, he kisses the skirt
of her dress, we feel as though we touched it with our
lips to stay our goddess from soaring away into the very
heavens.   And when they plight their troth and break the
piece of gold, it is we—not Edgar—who quickly exchange
our half for the half she was about to hang about her
neck, solely because the latter has for an instant touched
the bosom we so dearly love.   Again, in the Lady of Lyons:
the picture on the easel in the poor cottage studio is not
the unfinished portrait of a vain and arrogant girl, but
becomes the sketch of a Soul's high ambition and aspira-
tion here and hereafter.

Picturesqueness is a quality above all others pervading
Mr. Fechter's assumptions.   Himself a skilled painter
and sculptor, learned in the history of costume, and informing those accomplishments and that knowledge with
a similar infusion of romance (for romance is inseparable
from the man), he is always a picture,—always a picture
in its right place in the group, always in true composition
with the background of the scene.   For picturesqueness
of manner, note so trivial a thing as the turn of his hand
in beckoning from a window, in Ruy Blas, to a personage
down in an outer courtyard to come up; or his assumption of the Duke's livery in the same scene; or his
writing a letter from dictation.   In the last scene of
Victor Hugo's noble drama, his bearing becomes positively

inspired; and his sudden assumption of the attitude of
the headsman, in his denunciation of the Duke and
threat to be his executioner, is, so far as I know, one of the
most ferociously picturesque things conceivable on the stage.

The foregoing use of the word "ferociously" reminds
me to remark that this artist is a master of passionate
vehemence; in which aspect he appears to me to represent,
perhaps more than in any other, an interesting union of
characteristics of two great nations,—the French and the
Anglo-Saxon. Born in London of a French mother, by
a German father, but reared entirely in England and in
France, there is, in his fury, a combination of French suddenness and impressibility with our more slowly demonstrative
Anglo-Saxon way when we get, as we say, "our blood
up," that produces an intensely fiery result. The fusion
of two races is in it, and one cannot decidedly say that
it belongs to either; but one can most decidedly say that
it belongs to a powerful concentration of human passion
and emotion, and to human nature.

Mr. Fechter has been in the main more accustomed to
speak French than to speak English, and therefore he
speaks our language with a French accent. But whosoever
should suppose that he does not speak English fluently,
plainly, distinctly, and with a perfect understanding of the
meaning, weight, and value of every word, would be
greatly mistaken. Not only is his knowledge of English—
extending to the most subtle idiom, or the most recondite
cant phrase – more extensive than that of many of us who
have English . for our mother-tongue, but his delivery of
Shakespeare's blank verse is remarkably facile, musical,
and intelligent. To be in a sort of pain for him, as one
sometimes is for a foreigner speaking English, or to be in
any doubt of his having twenty synonymes at his tongue's

end if he should want one, is out of the question after having been of his audience.

A few words on two of his Shakespearian impersonations, and I shall have indicated enough, in advance of Mr. Fechter's presentation of himself. That quality of picturesqueness, on which I have already laid stress, is strikingly developed in his Iago, and yet it is so judiciously governed that his Iago is not in the least picturesque according to the conventional ways of frowning, sneering, diabolically, grinning, and elaborately doing everything else that would induce Othello to run him through the body very early in the play. Mr. Fechter's is the Iago who could, and did, make friends; who could dissect his master's soul, without flourishing his scalpel as if it were a walking-stick; who could overpower Emilia by other arts than a sign-of-the-Saracen's-Head grimness; who could be a boon companion without *ipso facto* warning all beholders off by the portentous phenomenon; who could sing a song and clink a can naturally enough, and stab men really in the dark,—not in a transparent notification of himself as going about seeking whom to stab. Mr. Fechter's Iago is no more in the conventional psychological mode than in the conventional hussar pantaloons and boots; and you shall see the picturesqueness of his wearing borne out in his bearing all through the tragedy down to the moment when he becomes invincibly and consistently dumb.

Perhaps no innovation in Art was ever accepted with so much favor by so many intellectual persons pre-committed to, and preoccupied by, another system, as Mr. Fechter's Hamlet. I take this to have been the case (as it unquestionably was in London), not because of its picturesqueness, not because of its novelty, not because of its many scattered beauties, but because of its perfect consistency with itself. ·As the animal-painter said of his favorite picture of rabbits that there was more nature about those rabbits than you usually found in rabbits, so it may be said of Mr. Fechter's Hamlet, that there was more consistency about that Hamlet than you usually found in Hamlets. Its great and satisfying originality was in its possessing the merit of a distinctly conceived and executed idea. From the first appearance of the broken glass of fashion and mould of form, pale and worn with weeping for his father's death, and remotely suspicious of its cause, to his final struggle with Horatio for the fatal cup, there were cohesion and coherence in Mr. Fechter's view of the character. Devrient, the German actor, had, some years before in London, fluttered the theatrical doves considerably, by such changes as being seated when instructing the players, and like mild departures from established usage ; but he had worn, in the main, the old nondescript dress, and had held forth, in the main, in the old way, hovering between sanity and madness. I do not remember whether he wore his hair crisply curled short, as if he were going to an everlasting dancing-master's party at the Danish court ; but I do remember that most other Hamlets since the great Kemble had been bound to do so. Mr. Fechter's Hamlet, a pale, wo-begone Norseman with long flaxen hair, wearing a strange garb never associated with the part upon the English stage (if ever seen there at all) and making a piratical swoop upon the whole fleet of little theatrical prescriptions without meaning, or, like Dr. Johnson's celebrated friend, with only one idea in them, and that a wrong one, never could have achieved its extraordinary success but for its animation by one pervading purpose, to which all changes were made intelligently subservient. The bearing of this purpose on the treatment of Ophelia, on the death of Polonius, and on the old student fellowship between Hamlet and Horatio, was exceedingly striking; and the difference between picturesqueness of stage arrangement for mere stage effect, and for the elucidation of a meaning, was well displayed in there having been a gallery of musicians at the Play, and in one of them passing on his way out, with his instrument in his hand, when Hamlet, seeing it, took it from him to point his talk with Rosencrantz and Guildenstern.

This leads me to the observation with which I have all along desired to conclude: that Mr. Fechter's romance and picturesqueness are always united to a true artist's intelligence, and a true artist's training in a true artist's spirit. He became one of the company of the Théâtre Français when he was a very young man, and he has cultivated his natural gifts in the best schools. I cannot wish my friend a better audience than he will have in the American people, and I cannot wish them a better actor than they will have in my friend. [1869]

INTERNATIONAL COPYRIGHT.

TO THE EDITOR OF *THE TIMES*.

SIR,—In your paper of Saturday you thought it worth while to refer to an article on my "American Notes," published in the recent number of the *Edinburgh Review*, for the purpose of commenting on a statement of the reviewer's in reference to the English and American press, with which I have no further concern than that I know it to be a very monstrous likening of unlike things.

I am anxious to give to another misrepresentation made by the same writer, whosoever he may be—which *is* personal to myself,—the most public and positive contradiction in my power; and I shall be really obliged to you if you will allow me to do this through the medium of your columns.

He asserts "that if he be rightly informed, I went to America as a kind of missionary in the cause of international copyright." I deny it wholly. He is wrongly informed; and reports, without inquiry, a piece of information which I could only characterize by using one of the shortest and strongest words in the language. Upon my honour the assertion is destitute of any particle, aspect, or colouring of truth.

It occurred to me to speak (as other English travellers connected with literature had done before me) of the existing laws—or rather want of laws—on the subject of international copyright, when I found myself in America, simply because I had never hesitated to denounce their injustice while at home; because I thought it a duty to English writers, that their case should be fairly represented; and because, inexperienced at that time in the American people, I believed that they would listen to the truth, even from one presumed to have an interest in stating it, and would not long refuse to recognize a principle of common honesty, even though it happened to clash with a miserably short-sighted view of their own profit and advantage.

I am, Sir, your obliged Servant,

CHARLES DICKENS.

1, Devonshire Terrace, Sunday, Jan. 15. [1843!

THE EARLY-CLOSING MOVEMENT.

Devonshire Terrace, York Gate, Regent's Park,
28th March, 1844.

GENTLEMEN,

I beg to assure you, that it gives me great satisfaction to have the honour of enrolling my name among the Vice-Presidents of your association.

My engagements will not permit, I regret to say, of my attending your Meeting at the Hanover Square Rooms, on Monday Evening.' But, though absent in the body, I am with you in the spirit there and always. I believe that the objects you have in view, are not of greater importance to yourselves than to the welfare and happiness of society—in general; to whom the comfort, happiness, and intelligence of that large class of industrious persons whose claims you advocate, is, if rightly understood, a matter of the highest moment and loftiest concern.

I understand the late-hour system to be a means of depriving very many young men of all reasonable opportunities of self-culture and improvement, and of making their labour irksome, weary, and oppressive. I understand the early-hour system to be a means of lightening their labour without disadvantage to any body or any thing, and of enabling them to improve themselves, as all rational creatures are intended to do, and have a right to do; and therefore I hold that there is no more room for choice or doubt between the two, than there is between good and bad, or right and wrong.

I am, Gentlemen,

Your faithful Servant,

CHARLES DICKENS.

The Committee of the
Metropolitan Drapers' Association.

FAMILIAR EPISTLE FROM A PARENT TO A CHILD, AGED TWO YEARS AND TWO MONTHS.

MY CHILD,

To recount with what trouble I have brought you up, —with what an anxious eye I have regarded your progress, —how late and how often I have sat up at night working for you,—and how many thousand letters I have received from, and written to your various relations and friends, many of whom have been of a querulous and irritable turn,—to dwell on the anxiety and tenderness with which I have (as far as I possessed the power) inspected and chosen your food; rejecting the indigestible and heavy matter which some injudicious but well meaning old ladies would have had you swallow, and retaining only those light and pleasant articles which I deemed calculated to keep you free from all gross humours, and to render you an agreeable child, and one who might be popular with society in general,—to dilate on the steadiness with which I have prevented your annoying any company by talking politics,—always assuring you that you would thank me for it yourself some day when you grew older, -to expatiate, in short, upon my own assiduity as a parent, is beside my present purpose, though I cannot but contemplate your fair appearance—your robust health, and unimpeded circulation (which I take to be the great secret of your good looks) without the liveliest satisfaction and delight.

It is a. trite observation, and one which, young as you are, I have no doubt you have often heard repeated, that we have fallen upon strange times, and live in days of constant shiftings and changes. I had a melancholy instance of this only a week or two since. I was returning from Manchester to London by the mail train when I suddenly fell into another train—a mixed train—of reflection, occasioned by the dejected and disconsolate demeanour of the Post-office Guard. We were stopping at some station where they take in water, when he dismounted slowly from the little box in which he sits in ghastly mockery of his old condition with pistol and blunderbuss beside him, ready to shoot the first highwayman (or railwayman) who shall attempt to stop the horses, which now travel (when they travel at all) *in*side and in a portable stable invented for the purpose,—he dismounted, I say, slowly and sadly, from his post, and looking mournfully about him as if in dismal recollection of the old road-side public-house—the blazing fire—the glass of foaming ale—the buxom hand-maid and admiring hangers-on of tap-room and stable, all honoured by his notice; and, retiring a little apart, stood leaning against a signal-post, surveying the engine with a look of combined affliction and disgust which no words can describe. His scarlet-coat and golden lace were tarnished with ignoble smoke; flakes of soot had fallen on his bright green shawl—his pride in days of yore—the steam condensed in the tunnel from which we had just emerged, shone upon his hat like rain. His eye betokened that he was thinking of the coachman; and as it wandered to his own seat and his own fast-fading garb, it was plain to see that he felt his office and himself had alike no business there, and were nothing but an elaborate practical joke.

As we whirled away, I was led insensibly into an anticipation of those days to come when mail-coach guards shall no longer be judges of horse-flesh—when a mail-coach guard shall never even have seen a horse—when stations shall have superseded stables, and corn shall have given place to coke. "In those dawning times," thought I, "exhibition-rooms shall teem with portraits of Her Majesty's favourite engine, with boilers after nature by future Landseers. Some Amburgh, yet unborn, shall break wild horses by his magic power; and in the dress of a mail-coach guard exhibit his Trained Animals in a mock mail-coach. Then, shall wondering crowds observe how that, with the exception of his whip, it is all his eye; and crowned heads shall see them feed on oats, and stand alone unmoved and undismayed, while courtiers flee affrighted when the coursers neigh!"

Such, my child, were the reflections from which I was only awakened then, as I am now, by the necessity of attending to matters of present though minor importance, I offer no apology to you for the digression, for it brings me very naturally to the subject of change, which is the very subject of which I desire to treat.

In fact, then, my child, you have changed hands. Henceforth, I resign you to the guardianship and protection of one of my most intimate and valued friends, Mr. Ainsworth, with whom, and with you, my best wishes and warmest feelings will ever remain. I reap no gain or profit by parting from you. Nor will any conveyance of your property be required, for, in this respect, you have always been literally "Bentley's" miscellany, and never mine.

Unlike the driver of the old Manchester mail, I regard

this altered state of things with feelings of unmingled pleasure and satisfaction. Unlike the guard of the new Manchester mail, *your* guard is at home in his new place, and has roystering highwaymen and gallant desperadoes even within call. And if I might compare you, my child, to an engine (not a Tory engine, nor a Whig engine, but a brisk and rapid locomotive); your friends and patrons to passengers; and he who now stands towards you in *loco parentis* as the skilful engineer and supervisor of the whole, I would humbly crave leave to postpone the departure of the train on its new and auspicious course for one brief instant, while, with hat in hand, I approach side by side with the friend who travelled with me on the old road, and presume to solicit favour and kindness in behalf of him and his new charge, both for their sakes and that of the old coachman.   Boz.

[1839]

GEORGE REDWAY'S Announcements

AUTUMN 1897

Candide, or All for the Best. A new translation from the French of VOLTAIRE, with Introduction and Notes by WALTER JERROLD and sixty-two vignettes and an etched frontispiece by ADRIEN MOREAU. [Net **£1**

Of this superb edition of Voltaire's masterpiece ("the wittiest book in the whole world") only 475 copies are for sale in Great Britain. Of these seventy-five are printed on large paper (Japanese vellum) with extra set of the *en-têtes* (India paper proofs in colour).

Great Teachers. A Series of Biographical and Critical Essays on Ruskin, Carlyle, Shelley, Burns, Coleridge, Tennyson, Emerson, Browning. By JOSEPH FORSTER. Crown 8vo. Cloth. · [Net **6s.**

The author's previous volume, "Four Great Teachers," is now out of print; it is here reprinted with additional essays.

The Story of Our English Towns. Told by P. H. DITCHFIELD, F.S.A., Author of "Old English Customs Extant at the Present Time." With Introduction by the Rev. AUGUSTUS JESSOPP, D.D. [Net **6s.**

On British and Roman Towns—Saxon Towns—Church Towns —Castle Towns—The Guilds—Mediæval Towns—University Towns—Palatinate Towns and Cathedral Cities Cinque Ports and Harbours—Memorable Sieges of Great Towns. An attempt to summarize in a popular form the main results which the labours of experts have arrived at.

The Stamp Collector. By W. J. HARDY, F.S.A., and E. D. BACON. [Net **7s. 6d.**

New volume of "The Collector Series." Mr. Hardy is well known as the author of "Bookplates," and Mr. Bacon is the expert in charge of the Tapling collection of stamps in the British Museum.

A Tragedy of Grub Street and other Bohemian Stories. By S. J. ADAIR FITZGERALD. Crown 8vo. [Net **3s. 6d.**

The Morality of Marriage and other Essays on the Status and Destiny of Woman. By MONA CAIRD. 8vo. Cloth. [Net **7d. 6s.**

Mrs. Caird is well known for her letters to the *Daily Telegraph* on the marriage question. Her book is based on articles contributed to the *Nineteenth Century* and other important reviews.

Sporting Society, or Sporting Chat and Sporting
Memories. Edited by FOX RUSSELL. Illustrations by R. CAL-
DECOTT. 2 vols. Crown 8vo. Cloth gilt. [Net **12**s.
Among the contributors are Sir Courtenay Boyle, Old Calabar,
Alfred E. T. Watson, T. H. S. Escott, Capt. R. Bird Thompson,
Fox Russell, G. Christopher Davies, Capt. Redway, and Clive
Phillips Wolley. The subjects dealt with are Hunting, Steeple-
chasing, Angling, Shooting, Pedestrianism, Racing, Salmon-spear-
ing, etc.

Travel and Big Game. By PERCY SELOUS, with
two chapters by H. A. BRYDEN, and six original drawings by
CHARLES WHYMPER. Royal 8vo. Cloth. [Net **10**s. **6**d.
On Hunting and Trapping in Canada, Desert Hunting, Leopard
Hunting in Bechuanaland. After Grizzlies in the Rockies, Hunting
Wapiti and Moose in North America, Lion Hunting in South
Africa, Shooting Rhinoceroses and Hippopotami, Giraffe Hunting.
After Buffalo and Zebra, etc.

Curiosities of Bird Life. An Account of the Sexual
Adornments, Wonderful Displays, Strange Sounds, Sweet Songs,
Curious Nests, Protective and Recognitory Colours, and Extraor-
dinary Habits of Birds. By CHARLES DIXON. Crown 8vo.
[Net **7**s. **6**d.
Mr. Dixon is well known as the author of numerous popular
books on Birds. An excellent book for a present.

Notes on the Margins, being suggestions of
Thought and Enquiry. By CLIFFORD HARRISON. Crown 8vo.
[Net **5**s.
The author of this volume is the well-known reciter and the
friend of Charles Kingsley. His brother, the late Mr. Harrison,
married "Lucas Malet," daughter of the author of "Alton Locke,"
and it is understood that Mr. Clifford Harrison has consulted
their wishes in permitting its publication.

To be read at Dusk, and other Stories, Sketches
and Essays. By CHARLES DICKENS. Hitherto Uncollected.
Crown 8vo. [Net **6**s.
Mr. F. G. Kitton, the well-known student and collector of
Dickens' works, has discovered nearly fifty articles, essays, and
stories, which have hitherto escaped the notice of bibliographers.
Such of these as are not protected by copyright in America will
be published in New York; and the pieces in which British
copyright has lapsed will be found in this volume.

Common Ailments and their Cures. By
Dr. ANDREW WILSON. [Net **1**s.

A marvellous shillingsworth of medical advice by the popular lecturer on health, revised by an experienced medical practitioner. The volume gives in 260 large pages as much information as many a book for which seven and sixpence is demanded.

The Beauties of Marie Corelli. Selected and
arranged. By ANNIE MACKAY. Cloth gilt. [Net **2**s. **6**d.

A choicely-produced little volume suitable for a Christmas present or New Year's gift : it contains the "gems" from all the published writings of this favourite author, who has carefully revised the proofs.

Demon Possession and Allied Themes. By
the late Dr. JOHN L. NEVIUS, a Chinese Missionary. Large Crown 8vo. pp. 530. [Net **7**s. **6**d.

A new edition of this valuable work full of first-hand testimony as to certain psychical phenomena occurring in the Shantung province. The introduction is by the Secretary of the Board of Foreign Missions of the Presbyterian Church. Its value to students of theology is immense, and Mr. Andrew Lang made it the subject of a leader in the *Daily News* when it first appeared, recommending it to members of the S. P. R.

How to Publish a Book or an Article and how
to Produce a Play. By LEOPOLD WAGNER. Crown 8vo.
[Net **3**s. **6**d.

This is a thoroughly practical guide to the young author, and is *not* written in the interests of a printing firm or of an authors' society. It aims at answering the questions that are upon the lips of every young author—"How can I find a publisher for what I have written?" "What shall I write that will ensure acceptance by an editor?" Mr. Wagner has been assisted by publishers and their readers, by editors of magazines and newspapers, and by managers of theatres.

The Secret Societies of all Ages and Countries.
A Comprehensive Account of upwards of One Hundred and Sixty Secret Organisations,—Religious, Political, and Social,—from the most Remote Ages, down to the Present Time. By C. W. HECKETHORN. New Edition, thoroughly Revised, and greatly Enlarged. Two volumes. [Net **£1 11**s. **6**d.

The nucleus of the present work was issued twenty-five years ago and is now out of print. Mr. Heckethorn has spent a lifetime in accumulating and digesting the materials for these monumental volumes.

The Actor's Art: Theatrical Reminiscences,

Methods of Study, and Advice to Aspirants. Specially Contributed by Leading Actors of the Day. Edited by J. A. HAMMERTON. Prefatory Note by Sir HENRY IRVING. Crown 8vo. [**6**s.

To each original article is appended a fascimile of the author's signature.

Rhymes of Ironquill. Selected and arranged by

J. A. HAMMERTON. Imperial 16mo. Uniform with Cotsford Dick's "Ways of the World". [Net **3**s. **6**d.

"Ironquill" is the Hon. Eugene Ware of Kansas whose name is a household word in the Transmissouri and whose masculine poetry has been highly praised by W. D. Howells and other eminent critics.

Reminiscences of Miss M. Betham Edwards.

One volume. 8vo.

Miss Betham Edwards is best known as the author of "Kitty." Her account of the home life of George Eliot, of Liszt, and other celebrities, should serve to attract considerable attention to this volume.

The Early Days of the Nineteenth Century.

By W. CONNOR SYDNEY. 2 vols. 8vo. [Net £1 **4**s.

A brilliant review of the manners and customs of our forefathers by an author whose previous work has been highly successful.

Concise Dictionary of English Literature,

Biographical and Bibliographical. Being a Compendious Account of the Lives and Writings of 700 British Authors between the years 1400 and 1897. By R. FARQUHARSON SHARP, of the British Museum. [**7**s. **6**d.

No bookseller, librarian, publisher, editor, journalist, or professor, or student of literature, can possibly afford to be without this book. Nothing like it has ever been attempted in Great Britain. It is "Allibone," "Lowndes," and the Dictionary of National Biography condensed into a handy volume. Mr. Sharp has laboured assiduously for two years to complete it.

Old Violins. By the Rev. H. R. Haweis.

[Net **7**s. **6**d.

New volume of "The Collector Series," by the popular author of "Music and Morals," whose knowledge of old fiddles is well known, and has been supplemented by the enthusiastic help of Mr. Arthur Hill of the famous Bond Street firm.

Dealings with the Dead. Selections from "La

Légende de la Morte en Basse Bretagne." Authorized Translation by Mrs. A. E. WHITEHEAD. Preface by ARTHUR LILLIE. Crown 8vo. [Net **3**s. **6**d.

A very curious book of interest to the theologian, the mystic, and the folk-lorist.

The Connoisseur: Essays on the Romantic and
Picturesque Associations of Art and Artists. By FREDERICK S.
ROBINSON. [Net **7**s. **6**d.

The author has been considerably assisted by his father, Sir
Charles Robinson, H.M. Surveyor of Pictures, to whose fine taste
and energy the nation is mainly indebted for the Treasures of
South Kensington Museum.

Tobacco Talk and Smoker's Gossip. [Net **1**s.

This amusing miscellany of fact and anecdote about the great
plant in all its forms and uses, has now been reissued at a Shilling
in paper covers. It is printed throughout in green ink. Many
thousands have been sold during the past ten years. Ladies buy
it to give to their men friends.

The Symbolism of the East and West. By
H. MURRAY-AYNSLEY. With Introduction by Sir GEORGE
BIRDWOOD. 4to.

On Sun Worship—The Svastika—Sacred Stones—Snake Worship
—Sacred Trees—The Evil Eye—Architectural and other customs
—The Cross as a Heathen and a Christian Symbol, etc., etc.

The Symbolism of Heraldry, or a treatise on the Meanings and Derivations of Armorial Bearings.
By W. CECIL WADE. With about 80 Illustrations.

Contents:—Origin of Armorial Bearings—The Symbolic Side of
Heraldry—Heraldic Colours and Metals—The Furs of Heraldry
—The Meaning of Heraldic Lines—The Symbolism of the Ordi-
naries—The Division Lines of the Shield—The Colours of the
Common Charges not Emblematical—Symbolism of the Common
Charges—Examples of Symbolic Arms—Cadency or Differencing.

REDWAY'S OCCULT SERIES.

The Book of Black Magic and of Pacts. By
ARTHUR EDWARD WAITE. [Net **£2 2**s.

Mr. Waite's numerous books and translations have placed him
in the front rank of modern writers on occultism; and this
magnificent quarto with nearly 200 illustrations will be eagerly
welcomed by the richer class of students.

The Catechism of Palmistry. By Madame IDA
ELLIS. Crown 8vo. [Net **2**s. **6**d.

Contains answers to over 600 questions on Palmistry by the
well-known expert. With nineteen plates.

The Hidden Way across the Threshold: an

explanation of the concealed forces in every man to open the temple of the soul and to learn the guidance of the Unseen Hand. Large 8vo. pp. 598. By J. C. STREET. [Net **15s.**

Third edition of a valuable work by an American adept. With illustrations.

Spiritualism. By Judge EDMONDS and Dr. C. T.

DEXTER. 2 vols. 8vo. With portraits. [Net **10s. 6d.**

A new edition, with alterations, of a famous American work which has long been selling at a premium.

Human Magnetism, or How to Hypnotize.

A practical handbook for students of Mesmerism. With 10 plates. By Professor JAMES COATES. Crown 8vo. [Net **5s.**

A thoroughly practical and up-to-date book. The author repudiates the idea that a mesmerized person can be made to commit crime.

New Manual of Astrology. A complete guide

for students. By WALTER OLD ("Sepharial"). [Net **10s. 6d.**

The large sale of old-fashioned books by Lilly, Raphael, Zadkiel, and others, prove how popular this study has become, and the need for a book in modern phraseology and adapted to the *fin de siècle* reader.

The Gift of the Spirit. Essays by PRENTICE

MULFORD. Crown 8vo. [Net **3s. 6d.**

Essays on mysticism and theosophy by an American whose fame has reached Europe as the author of "The White Cross Library."

Fortune Telling Cards. A pack of 32 cards

specially prepared for use by divinators. By "MINETTA," the fashionable "fortune-teller." [Net **3s. 6d.**

With accompanying booklet explaining the use of the cards.

Handbook of Cartomancy and Divination.

By GRAND ORIENT. [Net **2s.**

This is a reprint of the little book to which Mr. J. Holt Schooling, the expert in statistics, recently devoted an article in *Pearson's Magazine.* He had been told by "Minetta" of four things that would happen to him within a week or so. "Well, these things *did* happen within a week or so. A facer, I admit." Working out the odds against this quadruple event "coming off," Mr. Schooling found them to be 946,763 to 1—rather long odds to pull through. He adds, "I do not attempt to explain this, but I think it fair to state the facts."

GEORGE REDWAY, Publisher, 9, Hart Street, Bloomsbury, LONDON.